BEAUTIFUL CHILDREN

RANDOM HOUSE | NEW YORK

BEAUTIFUL CHILDREN

A Novel

CHARLES BOCK

Published in the United States by Random House,
an imprint of The Random House Publishing Group,
a division of Random House, Inc., New York.

RANDOM HOUSE and colophon are registered
trademarks of Random House, Inc.

Grateful acknowledgment is made to Linda Music for
permission to reprint a lyric excerpt from "Free Money,"
written by Patti Smith and Lenny Kaye, copyright © 1975 by
Linda Music (ASCAP). Used by permission. All rights reserved.

LIBRARY OF CONGRESS CATALOGING-IN-PUBLICATION DATA
Bock, Charles.
Beautiful children: a novel / Charles Bock.
p.   cm.
ISBN 978-1-4000-6650-6
1. Boys—Fiction.   2. Missing children—Fiction.
3. Deserts—Fiction.   4. Las Vegas (Nev.)—Fiction.
5. Psychological fiction.   I. Title.
PS3602.O3255B43 2008
813'.6—dc22   2007004166

Printed in the United States of America on acid-free paper

www.atrandom.com

1 2 3 4 5 6 7 8 9

FIRST EDITION

Book design by Dana Leigh Blanchette

For my parents,
Caryl & Howard Bock

PART ONE

1.1

The lens zooms in, then draws back. The images are shaky: a celebration, that much is clear; children in bright orange jerseys and matching base-ball caps, some worn backward, or with bills to the side. They chatter and jibe, passing pitchers of soda, reaching for slices with favorite top-pings. Chins shine with grease. Smiles glow as if smeared with lipstick. One boy sits a bit away from the rest, toward the end of the table. He is pretty much the same size as everyone else—pudgier than some, smaller than others. He's not wearing a cap, though, and the poor resolution of the camcorder makes it look as if the top of his skull might be consumed in flame. But no. Another second shows nothing more dangerous than a mass of bright red hair. The child leans forward now, his jersey bunching around his shoulders. Attempting to convince the nearest teammate to unscrew the top of a salt shaker, his freckled face is animated, lively. *Dude,* we can hear him say. *Come on. Come on, dude.* A punch to the shoulder answers him. He squeals, though not unhappily. *Dick.*

The camcorder's microphone catches the tail end of a reprimand from an unseen adult. It catches the boy's protest, *It wasn't me!* By this time, though, focus is shifting, swinging toward the middle of the table, where coaches and other adults subdue a slap fight. After a few seconds, a semblance of decorum is reached; the presentation of the next trophy begins, and the camera pans down the length of the table, showing children in varying states of interest. And here judicious use of the fast-forward cues a final appearance by the redheaded boy, for just a few seconds, a short sequence—he directs a sneering remark toward the action; when his neighbor does not respond, the boy sinks into his chair. The flesh of his cheeks lengthens, goes slack. Small eyes cloud, turn dark.

This sequence, these scant seconds, are why the Ewings tracked down that videotape. Because recent photos were supposed to work best, were supposed to give a potential witness the best chance at identification. So Lincoln and Lorraine would stand at the front door of a nice couple whose names they had memorized on the ride over. Nodding soberly, the Ewings would thank the couple for all their help. They would try to make small talk. The delighted shrieks of children would interrupt, breaking out from upstairs, bodies tramping, at play. Then designer sunglasses would not be able to hide Lorraine's tears. And then Lincoln would take his wife into his arms. Gently he would stroke her hair and gently he would guide her back down the walkway, her face staying buried in his shoulder, her mascara running, just a bit, onto his suit's lapel. No words between them, just his arm delicate around her waist, their long, twisted shadow slipping diagonally through the trim, open yard. And yes, that black cassette, it would be Lincoln's possession: in his opposite hand, as far from Lorraine as possible.

In a short amount of time that section of videotape would be transformed into a series of stills, frames scanned into a computer. A single frame would be enlarged, then Photoshopped, resulting in the image of a slouching, unexpressive child. This image would be circulated in e-mail attachments, faxes, and flyers; it would be posted in arcades and student unions and youth hostels; in post offices and convenience stores and drop-in centers for the homeless and indigent. And at some point fairly early on in this process, Lincoln Ewing would be reminded of the damndest piece of information. A drop of conventional wisdom that, honestly, Lincoln had no clue where he'd picked up. It concerned Native Americans. Supposedly, when photography was invented, they believed each picture from the white man's magic machine removed a piece of the subject's soul.

This was precisely the kind of thing Lincoln didn't need in his head. Yet, just as a tongue cannot resist probing the sensitive area of a cracked tooth, Lincoln would find himself returning to that god-awful piece of information: gnawing on it when a police officer misread his son's birth certificate, causing the boy's middle name to fall by the wayside, becoming as forgotten as the great-grandfather who had inspired it. And when mention of the boy's twelve years of age was replaced by his date of birth—this distinction small, but especially painful, however pragmatic; done, it was explained, as a matter of protocol, to acknowledge a grim reality: *nobody can say how long a child will be missing.*

Lincoln would watch the police spokesman squinting in front of a phalanx of floodlights and tripods, stumbling through a prepared statement that asked for the public's help; he'd watch the vacuous broadcasters with their melodramatic pronouncements. He would gather up the stuffed-animal bouquets, attend the candlelight vigils. Lincoln would offer rewards and set up 1-800 hotlines. Steps taken for a righteous purpose, in the ostensible hope of solving this tragedy; steps that placed more and more distance between the flesh and blood of Newell Ewing and the cautionary tale his name would come to signify, between the child from that pizza party and the embodiment of every parent's worst nightmare.

And when that soulless stare had been reproduced hundreds of times; when thousands of Xeroxes had been made off hundreds of copies, most of them done on machines perpetually low on toner; when another copy of a copied copy had created further blurring, new smudges; after all this, Lincoln Ewing would be left to wonder. What was left of his son? What did he have?

This would be later.

A hundred and five outside for the ninety-ninth straight day. That dry desert heat, a wall that hit the moment you stepped outside, then pounded relentlessly. To get local fanboys away from their liquid crystal screens, out of their air-conditioned living rooms, and into their air-conditioned cars, management at Amazin' Stories had been importing the biggest names in the fantasy game. Every Saturday afternoon, there were free meet and greets, autographs, happily personalized little doodles, and, sure, loads of stock for sale. So long as nobody went crazy and wheelbarrowed in every comic an artist had done, collectors could even bring their own back issues to be signed. It was a pretty sweet deal, and an effective one, so much so that each weekend, men in their early to middle twenties shuffled self-consciously into the store, half-embarrassed but also nervous, wired, as if the warm spots they possessed for their childhood heroes were stains of gum they'd stepped into and now were unable to free themselves from, the hard and powerful colors pulling, urging them to revisit the ritual of standing inside a store of illustrated books; of reading; of fantasizing and being swept away.

All of twelve years old, Newell was in the bloom of his enchantment. Except for a few times when his parents had made him clip on his tie and go out to brunch with them, he'd spent most of his Saturday afternoons in Amazin' Stories, squirming through the larger, taller bodies for a better view of the autograph table, hanging on every spoken word from the makeshift lectern, laughing on cue with everyone else. When the iconic septuagenarian had good-naturedly regaled the overflow audience with golden-age reminiscences for a good hour longer than scheduled, Newell had had a primo view. And when the year's hottest illustrator had repeatedly checked his watch, deflected most questions as "irrelevant," and repeatedly referred to his upcoming *Vanity Fair* photo spread, Newell had been on hand for that, too. After a summer of insider tales and celebrity name-dropping, honestly, it wasn't exactly easy to get jazzed about Bing Beiderbixxe.

From the looks of things, Newell wasn't alone in this opinion. The store was largely empty, just a few underclassman types solemnly wandering the new arrivals racks, and three or four guys standing at a respectful distance from the autograph table, nodding and listening, but seeming unconvinced, reluctant to come in any closer. Newell couldn't blame them. Why the illustrator and creative mind behind *Wendy Whitebread, Undercover Slut* had been booked, he had no clue. Beiderbixxe's comic was this cheapo deal, printed on rough paper, published by some rinky-dink outfit. Word of mouth claimed the bizarre name had been lifted from an obscure porno comic, and if that was true, Newell had to admit, it was pretty cool. Too bad the rest of *Whitebread* bit so hard. The ditzy blond policewoman with the badge over her crotch never did anything fresh. Every single panel had been ripped off from some way-better comic. Every pose was a pose of a pose. Newell had complained about it to Kenny, who was older and knew a lot more about this stuff. *They must not have been able to get anyone else to come,* Newell had said, referring to Bing as *Bonerbite. Bonerbite sucks goat balls. The hairs from goat balls get stuck between his teeth and Bonerbite walks around sucking on them, getting all the taste he can.* Kenny had listened, and after a few moments, in that halting and unconvinced way of his, had admitted he didn't completely understand, either. He'd taken his time, negotiating and making order of his thoughts, starting over a few times, correcting himself a few more, and finally, Kenny had said the references in *Wendy Whitebread* were some sort of map, he guessed, and the books were a kind of tribute, he thought, but like a commentary, too. "It's supposed to be funny. But in a serious way. You know, where not giving away the humor is part of the joke?"

Today, while waiting around, in deference to his friend, Newell had given *Wendy Whitebread* another chance, examining some of the panels, paying attention to the connection each might have with its source material, trying to figure out, as Kenny had suggested, why Bing might have chosen that specific panel for inspiration, what the changes might have meant. Bing's logic remained a shelf Newell could not reach, no matter how he strained from the top of his mental tiptoes. Still, the boy had gained enough appreciation for the guy's work that, presently, from his vantage point, about halfway in the store, he watched the comic book artist with more than a middling interest: Beiderbixxe, hefty and balding, his face large and fleshy, pale and pinkish. Behind boxy black eyeglasses, he appeared intelligent, welcoming even; busily weaving some sort of tale, trying like hell to appeal to each of his few audience members. "In the fifties," he was saying, "these two, they'd end up beats or novelists or something. In the sixties, they'd be, what, hippy rock stars, Warhol figures. The seventies they become filmmakers. The eighties they get into rap or maybe indie rock. The nineties, that's easy, they're hacking the World Bank's source code."

Newell half-listened, but was a step behind the story, unable to follow along, and, truth be told, not all that interested. Bing's meaty left hand wasn't helping—it kept making this rolling motion, as if this would spin the guy toward his point more quickly. Newell got distracted by the hand, and then his eyes wandered some more, toward the table, near the artist's elbow, where a plastic bottle was mostly empty, a sluice of fluorescent liquid along the bottom.

"Just putting it out there," Bing said. "Is it at all possible that these *bad kids* are the latest installment of avant-garde, that two killers just might be nothing less than evolutionary forerunners?"

The boy gave up now, turning away, looking through the glass door and picture window at the shopping plaza, still and dead, the rows of parked cars, nobody coming or going. The day outside was bright and oppressive, and the boy's face felt warm. He reached for the vinyl case, which hung from the side belt loop of his jean shorts, and withdrew a small silver device. The tip of his tongue peeked out of the corner of his mouth; his fingers danced a familiar pattern. He listened for three rings but did not leave a message, instead quickly pressing the button in the upper right corner of the pad. More punching now, each digit entered with increasing force. The phone went back to his ear; a longing swelled through him. For a moment he resented the universe for all the things he did not understand. He listened for a time, managed to keep from stomping his foot, and then looked once more to the store's entrance, a longer, harder look this time, one that concentrated and focused his building energies. Impulses pulsed through Newell, telling him to whirl around, throw his phone at Beiderbixxe, mute that stupid droning voice. Instead the boy pressed a control button on his phone, switching modes.

His high score on the phone game was 730 million, and Newell was on his way to clearing the first screen when a stray missile infiltrated his defense system, obliterating his home base. He snorted a vulgarity, swung his leg as if to punt away the small silver box, and corkscrewed in place. Newell had an impulse to scream at some guy who might have been looking at him. Then his shoulders sagged. The boy sulked and fumed and desultorily hit the RESET button on his phone. He was about to start the game over when, from the front of the store, the jingle and clank of small metal bells sounded.

Prodding the door with his shoulder came an odd collection of lines and angles. Gangly, wiry, a little weird-looking, even for this place. Hair was spackled to his forehead in darkish streaks. More hair fell over his eyes, covering his ears, winding down in oily tendrils toward his shoulders. Arms white and thin, like limp strands of uncooked spaghetti, stuck out from a used and faded T-shirt, itself damp, clingy. He wore the same jeans he always did, the only person Newell knew who wore jeans in a hundred-and-ten-degree weather.

"FINALLY, NIGGA. *Where the fuck you been, Kenny?*"

With unteachable comic timing, the odd lines folded upon themselves, collapsing with an uncoordinated ferocity. Kenny did this strange, desperate wingy deal with his other arm, to no avail—the sheets continued their descent, slipping out from beneath the crook of his arm that had held them.

"Whoa . . . Hey—"

Newell arrived in time to grab the diner place mat. "I got it," he said, easing a crumpled yellow flyer from the inside of Kenny's underarm.

"YO, KENNY," he said. "You made it! *My MAN.*"

Kenny's body unclenched; he exhaled, allowed the boy to take the papers, said "Thanks." Stepping into the store, he raised his head, let the air-conditioning run over him. Newell saw cheeks flushed to the shade of a ripe plum and sparkling with sweat, the bony surface of Kenny's features appearing raw, irritated.

"*Dude.* I was fuckin' *bugging.* I thought for sure you'd wuss out again."

Kenny yanked the hair out of his eyes and back behind his ear. A long breath and he began to compose himself. Anxious eyes quickly scanned the store. "Couldn't get the Reliant started," he said. "And I wasn't sure which to bring. I hope they're okay."

Newell turned over the place mat, stared at it, then pressed the rumples against his knee. "Dude. If you could afford real drawing paper, you'd really be something. You know that, right?"

The words hung for a long moment. Kenny started to smile, but it was sheepish, and went uncompleted. He glanced down at his sneakers, noticing the ripped fringe of his jeans, inexplicably caught up and tucked inside his baggy gray socks. His laces, untied and dirty, were sprawled limply along the thin carpet.

"Oh. Fuck. I didn't—No, really. This is *way* better than any of Bonerbite's stuff," Newell insisted. "I'm *telling* you. *WAY* better than *all* those guys. SERIOUS." Newell flared now, punching Kenny on the arm. "*Fucker.*" Bouncing on his toes, his every movement built on itself, generating more energy, more excitement. Now the boy's face exploded. "*Yeaaah-boiieyyyy.*" He grinned crazily, and looked past an embarrassed, confused Kenny, toward the autograph table. "Here we go. *Fucking awesomeness.*"

1.3

After her son's sneaker tracks had been found in the desert, Lorraine began to peek. Once the neighbors had stopped staring and the first round of leads had come up vapors, during the quiet hours before the dawn, when Lincoln was upstairs, passed out in the guest room. Or she would look during the lazy part of the afternoon, when the house was empty and her defenses were down. True, they'd agreed to let sleeping dogs lie, but she knew Lincoln did it, too: late at night, after he'd come home from the office, the police station, or a meeting with the latest in a series of infuriatingly incompetent private investigators. He watched when the house was dark and Lorraine was safely locked away inside what Lincoln still thought of as *their* bedroom. As often as not, he left the evidence inside the machine, where she discovered it the next day. Nor was it out of the realm of possibility that Lorraine had forgotten to put the tape back. Days might pass before one of them finally hit EJECT, tucked the cassette back into its little white sleeve, and placed the package back inside the pantry. There was no discussion. Pretenses had gone by the wayside. Watching wasn't the kind of thing she could help and it wasn't the kind of thing he could help. The button was pressed, the images ran: Newell sinking in his chair, chin gleaming, small eyes clouding.

Everyday banalities numb perception: with daily and continual exposure to someone, you do not see that person, but a compilation—memory and presence and projection, the embodiment of your feelings about the idea of that person. With this in mind, the charitable thing would be to report that Lorraine, and Lincoln too, when he watched—separately, in the deep of the night, his mind buzzing with desire and remorse and, not infrequently, from a few belts—that *each* parent recalled every physical change, no matter how minute, their son had undergone in the months between that taped Little League party and his disappearance. The charitable thing would be Newell alive in their memories in his most recent form: his hair still fresh from its back-to-school cut; his skin the milky, almost unhealthy white of a boy who'd spent his summer cooled by air-conditioning; the extra bit of languorous heft to his face. That would be the charitable thing. But with the passing of time, the sad truth is that each physical discrepancy would double and redouble in importance for Lorraine, and instead of a vehicle of generosity and relief, memory's precision would become a form of torture, not so much a reminder of what had been, but a rejoinder to all that was being missed— the distance between Newell and that tape widening even as Lorraine watched it once again.

Still, what was she supposed to do?

1.4

Dawn had broken, the dew still glistening on sun-browned lawns, his epic trek waiting, spread before him like some marvelously set picnic. Mindful of the sustenance he would require, Bing Beiderbixxe had disregarded his diet and purchased a drive-through sausage-and-egg sandwich. Just for kicks, he'd picked up sixty-four ounces of caffeinated carbonation. Then he'd set off, onto the normally knotted 405. Even on a Saturday morning, even as the sky above the cement husk of freeway was turning lighter shades, the four largely barren lanes had been a pleasant surprise for Bing, who, accelerating steadily, had driven with his sandwich in his free hand and the giant soda cup nestled between his thighs. A life-size cardboard cutout of Wendy Whitebread was crammed across the rear of his hatchback, a milk crate of comic books sat shotgun. Bing's newly purchased "going out outfit" (silver cabana shirt, black designer jeans) lay carefully draped over the crate. He'd headed north and east, making good time, passing Anaheim's tawdry theme parks and Corona's clot of auto malls, and then Riverside, which didn't have a river or any sides, but only, improbably, even more auto malls. Rough calculations had him reaching the Mojave well before the sun hit its zenith, which would allow him to avoid the desert's most intense heat, and keep his crappy little engine from blowing. Terrific. The scope of Beiderbixxe's genius did not include impromptu gasket fixing.

The yucca trees and sagebrush and cacti; the sand dunes and pebble heaps and drum-hard earth; the breathtaking and seemingly endless desert; the emptiness; the lull. Six hours. Plenty of time to settle into a rhythm, to retreat inside the maze of his own thoughts, to straighten out just when he was supposed to hold 'em and why he should fold 'em; to recall the guideline about bringing into a casino only the cash he could afford to lose; to extrapolate how much this was, given his circumstances; to revise the figure to reflect worst- and best-case scenarios. Bing had played his latest favorite CD four times in a row. He'd learned the lyrics to all the songs and, for the sheer pleasure of it, indulged venomous thoughts about how much he disliked his two housemates. He'd fantasized about getting his own place and, then, about creatively carnal ways to piss away his gambling winnings.

Yellow ribbons alternated with American flags, hanging from every other telephone pole and billboard. Eighteen-wheelers passed from the opposite direction, the hatchback shaking in their wake, the car threatening to run off the road. Somewhere around Barstow, with skeptical thoughts forming around whether the store would have any window promotion, Bing had wondered, too, if anyone would even bother to show.

Male-pattern baldness had kicked in uncommonly early for Bing. When classmates had started expressing their personalities with hair sprays and tubes of dyes and even the occasional muttonchop, his wheat-brown hair was already receding from his temples, thinning around his crown, clinging to his shirts, and floating into his cereal. His increasingly shiny head served as an exclamation point atop what he saw as an already staggering assembly of bodily injustices: asthma; a mealy voice; a nearly pathological aversion to sweating and sweat-related activities; nearsighted *and* farsighted. As a child Bing had been challenged in the height department, though his tummy had been given no such restriction. His ass was the size of an elephant's skull. When nobody was looking, Bing sucked his thumb; when people were, he picked his nose. And that name! So what if his parents had loved jazz: what kind of goddamn name was that to pawn off on your kid?

Was it any wonder that, even as a grade-schooler, Bing had felt far less comfortable with people than with images and technologies? That his developing intellect and nascent personality had suffered so greatly upon entering the arena where sex became a possibility? Even now, Bing couldn't offer a definitive answer about this stuff. This much was sure: where his older brothers, Satchmo and Jolson, had been gregarious and well-adjusted teenagers, where younger sisters, Dizzy and Bird, had been scholarly and well-liked, Bing had been awkward and ill-equipped, retreating from and, in fact, surviving his adolescence via pop culture's many alleyways, entertainments that were neither fully active nor passive, obsessions that weren't social but, rather, *a*social. He collected every comic under the *X-Men* umbrella (purchasing duplicate copies—one to read, one for posterity). He religiously updated his library of science fiction and pulp novels with the latest installments of each series (no matter how sloppy and half-assed each successive volume may have been). He constantly referenced the dialogue of sitcoms he'd memorized during afternoons of syndicated reruns (shows that hadn't been all that funny the first time he'd seen them). Bing inhaled kung fu videos and pay-per-view wrestling extravaganzas until vicarious testosterone all but burst through his flabby arms, then he headed out and played old-school stand-up arcade games until skill allowed him to stretch a quarter for like a week. On a daily basis, for three consecutive months, in an infamous phase whose mere recollection, to this day, still caused him physical pain, Bing Beiderbixxe had donned a cape. Beiderbixxe the Misguided! Bing the Misunderstood! The listless fat kid who could get only as close to a naked woman as the nearest *Sports Illustrated* swimsuit issue, *Maxim* subscription, or *Cinemax's Max After Dark* episode would allow. The quiet, unthreatening loner who was told by the plain brunette at the next desk, *"I like you—as a friend."* The wisecracking antihero who had convinced himself he would overcome insurmountable odds and rescue the planet from undefeatable evil and, in the process, melt the heart of the unwinnable babe! The bitter jaded mess, so deluded by television and movies, he actually believed himself capable of landing supermodel-caliber women and therefore refused to adjust his standards!

No, he had not been the finest dandelion in the field. His diorama had not been in contention for the blue ribbon. And toward the end of his senior year, a certain genre of computer game had completely blown the petals off Bing's winsome little diorama. First-person shoot-'em-up was the genre's technical label; *Deathmatch,* the colloquial term. Originally, Deathmatch games seemed like little more than variations on the traditional hero-against-everyone battles; however, the genius of the genre, and the source of its addictive appeal, lay in its perspective. For as with the scene in a horror movie where the camera assumes the point of view of the killer, Deathmatch games provided the three-dimensional experience of being inside the battle, moving through some sort of darkened and foreboding domain. Advances in home computers made an encompassing, immersive perspective possible, the action blurringly disjointed all around you, bobbing and zagging as you inched around corners, performed leaping somersaults, searched for ammo and weaponry, and, most important, hunted. The goal was fresh meat. For disenfranchised males between the ages of twelve and twenty-eight, the games were a godsend. They gave you violence, constant and tangible, graphic and over-the-top, the splatters of blood never failing to impress and amuse, the physical recoil of victims always providing easy, guiltless thrills. Head shots were especially cool, but then again, *everything* about these games kicked ass.

Thus, Bing had dabbled. He'd lost track of more than a few afternoons, blasted his way through more than a few nights, even participated in his share of weekend-long marathons at a nearby hotel convention center, competing against teenagers and scruffy twentysomethings who, from their dilapidated station wagons, wheeled in hard drives the size of mini-fridges. Bing's involvement had extended through his senior year and into the first of his six years at a small southern California college whose liberal arts curriculum had also produced Richard Milhous Nixon. Which isn't to say the game was the entirety of his campus life, mind you. Bing also had a work-study job in the computer center. He had a full schedule of classes in art, art history, art appreciation, graphic arts, life drawing, portraiture, and still life. He had aspirations to nothing less than the creation of sensitive, artistic, emotionally honest pictures that, just maybe, would get him laid. There was also a small island of friends with whom Bing shared his dreamy hopes—five or six castaways like him, fellow travelers from high school who'd scattered to different colleges, as well as a few new buddies, like-minded thinkers that Bing had found on campus. Brought together as if responding to a siren audible only to them, they hung out; often in person, but just as often electronically, congregating in a chat room, chewing the fat during late-night bull sessions, forming and closing a small tight circle. The Knitting Room, they called themselves, since knitting was about as boring as anyone could come up with, and all the chat rooms with sexy and violent names were continually filled. Inside the Knitting Room, commentary went uninterrupted and undisturbed (sigh); the tone was unfailingly cynical. Each Knitter was a master in one-upmanship, secure in his superiority to the rest of the world, confidently voicing opinions on anything from rock and roll:]1450SAT: Iz it possible tht Elvis Costello truly dzn't know what's so funny about peace love & understanding? to young celebrity hotties:]DOMINATR69: I'd put it in her fartbox. Even ideas for reality game shows:]KC_FTT_B: Ten big good looking d_des on an island. All testosterone machines, policemen, firemen, marines. They're homophobes, and there's no women on the island, only these ten d_des and a flock of sheep. Evry day the contestants get fed Viagra and Exctasy. Last one who doesn't bang a sheep wins a million dollars.

Then came instances when someone needed a way to avoid a term paper, and a late-night missive would go out. The Knitters would meet at the computer lab. Flavored chips were mandatory, as were Big Slams of Mountain Dew, and carry-packs of Red Bull. By breakfast time, everyone would be so twitchy and wired and fucked up that there was no way back to the cerebral, internal processes that schoolwork demanded.

You look back, you understand. But at the time, there's no way. Not while you're trapped, not from the middle of it.

The first warm morning of spring. Around campus, Bing was commonly referred to as the Dork King, Butterbixxe, and the Creepy Loser in the Cape. Running late for class, he had come down from his room unshaven, fumbling with his backpack and notebook. The dorm lounge was on the ground floor, you had to pass through it to get outside, and five, eight, people were standing around the television, which was mounted in the corner. One frizz-haired girl stared in shock, which was bizarre since her intellectual energies were usually devoted to the latest twists in celebrities' private lives. Another moron—his long white T-shirt reading PARTY COED NAKED LACROSSE—kept saying how unbelievable it was.

A glance explained nothing. The screen was filled with the front of a sprawling, modernish building, a distant shot of wide cement steps leading up to a drab entrance, a series of double doors. SWAT troops were positioned along the perimeter, rifles trained. For long seconds nothing happened, then the scene shifted, to a half-open window on the top floor. The view shifted again to overhead, from a helicopter flying above; then to teenagers outside the school, standing behind barricades, crying and hugging one another. Then to stretchers loaded onto ambulances; frantic parents; more cops with guns.

A crawl along the bottom of the screen provided cursory details: two instigators were believed responsible, a pair of students from the high school, part of a group known for wearing trench coats and indulging in computer games. A network announcer relayed the contents of cell phone calls made from students inside the school, which provided some sense of what was happening.

Bing commandeered a love seat across from the screen. Seemingly born to opine about events like these, he refrained from providing a running commentary or so much as updating a newcomer on a new development. Rather, he settled in on the sagging couch and missed Comp Lit. In the day's ensuing hours, and then the week's subsequent days, through updates and reports and special investigations, Bing would gather more facts surrounding the true scope of what these young men had done, more information about the magnitude of their act. Bing would learn that this had not been a simple case where some postal employee had lost it. This had not been a prank phone call, or some copycat bringing Daddy's pistol to homeroom. Rather, the two high school students in question—each seventeen years of age—had procured the architectural blueprints for their school; they'd sawed down shotguns, used pliers to widen ends of CO_2 cartridges. For fourteen months, they'd planned, they'd labored.

Like the lady who protests too much to a rich suitor on their first date, Bing railed against the subsequent media focus on Deathmatch games. *Sure,* he told anyone who'd listen, *the killers had been experts at the games. But everyone who saw* Old Yeller *didn't go shoot their dogs, did they? How many fans of the Road Runner sprinted off a cliff and expected to float on the air?* Bing made sure to note the gap that existed between making a joke about blowing up your high school and actually trying to blow up your high school; the significant difference between a socially feeble and mixed-up kid who nursed a grudge against his teenage years and a cold-blooded mass murderer. And while, yes, it was true that, on occasion, one of the perpetrator's journals elicited sympathy—*I hate you people for leaving me out of so many things*—and while, admittedly, the second perp's website included a number of heartrending posts—*You don't know how many hours I spent on this. Would someone please play it?*—in the hard cold light of what became known as twentieth-century America's worst school yard slaughter, empathy had to be with the victims and their families. Bing Beiderbixxe understood this as much as anyone.

But what Bing did not tell people, what to this day still freaked him out more than a little bit, was that he also possessed a firsthand understanding of the ways in which an act of destruction can be viewed as a piece of creation, the means by which an act of violence might translate into a perfect piece of art. Bing Beiderbixxe did not tell people that when he had come down from his room that morning and discovered the slaughter, he had done so after huddling all night in front of his computer, working on a special version of Deathmatch. Bing's version of the Deathmatch game was to take place inside an exact re-creation of his dormitory; his starting point was to be the dormitory lounge. But Bing did not mention this. Furthermore, he did not tell anyone that he'd watched the real-life slaughter play itself out while surrounded by the same neighbors whose doppelgängers were to be chased through his computer game's virtual hallways, who were to be cut down in his re-created stairwells and bedrooms—the exact people whom Bing had identically rendered, specifically so he could inflict bloody damage upon their images.

This was Bing's dirty little secret, and he had shoved the zip disc that held it into the bottom drawer of his desk, burying the fact of Dormitory Deathmatch beneath loose papers and envelopes, hiding all evidence of his flirtation with the dark spirits, and spending years pretending the dance had never happened. Horrified by what he'd almost done, Bing had tried to change the way he thought about the people he interacted with, and he had tried to address the way he moved in and through the world. Bing had suffered his share of bad dreams since that day, and had learned his lesson, and knew this lesson had taken hold, because years later, on the awful morning when terrorists flew those planes into the twin towers of the World Trade Center, Bing Beiderbixxe remembered that part of the teenagers' original plan had involved hijacking a plane, which they'd wanted to fly into a New York skyscraper.

After which he immediately thought about the one and only time that he'd removed the zip disc from his desk and shared the story of the half-finished program.

He thought of the woman to whom he had first spoken the magic words *I love you.* She'd relocated to lower Manhattan, Bing remembered, and it took a fraction of a second for all his bitterness—including his morbid fantasies where she got it on with three stockbrokers in the dugout seats of Yankee Stadium—to dissolve. And it was with the world in chaos around him that Bing fired off more than a few e-mails to friends of his onetime love, making sure she was okay.

So many things Bing wished to make right.

He was more than ready to be finished driving when the first wave of billboards hit, leaping out from the washed-out desert to intrude on his ruminations: advertisements for entertainers who were famous or once had been famous, for 99-percent-return rates on slot machines and no limit hold-'em poker, for gentlemen's clubs and adult cabarets and top-less reviews. Bing gawked at each and every one of them, happy to have something distract him from the road's grind, from the workings of his mind. Ahead, gray and dusty grids appeared in an intricate sprawl: starter homes and tract homes, optimistically titled subdivisions and in-sipidly beautiful incorporated communities. Spanish tiled roofs were the law of the land. Sunlight glinted off a thousand backyard pools at once. Both sides of the road were dappled with dingy motels, coming and going at wide intervals of empty space, their paint jobs faded and crack-ing. And then, rising on the horizon, looming over the flat and wide basin from the moment they appeared, shining towers and popish theme-park façades. Built at a scale that was out of proportion with the rest of the city, they were impossible to ignore, newly unwrapped and shining toys amid a room of small wooden carvings. Forward Bing drove, toward their glitter, moving up the southern and outermost edge of the Strip, passing a visitors' information center where tourists could get maps and make hotel reservations, then a one-story storefront hawking prop plane rides to the Grand Canyon, and then this weird little building that, in ancient neon, blinked out an offer: FREE ASPIRIN AND TENDER SYMPATHY.

At the base of a skyline that was far too ornate to take in at once, his eyes came upon that familiar benchmark. Sticking out of the middle of an otherwise barren traffic median, the sign was smaller than he'd thought it would be, but every bit as iconic as it looked on television.

Was there any way to jump-start a libido quicker? Any other place on the planet that instantly offered the chance to reverse fortune and end losing streaks, the chance to set right a lifetime of disappointments? How could one read the gracious message—WELCOME TO FABULOUS LAS VEGAS, NEVADA—and feel anything but tingling anticipation?

The first pulse, high-pitched and melodic, caused each young man to reach toward his waist. By the time phones were out, the customized ring tone had distinguished itself.

"Shit. Whenever I'm about to do anything—"

Checking the screen confirmed what he already knew to be true. Newell brought the device to the side of his face and did not wait for a greeting. "Ten more minutes?" he asked. His eyes found Kenny, rolled for his friend's benefit. "Mom? Maaa*wwwmm*. . . . Come *awhnnn*—"

"But you said FOUR. It's only—"

He scanned for the store clock, saw what time it was, and expelled air through his nose. His hip slung to the side. Newell went silent and sullen. He listened.

"I know," he admitted. "I know. . . . But he just got here, Mom. . . . I been waiting all summer for this. I mean, that's the whole—

"No," he said, brusquely. "I *know* it's not your fault he was late. . . . All right. . . . *All right*. All right already, FAWCK."

Slamming the device shut, Newell stomped away from Kenny, shoved the glass door with enough force to whip its metal guard against the store's outside wall, and ignored the banging impact, trudging outside, into the vivid brightness. Beneath a sun-beaten awning, the boy paused on a stretch of shaded cement, near three complicated-looking mountain bikes, each of their front treads locked into a slot on the dull metal rack. Newell feebly kicked the nearest tire, and took in the relative stillness, the shopping center's long rows of parked cars, metallic surfaces gleaming beneath the unforgiving sun. He put his hands on his hips, cocked his head. Defiance gave way to a plunging inevitability as his eyes trained on a single object: gliding like a wraith along a long row of parked cars and light posts, taking each speed bump with methodical ease.

Store bells jingled behind him; a presence arrived next to him. Newell continued his surveillance.

"It's not fair," he said.

"Yeah."

"I wanted to be here to see."

"You were here. I was late."

The boy remained still as a rock, then exhaled air through his nose, snorting. "But I never get to do *anything*."

His holster was clipped into jean shorts that, by design, were far too baggy for his body. When he jammed the phone back into place, the fabric slid down, just a bit. Newell gave a halfhearted smirk, watching as the black luxury sedan slowed, pulling toward the curb. Presently, its heavily tinted driver-side window descended. In the newly created opening, a salad of strawberry blond hair tossed lightly. Reflective lenses of designer sunglasses danced with light.

The last time she'd ventured inside Amazin' Stories, her tanned flesh had all but spilled out of her baby-blue swimsuit top, and her wraparound sarong had been clinging to her in something straight out of a sophomoric dream. Newell still got upset about the way the whole store had gone dead, and he refused to let anyone so much as bring up the subject of his mother. Still, on the rare occasion when Kenny sensed his young friend was in a receptive mood, and wouldn't freak out too bad, he'd remind Newell of harmless details—like how the flip-flops had matched her toenail polish. He did it only when they were alone, though—around other people Kenny got flustered; even around Newell he wasn't exactly vocal, a clamped fist that refused to open. And if there was even a hint that Newell had taken his joke the wrong way, he'd retreat, mollifying the boy, claiming he understood why Newell's mom had to pick him up in the parking lot. That having a prearranged signal was a *super* idea.

Kenny stared over at the sedan, its engine idling with barely contained power. After a long moment, embossed lips smiled tightly in return.

"Hey," he said, addressing Newell casually, almost absently. "What are you doing later?"

"Dickfuck. Why?"

"I thought, dunno, we could—a movie? Maybe just drive around. Hang or whatever. I mean, it still won't be anything, but, you know, something."

Newell's freckles turned a deeper color, and it looked as if his face were glowing, lit from inside. "For reals?" Newell asked. "Dude. Aww. You *rule.*"

"I have to get my aunt from work. Figure I'll come by between seven and eight—"

The bleat that interrupted them was short, and sharp, and scattered small black birds from their lamppost perch. "I gotta go," Newell said. After pounding Kenny's hand with his fist, he took off, a spark in his stride now, this coherent, optimistic agility. His shorts were slipping but he did nothing to stop them. Before disappearing into the backseat, he quickly looked back and over his shoulder. Cupping a hand to his mouth, he called, *"Don't wuss out."*

The sky that afternoon was perfect and blue and stretched endlessly in all directions, and it was as if the day's brightness and intensity brought each detail into a crystalline focus: the onetime franchise diner from an era of ice cream socials; the massive main lot, just a bit more than half-filled, most of the cars showing themselves as white, gray, light blue, or some other color the sun could not ruin. Kenny stood there for endless seconds, letting the last shouts (*"Yeaah boiiey! You the man!"*) fade. He dutifully watched the sedan disappear into traffic, brushed a stray coagulation of hair from his eyes, felt the sun wide across the middle of his forehead and in a sharper crease between his eyes; he felt anonymous, a loneliness gripping him, this sense of intense emptiness— rooted in his stomach, it spread outward, threatening to swallow him whole. At the same time, Kenny felt something else: the small and penetrating type of failure that comes exclusively when a person must face a question, the answer of which terrifies him.

Kenny's hands were clammy; and he realized that at some point during his conversation with Newell, he had rolled his drawings up into a tight scroll. He dropped to one knee now, and pain flared where he made contact with the sidewalk, and he began smoothing out the damp pieces of paper. Then he wiped his hands on his T-shirt. His head ducked; simultaneously, his arm raised. A quick whiff. Of all days to forget deodorant.

A few months before the World Trade Center was attacked, an angry man of Arabic descent told a librarian in Hamburg, Germany, *Thousands will be dead and you will think of me.* This warning reminded Bing Beiderbixxe of one issued from that high school parking lot—*You don't want to be at school today. I'm telling you because I like you.* And that line never failed to lead Bing back to something he'd read in one of his favorite novels: *Beckett is the last major writer to shape the way we think and see. After him, the major works involve midair explosions and crumbling buildings. This is the new tragic narrative.*

He did not know what, if anything, any of it meant, if those examples weren't just cases where coincidence and human nature created overlapping similarities. Lots of times, the conclusion a person makes tells you more about how they think, as opposed to revealing any kind of grand scheme. After all, someone steps on a butterfly, that doesn't mean he caused an earthquake halfway across the world. Only, this was not butterflies and this was not earthquakes.

Bing Beiderbixxe was now three months shy of his twenty-fifth birthday and nowhere near the finished and mature person he wanted to be; yet he honestly could claim he was working on it, evolving, taking the slow and arduous baby steps that were mandatory for the transition from self-consciousness to self-awareness, coming into the distance necessary to have some perspective on his past, all that self-help shit. Problem was, at the same time, he was slaving away on an undertaking that just wasn't succeeding, a project that, no matter how good an idea it might have been, just wasn't getting through. Two weekends of each month in a storefront in some strip mall, wasting his afternoons at fold-out autograph tables, sitting beneath too bright halogen lights and dealing with obsessive types who believed that maybe one day his autograph on the first issue of this failing comic book would be worth something, four hours at a time, making small talk with college kids who had little else to do, staring at primitive drawings made by young men who thought his job *was* glamorous, slugoids who for whatever reason wanted his career, wanted to be Bing—which they were more than welcome to be, only then Bing would have to figure out what the hell else he was going to do.

Bing smiled big and pretty. "No," he said, "of course I don't mind personalizing the greeting. To whom do I make this out?"

Searching for his pen, he made light of his forgetfulness, then scribbled out yet another signature, and asked, *What's it like living here in Vegas?*

Shy teenagers shrugged and said they'd grown up here, they didn't have anything to compare Las Vegas to. Know-it-alls looked at Bing like he was batshit crazy, as if he'd asked them what it was like to live in Crapsville, North Dakota.

Whatever they said, Bing listened. However strangely they acted, he responded with practiced sincerity and understanding and the momentary pretense of thought. Beiderbixxe the Curious. Bing the Attentive. A final sip of his Big Slam. Another bite of a high-protein energy bar that tasted like a combination of chocolate and chalk.

Surely life had to hold more than this! Rock and movie stars got nubile groupies in thong underwear, after all. Rappers traveled with posses of Uzi-toting steel-fanged homies. Even young women with acoustic guitars and songs of female teen angst didn't do so badly, attracting younger women with glandular problems and metal lunch boxes stuffed with dead white roses. But your friendly neighborhood comic book illustrator? All he got were these long-haired mongoloids, lurking in the background, trying to summon the intestinal fortitude to approach him. How the Bingster yearned to break free of labels and limitations! How much *more* than a simple illustrator he knew himself to be: a scholar and a gentleman, a chronicler of metaphysical conundrums, and a devotee of historical arcana. Did the surrounding flotsam have the slightest idea that Der Bingelot not only had built, but maintained and governed, his own virtual Roman empire? That he was now proficient in JavaScript, HTML, C++, and rudimentary bump mapping? That after only two months on free weights, he had lost five pounds while increasing his arm-curl workout by ten?

And did any of his so-called fans, in any way, shape or form, know which burlesque house was nearest his motel?

The espadrille eased down onto the gas pedal, moved to the brake, and did the same thing, the sedan inching ahead. Lorraine stared forward, without energy. In front of her, a blood-red pickup sat high on raised tires, its gleaming bumper festooned with stickers. One announced that freedom was not free. Another promoted 92.3 KOMP as the rock of Las Vegas. Especially eye-catching was the sketchy outline of a spike-haired boy—he had a devilish look, and was urinating, in an arcing stream, onto the name of a foreign automaker.

Ahead a bit and to the left, some poor bastard was standing in front of a raised hood, waving through black-and-white billows. But he wasn't responsible for all the gridlock. It was a gruesome scene, spanning all four lanes in each direction, with rows of brake lights and blinkers washed out by the sun, and an oppressive glare reflecting off hoods and windows. Even the air along the road was gray and dingy and gross, for pollutants had collected for months without any rainfall to wash them away. Median foliage, fortified by so much carbon dioxide, was in full bloom and covered in soot, with the weaker, newer branches buckling beneath layers of dirt. Mobile calls constantly juxtaposed and faded. Kerosene mirages were not uncommon.

Lorraine checked her rearview and silently cursed her judgment, taking Sahara in the middle of the afternoon. By the time she'd seen this was the wrong decision, it had been too late. Now she was stuck, halfway up the overpass, unable to tell what color that traffic signal was. She guessed it didn't matter. Listlessly, she flicked the switch for her turn signal.

Halfway down the backseat, Newell was hunched over something or other, sulking maybe, perhaps manipulating a handheld stylus, playing one of his games. Was it possible he was immersing himself in the pages of some comic book? Perish the thought. He'd just come from a comic book store, absurd to think he'd be looking at a comic book. At least then he'd be reading. Lorraine adjusted her rearview mirror.

"Quit staring," he said.

She chalked it up to his age. *Almost twelve and a half,* the boy liked to brag, as if the six months made a difference, as if anyone besides his mother cared. That stretch where he would rather drink urine than sit up front with her. Like Muhammad coming down from the mountain if he deigned to argue about which radio station's commercials he wanted to hear. Whatever he was doing back there, it was sure to ruin his posture, keep him preoccupied for a little while.

"What? Quit it."

Jesus. She was never going to get into that lane.

Within sight yet impossibly far away, the intersection's two nearest corners were anchored by convenience stores, while its two far corners were occupied by gas stations. The convenience stores had gas pumps, the gas stations had mart attachments, and each of their bright color schematics promised pleasure and reliability, a smile with your receipt or your money back—if you could manage to make it three blocks.

"Momz?"

. . .

"Mamasita?"

"So you're talking to me now?"

"Come *aww-hhn.*"

"You know the rules."

"Please. Pleeeeezzze."

"The doctor says—"

"*FPhhf.*"

"And your teachers—"

"*FFFFfffphhhfffft.*"

"Well," she said, trying to sound cheerful. "I think skim milk is tasty."

"Knock yourself out, then. Don't let me stop you."

"Besides, it looks to me like you're already sugared to your hyperactive little jowls."

"MOM."

She could not help but laugh a little, feeling a small measure of satis-faction, and eased her foot, for a pulse, onto the gas. "What's the matter, sweetie, the way you dish it out—"

He was brooding, pushing his hand on his cheek. Was he really checking to see if he had jowls? The possibility was so cute that Lorraine felt her heart break.

"You know, maybe if you'd stop being obnoxious, you might be al-lowed to get Slurpees."

"YEAH. Maybe I'll do that. OKAY. And maybe I'll grow lips on my butt. I won't need a Slurpee then. I'll spend all day kissing my own—"

"Language."

A rancher with a comb-over had been checking her out for a while. From his secondhand Ford, he waved her into the lane. Lorraine thanked him with a dip into the shallow end of her endless reservoir of forced smiles. Still good-looking enough to set hayseeds and horny teenagers drooling, it was true. Her palm guiding the steering wheel, she flashed a glance at herself in the rearview mirror, and immediately fixated on small truths she could not avoid: eyes that stayed rigid around the corners; cheekbones that used to smile easily through kick steps, now puttyish.

"You know, Newell, you don't *have* to get anything."

"What do any of us have to do? Huh, Ma?"

"Don't be smart."

"Rilly. Why *are* we here?"

A terse smile. She kept her foot flexed on the brake. Was it the worst question?

"We are here," Lorraine said, "because your perfect mother made the mistake of turning onto this road in the middle of the afternoon. That is why we are here."

"He could have taken me home, you know."

She felt an aftertaste in her mouth, perhaps the onset of car nausea, and dutifully flicked the console, turning the air-conditioning system to a lower setting. A look in the rearview showed her son was actually staring back, waiting on an answer. She puckered her lips, checked her lipstick.

"How many times have I told you—"

He answered with a snort.

"Well, maybe if you explain it to me again? He's old enough to drive, but still hangs out in comic stores?"

"Maaa."

"How about we change the subject. How was this week's . . . drawer? Did he do the . . . autographs? Like you wanted?"

"I don't even care about him. Bonerbite's lame. You should see the stuff Kenny's been doing."

"Something else, Newell."

"Serious, though. It's *awesome.* And he's cool to me. I don't—"

"I said . . ."

A vacant lot between two of the strip malls on the near side of the street: tumbleweeds and jetsam and landfill; a chipped fiery bird painted across the weathered hood of an orange Camaro, a small black-and-red FOR SALE BY OWNER sign taped to the tinted windshield. One one thousand, Lorraine counted, a trick that allowed her to control her anger. Two one thousand. With a measured, almost forced cheeriness, she said: "You understand there's a dramatic age difference between you and Kenny."

The boy kept staring out of the window. A strong vein down the side of his neck tensed.

"He's nice enough, Newell. I'm not disagreeing with you, honey. But I don't think I'm being unreasonable, wanting to know where you two are going tonight."

Broken glass sparkled in random constellations; the outline of tract homes and subdivisions through the background was faint, but undeniably present, the purple mountain ranges apathetic across the far distance.

"Newell?"

. . .

"At least explain why I'm so out of line, then."

. . .

"A phone number. Where his mother can be reached."

His silence broke softly, with the declaration: "He doesn't have parents, Mom."

"Oh . . ."

"Yeah."

"I'm sorry, honey. I didn't know."

"He's a mutant sewer dweller."

"NEWELL."

"A *total* perv."

"YOUNG MAN."

"Serious. He's gonna take me out tonight and abuse me."

"THAT'S ENOUGH—"

A snort. A cackle. The boy slapping his knee. "He told me so. Burgers, then anal penetration."

1.6

Anal rape was actually the phrase Lorraine would first remember, though she also would recall hamburgers had been involved in some strange way. Certainly, Newell's spoken words would not be her foremost memory of the day he went missing (that honor would go to the phone call, received deep in the night, those screams, malicious, cackling, a celebratory spew of profanities). However, throughout the ensuing months, as Lorraine obsessed, she would, in a tedious and meticulous and thoroughly round-about manner, reconstruct the entire sentence in all its snotty glory, with every one of the untold layers of torment that words contain.

Burgers, then anal penetration, would remain a sticking point for her, leaping out from her reflections of that afternoon's gleaming heat. Though Lorraine had immediately reacted in the car, firmly putting an end to Newell's little rebellion, when she looked back on it, she was vexed by how much there had been for her to clamp down on—the ugly fact of her child saying such an obviously inappropriate sentence; the uglier fact of her child disrespecting her, blatantly challenging her; and because her boy—*her son*—had even been capable of saying something so wrong.

Then again, why should she have read more into it than the obvious?

It was a crude joke, nothing more, uttered during one of those rock-and-a-hard-place meltdowns that every parent and child get caught in. A kid hears things from older kids. He repeats things from off cable. That doesn't mean he knows what he's talking about. How the hell could he? A child's world is a ripe grape waiting to be tasted. His youth is eternal, his life an adventure in which he is the hero and the star. A child imagines what the future will be like, naturally, but he sees only swashbuckling adventures, true love, hundred-room mansions atop seaside cliffs. His contemplations must be informed by the viewpoint of youth, and therefore, by their very nature, must be flawed in the most beautiful and optimistic ways. The real meanings of words, the weight of consequences, *adulthood,* with all its responsibilities and implications, is as impenetrable to a child as martian trigonometry. That is one of the beauties of youth. And it is why someone has to be there, vigilant.

Kenny had glimpses naturally, in nibbles and morsels and bite-size portions, arriving with the aunt who filled uncomfortable silences with innocuous, if equally uncomfortable, questions; with the trade school representatives and army recruiters who regularly prowled the cafeteria of his vocational high school. The future was thirty seconds during late-night syndicated dating shows where a low-rent spokesperson talked about the career in the exciting field waiting for you. It was some huge and unknowable network of people who were key to getting cushy summer jobs, like, say, being a lifeguard at a hotel pool. It didn't matter how much you wanted the whistle around your neck and the perch above all those oiled bodies. Like, like . . . like how you got it? The procedures involved? They were beyond Kenny, he didn't know how they worked or where to begin. The future was nebulous and large and halfhearted. It was a promise to get his shit together. Right after the commercial. After the show. Five more minutes. Kenny tried not to think about the future. Thinking—*wanting*—only hurt worse.

Shit happened, then more shit happened. *That* was the future.

The easiest way to deal was to stretch out across the floor along the far end of his dad's trailer and press his chest against a throw rug that in no way cushioned him from the hard floor. Occasionally, Kenny warmed up with a light sketch, say, a front porch—the house cat up on blocks in the driveway, the rusting jalopy trapped in a tree. Eventually his attention would turn toward his father's illicit pleasures, stashed in a cardboard box. His dad would be in some church basement for one of his "meetings," he'd be relapsing at some penny-ante blackjack table, and Kenny would surround himself with soft-focus photographs on high-glossed pages: the syndicated bombshell lolling amid a frothy surf; the televangelist's infamous secretary straddling a pew; the airbrushed bodies that melted, as if by magic, into bearskin rugs; girls of the Ivy League, their pleated skirts tantalizingly raised; would-be starlets, more than eager to show a rosy cheek.

The harder stuff, it was there, too: magazines that were lusterless and brittle with dried misuse; women who were not bunnies, or pets, but haggard. Inhumane hairstyles. Eyes raccooned with dark circles. Page one seventy-six of a prehistoric *Swan* revealing a cigarette burn along a stringy, pockmarked forearm; the foldout from January's *Cheri* showing a deep bruise on the back of a thigh. On the rare—indeed, miraculous—occasion when a woman still wore panties, inevitably the fabric was flimsy, and the model always pulled it to the side. Using her index and middle finger, she'd spread apart the gates to what should have been her most private self.

A singular photograph had preoccupied Kenny for a good while now, most of the summer, really. It took up a full, loose page, which had been freed from the magazine's confining staples. Basically, the photo was a woman's head, a close-up. She had an oblong head, long and thin, with platinum curls framing her features in the manner of an ancient football helmet. The woman wore way too much makeup but you could still see pockmarks on her skin. Collagen bloated her lips beyond the cracking point. And there was something else—inside the squinting slits that doubled as this woman's eyes. This strange, almost unquantifiable quality. It brought a cohesion to her expression, it seemed to Kenny, a clarity to her pain, all but transforming her dried, crack whore face, creating a statement, a message that Kenny could not give words to, yet somehow recognized.

Stretched out in his father's trailer, sitting at his mom's kitchen table, trying to get away from all the drama by crashing with his aunt, using the loose magazine page in front of him as a guide, working from and relying on his memory, Kenny would clutch a nub of pencil and ignore his more carnal instincts. A yellowed white pages might serve as his table, the back of an unsolicited flyer as his canvas. With fastidious delicacy, he would reproduce the woman's chins of loose flesh. He'd take great pains to render her nostrils as bloated, and scribble a flush into her cheeks, so it appeared she had recently concluded a vigorous workout. Often, he tried to shade her gaze with what he felt to be a proper desperation. Then he might go back, augmenting her hatred, adding to it the first traces of a saddened poise.

Here and there a tangled forelock would fall in front of his eyes, and less often than this, he'd brush the annoyance behind his ear, and through every second he would become less aware of the water pump's arrhythmic hum. Further he'd retreat, further, until he entered a locale without matter or dimension, without thought or awareness of thought, this almost spiritual calm, where sound was black and the earth no longer rotated around the sun, and he was not ashamed of being a perv who rummaged through his dad's cardboard boxes for dirty magazines; indeed, in this realm of his own creation Kenny did not worry about the currents that run between a naked woman, the guy doing her, and the voyeur getting off on the scene. He did not worry about the fact that he had never kissed a girl.

The inside of his right hand became smudged with lead. His left sneaker lolled in slow, counterclockwise circles. He refused to think about whether letting Mom know about Dad's latest binge would end custody weekend visitations. He refused to think about senior year or anything that might happen afterward. Noticing a flaw, Kenny would quickly double back. Persistent, short jabs of his eraser would reconfigure the glop that sat, iridescent, on her soft jewel of a tongue. Broad strokes might reduce the ejaculate along her chin. Once in a while he even lucked out. The insulting connotations that accompany exaggerated humor would actually disappear, and the woman's face would be left with a stressed, fundamental humanity—the nobility inherent in struggles that cannot be won.

Problem was, about the only serious feedback Kenny'd ever gotten about his work had come on a school desk, scribbling back and forth with some dude who had a later class in the same room. You couldn't exactly know if you were any good when your only responses came from a person you'd never met and didn't know anything about. When the only real, live person who'd ever seen your sketches in person was all of twelve years old. Kenny had to get opinions from someone who mattered, he knew this much. All summer long, he'd counted down the days toward each weekend, figuring out which pictures were best suited for that particular visiting artist, coming up with new drawings, tweaking old ones, improving them right up until he'd gone too far. Kenny had ruined an embarrassing amount of his most promising stuff and then he'd acted as if it were no big thing, consoling himself with the idea that the whole deal was kind of stupid anyway. He sabotaged himself in other ways too, volunteering to take his aunt to a swap meet on a Sunday when a particular visitor was supposed to be receptive to amateur work. The Reliant hadn't started. He just plain didn't show up and Newell asked where he'd been, and he had no response, not anything believable. Newell shrugged, he answered, *Sure,* and from the hurt in the boy's eyes, Kenny saw that his friend believed in him just a little bit less, maybe Newell didn't even believe in him anymore, Kenny couldn't blame him if he didn't, retreating the way he did always made Kenny feel terrible and disappointed in himself, the biggest coward the world had ever known. But he couldn't help it. The thought of a reckoning was just that terrifying.

Beneath the awning outside Amazin' Stories he took his time and retied his sneakers. He flattened out the drawings that had begun to curl up at the edges and rearranged the order of the sheets. Kenny felt along the war zone of his chin. His fingers ran over hairs he'd missed the last time he'd tried to shave, fledgling hairs that had grown in since then, and finally, a triangle of three small pimples. A deep breath. A ginger step forward.

His strategy, as much as he had one, was to hang in the back, wait for everyone to leave. That got shot to hell when he saw that the area around the table could not have been more deserted—just Bing there, alone, slumped in his seat, staring down at nothing in particular. Gravity seemed to be pulling extra hard at the flesh of the comic book artist's cheeks and chin, for it loaded his jawline with extra weight, and made his face look really heavy. Kenny watched him remove his glasses, let out a breath that was more like a sigh, and rub the corner of his eyes with the inside of his palm.

But then the guy looked up. He said, "Oh. Hey."

"Um. Am I—"

"No. Of course not."

"I didn't mean . . ."

A hand extended, waving him forward. "Please." A smile at once apologetic and welcoming: "Bing. Bing Beiderbixxe."

"Right. I know, hi."

"Sorry about that. Long day. Kind of hit a wall, I guess."

"Don't worry about—it's—I mean—"

"What's your name?"

"Oh. . . . Kenny. My—I . . . Kenny."

"Hi, Kenny. Nice to meet you."

"Yeah, hi. Right. Nice to meet you, too. Ah, I want—wanted to—I was hoping . . . What I mean—" Kenny stopped, gathered himself. "I thought your last issue was real excellent. How you did the Sienkiewicz and all . . ."

"Thank you, Kenny. What a nice thing to say."

Bing cocked his head slightly, as if waiting for the next step. Kenny shifted from one foot to the other. He started to speak, but the wires got crossed, on the way from his brain to his mouth, the map turned upside down. Bing's face remained patient, plastered with indulgence. For a moment he smoothly rubbed his eyeglasses against the part of his shirt where the fabric lapped over the buttons.

"Anything you'd like me to sign? That's what I'm here for."

"Oh—Oh, *shit.* I can't believe—Mr. Bidderboxxe, I swear I had them out to bring. I—I set them out."

"It's all right, Kenny." Bing put his glasses on now. As if he were a veterinarian putting a suffering pet to sleep for its own good, he nodded toward Kenny's chest. "And what do we have here?" He reached out for the crumpled papers and set them down in front of him, and here it was, the future arriving with the next moment and the next: Bing trying to smooth out the place mat so it didn't roll up at the edges; Bing giving up on the rolling edge and taking in the drawing, his brow crinkling into a pointed arrow, the comic book artist squinting a bit, pursing his lips. "You did this?"

It was as if Kenny were anesthetized, as if he were going through the motions of being himself. Bing did not seem to care, he was raising his hand and extending a finger, nudging his frames back up the bridge of his nose. He was remarking about Kenny's touch with a pencil, how sophisticated the shades of her hair and cheeks were, their contrasts. "Her expression is really great," Bing said. "And I really like what you did with her eyes. Most of the time, when someone brings me a naked woman, they're not women, you know? Not flesh and blood. This is real. Really nice, Kenny. Let's see what else you have here."

He emerged into the parking lot in time to watch a *V*-pattern of birds ascending above the disappearing horizon of traffic signals. The shopping plaza appeared as a large stucco corral, reining him in on all sides. The asphalt lot was a lake of shining tar. Kenny's head swam with the unlimited possibilities of a dreamer's imagination. If he'd known how to whistle, man would he have been whistling.

In the grand scheme, the whole thing was like a very special afterschool television presentation. He saw this: the wily pro recognizing the potential that lay inside this unacknowledged and rough diamond, the grizzled vet taking an obviously troubled and shy and awkward pupil under his wing, helping someone step forward while at the same time helping himself let go. The feel-good story of the year. It had everything except the group hug while the music swelled and the credits rolled.

So maybe that had been expecting too much. Entirely possible that Bing Beiderbixxe's generosity and interest, no matter how legit it had been, also was practiced, standard. Asking about rumpled papers was part of the gig. Giving advice helped push units.

And really, how hard is it to say something nice about one or two drawings? How hard is it to show someone a different way to grip his pencil? To tell someone, keep up the good work?

Bing had not offered him a job, that was for sure. He hadn't provided a name to contact, a number to call, or an address to e-mail. In no way, shape, or form had the guy bestowed entry into any kind of future or profession. The facts were plain: he was right where he always was. Outside, alone, lost again, looking for his Plymouth.

Yet he felt everything had changed. He hadn't gotten what he'd come here for. But he'd gotten something, that was for sure.

The beat-up, boxy two-door was a relic from the eighties—the more paranoid stoners at Vo Tech thought it was an undercover FBI car. Eventually, it turned up on the other side of the lot, in a row and space parallel to where Kenny had been looking. He headed around to the passenger side, and wrapped his hand in his shirttail. He pulled open the creaking door, watched a crushed Big Gulp cup fall out.

All over the car's bucket seat and the floor, Kenny saw parts of other crushed Big Gulps, many with scenes from a crappy summer movie on their sides. He saw segments of tangled ribbons from cassette tapes. He saw loose magazine subscription cards and the hardened remains of deformed french fries. Assorted coins were in there, some of them shining, others moldy and green. And plastic soda container lids. And a corroded and ripped egg carton that once had been blue. And twisted straw fragments. And the ripped partitions of various diner place mats (pencil etchings invariably running along their margins). And the disconnected and free-floating spiral spine of a notebook. And the casings of two shotgun shells that Kenny had found when he'd been wandering through a vacant lot behind his mom's apartment complex. A sick recognition took him, heavy, pulling. The inside of his mouth was impossibly dry. He tossed a few more empty and crushed soda cans onto the cement. He threw out a pair of burger wrappers that seemed to have been fused together with dried condiments. He carefully placed his drawings in the newly created space in the front seat. He climbed into the car and struggled to cross over, into the driver's seat, without putting his knee through the drawings.

What really sucked was, not only did the FBImobile not have air-conditioning, but ever since his dad had sideswiped that light pole, something had been wrong with the driver's side, so the driver-side door wouldn't open, and something electrical had shorted out, so the driver-side window wouldn't roll down. Which meant that as the engine turned over on the fourth attempt, as balding tires backed over the cardboard with a dull *pop,* and Kenny started off to go get his aunt, not only did he *not* enjoy a refreshing swoosh of air onto his face, but he received *magni-*

fied sun, *concentrated* heat. It meant the FBImobile was basically a mobile furnace.

It took less than a block before he pulled into the Jack in the Box drive-through circle, and by then his pit sweat was worse than usual, the back of his T clinging to him like a second skin. A late model Mazda sports car was idling ahead, at the farthest window. While Kenny stared at the menu and waited for the first noise from the microphone clown head, a car pulled up behind him. Kenny felt the beads of perspiration forming, then dripping down his forehead. His thighs were roasting inside his jeans. He distracted himself by anticipating all the certainties of a drive-through exchange, not the least of which was the polite greeting, the simple pleasure of being asked what you wanted: *Hello, may I take your order please.*

Except the FBImobile's driver-side window would not roll down.

And the driver's door would not open.

Kenny didn't know how he would be able to answer the clown head, if it ever asked him hello, may I take your order please, which didn't seem to be happening anytime soon, anyhow. His hand tapped against the steering wheel. His temples pulsed and pounded. Here he was, a promising artist—hadn't he just been told he was promising? And he was trapped in place, stuck in this stupid box of trash. Promise wasn't enough. Promise wasn't a way out.

About the last thing Kenny needed right now was to have to scream through a closed window for his stupid soda. Why was getting a stupid Pepsi turning into a problem-solving quiz? If the FBImobile didn't get moving soon the steering wheel would start shaking.

Shifting the car into park, he started scooting across vinyl upholstery. And was met by the safety belt, its searing heat penetrating the denim of his jeans, scorching the soft skin inside the back of his knee.

From behind him came the tinnish bleats of car horns.

"HEY?" Kenny screamed back at the raised window. Bellowing now, from the depths of his lungs: "HELLO?

"WOULD SOMEBODY HELP ME ALREADY?"

I WILL NEVER BE ABLE TO DO
ENOUGH FOR MY CHILD

6:30–8:30 P.M.

2.1

They were drowsy on the four-poster bed, their first time like this in longer than Lorraine cared to remember. She nuzzled into her husband's side and felt the beat of Lincoln's breath faint in her ear, warm on her cheek. Lorraine slipped a hand between the buttons of his work shirt, laying her palm on Lincoln's chest; she felt him take a deeper breath, knew he was inhaling the fragrance of her apple shampoo. Her hair was still damp, fanned out near him in dark, soggy tendrils. Her robe was loosely tied, slack enough for the cotton to part, the edge of her nipple brushing against his side.

So simple, what was unfolding, layered with pleasures: the joy of pet-
ting, for one thing; this rekindled aspect of their closeness, for another;
and the sheer comfort of knowing that despite the difficulties, they still
were drawn to each other; the affirmation which such knowledge brings.
Satisfaction bloomed inside Lorraine, a serenity that was tactile, clean, a
peace both private and shared. She released a giggle into the meat of Lincoln's collarbone, picked back up on her train of thought.

"I'm just not sure it's a good idea."

The overworked hum of the air conditioner was audible throughout
their bedroom. Lincoln kissed her shoulder and received no response. He
eased his forearm from behind her head, began shaking his hand to get
some circulation back, weighing and considering each prospective word.

"I hear what you're saying."

A series of thumps—descending the stairwell, the boy disobeying orders once more, straying from his room. Lorraine withdrew from Lincoln and away from eye contact. He rustled behind her. When his palm
skimmed the curvature of her shoulder, she flinched. He continued,
pressing lightly into the muscles on each side of her neck.

"Sometimes family means compromise, Lor."

"What—so this is my compromise?"

"Someone's got to be the adult. I'm saying: we might as well enjoy it
once in a while."

His fingers moved underneath her hair, to the base of her skull, where
they began making small, circular rotations. Lorraine remained still. Re-
fraining from encouragement or appreciation, she willfully directed her
attention toward the open yard of space where the drapes were not completely closed. The first shades of twilight were cascading through, and
Lorraine could see down to the backyard; water calm in the pool where
no one had swum this summer; the floating chair's shadow creeping
across the deep end.

She felt his fingers tracing down her neck, arriving at its base, where
they dug into the twin reservoirs of tension, attacking Lorraine's knots,
kneading.

"He asks why I don't leave you, Link."

"Yeah," he admitted. "He asks me that too."

"And I don't know where he *gets* that type of language, but . . . He's acting worse and worse. I can't control him and—"

"All kids that age are obnoxious, Lor. They all want to kill their parents. I sure as hell did. That doesn't mean he's whacked in the head. It sure doesn't mean we have to live like hermits."

Beyond the brick wall of the backyard, an endless grid of lights awaited, the violet night deepening, melding with the mountain ranges. Lincoln zeroed in on her troubled spots, rocking over them, lightly at first, then applying more pressure. An affirming murmur escaped her lips. Her thoughts momentarily fell away. Now she felt new contact, warmth and weight against her rear, his waist beginning a slight grind against her lower back. Against her better judgment Lorraine shut her eyes, allowing the soothing colors to start through her.

"I don't like how he talks to me."

"I know."

"And I don't want you rewarding him."

"I hear you."

Now her backside pressed back into him and she leaned against him, feeling his erection on the small of her back. She mewled, going a bit high and giggly. "It's tempting. But a Saturday night? With all the loonies running around out there."

From beyond the house's opposite end, the neighbor's Rhodesian ridgeback started its nightly howls.

"I just want to make sure we're on the same page," she said.

Truth be told, they hadn't been on the same page for a while now. But as far as Lincoln Ewing was concerned, things had really started veering south when Lorraine had stopped putting it in her mouth. Which maybe wasn't exactly the fairest assessment—Lincoln could admit as much, adding that dating back to their courtship, Lorraine had never been, oh, *enthusiastic* about having it in her mouth; never confident in its handling and manipulation. The difference, however, was that while her efforts traditionally had been somewhat token and tentative, they nonetheless had been *efforts,* undertaken in the interest of reciprocation and the spirit of fair play, as an outgrowth of her affection—both for Lincoln and for this bond they had forged. Fact is, there used to be something poignant in the way she fumbled with it, something sentimentally beautiful in the awkward kiss she'd plant on its tip, and then her mouth's enveloping warmness, Lorraine keeping it in her mouth for stretches whose protracted nature somehow heightened the effect: long enough for the act to be a thrill, but not so long that her inexperience showed, less literally turning out to be more as far as he had been concerned. And sure over the years there must have been some reduction, a gradual tapering of her oral proclivities. But Lincoln had a mortgage to pay and a child to raise and some fifty thousand square feet of convention space and meeting rooms to book every weekend, so he might be forgiven if his wife's infrequent desire to blow him had simmered on the back burner of his subconscious. The fact was, their union had flourished and their lives had continued, and if the passion had died down over the course of twelve years, well, that was normal enough wasn't it, so long as the embers still burned. Which they most certainly did, low maybe, but consistent, beneath all the kindling and paperwork and responsibilities. Sometimes Lorraine put it in her mouth and sometimes she didn't. Did. Didn't. The only thing, somewhere around the time of last tax refund's arrival, about the time where school had let out for summer, the boy had been at a friend's, and a video had led to pecking. And Lincoln and Lorraine had been on the couch, doing a little more than pecking, and he had, kind of, gently just sort of pulled on her blouse in a way that would get her heading southwards. And just as deftly, a smiling Lorraine had veered away from that region, and all of a sudden it occurred to Lincoln that he could not think of the last time she *had*—and he'd told his wife as much, doing so in a subdued and low-key manner, one that was not confrontational or in any way intended to cause strife. Just brought up the thought. Not the biggest deal, he said. More like, *Hey, you're at the amusement park, why not go on all the rides?* Lincoln sure as hell spent three-day stretches between her legs, didn't he?

"Symbolism, Link. Gender power structures." Lorraine explained she did not have a problem with putting it in her mouth, *per se.* "It's just, if

I'm going to have it in my mouth, I need the act to be *organic*. Not to have it in my mouth because you want it there, but because the beauty of the moment dictates that my mouth is the natural and correct place for it to be."

Lincoln had listened. He'd nodded. He'd even refrained from cracking how having it in her mouth felt pretty damn fine in the beauty of every and any given moment.

Right, is what he'd said. *Great.*

"Except, um, is there any timetable on just when this beautiful and perfect event might take place? Any ideas on when those planets are going to align? Because, sweet darling, from my side of the fence, that particular special's been dropped from the menu." The way Lincoln saw things, the mere option, the thought that Lorraine could *if she so chose* put it in her mouth, this no longer entered her mind. He went so far as to wonder if there was any chance that Lorraine's gag reflex was more mental than physical? "Maybe?" he prodded. "Just maybe?"

How clear it seemed to him now. As far as mistakes go, that particular ditty had fallen somewhere between President Announces Tax Hike and President Admits Getting Rim Jobs from Male Intern. Not just because Lorraine would not look at him, but had sat there, arms crossed so tightly that they squished what, in better moods, Lincoln still thought of as perfect breasts. More important, it had been a mistake because Lincoln had given her the perfect opening and justification to get all indignant and self-righteous the way she liked to. And simple as Simon, just because his brain had locked for five seconds and he had inserted his ass into his mouth, the subject of conversation no longer was Lorraine getting lovey on his nuts, nor was it Lincoln's urges, nor even the undiscussed but not-insubstantial problem of Lorraine only liking sex in the missionary position. The subject was not that Lincoln would have given his left testicle for something besides plain one-scoop vanilla sex and it was not the sheer volume of Lorraine's hesitancies and it sure as hell was not Lincoln's fear that all of these hesitancies pointed to deeper issues that needed to be addressed in this marriage, questions about limits and boundaries and how far she was willing to go to please. No. Because of a blunder that Lincoln, dumbass that he was (he was *such* a dumbass), knew better than to make, things had firmly and irrevocably moved into Bad Man Makes Girl Cry Territory. Pig Territory. Which was a howling shame. A minor tragedy. Because when he got to those pearly gates and Saint Peter opened the book on his life, Lincoln Ewing was more than a little sure the record would show he took great pains to be supportive of Lorraine, understanding of her emotions, sensitive to the slightest movements of her moon; the record would show he was a loving husband, a proud parent, a first-rate provider, one of those guys who lived on that intellectual and emotional plane where sexuality was merely a part of his larger marriage and family structure. Never bitched about stretches where he and Lorraine were not intimate (if he did, it was usually good-natured). Never moaned about junctures where the intimacy was perfunctory and did nothing for anyone's libido. Without question he respected the value of privacy in a marriage, understood an individual's need to maintain his or her sense of self, yet at the same time he did not want limitations on honesty, nor boundaries on intimacy. He made all these concessions and he aspired to all these things, and what did it get him? Not a hummer on a crisp summer night, that was for goddamn sure. What he got was trapped in another Politics of Marriage Conversation, one more evening tactfully countering Lorraine's points and defending himself, apologizing and then pleading and then groveling.

When he got down to it, when he'd calmed down and was off somewhere nursing a good stiff drink, Lincoln was introspective enough to admit this dynamic was nothing new, but in fact went back to when he'd first noticed Lorraine. He'd been a lightweight, twenty-two, just another former athlete turned glorified salesman. Hadn't even known better than to give convention reps those souvenir pens with the dress disappearing from off the showgirl's body. He used to bring prospective clients backstage to the Lido show—corporate reps were always thrilled to get introduced to the dancers, the combo of sex and glamour and exclusivity was just the thing for greasing a deal. The chorus girls were used to it, they'd received attention and kindness from men for so long that they took a certain amount for granted. It was not all that uncommon for showgirls to use their sexual allure, hustling themselves clothes and jewelry and a run of the high life. Only, where they'd turned haughty and jaded, Lorraine appeared genuinely conflicted by the whole routine. She did her part, glad-handing and smiling big as per orders from above; however, it seemed to Lincoln that she was uncomfortable with her sexual power, at odds with the attention it drew. Backstage, he'd watch her shake hands and smile and give nothing of herself, saw that she was holding back, guarded, defensive, sometimes even hostile toward this part of the job. They'd discussed it over the years, carrying out a running debate over whether she'd been there to be a dancer or a consort; what was the harm in acting decently toward people who were in a position to keep your employer's business successful. The issue never had been completely put to bed between them, their debate never concluded. Equally unsettled were Lincoln's attempts at getting beyond her natural recalcitrance, his perpetual mission to satisfy and—why not—please her. Somewhere along the line, this had found its own life. Without either party paying attention, the dynamic had grown into one of the sustaining patterns of their marriage, its own game, replete with its own rules—Lincoln trying harder, making Lorraine more unsatisfied, which in turn made Lincoln more determined.

Oh, the sex they used to have working their tempers off on each other! How she used to wail! Sitting upright, Lorraine wrapped around him; her body convulsing; Lorraine sobbing, weeping in release, finally giving herself to him, finally his. If there was something inside her that needed to be won or taken, then something inside of him also needed to win her or take her, and once he had, once all barriers were broken through and all games had been played, then there were no limits, no constraints; rather, there was the way he rolled her around in his mouth; the music he sent through her body; the first time she stuck her finger in his ass at *just* the right moment. . . .

In the days that had followed what Lincoln came to think of as the Argument, he'd mused wistfully on the complicated dimensions of his wife's sexuality. Cute little skirts kept power walking into his office, relaying and picking up the latest departmental memos, and Lincoln had watched their twitching backsides with conflicted interest. It's not like there's ever a good time for your marriage to go through a sexual crisis, but the onset of summer in Las Vegas certainly wasn't ideal. The Consumer Electronics Show bids were also coming up, and Lincoln was the hotel's point man, responsible for coordinating myriad schedules and agendas into a coherent game plan, something that would uniformly hypnotize companies attending the show, convince them to book the Kubla Khan's hotel rooms, its convention spaces, its banquet halls. Under optimum conditions, it was a grueling burden, with deadlines on top of deadlines. There were teleconferences. Videoconferences.

In the wee small hours, Lincoln would ease his sedan through a maze of sweetly named capillary roads and into his moderately prestigious neighborhood. Leafy and fruitless trees provided camouflage for the cul-de-sac of spacious ranch-style homes. Usually the house was dark and silent by the time Lincoln got back, with moths congregating around the near streetlights, and a private security guard parked on a side street, curled asleep in the backseat. Pulling up usually woke the neighbor's dog and set it barking, and Lincoln would turn off the fuzzy sounds of a long-distance baseball game that had kept him company for the drive. His ass dragging down to the cement, his shirttail untucked, Lincoln would trudge up the stairs and find the door to the master bedroom shut—Lorraine was a light sleeper, it was true, she was susceptible to tossing and restlessness, and had been known to shoot up out of dreams, awaken to the lightest peck on the cheek. Still, a certain promotions and marketing executive would manage, even after ten hours of mind-numbing work, to ease the bedroom door open without any creaking. He'd slip under the minority of covers that she had not appropriated. Maybe he'd be daring and kiss her shoulder. Lincoln would stretch out in his bed and look up into the darkness of the ceiling and soon enough his mind would begin to unwind and unpack. And underneath the down comforter and the one-thousand-thread-count linens, his feet, at the toe and ankle, they'd kinda, of their own accord, *twitch*. And if neither the neighbor's barking dog nor the creaking bedroom door nor even the peck on the shoulder had awakened Lorraine, then the twitches were sure to do it; and by the same token, if all the noise and activity already had roused Lorraine, well, his vibrating feet sure weren't going to help get her back to sleep. And so, one night toward the end of May, it simply had been easier for Lincoln to retire to the guest bedroom. The more considerate thing. This although the bed in the spare bedroom had been unfamiliar and unforgiving. This despite the fact that Lincoln truly enjoyed sleeping with the mother of his child, despite the fact that everyone and their sister knows separate beds are a barometer for a relationship in trouble. Lincoln headed into that spare bedroom and he inserted himself upon that crappy fold-out, and whatever sense of independence an expanse of mattress might hold when you've been keeping to your side of the bed for twelve years, whatever sense of freedom might come with being able to wrap yourself in as many sheets as you please, these were small consolations indeed.

The next morning, water boiled. Hormone-free, ranch-raised chicken embryos scrambled over a medium flame.

Lorraine greeted him with a mouth slightly open, eyes calm and small.

She started to say . . .

He interrupted and faded. . . .

There was regret. Embarrassment. Silences and false starts. Each party tried to put his/her best face on the event, advocated certain truths of whose veracity he/she was unsure. A sacrifice *on their part* developed as the company line; each telling him/herself that it made the other's life easier, logistically, if Lincoln slept alone in the other room. It was temporary. Just during the rush at work. When he came home so late. Successive nights. Then successive weeks. Temperatures climbed into the nineties, and then triple digits. The turn into that spare bedroom became progressively easier for Lincoln. Without so much as an attempt to address whether either of them actually *wanted* to be sleeping apart, the distance and regret between them multiplied. And Lincoln understood that Lorraine's remoteness was caused by some sort of insecurity, some type of deep inner unhappiness; he felt it was his job to get through that remoteness, heal that pain. Even when Lorraine started losing her shit, unloading on him for piddling garbage—running out of coffee filters and the like—even then Lincoln weathered her storms, adjusted to her whims. He flowered her with calm, showered her with exotic baked goods; with reservations at restaurants whose kitchens had been re-

vamped by celebrity chefs; with a diamond tennis bracelet; with matching earrings. Lincoln busted his ass to please Lorraine and his efforts
suffered as all things do under the law of diminishing returns: polite
smiles, the platonic squeezing of hands, Lorraine retreating deeper into
silence, erecting more barriers, becoming more distant, more withdrawn,
gradually turning rigid as calculus. It wasn't funny anymore, it wasn't a
game; almost as if she were making a statement, as if it were important
for Lorraine to convey that her will to *not* be pleased was superior to Lincoln's will to make her happy. Incrementally and in stages and all at once,
the possibility hit Lincoln that his wife had hardened her heart, that inside Lorraine was a kernel of unhappiness too profound, too ingrained
for him to be able to affect. Generally, Lincoln possessed an athlete's
confidence, but he started questioning how he acted around his wife,
second-guessing his decisions. He felt himself becoming overly sensitive
to her slightest act, hypercritical to the most basic of exchanges. Like
how she never thanked him for anything, but rather *appreciated him
doing it.* Or when she said, *You know what? Actually, your advice worked
out real well.* Well, maybe he was being a little extreme with that one.
Maybe he was hearing different things from what Lorraine was saying in
some individual cases. But he sure as shit wasn't imagining how she always sat at a distance from him, went cold at his simplest attempts at
physical articulation. Wasn't being overly sensitive to all those excuses she
made— *"We'll wake the boy," "I have to be up early," "I just did my nails."*
And then, on two occasions when the stars actually had been aligned and
the moon was in its proper orbit and, at the suggestion of sex, lo and behold, Lorraine did not freeze up like a cheap computer, even then, forget
about it ending up in her mouth, about the only time she'd moved was
to yawn, or wipe her eyes.

And so finally, one morning—like a week or so ago—they'd been in
the kitchen and the kid had been getting ready to go to wherever the hell
she was shuttling him off to that day, and Lincoln was putting the finishing bites to one of them burnt pieces of toast, and when he rose from
their dinner table, he happened to check out Lorraine's backside. She was
wearing these ballooney palazzo pants, they were unflattering and made

with chintzy fabric. And all of a sudden Lincoln had the tactile sensation of not wanting to be there. He literally regretted every major personal decision he had ever made.

It was a passing emotion, one he was ashamed of, acted against, in opposition to. No matter how goddamn miserable Lorraine's unhappiness made him or what an awful burden her unhappiness was, no matter how many times he lashed out and shoved his foot in his mouth (asking her to please, please, *please* stop being such a cunt), the simple heart of things was that his wife remained the sun around which his universe orbited. The first person he thought of when he heard good news or juicy gossip. The wall he bounced ideas off and the ear upon which his worries fell; literally, the bottom to his line. She had introduced the son of a ranch hand to sushi, helped transform a minor league ballplayer into a corporate executive. Lorraine had shown him there were fine things in life, made him understand he was entitled to enjoy them—to say nothing of the importance of *looking* as if he were entitled to finer things. Lincoln's opinion on the war varied day to day, hour to hour, depending less on news from the front than on whether he wanted to piss her off or not; his relationship to immediate history was based on each particular event's relationship to *their* marriage. Even when black rage took him, when he thought of chucking it all—taking their meager savings and boarding a plane and starting over somewhere—what Lincoln imagined was not his new life on some faraway shore, but Lorraine's reaction; more specifically, he imagined the reaction he would have liked to see: her torn up, heartbroken, loving him with the same intensity as he did her.

Thirteen years ago, when she had insisted on keeping her last name, he had not been able to complain. And thirteen years later, the simple sight of Lorraine wandering through the bedroom naked with that little Tampax string dangling from between her legs, this never failed to send an unspeakable, almost giddy affection through him.

He leaned forward now, his arms coming to rest on his thighs, which were partially covered by the rumpled sheets. His head hung a bit and he looked out horizontally, at some unknowable point beyond the confines of the darkening bedroom. Lincoln rubbed his forehead with his palms, as if trying to will a thought into being. When he finally spoke, it was soberly, with a sad gravity, one that was not directed at Lorraine, nor at himself, but at the concept of what was true, as if he were trying to do justice to the notion of truth itself. Marriages have peaks, he said. They also have valleys. Sometimes you . . . sometimes *we* get caught in a valley. He took Lorraine's hand and his fingers, still callused after all these years away from the batting cages, entwined with hers, so delicate, manicured, perfect. He said if something was wrong with the kid, they'd deal with it. They would do whatever had to be done. Lincoln said he was tired of the spare bedroom. He'd spent six hours with clients today. Six hours on a Saturday. We get out without the kid, what, once a month, if that? Lincoln wasn't saying sex, not so much. Maybe sex in the way that the warmth of a body is sexual, the way that being here with you is nice. Was this so bad? A nice night with his wife? "We could go to Commander's Palace. Or the new place over at the Venetian. We'll pay too much for a tepid Beaujolais. Does this really sound so bad?" And now Lincoln Ewing faced his wife, intent on saying the right thing for once, this one time getting it right; fighting for what mattered most.

2.2

———

]BBIXXE: He used a photo from some porn mag. Only his drawing wasn't
                  lewd or cartoony. Nothing like that. A legitimate attempt at
                  sensitively rendering a pornographic scene.

]KC_FTT_B: How were her tits?

]BBIXXE: I mean, you know how it is. If he goes to art school and puts
                  in the work Homer put into the Odyssey, he might end up w/
                  something.

]1450SAT: You told him this?

]BBIXXE: Well, he wasn't really verbal.

]1450SAT: Some would argue this is more reason to encourage him.

]BBIXXE: Do you have the slightest idea how many drawings people show
                  me at these things? Most guys can draw, a little, I guess, but not
                  where they know what they're doing, not seriously, you know?

]1450SAT: Again, this is more of a reason not less.

]BBIXXE: I said he should keep up the good work. Stop riding my ass
                  already.

]DOMINATR69:   Bingle, I thought this was spposed 2 b some earth rockin
                  theory.

]BBIXXE: I was burnt out, to be honest.

]KC_FTT_B: More like rockin like Dokken—and that aint rockin at all my
                  friend.

]1450SAT: I still don't understand. Some quiet HS'er shows u this halfway
                  decent drawing of a beaver shot on the back of a placemat, &
                  all of a sudden you're quitting the biz for a get rich scheme?

]BBIXXE: Not a scheme. More of a hypothesis. See, what happened, my
                  cheapo publisher's got me booked into this shitty motel at
                  the bottom of the Strip. On my way back there from the
                  store, I started thinking about the drawing. Like I said,
                  a pencil drawing, only well shaded.

]KC_FTT_B: I give a crap beca_se dot dot dot

]BBIXXE: At first I just thought the pencil work would make a seriously
                  nice tattoo. Really elegant and well done. But driving down the
                  Strip, all those signs were shining down on me. & maybe because
                  I was so exhausted, it looked like this huge surreal collage,
                  crazy w/light and colors. It sorta felt like they were all leaping
                  out at me. I guess I made a connection. You know how I do.

]DOMINATR69:   Your bizarre ramblings have me scared, yet oddly captivated.
                  I am repelled, but cannot look away.

]BBIXXE: Think about a tatt—a really detailed cool one. Now give it
                  depth. Give it perspective.

]1450SAT: You mean a rgular painting, imbedded on my bicep?

]BBIXXE: Better even. If it has dimension & perspective, it kind of stops
                  being your average tatt. The medium of what is or isn't
                  tattoo evolves.

]1450SAT: I get it. You want a 3D tattoo.

]DOMINATR69:   You're saying real live body art?

]BBIXXE: *True* body art.

]KC_FTT_B: Sweet mother of Van Halen! This does act_ally rock!!

]DOMINATR69:   I just soiled myself, it rocks so hard.

]BBIXXE: Thank you senoritas. I figured it was worth running past you ladies before I power nap & hit the town.

]DOMINATR69:   Every headbanger with tatt sleeves down their arms will want one. every hipster alt-wierdo. If they have a tatt, they'll want this.

]KC_FTT_B: Yo_cld have it so this arrow's sticking frm yr forehead & blood's g_shing all over yr face. People'll b all trying 2 get th arrow from owt yr head. But then they'll see & be like: *'Oh snaps. It's so real looking. How do I get that shit for myself?'*

]DOMINATR69:   We patent the technique. We'll b rollin in cash!

]1450SAT: I'll be able to quit this suckass techie support shit.

]BBIXXE: KC_FTT_B might even be able to fix his U key!

]KC_FTT_B: I totally say we go 4 it!!!

]BBIXXE: The big technical question I have is about shading. In drawing and painting, shades create the illusion of proportion and dimension. But in a comix, every color has to be separated by a black line. The inside of this part of Weather Report Girl's costume is red. The outside b yellow. A black line separates red & yellow. That portions off those shades. & the effect is flattening. Everything becomes two dimensional.

]1450SAT: I got you. Black sets yr image. Which is probably why black's the best color 4 a tatt—because it's perfect 4 defining an image on flesh.

]DOMINATR69: And U just know flesh can't be the easiest surface to print on.

]1450SAT: So our problem's not that we can't use black. More that if we want real 3D tatts, we have to have those shades and tones.

]BBIXXE: Right. I don't know if that's possible on skin.

]KC_FTT_B: D_de. My co_sin works in a parlor in Reseda. yo_ definitely can mix the colors of a tatt.

]DOMINATR69: What was that?

]1450SAT: They mix the inks on the thing, the palette. Right before they dip the needle.

]DOMINATR69: Oh baby. I just soiled myself again.

]1450SAT: It is SO on.

]BBIXXE: Well, being able to mix inks is nice, but it doesn't really solve the real big questions.

]DOMINATR69: Here he goes again.

]1450SAT: LIVE, directly from my sphincter, it's *Buzzkill Beiderbixxe.*

]BBIXXE: Bitch all you want. But there's a moral issue here. A tattoo gun is basically like a twenty watt dentist drill zapping giant sharp ass needles into human flesh.

]1450SAT: Give Buzzkill a million dollars & he'll complain about the paper bag it got delivered in.

]KC_FTT_B: B_zzkill's in bed w/a Pentho_se Pet—worrying if the whipped cream is past the expiration date.

]BBIXXE: You dip the point of this sharp ass needle into a basically toxic substance, power up the drill, and *inject* the toxic ink in2 the skin, one dot at a time.

]DOMINATR69:   Watch as Buzkill goes to VEGAS. On SATURDAY NIGHT. And spends all his time IN A CHATROOM!

]BBIXXE: Suck my fuck. Do you even know what I've been through today? I've been eating shit since before dawn and glad-handing with mongoloids all day, and now I get to this crappy motel and take five minutes to check in with you and you guys just don't let up.

]KC_FTT_B: Serio_s brah, when yo_ get all whining like this, yo_ sound like a total pre-op. It's kind of a t_rn on.

]BBIXXE: Just how much do you expect a person to take?

]DOMINATR69:   Poor Bingle. Maybe you should bust out the cape. For old times sake. It'll make you feel better.

]BBIXXE: I mean really. With me & with the poor bastard getting drilled in three dimensions, is there a limit to how much abuse they can realistically be expected 2take?

]DOMINATR69:   Hitting Vegas in a cape: that's an answer if I ever heard one

]1450SAT: Know what I never understood about LV? Honestly: they got slot machines in the front of supermarkets right? In the convenience stores. Y not just put them in the hotel rooms? If they put video poker in yr john, you could like sit on the toilet & play at the same time.

]KC_FTT_B: D_de. That toilet thing wld be cool. Like: *Holy shit. I got a jackpot.*

]BBIXXE: I've got to get some new friends.

]KC_FTT_B: Get it? Slots in a toilet: *Holy shit. Jackpot.*

]DOMINATR69:   Don't get all Amnesty International Bingawumba. This was your idea remember.

]BBIXXE: Because what you're talking about doesn't even make sense. Just off the top of my head, how are you going to mix ink *after* it's been injected into flesh?

]1450SAT: What if we went with layers?

]BBIXXE: xghlph?

]KC_FTT_B: f_ckers, don't even know what f_nny is.

]1450SAT: I'm telling you, layers. Inject different colors & shades into different levels of skin. That might allow us to superimpose images, construct depth.

]KC_FTT_B: Know what—they got machines that drill w/lotsa needlez at once. 7&9&15 needlez. It co_ld do the art way faster.

]DOMINATR69:   That's what I'm talking about! There's what, a dermis right? There's a epidermis. And I've heard of subcutaneous levels of skin. Are there cutaneous levels?

]BBIXXE: Um. Ud die

]DOMINATR69:   wld nt

]BBIXXE: that much toxic ink in yr body? That much abuse?

]DOMINATR69:   Who says all ink is toxic?

]BBIXXE: It's lead and carbon based. Can't be nutritious.

]KC_FTT_B: What if we treated the skin? Like ancient indians treating deer pelts.

]1450SAT: Deer pelts are dead, retard.

]DOMINATR69:   Are there different types of tattoo ink? Diff mixtures?

]BBIXXE: Okay. just for shits and giggles, let's say I admit that it is possible to inject shades and nuances into the human skin. Say we pretend you could do these tattoos at a size that allowed for volume and detail *but that at the same time* did not overload the body with poisons.

]KC_FTT_B: Woo hoo! We win!

]BBIXXE: For argument's sake, let's also forget about the mind-numbing time it'd take to individually mix the shades into nuanced fractions, then inject every single dot of skin w/ single dots of nuanced shade. Let's forget about the pain of such an enterprise on the subject. Ignore the unconscionable wear & tear & agony that'd come with sitting for hours while

not one but FIFTEEN electricity-laden needles injected
marginally toxic chemicals into LAYERS of skin.

]DOMINATR69:   Do you actually have a point?

]BBIXXE: After all this forgetting n ignoring all these faults and holes,
my dear, demented Jedis, just who in their right mind is
gonna let you drill them?

]1450SAT: who says they have to be in their right mind

]KC_FTT_B: who says they have to let _s

]1450SAT: maybe someone who likes the pain?

]DOMINATR69:   Some S&M freak who totally gets off on pain

]KC_FTT_B: some hardcore hardass

]1450SAT: a bum

]DOMINATR69:   a loser

]KC_FTT_B: an addict, all not feeling nothing

]1450SAT: it'd have 2b some1 who doesn't care about himself

]DOMINATR69:   How about some1 who can't escape.

]KC_FTT_B: R_naways d_de. Nobody cares abowt r_naways.

With stiff knees and sore behinds, Kenny and his aunt would disembark from the third bus of their journey, getting out where Main met Fremont. *"Howdy, partner. Welcome to downtown Las Vegas,"* always greeted them, booming through an overhead speaker system in a folksy western accent, the message delivered courtesy of the Pioneer Club, and its large mechanical figure, Vegas Vic. Vic wore a cowboy hat and a smile. His right eye winked suggestively and his mechanical arm waved visitors inside.

Kenny's aunt knew better than to take the bait. Tucking her black pleather purse underneath her armpit, she'd wrap a meaty hand around Kenny's wrist as if she were holding a twig. Her sweatpants rubbing together at the thighs, she'd start down the gulch, leading the eight-year-old boy she called her *little trooper* underneath the first in a row of metallic awnings, rows of bulbs showering warm light onto the pedestrians. From inside each darkened open-air entrance, cool winds hummed.

Past the Pioneer Club and Slots-O-Fun, too, she and Kenny ignored the costumed barkers who promised a free spin at the fortune wheel. They did not comment on the early-morning tourists who wandered, gape-eyed, half in the bag, holding Bloody Marys. Past Sassy Sally's now, and the Four Queens. Even the Horseshoe, host of the famed World Series of Poker. Finally they'd arrive outside the small one-story storefront, where at least two or three other people lingered, hands deep in their pockets.

If Kenny had to pee, his aunt would say he should go now, around the side.

In the large window that Kenny's aunt claimed bullets could not shatter, an aged man ignored the stares from outside and continued with his business, deliberately setting up the displays, cracking open small black boxes to reveal bracelets and rings that glittered against dusty velvet. This man, whom Kenny's aunt called *the Jew*, had a thick, pale face, blotched with red veins and dominated by a bulbous nose. His barrel of a belly stretched the polka dots of his wide-collared/rayon shirts. Making his way from the window, his attention would turn to a warden's ring of keys.

Once the gauntlet of locks was run and the store was open, Kenny's aunt would compete for a place in line at the front counter, where all serious business was conducted. The boy's minute attention span would launch Kenny in the opposite direction, heading down the line of showcases, scanning walls yellowed with age, inhaling mothballed air. Kenny was too small to peer over the glass countertops, but he could still take in plenty: rope chains with glittering diamond pendants that spelled out the names of Arab sheiks; racing silks and rider's goggles from Del Mar and Hollywood Park; cigar boxes overflowing with war medals and fancy Confederate ribbons.

Sometimes, when the store was empty, if Kenny was on his best behavior, the Jew might emerge from the back room with his tray of glass eyes. Other times he made a silver dollar stick to his forehead, shot nickels from his nose and ears, or stacked eight quarters on the back of his spotted hand, and then, whipping his wrist, caught them. Kenny's favorite was when those marvelously large hands blurred, crossing and recrossing. *Follow me closely,* the Jew growled, his hard consonants stressed and overpronounced. *Where's the quarter, come on. You sure?*

More often, the Jew had to deal with the foot traffic of tourists, gawkers who wanted to see this ring, asked for prices on cameras they didn't know how to use. The high roller on a hot streak who'd come to get his Rolex out of hock; the same high roller, head low, bringing back the watch. One time a smelly recluse opened a briefcase, revealing gemstones of such quality that the Jew kicked everyone out, locked the store, and engaged in private negotiations. Usually, though, it was weekend warriors on the other end of a sleepless binge. Men who'd emptied their wallets and cashed in their plane tickets, and were in need of enough money to get back to the tables. Standing in line they yawned, wiped red eyes, nursed hangovers.

Behind the counter, the Jew would take out a magnifying glass. Examine a thin band.

"I paid two thousand dollars for that," its owner would volunteer.

"The gold isn't a great weight."

"Two thousand dollars I paid."

"Maybe. But the weight isn't there. And see this—the diamond, it's more than a little yellow."

"Ten years ago I bought that ring."

"I can give you four hundred."

The guy's face would flush. For a moment, it would look like he might weep.

"Please, man. Have a heart."

"Maybe you should go around the corner."

"It's her *engagement ring.*"

"They'll take care of you around the corner."

"MOTHERFUCKING KIKE."

Even as an eight-year-old, Kenny was no stranger to epithets, late-night screams filtering in through the cheap stucco of his bedroom walls, his mother complaining that if his dad would quit drinking for a month, maybe he could hold down a job, his father answering that if she'd stop blowing his money at roulette, maybe he'd have a reason to quit drinking. Inside the pawn shop, however, there were no sheets to hide beneath, no darkened closet to disappear into, only his aunt's ripe body, her ratty sweatpants, and these provided little camouflage. It never failed, though: the shouting would subside, the offended man would storm out. While the air might remain charged, the threat of violence would disperse slowly, like a cloud of cigarette smoke.

Approaching the counter, his aunt would say the rent was late. Or it was the electric bill this time. Maybe she just didn't know anymore. She mixed familiarity with a tired resignation, and the Jew usually responded in kind, for Kenny's aunt had been coming to him for years, pawning her mother's communion ring, sometimes her grandmother's pearl broach and, also, when she was in dire straits, a small golden locket that she kept wrapped in the Sunday funnies. The loan amounts had long been set, and if Kenny's aunt needed an extra month to redeem her goods, it was understood this wouldn't be a problem. Placing the bills on the counter one by one, the Jew would explain the vagaries of compound interest.

He'd put each item inside a manila envelope specifically designed to hold jewelry and/or folded money. Examining Kenny's aunt, he'd wink suggestively. "You here to stay? Just to play?"

"Stop it. What I really need to do is quit playing the slots. Otherwise I'm gonna end up a bum."

They made this journey—*their adventure,* his aunt called it—visiting downtown, Vegas Vic, and Fremont Street each month, sometimes more often, their bus route and routine holding true whether auntie picked up Kenny to give his parents some quality alone time, or because she felt a child should not be in the middle of a war zone. Through the stints Kenny's father did in rehab and the times he stumbled back down the proverbial twelve steps; through his mother's attempts at night school and then her stops on Las Vegas's cocktail waitress circuit, and also the times she got really, really sad and cried all night and ended up getting high for a week and shacking up with some guy she barely knew. Through each of his parents' trial separations, and every aborted reconciliation; through back-to-school shopping excursions spent among the sale racks at the outlet mall, and Christmas gifts from his aunt that Kenny recognized as coming from the pawn shop (an outdated Nintendo system whose right controller didn't work; knockoff brand CD players that fizzed out after a month); through Kenny's emerging awareness of his own pubescence, and that stunning first discovery of Dad's stash of explicit magazines. Through all the fare increases and missed transfers and convoluted detours, without fail and despite occasional interruptions of prosperity. Each trip took them beyond the unofficial demarcation point where the world famous Las Vegas Strip ended and Las Vegas Boulevard picked back up. Beyond the juncture where the gleaming hotels were replaced by an expanse of sky. Through the cheers of the paying multitudes and then those pitiless implosions, as each ancient hotel on the Strip became one with the true sands and dunes of the desert. From the viewpoint of unforgiving seats, through the darkened windows of public transportation, Kenny and his aunt made their trips, watching as each new generation of hotel and casino resorts slowly reconfigured the city's skyline—towers sculpted to appear as structural interpretations of department store birthday cakes, towers created as pop art oddities and streamlined glass palaces, the world famous Strip stretching even farther southward along its axis, moving farther away from downtown.

The year Kenny turned fourteen, the fighting in his home reached a breaking point, and after a whole lot of fireworks, his dad moved out. Not long afterward, with much less ceremony, and a whole lot less screaming, a middle-aged woman appeared behind the front counter of the pawn shop. She was small, the woman, slight as a bird, with salt and pepper sprinkling unkempt bangs, and dog hair clinging noticeably to a coffee-stained blouse. She possessed the Jew's deeply set eyes, his sloped shoulders, and hard accent. Kenny's aunt asked what happened. "You want to interrogate me," snapped the woman, "or you want to do some business?"

Follow-up visits revealed her to be perpetually nervous and defensive. More than once she threw a customer out of the store for reasons Kenny could not figure. He'd stay as far away from her as he could, and stare anywhere but at her, avoiding all contact. Whenever she acknowledged his existence and wanted to know how he was doing at school, Kenny, unable to comprehend her attempt at kindness, answered in scared one-word exclamations. His darting eyes glanced over the shop's subtle changes, overlooking the china dolls that had been placed inside showcases, the lilacs and potpourri next to the gun rack.

By the following spring, a painted portrait of the Jew wearing an unfamiliar silver toupee hung on the wall behind the front counter, near a framed proclamation, signed by Governor William Jefferson Clinton, which declared the Jew an official Arkansas Traveler. Kenny looked at the old document while his aunt explained how she usually kept her pawn ticket in her purse. "Wasn't until the bus was at Charleston, I realized I musta forgot."

The woman muttered an undecipherable judgment. Opening a file cabinet, she withdrew a series of index cards, and then saw the initials. Untold incarnations of the same two letters, variations on a theme: the strong, illegible script of a confident man with things to do; the distracted scribbles that landed halfway between the lined columns; the weak scratches of a cheap plastic ballpoint running out of ink; the luxurious thickness of indelible black marker. Always capital letters. Always slanted to the right. As the pair of initials descended the card's final columns, each of the Jew's signatures appeared progressively gnarled, further and further cramped.

"Oh, Daddy." The woman's voice was halting, hesitant. "All those years. Back and forth. The same nickels. The same junk."

"I know it's not the best stuff," said Kenny's aunt. "But it helps me get through."

From the back room a phone stopped ringing. The Jew's daughter's eyes had dilated and were wide as an ocean. They were soft and moist and she glanced back down at the ledger, her finger pressing the edge of the page.

"You have a criminal record?"

"Hmh?"

"I asked if you have a record."

"No. No record."

"You a drunk?"

"Not a drunk, no ma'am."

Again the Jew's Daughter looked down at the column. Again back at Kenny's aunt.

"Maybe you need a job?"

This was how the second seat appeared behind the counter. Mondays through Saturdays, eight A.M. to six P.M., Kenny's aunt rocked back and forth with a loaded Beretta in her lap. She moved in and out of the large walk-in safe, helping to carry heavy televisions and stereos into the back room. Whenever there were too many customers for the Jew's Daughter to handle alone, his aunt showed jewelry, answered questions, and simply waited people out. Whenever a gypsy family flooded the store—their diapered children crawling all over the floor, the adults spreading out, hovering over different showcases, demanding to see this ring, that bracelet, every damn one of them searching for the perfect opportunity to make a pendant disappear—whenever this happened, Kenny's aunt guarded the door, kept an eye wherever the Jew's Daughter could not look. She polished jewelry and made coffee, ran around the corner to get a new carton of 2 percent, and watched the clock, making it her business to beat the rush of dealers to the Horseshoe snack bar for lunchtime sandwiches. If a pawn ticket envelope went missing, Kenny's aunt helped search, assuring the Jew's Daughter they'd find it, the envelope had to be there. If the afternoon was empty of customers, his aunt provided a running commentary on the old movie that the two women watched on a television with wavy reception. Sometimes the Jew's Daughter would vent about her children, complaining that they did not understand the sacrifices she was making every day on their behalf. Kenny's aunt would answer, calmly, sincerely, that she was sure the Daughter's children were more grateful than the Daughter could ever know. Whatever kept the Jew's Daughter from feeling too much pressure, Kenny's aunt tried to provide. Whatever talked her down off that day's ledge.

It was no small order. The county had deregulated pawn licenses, and hock shops were popping up in just about every residential neighborhood, tripling inside the city limits alone. This was in addition to the bank and credit card machines that could be found inside any casino. And a burgeoning industry where, in exchange for a cash advance, workers could sign over paychecks they hadn't yet earned. "It changes who comes in," Kenny's aunt would explain, on their long bus rides home. Venting, bitter with exhaustion, she'd repeat what the Jew's Daughter had told her. "We got less people coming downtown, first of all. And two, less people using pawn shops. It adds up, you know?"

Kenny could not help but feel the weight of the past as he eased the FBI-mobile out of Main's final bend. Presently, flimsy motels advertised hourly rates and bail bonds shacks touted round-the-clock service. Adult bookstores—their windows black with shoe polish—came and went, followed by liquor places with iron bars over their doors.

As the thoroughfare opened, flat fields of dormant automobiles fanned out, a new cluster of towers breaking into the horizon. A multi-million-dollar dome now hovered over them, covering Fremont Street in the latest attempt to draw crowds. Like everything else, though, this gimmick wasn't working. Downtown mostly attracted nickel-and-dimers these days: busloads of Asian tourists in from California for weekend binges, bargain hunters who finagled cut-rate packages from floundering Internet travel agencies.

Kenny took a long sip, the flat soda swishing warmly through his mouth, the cardboard cup saturated, flimsy in his free hand.

Behind a clothing store that sold dealer slacks to casino workers, a crusty old man had a special agreement with him: if Kenny parked the Reliant there for more than ten minutes, the old man agreed to begin charging. Climbing out of the FBImobile, Kenny walked past the small booth where the guy sat, listening to the radio. The guy ignored him. Kenny returned the favor.

Dusk was eking across the horizon in pale purple swaths. Music had just started from Fremont Street, signifying the commencement of the animated movie along the dome. For an instant Kenny remembered the deep, throaty voice: "*Howdy, partner. Welcome to downtown Las Vegas.*" It had been gone for years now, but he resented its absence. He couldn't exactly say why.

He started down the street. From a block away, painted red letters were visible on the side of a white brick building: 6 % INTEREST. LOWEST IN TOWN.

Sometimes when the afternoon was dead, they closed early. If the grating was already down in front of the shop, Kenny knew to duck between the beef jerky store and the place where they sold Nazi memorabilia. Inevitably, inside the liquor mart's front entrance, his aunt would be on a small stool, sagging like a sack of potatoes; she'd be feeding nickels into her lucky slot machine, her arm heavy and listless, her eyes bleary, red at the corners. And Kenny was more than fine with this. If he had to pick up the old bag, he'd rather pick her up in the liquor mart.

A pair of teenagers argued loudly on a far corner—the boy tearing his hand from his girlfriend, screaming: " 'Fuck that' *is* my answer for everything." Kenny looked down at the cement. His pace quickened, even as he began steeling himself.

Was today the day for the streetwalker whose baby needed asthma medicine? Had today marked the return of the fey cowboy who habitually called the police, claiming THIS OLD BITCH had switched the charm bracelet he'd pawned with a PIECE A CRAP? Was it another day for homeless men to intimidate a pair of aging women, refusing to leave until they'd received enough money for a night of binge drinking? Had a different bunch of vagabonds come by, claiming that for a fee they'd protect the store from those bums? Maybe the sheriff put an end to all the shake-downs, even as he checked on whether any rifles were worth "confiscat-ing." Always another story, the latest hard-luck account, the newest and angriest plea—people without checking accounts or savings accounts or IRAs who had arrived specifically at this place because there was nowhere else to go, and 6 percent less interest a month just might end up the differ-ence between getting back their engagement band and getting a divorce.

But today, today Kenny was the one with a story to tell. He was the one with news.

His aunt had just finished stacking the jewelry trays of a showcase, and was gingerly carrying them, limping toward the huge walk-in safe. Figuring it was best to wait for her to return, Kenny nodded toward the Jew's Daughter, who was behind the front counter, trying to enter the day's totals into the computer, receiving in return a series of beeps and bloops that didn't sound promising.

Hair now faded, eyes sunk deeply into her skull, the Jew's Daughter was visibly tired, worn down by the day, by years of days like this. She muttered something—Kenny did not know if it was in response to him, or at the computer, but he left well enough alone and, as if by habit, headed toward the showcase.

Televisions, guitars, golf bags, and stereo equipment were scattered along the store's back shelves like the remains of a bad garage sale, but today they did not seem as overwhelming as usual, and as Kenny waited for his aunt to return, he perused the half-empty displays. Normally the jewelry appeared dingy and lusterless to him, the wedding rings seeming to be stories of love abandoned, the rows of unattended charms, talis-mans of squandered affection. Often Kenny would stare at them and it was as if all of their romantic memories and inscribed tales of personal significance had been stripped, peeled away by desire and weakness and the hard cold eyes of penny weight and cash value. Today, though, he saw something different. Maybe it was simply the way light reflected off the watches and rings. Maybe it was something else. But for some reason Kenny looked at the bands and charms and was aware of the opportunity that waited inside of them all—the new romances, the memories that had not yet happened, the untold people out there, ready to walk in at any moment and give meaning to those rings.

"So."

He projected his voice toward his aunt, who was out of the safe now. "I—me and my friend . . . went to this artist guy today. He's an illustrator for this comic book. No big deal, not really. But I . . . I showed him some of my drawings."

From the computer, eyes darted, large and ferocious in their helplessness. Immediately his aunt defused things. "One second, Kenny. Just give us a sec, okay?"

Clicking sounds picked back up from the keyboard. His aunt hobbled toward him now, her arthritic legs groaning beneath what now were years of extra weight. Stopping briefly at a small, messy table, she reached into her purse, and came up with a handful of pink frosted cookies.

When she was within arm's length, she whispered. "You got to hear this one. Woman comes in. Her husband borrowed two dollars from her purse. Says he's going to get toilet paper. Disappears. A week later he comes back. Stinks to high heaven. Booze. Perfume. The whole nine. This ain't enough, she discovers he's got a ten-dollar poker chip shoved up his ass."

His aunt paused, shoveling two cookies into her mouth. She chewed and began speaking at the same time. "I tell the woman, don't put up with those shenanigans. Guess what she goes?"

From the front counter there were more beeps. Harder clicking.

"Who's complaining? He's a winner, isn't he?"

His aunt started laughing, her guffaws sending cookie bits all over her blouse. A hard bang interrupted—from the counter:

"This fucking thing!"

The Jew's Daughter pushed the keyboard away. "I never wanted to do this. I never wanted to be here."

Kenny's aunt looked at him as she chewed. "What were you saying about your friend?"

He stared back, rooted to the ground, something seizing inside of him.

2.4

During those first, frantic days after Newell disappeared, Lincoln and Lorraine survived because of each other, the problems and troubles of their marriage giving way to its core strengths, chief of which was tenderness. Born of history, reaching beyond language, these bonds provided some small measure of shelter, and allowed the couple to weather so much niggling and unreality: friends and relations descending upon the house like a well-intentioned swarm; officers tramping clumsily through each room, unfailingly leaving the toilet seat up. Neither Lincoln nor Lorraine could bring themselves to eat more than a muffin here or there. Sleep was sporadic, coming when it could not be kept at bay any longer. Yet they had that tenderness, those small private moments: the afternoon they'd successfully gotten Lorraine's parents onto their flight back home, for example. And the morning Lincoln's dad had packed up his camper and hugged his daughter-in-law. After he was gone, they'd been able to sit at the kitchen table and pick over a tray of banana bread that someone had dropped off, just sit there and wait for the next pot of coffee to brew, exhaling as much as possible. Being with each other. Being there for each other.

Still, she was not ready to have him back in what she privately thought of as *her* bed. She was sorry for this, but it didn't feel right to her, not just yet. Lincoln's disappointment was as wordless as it was obvious; nonetheless he respected her feelings and bided his time; he slept in the guest bedroom and shaved in the guest bathroom; he dressed and went downstairs each morning, kissed his wife on the cheek, gave her a hug of support, and went over whatever details needed to be discussed. And then Lincoln went off to work, leaving her alone in the silence, alone inside her own head. The relentless August sun was giving way to September days that were as unremarkable as sunlight, days that were as beautiful as any that this planet had seen. Their beauty tortured Lorraine. And no matter how much she promised herself she would stop, she found herself watching videotapes of Newell.

She couldn't help it. She had to see her son.

He is not yet two: they are naked and soapy in a tub filled with bubbles. On her lap, he giggles. She holds him by his armpits. Newell is still all rolls and softness, his face bright and wet. He has her flecked green eyes and they sparkle with unabated joy. He has his father's snub nose and happy, fat cheeks. Lorraine watches a younger, almost perfect version of herself lift her son and raise him up and down and call *ELEVATOR.* She hears her own voice make gurgling noises, ridiculous sounds. Her son's head is one large grin. Now he notices something. Looking directly into the video recorder, the focus of the device upon him, the boy seems intrigued, mildly perplexed. He paws for the camera. His face breaks into a wide smile and he claps, giggles, and starts splashing, furiously, satisfyingly, water all over Mommy, who squeals, not unhappily, water toward Daddy, who can be heard laughing from behind the viewfinder, *Well, all right, little shooter. Baths ARE exciting, aren't they?*

Twenty-five minutes of this. Lorraine could watch until the end of time.

She could get just as lost inside the eight minutes of Newell working to stand up on his own, walking unsteadily, teetering with each ridiculously adorable step, almost losing his balance and going faster, reaching and then hugging the base of a tree in their front yard. An unbearably cute little boy, this pudgy person in miniature: hair the orange of carrots curls in loopy directions; his face is plump as pie, soft and white as powder. He is bundled up in a puffy blue jacket whose obscene price Lorraine, each time she watches, recalls. She remembers the joy of shopping for each piece of that little outfit.

With time she and Lincoln had become sloppy; one taped memory would move beyond the crux of the moment they'd intended to capture; then the static would be jarring, the image would change, red numbers in the bottom right-hand corner documenting different times and dates. (Lincoln had spent an afternoon wrapped in the unfolded pages of the manual, learning the camera's functions, and he never failed to make sure the date was on there, as if to prove he had mastered the machine.)

September 19; 3:54 P.M.; eight years old; an adult T-shirt that fits him like a dress, hanging down over his elbows and to the middle of his legs. He is wearing shorts with all sorts of pockets. Black pads swell his elbows and knees, and his head is protected by a shining fiberglass helmet designed in the style of a comic book hero. He stands out in front of the driveway, where Lincoln's beloved old truck is parked, during a phase when her husband refused to get a new one. Newell shouts, *MOM,* and starts rolling on his skateboard, gathering speed for a trick. *ARE YOU LOOKING?*

March 4; 7:52; the camera peers through an open sliver into his bedroom, a clandestine segment, Lorraine joining Lincoln as silent voyeurs, watching the child—he is stretched out on the carpet, on his stomach, his school books ignored next to him in a pile while he maneuvers different action figures through a complicated sequence of events. Lorraine watched a presentation Newell made for third-grade science class that involved sugar and the prolonged effects of light. She watched her son push his back straight against the pantry wall, discover the new pencil mark on the pantry showed him to be exactly the same height as the last time they'd checked, and have a minor tantrum. Lorraine watched a homemade rap video of him mugging and jumping around and ecstatically shouting rhymes. She watched her extended family, all seated around the antique table in the off room that was saved for special events. Everyone was dressed in their Thanksgiving best and anxious to eat, trying to survive to the end of Grandma's rambling thank-you to the Lord. Newell's eyes open. He scans the table. Noticing that his father is filming, the boy sticks his tongue out of his mouth. Lorraine watched this video and she watched one more and after that one she went to the kitchen cabinet and, just this last time, took the last cassette out of its white sleeve.

Inevitably, she would find herself in Newell's bedroom, on any pretext. Just walking in there was almost more than she could take, for the space was lifeless and barren in a way that a child's room never should be; it was a shrine, a mausoleum, a kingdom awaiting the return of its rightful monarch: the small single bed frame running lengthwise beneath a drawn picture window; the posters Scotch-taped on pale yellow walls; the marks and scuffs from where Newell had kicked and thrown objects.

Lorraine would stretch out on her son's mattress and try to summon the remnants of his energy. She would open files on his hard drive. A half-finished school science project sat gathering dust in the room's far corner. A laundry bin was packed with state-of-the-art toys of interstellar destruction, none of which the boy had touched in months. Lorraine went through his dresser. She refolded undersize versions of designer jockey shorts, each of which cost as much as sweatshop workers made in a month. She coordinated and scoured through the contents of his closet—the housekeeper couldn't be trusted; who knew what she might steal or screw up. Lorraine searched his bookshelf and his school primers. She left the rows of comics untouched in their plastic wrappers, but every so often picked up one of the painted die-cast metal figurines that swarmed the middle shelf (positioned in a titanic last stand: eight or so druids, sorcerers, and knights defended themselves against a miasma of Hot Wheels miniatures, stretchable wrestling icons, and hand-painted revolutionary war soldiers). Lorraine would examine the honest, if clumsy, attempt her son had made at painting the druid's beard, the colored blop that substituted for a coat of arms on a warrior's shield.

It was not uncommon for her to find a stray sock and go to pieces. What was uncommon, though, was the afternoon she noticed a number of dimes and nickels loosely pooled on his dresser. She started to tremble, her body unable to handle the shock. Then she realized they were Lincoln's coins, and she was not the only one making pilgrimages.

Pulling out the drawer of Newell's desk, she found, amid the scattered suits of a loose and incomplete deck of playing cards, a manila envelope, large enough to contain a ring. Lorraine tried to come up with reasons for it to be there, places it might have come from. She jabbed a finger inside, and turned it over, and then saw the pencil sketch: a giant skull with a complicated set of braces across its bony teeth. Speeding down those braces was a miniature locomotive; rows of tiny arms waving in terror from its windows. The train's smokestack trail was shaped like billowy skulls, and leaning out of the front of the engine was this tiny wolf—he wore a conductor's hat, his eyes popping in cartoon terror.

"It has to be a clue," she insisted.

"Yes, ma'am," the case officer said.

"Don't you think? So many tiny hands, just waving like that?"

She followed up on her call, and kept calling—every afternoon, as many as three times on one particular day when her mind refused to let go of this supposed breakthrough, and she ranted into the speaker end of the phone, annotating each nuanced aspect of the drawing for the case officer, speculating on the possible significance of eyes popping in cartoon terror, the many interpretations of a *train chugging toward the end of the world.* She digressed into memories of the boy at five, as if this whole nightmare would be wrapped up once the case officer understood that Newell had a reddish birthmark on his right calf. The case officer's end of the phone always was filled with background clutter and police business, yet no matter how busy he seemed or how many times he'd heard a piece of information, he always seemed to listen, and thanked Lorraine for the call, saying he hoped this would help, and if there was any news, she would be the first to know. The case officer was a father himself, girls, six and eight. He was decent and understanding and Lorraine stopped calling.

For part of an afternoon, she pulled herself together. For three full consecutive days she stayed under control. Unexpectedly the phone rang.

This was it. This was her child.

"Hi. Can I please speak to Mr. or Miss . . . ah . . . Blewing?"

"You are speaking to Mrs. Ewing."

"Hi. My name is Ron. I'm calling on behalf of public broadcasting. We're doing our annual pledge drive and—"

Her son had been trouble from the beginning: a breech birth; three weeks early; Lorraine had unexpectedly dilated and then the child had been reversed in her uterus, caught in his own umbilical cord; Lorraine had been cut open and the cord had been unwrapped from around his feet and the fetus had been physically removed from her body, and she had been all of twenty years old. That had been the end of her in a two-piece bathing suit, the end of any possibility at a swimsuit modeling career. (*They can airbrush,* Lincoln had said, *it's no big deal.*) She'd wanted to be a good mother, wanted a healthy baby, and she didn't want a boob job afterward, so goodbye to her life as a showgirl. Now her child did not call, did not let her know he was alive. Silence held the limitless depths of torture for Lorraine; silence was its own hell, its own purgatory, the definitive confirmation of Lorraine's shortcomings as a parent, the final result of every obnoxious trait she had ever let slide, the character deficiencies she had not been able to control. Had she been overprotective? Too permissive? Had she given the boy too much attention? Not enough?

She was not able to drive past a school yard without breaking down, and she could not prevent herself from cruising school yards, from going by that comic book shop. The boy had never been to a Hooters, but he had known that men liked Hooters, and whenever Lorraine used to drive past, he had enjoyed chanting *Hooters, Hooters,* and therefore she no longer could turn right on Lindell. She could not look across a grass field without thinking of trying to get him to play outside, and she could not look upon a skyscraper because it was not grass. The news broadcasted reports about what appeared to be the remains of a human hand being found in the Mojave Desert. Court TV had daily coverage of a drifter on trial (he was accused of taking a nine-year-old girl from a Stateline casino's child care center, then raping her in a bathroom stall). Lorraine could not look away. Even when exhaustion finally took her, she had complicated nightmares, and upon waking could not remember a moment of them. Instead she harangued her son in extended mental monologues, remaining angry at him for that last comment in the car that afternoon, for disappearing, for causing this ache, this hole inside of her. Never a barrel of laughs in the best of times, Lorraine became humorless, grim, her eyes growing haunted, even as she continued to hoard images that reminded her of reminders of her son, filling her purse with snapshots, and copies of the police report, and three randomly selected action figures from his shelf, her world shrinking by the day, reaching a point where any news that suggested the world did not revolve around Newell's absence repulsed Lorraine, and any object that could not facilitate his return was useless to her. Whether pushing a cart in the market or locked in her own bathroom, Lorraine would start bawling—inconsolable, gut-wrenching heaves. For a time she became militant about yoga, and grimly chanted the ninety-nine names of a god she alternately did not believe in and despised, praying to this god nonetheless.

Interest on Newell's college fund accrued unabated.

The days started getting dark earlier; and although it was still unusual to see people wearing light sweaters or jackets, the air had cooled noticeably, with the first carved pumpkins appearing in windows. The boy was just old enough to disdain trick-or-treating, but still was young enough to covet bags of candy. Lorraine remembered him in costume as a pirate. As the action hero from some movie whose plot she had pretended to follow. On something more than a whim, but certainly less than a plan, she found herself near the main branch of the public library. She could have visited a bookstore and asked for help. She could have looked online. She'd brought her son to this library for story time and after-school programs; went upstairs with him and watched puppet shows when he was just learning how to walk. Lorraine had checked out books from this library that had helped Newell learn to read and she had dropped him off and gotten all her shopping done and then come back to pick him up and found him underneath the stairwell, pretending to be a bank robber with one or two other children, hiding from patrons as if the adults were policemen, using their fingers to point and shoot as the supposed cops marched up to the periodicals. Entering the large open arboretum that marked the building's entrance, it occurred to Lorraine that she had not been inside a library without Newell for the entirety of her adult life. She took the elevator to the main floor. Senior citizens sat at tables, reading newspapers and magazines; middle-aged women listlessly pushed carts. Books about missing children. Memoirs on how person X got through tragedy Y. Lorraine eschewed the computer system and waited at the information counter behind a stooped old man, trying to be patient as he asked for help finding a book whose title and author he could not recall. She stared at the flyers on a nearby bulletin board. Tutoring Services Offered. Senior Citizen Reading Group. The gray image of a kitten. The many hardships stray felines had to endure during winter. Poor little darlings. Attracted to the taste of antifreeze, they foraged through trash bags outside auto body stores, licked the toxic remains from discarded plastic containers. In search of warmth they nestled underneath the hoods of parked cars, got mangled in engine gears.

Just taking the flyer would have been disrespectful so Lorraine purchased a copier card. She drove home and, for the first time in two months, thought about something other than her own pain. When Lincoln came home, she showed him the copy. He looked it up and down, considered the information, and did not appear to enjoy reminding Lorraine that Las Vegas winters rarely dipped below fifty degrees. He calmly explained that antifreeze automotive liquids were not necessary in desert environs, and that it was unlikely cats could find much of the stuff sitting around to lick. Evenly and with much sympathy he said that warmth-nestling wasn't really imperative in fifty-degree weather, and besides winter was a good two months away. What was she proposing, anyhow?

She did not answer. What good did it do to tell Lincoln her plans? Why tell him anything when he would shoot her down in that passive-aggressive shit-eating manner of his? Being around Lincoln exasperated Lorraine, and made her lose it, and made her so sad as to render her mute. And inevitably, once she had no more fury inside of her, once her sadness had been out in the sun for too long and had fermented, it made Lorraine hard. She could no longer tolerate Lincoln's throat clearing, his cautioned inquiries on her state of mind, pep talks so soggy that he barely pretended to believe them. He could talk until the end of time for all she cared, the facts remained: people *needed* to dispose of their antifreeze containers in a sealed and safe manner; drivers *had* to honk before starting their engines. Something *had* to be done for all the helpless kittens wandering those hard cold streets. Lorraine placed calls to local shelters, found out about vaccination laws, even started buying twenty-five-pound bags of cat food, fifty-pounders of kitty litter. And if her husband happened to feel a measure of relief in the sight of her beginning to come out of her shell, *great.* But by the same token, if the prospect of wholesale volumes of stray animals in his home concerned Lincoln, freaked him out, and/or made him wonder about her mental health, Lorraine told herself, she did not care. If Lincoln noticed what was going on and would have liked to talk with her about *this whole, you know, res-*

cue deal; if he himself was exasperated and near the end of his tether; if he felt all sorts of anger—toward himself, toward Lorraine, toward the whole stupid world—and was literally swimming in regrets, and as such was in no shape to deal with his own grief, let alone his wife's; if Lincoln knew he was a fucking mess and understood that Lorraine also was wrecked; if, to him, this meant they needed each other *more than ever,* if any of these possibilities, or a combination of them, or every single one, was true, it also was true that, at the end of the business day, the guy was around the house less and less. Said he was at the office. And Lorraine, she did not particularly feel the need to verify the truth right about then. *She had cats to save here, dammit.*

So let him judge her with cordial silence. Let him dig at her through his absence. Let him tell himself she had driven him away. But that son of a bitch was going to find out about the grand opening of the Newell Ewing Animal Rescue Shelter the old-fashioned way: his trifling ass was going to come home in the middle of the night and find twenty strays in that spare bedroom.

After couches had been shredded and neighbors had circulated a petition about the *illegally zoned cat compound,* and no less than three felines had met gruesome fates at the jaws of the Nelsons' Rhodesian ridgeback, finally, Lorraine was forced to admit the futility of her noble endeavor, and send the cages back to the ASPCA, at which point kittens gave way to a very strange flirtation with the Mothers United for the Protection of Unborn Children, and a bizarre meeting in a classroom at a church, where Lorraine sat uncomfortably in a metal folding chair and listened to a bunch of otherwise normal-looking people spew hatred with an intensity that was truly unsettling.

The next afternoon she drove to a large shopping center on East Tropicana and entered a small storefront office. Overhead lights hummed, the walls reflected the shade of curdled milk. Lorraine did not catch the name of the harried woman who came up from the back and took her name. After a time, the woman reappeared and guided Lorraine down a short aisle of sloppy, unmanned work cubicles. They sat at a table in the back. Slick posters, done in hard and dramatic colors, hung in cheap frames. The woman offered Lorraine coffee whose quality she apologized for. Mousy brown hair pulled back into a bun, unimpressive olive-green pants suit; early forties or so, Lorraine guessed. With a minimum of small talk the woman asked why Lorraine was there, and kept quiet when Lorraine explained about Newell's case. Every so often, the woman nodded slightly or asked a pointed follow-up. She commiserated and told Lorraine a little about the center and said, as Lorraine could see, they could use all the help they could get. Without any fuss, the woman walked Lorraine through the dos and don'ts of stuffing fund-raising letters into envelopes. "When you get finished, if you're up to it, maybe we'll get you a script and a mailing list. Try you on some calls."

A lopsided table, weighed down with incoming mail that needed sorting, mailing labels that had to be applied, work that was not important enough for a paid staffer to do, yet needed to be done. Lorraine applied. She sorted. The table was just around the corner from a small room with vending machines and a bathroom, and she bought herself stale pretzels and took breaks to use the facilities. She went through two boxes of stationery and also, for long stretches, stared at the old posters: Van Gogh's *Sunflowers* reprinted from an exhibit at the L.A. Guggenheim; a primitive crayon drawing of a teddy bear (block letters beneath it conveyed statistics concerning child abuse). She could not avoid a third poster, a teenage boy enveloped in shadows; he was huddled on a stoop, his elbows resting on the knee holes in his jeans, his Mohawked head hanging in his lap. Scrawling red block letters, designed to look like they'd been spray-painted on the wall behind him, read: LIFE ON THE STREET IS *SO* GLAMOROUS.

Police did not categorize Newell Ewing as a runaway. Nor did they classify him as a victim of kidnapping, nor a possible homicide victim, although they also hadn't eliminated any of these options. He was missing and his case was open and the officer Lorraine dealt with refused to lean one way or another. What had happened to her son was a Rorschach test that revealed the worst inclinations and fears of the person who considered the possibilities. Lorraine herself did not know if she believed her son had run away. She did not necessarily believe that Newell running away from home was preferable to the other choices. But that poster hit somewhere deep inside her. It brought a chill that no mother should experience. So Lorraine returned to the office of the Nevada Child Search the following day. And every day after that. The clock struck two and lunch hour ended and she drove east on Tropicana. And as she sat at that lopsided table and drudged through slush, bits of stories and pieces of information drifted her way: the counselor laughing about the guy who called in, thinking it was a psychic hotline; the disgruntled social worker who could not stop railing against bureaucratic idiocy. At the vending machines, Lorraine talked to a heavyset woman who had the hard, rough demeanor of someone whose life had been spent doing menial and physical labors. The woman told Lorraine about how she'd lived through a tough divorce and had worked up the courage and started dating again, and very slowly had fallen in love, so when her fourteen-year-old daughter claimed the guy followed her into a bathroom at IHOP, this woman had not known how to respond.

And other volunteers: the army mom who came in during mornings—her husband discovered their boy sold drugs and laid down a *my way or the highway* ultimatum; the grandfather who'd taken in kin as a last option, only to grow tired of calls from the police. Lorraine discovered that about every volunteer she talked with had either lost a child to or been a child of the streets.

She answered their inquiries without a tremor. "I don't know. He went out and didn't come home."

It was edifying in a strange way, almost empowering, really: the looming posters, the patronizing smiles of office staffers, the grim work of the phone counselors (talking to a worried parent, trying to guide a tweaking street kid). Any other place she went, Lorraine was isolated by grief, stranded on an island. Volunteer work not only eased, but also fed her suffering. Every time she came in, Lorraine politely asked a staffer if Newell had left a message. If anyone matching a description of him had been picked up. And could someone run a check through the police network? She supplied the coffee machine with gourmet blends, brought in expensive doughnuts, and even made a point of remembering each volunteer's favorites. Lorraine went so far as to volunteer for the thankless project of organizing the boxes and files in the back room, and spent hours on her knees amid dusty documents. If any of the tasks she per-

formed could indeed be considered a favorite, then her favorite was reading through the letters and printed e-mails that had come in to the
switchboard, picking out inspirational missives, examples that imparted
hope, and could be used in fund-raising or informational literature:

Dear Switchboard,

    My daughter returned on Tuesday and is back with her
counselor. I believe the only reason she came home is
because I left a message with you folks and after hearing the
message she knew we were here to help, no matter what.

Thank you & God bless.

Dear Nevada Child Search,

    I am so glad that the switchboard still exists. I ran
away in 1985 and when I was on the streets and living on
the run, you helped make things easier. It helped to call the
switchboard and get advice. The people I spoke with were
never pushy or preachy. They did ask if I was safe, but never
tried to tell me what to do. I can honestly say I do not know
if I could have survived without the switchboard. It meant
so much to be able and call and hear my mother's voice from
time to time without having her there to judge or question
me. Now that I am a mother myself I know how much it
helped her to be able to receive messages from me, too.
Thank you so much. Keep up the good work.

Street Teens
c/o: the Nevada Coalition for Homeless Teens

    Three years ago my son ran away. For nearly a year I
anxiously awaited his calls from many different places in
the country, not knowing what to expect from one day to the
next. Finally I received a call from him asking for money to

come home. I promptly wired him the money. Four days later he called back, saying he'd lost it. It broke my heart to tell my son that I didn't have any more to send, but I did it. I lived in fear of what would happen next and what the next call might bring. A month later I was contacted by your organization saying that my son had contacted you and was on the other line. The counselor not only arranged a bus ticket for him, but also helped develop a plan to assure that the problems which led up to my boy's leaving would be addressed. What the National Runaway Switchboard did was to enable my son to come home at his (and my) hour of need. Please accept this donation. I can never pay for what you gave me, but I can try to help others feel the gratitude I did on that December day when my son arrived home.

The first time Lorraine posted flyers at neighborhood stores, she cried the whole time and was so drained that afterward she promised herself this was it, no way she could do it again. A week later she was at the post office, staring at the ancient postings, children who had been missing from other states for no less than six years. As she waited in line for a clerk, then for an office manager, Lorraine felt assurance in the idea she was indeed doing something larger than herself. Blowing snot into the sleeve of a cashmere sweater, she taped up notices at her son's favorite comic book shop, inside the movie theater he most often frequented, and the pizzeria from the Little League party. On alternate weekends she staffed a table in Caesars Palace's glitzy shopping mall. Crowds passed her little space outside the food court, and their apathy filled Lorraine with righteous outrage, with self-satisfaction, even as it added logs and lighter fluid to the sense of culpability that constantly burned inside her. She grew accustomed to the hollow reverberations of dropped change inside a gallon jug, the leers of bored husbands. What never took was the sight of the teenagers. All those teenagers. Skulking. Effervescent. Awkward. Teenagers in monstrously oversize clothes and floppy hipster beach hats. Teenagers riding the escalator. Hanging out in packs, in pairs, cruising and flirting, laughing, wasting their afternoons like they had all the time in the world. It was too much. Too hard. She did not want to wish they were the ones who had disappeared but fuck help her she did. After her second weekend, Lorraine gave up the table and returned to the back of the old office. When the social workers took to the conference room, or had a junior high assembly to preach to, Lorraine read through three-ring educational binders. Used the wheezing desktops to pore through databases. And what she learned was that more girls ran away from home, 60 percent to 40. That California was the most popular state to run to and from. That call volume to the hotline increased by 50 percent at the beginning of each school year.

Is your teen sullen and nonresponsive? asked an advice nugget, found inside a three-ring binder, its pages among the few legal resources available to those who wished to help. *Has he/she changed friends and peer groups? Has there been a falling off in his/her personal hygiene?*

Lorraine suffered through each category, veritable *Cosmo* lists of parenting. "Listening to Your Child"; "Overcoming Hurdles to Communication"; "Can You Tell the Difference Between Normal Adolescent Rebellion and a Teen in Crisis?" She tortured herself with their earnest feebleness, their sugary and semiofficial language. *It is important to be active in your child's activities. It is imperative to be your teenager's advocate. The active advocate parent takes great pains to praise success and feed their youngster's sense of self, even as they vigilantly guard against that child acquiring a sense of entitlement. Children should be taught to ask questions, to think both de- and inductively, to explore the creative facets of their developing personalities, all without challenging authority. It is important to make sure your child has room to make decisions for him/herself, and learn from his/her own mistakes, although if your child is not working up to his/her capabilities, you are to confront your child, or even his/her school system, for your child should not be allowed to create a pattern of taking the easy way out. Remember: teenagers have peer pressure to deal with. They have friends and influences that may or may not be wholesome. Raging hormones. Body changes. Attractions and dealing with members of the opposite and/or same sex. Delineated sections of the runaway counselor advisory notebook deal with these problems. Should you so desire, you also are more than welcome to stay on the line and converse further with your teen crisis counselor. Otherwise, however, you are advised to continue as you are, dealing and coping, staying calm and supportive, being firm and strong, not sacrificing your dreams, but channeling them; you are to prostrate yourself and give everything you can and fight that good fight, to balance yourself on dental floss above a giant abyss, to work and slave and do the best that your limited and fallible self can, every night laying your weary head against a pillow and comforting yourself with the thought that you have given your all. You are to do all of these things and then one night you are to discover—that perhaps because you have done these things—your only child has not come home. And thus you are to face the stark and brutal fact that every single thing you've done in your life has been* WRONG, *that your child has fled and your marriage is a sham and your home reeks of cat urine and even the workings of your brain have turned against you. And when this happens, the only way out is to go downstairs and head to the kitchen cupboard and remove that fateful white sleeve from the shelf; only, when you do this, upon removing the videocassette, you will discover a rupture, loose ends of brown film dangling from each end of the cassette. You will discover the cassette has been destroyed. That bastard husband of yours, he's broken your videotape, oh he did it all right—though he will claim the machine ate it, say it was an accident, the thing just snapped, it got worn down. He will feign innocence and make his paltry excuses and you will know better. Whenever he passes your son's bedroom he closes the door. He drops oblique references to "the future." He's developed that hangdog look and taken to saying, "There's a lot we should talk about." You do not need his words. You do not even need your tape. You have your misery. Your endless internal monologue. Your running conversation. Your missing child.*

2.5

Against the wall, the boy was sitting maybe six inches from the television, staring right into that idiot box. Absorbed by the flashing images, he was ignoring the voice behind him.

From his relaxed position on the couch, Lincoln continued addressing the back of his son's head, explaining that eight hours was average for labor, usually a lot longer for a first child.

The story's subject kept looking ahead—he'd need glasses eventually, Lincoln knew. For Newell's sake, he hoped it wouldn't be soon.

"The nurses told me, if I wanted to take a break, Lorraine's parents were in with her, she wouldn't be alone. They even wanted to give me a pager. The second anything happened, someone would be in touch."

Shifting in place, Lincoln waded through a memory or two, and reported that he hadn't been able to make heads or tails of the nurse's accent. But he'd known that just like he'd done his part conceiving the kid, he was gonna do his job in the delivery room. Hell or high water, Lincoln was the rock for his wife's fingers to clutch, the flesh for her nails to tear. "I told them straight out where they could stick it," he said, turning up the macho a few notes, adding a bit of drama and bloodlust to this disturbance. "They tossed me right out of Humana Sunrise. Took three guards. I'm kicking and screaming, and they throw me right out of there, right out on my ass."

The last word brought eye contact from Newell—a sudden shared moment, both parties knowing the boy's mother would not tolerate that kind of language, that Lincoln used the word for precisely this reason. The code of men. The bond of fathers and sons. Newell's profile was bathed in the television's spooky half-light, frozen there, as if he were not quite sure how he should be reacting. Lincoln thought he saw a twinkle of bemusement in his son's expression, and for an instant wondered if he was laying it on too thick. But he also saw that he had Newell's attention.

"Oh, I was pissed," Lincoln continued. "Had half a mind to take my pickup right through the front of that hospital. If I'da had my thirty-eight in the glove compartment, I promise you, any son of a bitch dumb enough to keep me from what I love, what I created . . ." He leaned into a crouch. His hands came together in front of him, and his tone was more focused now. "I mean, we got this, this *happening* here. And you're nervous as shit. We've done the Lamaze and all that, got the breathing down, but it's different. Like going from a complicated game, dress-up and make-believe. It's the real deal here. A man can't help but wonder. The ultrasound says everything's okay but what the hell do doctors know? If they're such good doctors, what are they doing in Vegas, right? You worry, are Drs. Siegfried and Roy gonna pop you out one of them deformed freak babies, with the second head growing out of its neck or something?"

"Dad."

"What? You telling me you wouldn't have liked a twin brother?"

"Twenty dollars, please."

"Deal's a deal, hotshot."

"Kenny's going to be here *any* second."

"Well, when he gets here, I'll get my wallet."

From the hall bathroom, his wife's voice told him to stop torturing the boy. After a moment, Lorraine emerged from the open doorway, working at the clasp of one of her earrings. "And you," she said. "Listen to your father."

She fixed the clasp and started into the living room, toward the kitchen, where she walked in a nervous half circle around the dinner table, looking in each chair. If she was aware of the effect of her little black cocktail dress, she did not let on.

"Your mom sure cleans up nice."

"You haven't seen my purse?"

Lincoln pretended to make an effort to look, quickly got back to business: "This was when big prizefights still took place behind Caesars Palace. They used to build grandstands on top of the outdoor tennis courts, have the fights right out beneath the stars. Your dad didn't have the clout to get tickets then—I never had a lot of friends at Caesars—and you were on the way, so we didn't have any spare bucks for the pay-per-view."

As Lincoln spoke, he was aware of Newell glancing down into the shoe box in his lap, the game cartridges he'd been rummaging through when all this started. He was aware of the boy looking up and turning, searching out his mother and making eye contact. Immediately Lincoln knew she'd visited Newell's room, and while he did not know details of their truce, this glance gave him some idea. *We all make compromises,* it said. *This is part of the agreement.* This was almost enough to make him quit. To just junk it all and walk away. If this tale didn't truly deserve to be passed down, he would have given up right there. But damn if he was going to hand them victory, be denied the telling of such an excellent tale. His voice filled with forced goodwill, a hint of temper. "*So what I'd do.* I'd drive up and down I-15, where it runs behind the Strip, have the radio tuned to the sports station for the round-by-round updates. The closest parts of the freeway, between the sounds from the grandstands and the blow-by-blow recaps, it was just like being at the fights."

"What time are our reservations?" Lorraine asked.

"We're fine."

"I just don't want to be late."

Newell's head tilted back ever so slightly, the back of his skull making soft impact against the wall behind him.

"I drove around for a while," Lincoln said, "kind of light-headed. I was so pissed at myself for getting thrown out of there, letting your mom down. I don't remember driving, just that I ended up pulling into the employee lot at work, I think from repetition as much as anything. I had a copy of the Lamaze notes in the glove compartment and was going over them." He stopped now, became contemplative, the memory apparent to him as if he were looking at it through a thin sheet of gauze. "You know, your mom and I, we really didn't have a lot. She'd given up dancing to have you, and my bonus money had been just enough for the banks to let us go into debt for the house. We were getting by, not much more. We had health insurance but it wasn't going to cover it all, and that was just the beginning. Having a kid, you don't know what you're getting into."

Memories had him now, back in those moments, possessing him to the point where his affectations were stripped away, and he spoke candidly, honestly; to the point where he did not notice the changing tenor of the living room—his son going bone still, being sucked into the tale against his will, Lorraine coming to the edge of the kitchen, listening silently, her guard lowering enough to find herself occupied by her own memories, and a different tale of how that night went.

"This guy I know, Stromboli, was working the pit and I remember we talked for a while. Guess I was nervous, because Stromboli, and the craps dealer too, and pretty much every single individual around that table heard about the bundle on the way. I mean I blabbed. Getting kicked outta the hospital. The mutant two-headed flipper baby. If worrying made me a bad guy, and about not wanting a flipper baby—shouldn't I love the kid no matter what? This is to a full table, remember. All kinds of action going on. Money's at play. But you know what, every person around that table was pretty sympathetic. Concerned even. Then they wanted your old man to shut the hell up."

Lincoln chuckled at his own joke; Lorraine interrupted: "You're not wearing that tie."

"Looks that way."

"With *that* jacket?"

He turned away from her voice, away from the reality of a wife who habitually challenged and corrected his sense of style. *"Five's the point,"* he announced, assuming the barking voice of a croupier. " *'The point is five. New shooter here. New shooter coming out.'* I figure what the hell, right? Reach into my pocket. When I open my wallet, the damndest thing—this orange and red piece of confetti, I didn't know what it was. It carries up into the air, sweeps up in the air, just the damndest thing you ever saw, *it's a butterfly,* fluttering, unsteady above the crap table, right in the middle of all that smoke."

The smell of his wife's perfume and the weight of her presence were behind him; her arms wrapped around his neck.

"A moth," Newell said.

"Not many times in your life you honestly come across magic," Lincoln said. "That was one."

"I love that story," Lorraine said.

He looked up, admiring her for a count. She smiled—a bit sadly, he thought, before she broke the moment, straightened something on the adjacent table.

"I took those bones," Lincoln said, with renewed energy. "Straight off rolled myself a four and a three. Like something from the movies. You couldn't have scripted it any better." He felt a catch in his throat. "I'm telling you, whatever I needed, I rolled. It was insane. The crowd was cheering. *'Hot shooter. Make way for the hot shooter.'* "

"Why'd you have a butterfly in your wallet?" Newell's face betrayed interest, confusion. "I mean, if it's a moth the story makes sense. But a butterfly?"

"What time's your show?" Lorraine asked.

"Um . . . Seven-fifteen, I think."

"You'll be home by ten?"

"What if I get hungry and want to get food?"

"You shouldn't get hungry. You had dinner and your dad's giving you money for popcorn and snacks."

"He hasn't given me anything, *yet*."

"Don't rush me," Lincoln said, laughing. "I'm still trying to figure out why there was a butterfly in my wallet."

"Did or did we not agree, Newell?"

"Mom."

"You get to go out with your friend so long as you agree to be home by ten."

She did not break, no matter how long he studied her. Finally, if Newell did not exactly nod, the blankness of his face registered understanding, an unhappy acceptance of the terms, but acceptance nonetheless. He said, "Ten A.M. it is."

"Young man—"

Let them spar, Lincoln figured, let life and its messy details swirl. Rather than getting involved, instead of paying attention, he returned to a March night that did not feel all that long ago, a night when he had stayed at the craps table for five hours, when he'd won enough money to pay off all of his wife's hospital bills, and had continued to win, rolling so well that expecting baby or no expecting baby, the other players had not wanted him to leave the table, those bastards had wanted Lincoln to rattle them bones.

He'd about had to pull himself away, but pull himself away he had. He'd been exhausted and pumped, reeking with nicotine and drenched with sweat, riding on adrenaline and love and whiskey, while still sort of worried about flipper babies, how the delivery would go, which breathing technique went where.

He had told his son this story many times, it was true, overacting each time, stepping into his overblown tough-guy persona, painstakingly going over the details, ad infinitum, ad nauseam, so many times that he knew Newell was sick of the story, so many times that it was not uncommon for the kid to poke holes in his exaggerations, to roll his eyes, report, *I'm going into diabetic shock here.* Lincoln knew his son had become inured to how much the story meant to him, knew the emotion that the tale drew from him was repellent to his boy. At the same time Lincoln saw his son tempted, struggling with and repulsed by and suffocating with his own connections to the tale. The safe conclusion was that his dad was a big old softie. A lightweight. And maybe it was true. Maybe he was. Because Lincoln could not help himself. His voice breaking, he recalled the assuredness that overtook him that night on his drive back to the hospital.

"The word *blessing*," Lincoln said, "is flowery and unmasculine. I know."

But on that March night of twelve years ago plus change, be it boy or girl or flipper baby, he'd been sure that the coming child—yes, the very same one who was writhing now at having to hear all this, *you, you little pain in the ass*—surely was some sort of blessing. A blessed infant coming from some blessed place.

Even now telling the story made him more sure of it.

And what Lincoln did not say—what his wife did not now or ever correct him on—was that Lorraine had been in labor for only two hours.

He did not report that he'd missed the page from the hospital. That he had not been on hand for the birth—the *breech birth*.

Not while Lorraine was cut open. Not while his baby was unwrapped from its umbilical cord, forcibly removed from his momma's womb.

The fact is, he'd heard the news with his wife resting in hospital room seven. A glossed-over, secondhand version, accentuated by Jamaican lilts whose loveliness he still vividly heard: *Don't feel bad. The childe jes coulden' wait to come into the world.*

Newell Ewing would never know about these details. In the same way Lincoln never arrived at the blessed event itself, revisionist history would drop his absence from the story. Instead, what finally was mentioned, the last word in this little tale, was a postscript, a vow made when he had snuck away from his sleeping wife and their room of bounty, and had stood in front of the baby nursery's glass wall. *I will never be able to do enough for my child.*

The sound of a noisy engine pulling up to the driveway and idling. A wheezing horn. Newell could not move fast enough, shooting to his feet, extending his palm.

PART TWO

Chapter 3

FREE MONEY 9:30–10:30 P.M.

3.1

The neon. The halogen. The viscous liquid light. Thousands of millions of watts, flowing through letters of looping cursive and semi-cursive, filling then emptying, then starting over again. Waves of electricity, emanating from pop art façades, actually transforming the nature of the atmosphere, creating a mutation of night, a night that is not night— *daytime at night.* The twenty-four-hour bacchanal. The party without limits. The crown jewel of a country that has institutionalized indulgence. *Vegas on Saturday night.*

Nothing matches the spectacle of the four-point-six-mile stretch known as the Las Vegas Strip. Here, some thirty-five gaming resorts are gathered, each boasting more hotel suites than can be found in the countries formerly known as the Soviet Union. They operate like autonomous empires, each one packed with restaurants ranging from five-star gourmet to quickie snack bars, with walk-through shopping malls where high-end couture is as plentiful as suburbia's favorite brands, with amusement centers for the kiddies, thumping nightspots catering to those inclined to shake what their mommas gave them, and sports books whose giant-screen televisions and information boards rival the Pentagon's war room. This is only the beginning. Every amenity the mind, on a whim, might invent, is available. Every offering that might keep someone from heading into another resort.

Business may have been slumping that year with terrorism threats, a free-falling economy, and airline bankruptcies combining to drive most hotels' weekday occupancy rates to dangerously low levels. But on weekends, the city still overflowed as in the boom times, with occupancy rates spiking to above 90 percent. On Saturday nights, the price of a hotel room more than doubled. The cheapest blackjack tables were bumped from a two-dollar minimum bet to twenty. If you wanted to see Bill Cosby at Caesars, Bob Dylan at the Mandalay Bay, or *Nudes on Ice* at the Union Plaza, tickets were not only twice as expensive, brokers would tell you, but also twice as difficult to get. *Everything* cost more on Saturday night. On Saturday night everything was worth more. On Saturday night more was at stake, for players as well as the people serving them. Thus, the guy in the chef's hat at the buffet was more than happy to slice you an end cut. The bathroom attendants lowered their heads an extra subservient notch while offering selections of cologne.

Five out of ten livelihoods in Clark County depended on keeping visitors happy, and four of the other five were indirectly dependent. Which meant that at approximately nine thirty-five P.M. on the Saturday night of the second week of August, the blackjack dealer did not so much as raise his eyebrow at the prematurely balding guy who strained at the confines of a shiny lamé shirt (if the dealer had to guess, he'd say the shirt had been purchased especially for this trip). It meant that the dealer retained his poker face as this guy was dealt four consecutive hands of thirteen or fourteen; and that when this poor schlep, as per the instructions of his *Get Rich Quick Players Guide,* hit on the first three hands, and each time received a face card, he received the dealer's sympathies. It meant that during the fourth hand, when this guy stared at his cards, let out a deep breath, took off his thick black eyeglasses, and rubbed at his temples, when he said, *Okay, I'm good, hold,* and promptly watched what should have been his seven go to the next player, the dealer did not laugh out loud. And, too, it meant that when Bing Beiderbixxe, angry and dejected and more than a little abashed, left the casino, and asked the valet parking guy about the nearest strip club, he was not met with any sort of judgment. Just a sly smile, the wink of the complicit.

But remember, it's also Saturday night for residents of Las Vegas. And while a great many of the locals are busy dealing the wrong cards to the right people, there remain a large number of folks whose weekdays have been spent performing such tasks. When Saturday hits, these people are more than ready to let loose. Top tier pop acts perform at the university basketball arena. The city also is home to minor league teams in hockey, arena football, and baseball, as well as professional drag and stock-car racing tracks. Don't forget the drama companies, repertory ballet, the museums (art, natural, and regional history), or the zoo. All have their merits. Yet like the infamous founder of the Hair Club for Men, who on late-night commercials happily proclaimed himself to be not only the president of his club, but also a client, a great number of the people who live and work in Las Vegas are most captivated not by zoos and ballet, but by games of chance. On weekends, they leave the Strip to tourists, downtown to the unfortunates. The action heats up along the city's perimeter, adjacent to its many suburbs, inside the many casinos that specifically cater to locals, places like Sam's Town and the Palace Station, warehouse-size halls whose hotel rooms usually sell because the Strip has been overbooked. Here, the vibe is tangibly different from on the Strip: all the overblown pretenses and fantasies have been stripped away. Frequent-player slot clubs provide senior citizens with rebates at area grocery stores, and pick-the-parlay football contests require a Nevada driver's license to enter. Money still flows through the casinos; there's still enough energy in the air to rival any big-name joint, but out here the energy is shaded with blue-collar pragmatism. Career dealers and waitresses occupy untold seats around blackjack tables. Logrolling is constant, as is the business of watching, and washing, backs. You never know, the guy you broke in dealing poker with ten years ago could show up as a pit boss; the husband of your former secretary might end up a head waiter.

Lincoln Ewing happily thanked his old buddy with an arm around the shoulder and a twenty-dollar bill folded inside a handshake. A chair was pulled out for Lorraine. For more than a moment she allowed herself to be charmed by the dark and intimate table in the restaurant's far corner. Her husband's charisma impacted her as it had in the old days, his seemingly endless connections reminded her just how likeable he could be. Instead of checking her watch, she reached across the candlelit table, placed her hand atop his. The wine steward would be around shortly.

Hey, Kenny had asked, *what are you doing later?* And if Newell hadn't known what exactly a Saturday night entailed, he had known that Saturday nights were fun. What kind of fun, what exactly fun consisted of, what it was that made fun so damn fun as opposed to say, *neat,* or *nifty,* those were for someone else to worry about. Someone besides the *N* to the *E* to the dub to the *E* to the *L* to the *L*. And isn't that the essence of being twelve—being impressionable, blissfully ignorant of ramification? But Newell Ewing was also learning that, often, getting what you asked for meant getting *more* than what you asked for. He was on the Strip, *hell yeah,* descending the poorly lit stairwell reserved for employees of the Circus Circus Hotel & Casino and Family Entertainment Emporium, his footsteps resounding on the corrugated metal. Newell took another two steps in one leap, no longer fretting about the way his oversize and unbelted shorts kept slipping below the placement generally acceptable for a homeboy sag, nor the quarter-size nacho stain that his mom would blame him for getting on his fifty-dollar T. The concession stand of overpriced and undernuked cardboard foodstuffs. The arcade of video games that had malfunctioned and eaten his quarters. The rigged carnival games. The barkers who, whenever they'd gone on breaks, had made sure the stuffed bears were attached to the booths with metal hooks, so he couldn't ever snag one. These were behind him now. Oh he was runnin' with the big dawgs, strutting like a mack daddy, heading for fun of the serious and monumental and three-sixty-degree-slam-dunking variety. Fun that got blacked out by V-chips. The grade-A jollies he not only deserved, but was entitled to. *The fun that was supposed to be the whole point of a Saturday night out.*

Head start or not, Kenny wasn't about to let his friend get the best of him. His legs were longer than Newell's, and even if his strides were ungainly, he quickly made up ground, pulling even with Newell now, the pair of them running side by side for one, two, three steps down the stairwell. Kenny did not look over at Newell, he did not need to, for he felt his friend's breath rise and fall in syncopation with his, felt their legs moving to the same cadence. Kenny had an inkling to turn toward Newell and smile, but it also seemed that acknowledging the moment would ruin it. Bangs whipped into his eyes but Kenny did not brush them aside. He pushed off a step with his right leg and with an awkward leap pulled ahead—clearing the bottom three stairs, spending one blissful moment suspended, his legs spread wide and bent at the knees, his body pressing forward, feeling graceful and light, released, weightless.

With a thud like a baseball bat against the side of a car, he landed on the small steel platform, his momentum carrying him forward now, propelling him first into the maintenance door, and then into the great hall. Air glittered with nicotine and conversation; it dripped with hope and desperation and designer perfumes. Through the vague and blinking distance, keno ballasts flashed, the digital figures of progressive slot jackpot reader boards were in perpetual motion; the waterfall of coins into metal tins was resonant, continuous, an orchestral hymn.

Meanwhile, halfway across town, a girl sat in an ice cream truck.

If only it *were* possible to place her in the comic book shop earlier that day, to have her perusing the racks with a combination of fascination and haughtiness, to have her idly flipping through issues whose covers caught her fancy, then checking to see how fast the line was moving. She would have been bored, anxious to blow that metaphorical taco stand, hightail it over to the four-dollar matinee in time to buy popcorn and still make the previews. Absently she would have been fingering some of the stray fringe from where she had cut the sleeves off her Cub Scout shirt. She would have been shifting her slight body's weight from one sunburned sapling of leg to the other, then peeling small, transparent flakes of skin from the meat of her freckled arm, and then yanking on the back hem of her thrift-store skirt; maybe thinking about giving voice to her dissatisfaction with the slowness of the line, or simply plopping down onto the carpet, sitting on her knees and losing herself in one of the illustrated fantasies. She would have been weighing all these options, choosing none of them, simply killing time, her jittery, girlish mannerisms drawing just enough attention to get her noticed.

What can you do? The girl didn't like comic books. *Punk Planet* was more her speed. *The Anarchist Cookbook.* Moreover, there's something cosmically wrong with the girl being introduced by way of her location and activity. It is more appropriate to her personality that you meet her through negation, based on precisely where she was *not.* To wit: the distinction she insisted upon when discussing her skull. *Not bald,* but *shaved. Like a sprinkle of pepper atop an egg,* is how she phrased it. *Like the blades of grass that certainly will reclaim our scorched earth in the days following Armageddon.* The girl was more than happy to explain that the chickens raised at farms owned by Kentucky Fried Chicken had been genetically mutated—did not possess beaks, wings, feet, or feathers and, ergo, did not qualify for the *Oxford English Dictionary* definition of the word *chicken.* Easily and at the drop of a hat, she'd pontificate on the evils of red meat, dairy products, hormone-affected poultry, pesticide-sprayed fruits, genetically engineered vegetables, sugar or bean products gathered by exploited Central American workers, and any other foods she thought were connected to the worldwide conspiracy. Anyone who cared (and many who did not) had heard the girl with the shaved head explain that she'd pretty much existed on wheat and bottled water for three months now—and wheat was on shaky ground depending on how much she could download about this administration's policies toward corporate farm subsidies, and as for bottled water, *two dollars for fucking water?* Totally elitist. Another scam.

Can you hear the lilt in her voice? The musical insouciance that coated her doomsayings?

They were pissing away their Saturday night. Cruising the road to nowhere. Francesca had picked her up and they had landed in this dented old ice cream truck, which was parked across three spaces of the student lot at Edward W. Clark High School. They were hanging in the back—the girl plus Francesca plus a few others back there, seven or so. Self-proclaimed misfits whose indignation had at some point attracted hers. Like-minded thinkers whose interests extended into different subjects. Blokes who went out of their way to use the word *bloke,* calling each other at outrageous hours of the night and filling the dead air with whispers, who traded personalized mix tapes culled from hidden tracks on their favorite compact discs, delighted in the fact that the cassette tape was an ancient and disappearing species, and made sure to take special time and effort in their hunts through vintage shops for the forgotten postcard that would have a special, though not overt, significance to the receiver of the tape, thereby serving as that tape's *perfect* piece of cover art. Who played tag in graveyards and haunted the matinée shows at two-dollar theaters and made out with one another at random when there was nothing else to do, cutting class and sitting on top of their cars in the school parking lot, sneering at anyone who dared walk by, and loudly championing obscure bands because they were obscure, *because* they were signed to independent labels and run out of some garage and therefore removed from the drive-time prime-time socio-corporate-conspiracy: *Be Yourself, Buy Our Product.* The latest incarnation of suburban anarchists, their appearances painstakingly vandalized to reflect not an opinion of themselves but of the world; their respective and collective existences devoted to the embrace and celebration and exaltation of any fad, fashion, font, diet, drug, gossip, glyph, golden calf, black magic, method of self-mutilation, chat room signature pic, necromicon, exotic cosmetic accessory, erotic Universal Resource Locator, and/or generalized lifestyle choice that beyond a shadow of doubt proved they were *not in league with this fucked-up world.*

There was beer, a watery brand of dog piss that had been obtained through whatever machinations teens go through to get alcohol. There was a dime bag of really weak hash that had somehow gotten the nickname *Tijuana Worm*. Zydeco music played on a scratchy LP, though nobody was paying it attention, for they were too busy talking, of course, a bunch of teenagers slinging shit, would-be immortals in conversations that were destined to be carved on the sides of mountains. Voices still in the process of maturation cracked and reverberated off the metal hull, merging together; sentences overlapping, their echoes becoming jumbled, mixing in with the fiddles and banjos, this complicated, irrepressible tune.

The girl was in the far back, sitting on some sort of off-roading tire. Jagged treads were digging into the back of her thighs and she was squirming in place, trying to look like she was not squirming, pretending she did not care about getting her skirt dirty. A black plastic trash bag had been duct-taped where the rear window should have been, and shards of light were filtering in through the holes in the bag, creating columns of illumination, which fell upon her like water from a shower nozzle, this almost angelic effect.

This place sucks, she said. *I can't stand it here.*

She yapped intently, obliviously, as if she were the first person to come up with her idea, as if the notion of flight—*I can't wait till I'm old enough to blow this hole*—were not part of being young, as if the idea of running away were not part of the romance of youth, as natural as imagining your own funeral, telling yourself, *When I'm gone, won't they be sorry.*

Specifically, she was bitching about her home, *the eggshell-and-puke piece of cardboard her mom kept her trapped in.* Most definitely *not* her home, according to the girl with the shaved head. *Vegas was not the girl's home.* Vegas was a black hole. *A total fucking conspiracy.* The girl had done her research on this matter, and this research had fed her outrage, led to more researching, more uncovered transgressions, every one of which she'd dutifully transcribed into her diary, looping four-page sentences done with black marker: how each resort put the front entrance on one side of the ground floor, the hotel elevators on another, the restaurants on the third, and the shops on the fourth, so every time Mr. and Mrs. Tourist Suck wanted to do anything, they had to walk across the casino floor. How oxygen got pumped into the casino so gamblers wouldn't get tired. How there weren't clocks, so you didn't know how long you'd been playing, and didn't care if it was day or night. How poker chips replaced money so that after a while you wouldn't see the monetary value of what you were doing, but maybe got bored with playing only the red chips and wanted to play some blues, which were worth like twice as much. How waitresses gave out free alcohol-soaked drinks so the gambler would make good and sober decisions with all those chips that were not quite being seen as money. How oxygen, liquid, night, day, animal, vegetables, minerals, every and any single aspect of the casino resort environment, how all of them were skewed to keep a person on the floor of the gambling house—*all so you could win money from the casino.*

It galled her, the way her mother always harshed her flow, tried to get her to calm down. Sitting at the kitchen table, waving some sort of health food cracker at the girl. Saying, *"Oh, sweetie. SWEETIE."*

Sure her mom was a single parent, working full-time and trying to raise a kid and adjust to a new city and build a new life, doing the best she could with an English degree in a cheap frame and a shitload of debt on her mind. The girl's mother was prone to crying jags and panic attacks, and whenever the girl got rolling about everything that was wrong with their new home, her mom would cut her off, shouting back: "*What do you want me to do?* It's a miracle if we get an alimony payment. I moved here for a teaching job and the school district goes into a hiring freeze. The temp service hasn't called since the last time that spreadsheet program crashed. These are the facts, sweetie. So tell me what to do here. At least gaming school guarantees a dealing job when I graduate. It gives us a way to pay the bills. NO, THEY DO NOT STORE NUCLEAR WASTE ON THE STEPS OF CITY HALL. AND NO, I DON'T CARE WHAT YOU READ. THEY DO NOT STILL TEST HYDROGEN BOMBS RIGHT OUTSIDE CITY LIMITS. Oh, sweetie. SWEETIE. Please. Baby. You are asking the right questions. There's nothing *wrong* with the way you feel—I feel it, too. It's part of being alive. There's not any grand conspiracy. I mean, yes, but . . . Oh, baby."

The conspiracy of human frailty, was the phrase her mother used. And this usually seemed to have an effect on the girl. Like some magic elixir had been released, the tension would break, the two would embrace, the girl letting her mom cradle the sides of her skull, kiss the crag near the top of the back, letting her mother plant another one on her forehead, the girl finally breaking the embrace and holding her mom's hand for a count or so and then getting back to doing the dishes, or taking out the trash, the girl doing her chores and quietly telling herself things would be okay, trying to convince herself. *Seriously.* Just like she tried when they'd packed up the U-Haul, driven their crap in from Long Beach. Like she tried when her father called and explained that he was going to get married again, but of course he still cared about Mom. When he said that just because his schedule did not let him come down and visit, it didn't mean he didn't love her. Like with each guy her mother dated for longer than a week. Every bleeping time: the inevitable arrived and the girl dutifully stopped working on her latest poem or rant, she put out her cigarette (Death Cloves®, the profits of which went to a foundation dedicated to the abolition of smoking), made sure the ashes were hidden in the window frame, and lit up one of those incense candles endorsed by Amnesty International. She promised whoever was on the phone she'd call right back, muted the idiot box, put the stereo on auto select, saved and closed whatever file was open, undid her door chain, and let the poor schmuck enter. And never ever did she roll her eyes when he took a seat on the corner of her bed: *Um, hey, hey there. You know, your mom's a little concerned about your eating habits.*

But hanging out in the ice cream truck, see, that didn't take no effort.

Shadows subdivided the van's dented interior. Skunkweed and nicotine melded with the lingering scents of perspiration, urine, and leftover and rancid hamburger meat. From outside, the school bell blared for, like, the ninetieth time. What a school bell was blaring every half hour for on a summer night, who the fuck could say. Whatever. No point cursing it anymore.

"Doctors are fucked," the girl said. "Medical science is a plot."

Her words were directed next to her, to some kid whose name she may or may not have known, this lanky mawkish boy wearing an improbable stretch cap of bright green wool. Frail bone structure. Spectacles. A dramatic Roman nose. She wasn't sure, but it might have been the same face as this kid from her advanced-placement English class, this kid who never spoke and carried the same coverless, water-warped paperback wherever he went.

"Telling the truth would cost them customers and that would cost them money." The girl took a long swig of beer. She was pretty baked, her thoughts vomiting forth, shooting straight from her brain into her mouth.

"Forget their quackery. That shit about a lack of calcium and protein and essential daily vitamins preventing menstrual flow. I missed my last four periods because adolescent witches miss their periods. I'm thin because adolescent witches are thin.

"It's simple," she said. "The blood and nutrients go directly into my emergent spell powers."

Wool Cap Kid pursed his lips and the girl thought it was the same kid as from English class, definitely, which was both a worry and a relief, sort of—because he was kind of ugly and kind of cute at the same time, sitting there in a black V-neck, staring at her all astonished and all. The girl had always had a bit of a thing for him but had never wanted to screw things up by talking to him—that's how things went, once a boy thought you liked him, he wouldn't even make eye contact in the hallway, boys were weird like that, whatever.

His eyes, dark and shining beads, remained trained: the aperture of her summer vest's open and hanging collar, the upper embroidery and lace of her bra. She wondered if he was checking her out. Did he think her bra was just a fashion statement? Truly needed as a support garment? The hull's ovenlike state made the girl *seriously* question putting wool on your head.

"You're James, right?"

Slowly he nodded.

"We have Mr. Silvestri together. Fourth period?"

Residual light from a cracked lava lamp gave his profile an eerie red blush.

"Can I ask you something? Have you been reading the same book over and over all this time?

"I mean, it's okay if you have. That's better than carrying the thing around because the author has a big fancy Russian name or something, I guess. Or like if you maybe had one of those disorders, like in the after-school television specials—like where you maybe can't read and try real hard and stick with it and after all this time are on chapter five, although you *are* in advanced-placement English. I guess there has to be some mustard on that there hot dog."

A smile creased his thin yet kissable lips.

"I been meaning to ask for a while," she admitted, and felt her face getting hot. "Except the times I showed up for English class, you usually cut. And then, whenever we both blew off class and ended up here in the ice cream truck, mostly you stayed huddled in that corner. Only but now, well, here I am and here you am, all next to each other, so I thought, you know, what the hell." She fidgeted. "I hope you don't think I'm lame."

"Not lame." He flashed perfect teeth. "Just full of shit."

James spoke rationally and calmly, in no way unkindly, with the snap of a boy satisfied with his thought process, excited to be sharing it. "If you were a witch, you wouldn't need to ask about my book. You could just cast a spell. Peer into your crystal ball and see the answer."

The outlines of two, three figures moved ambiguously across the front of the truck. Some undefined form sat playing invisible drums to this song, which most definitely did not have drums.

"I'm full of shit?"

The girl heard her voice reverberating off the hull. "How the . . . How can anyone say that about anyone else?" She felt herself rising now. "You don't know. Nobody is anybody else, so nobody can know. Like, like, look at this ice cream truck. It's the exact same deal. Like, was the fucker found abandoned on the side of the road? Was it liberated from Mister Softee's regional HQ? Depends on who you ask, right? Depends on what they've been toking."

Eyes were on her now but fuck if she cared. "How is not a subject of debate," she said. "Truth is not a matter of interest."

Tugging on her arm. A shaft of light caught the piercing stud in Francesca's eyebrow, creating a momentary incandescence along her profile.

If she needed a ride, Francesca wanted to know.

"Truth is not what you know or what is rational." The girl continued, her fingers all but trembling with rage. "Some company line about why their product is so fucking wonderful. That totally lame excuse as to why your birthday card might be a little late this year. One more object a person can buy or sell or try to shuck off on you."

"I've got to get back," Francesca said.

"The truth is just like this big old dented piece of crap ice cream truck. It's a bunch of bumper stickers clinging to crappy pink spray-paint."

Her arms flailed, pointing in unfollowable directions. "Look at them. *Look.*"

CONSUME OR BE CONSUMED.

OBJECTIVITY IS SUBJECTIVE.

I DROPPED ACID IN THE GRAND CANYON.

NUNS WITH GUNS ♡ CHICKS WITH DICKS.

FIRST BANK OF NIHILISM, WE DON'T VALIDATE JACK SHIT.

WHATEVER GETS YOU THROUGH THE NIGHT.

Cheri Blossom planted one of her stilettos on each side of the new-comer's prematurely balding skull, and lowered herself into a squat that was not quite pronounced enough to pee from. Immediately, her taut and bejeweled tummy began a series of undulations, each wave stopping inches from his thick black spectacles. The newcomer's porcine features went slack, his pinkish mouth opened slightly, and Cheri watched as his mind literally receded into the world of private and carnal awe that men retreated into when women like her straddled them.

No biggie. She'd been at the game long enough that controlling a man was, as a process, about the same to her as cutting away the mealy part of an apple that had been left on top of the fridge overnight. Actually, it was more like when the sun was easing its way over the Sierra Nevadas, and a night of shaking her moneymaker was behind Cheri; like when she worked the final locks of her condo and opened the door and, lo and behold, her boyfriend was cooking the final foils of her stash. The similarity in these different situations being that however much Cheri's concern should have been with that particular moment, she always found herself occupied with *that moment's inherent dramatic value*—how the image of herself cutting away at that apple revealed her to be self-possessed and at peace; or, conversely, the dramatic depths of her tantrum, all the exasperation her boyfriend brought from her. Cheri knew it sounded strange, but she couldn't help it. Sometimes she almost felt removed from her body, as if she were in a multiplex somewhere, watching a person she knew to be herself on the giant screen; as if each day was nothing more than a procession of scenes, acts in the epic movie that was her life, *Cheri Blossom's Hard Wild Ride,* adapted from the best-selling autobiography, with audio versions available at fine stores every-where.

Tonight's installment featured Catholic school as her place of reckoning. Never mind that Cheri had not attended Catholic school, she hadn't attended much public school, either, and anyway, it was her movie, she could do what she wanted: wrap her white schoolgirl's blouse into a knot, for example, so that the heft of her breasts was both supported and accentuated. Or wear a skimpy plaid miniskirt with a fold along the crotch, so that when she squatted, the fabric parted down the middle, revealing her candy-pink panties. To thumping bass sounds, Cheri, if the whim struck her, could unwrap her schoolgirl's skirt. She could twirl her blouse above her head and chuck her bra at a table of nearby admirers. Could spread her arms in a crucifixion pose and tilt her head as far backward as it would go, arching back, extending the points of her bare and spectacular breasts toward the tinted spotlights. And here, as sweat dripped from her shadowed and glitter-covered outline, Cheri could wiggle out of her spangled G-string. Never mind that she'd sweated tonight's supply of painkillers out of her system. Never mind that when she shifted her weight, her yeast infection flared. Cheri was mentally strong; she could block out that shit.

An ecstatic yell. Cheri whirled the dampened pink swatch around her finger, swished her hips as if they were windshield wipers, and pranced around the runway in an arcing circle, throughout keeping an eye on everyone gathered at the foot of the stage, watching to see which ones were placing down bills. When she had this figured, Cheri made her way back to her newly discovered mark—that prematurely balding guy, his glasses a bit askew.

He looked like the type who usually stood near the back. Maybe it was his big night out in Vegas (that would explain the shirt). Well, Cheri was in the mood to help, and parked her dimpled and peachy rear in front of his blushing face. She gave a pepper-mill grind, widened her legs out into an *A* and, in a smooth quick motion, bent over. Cheri's tight little gluteus was spread out all maximus-like, and her sex was juicy and engorged and hanging right in front of this guy's nose. She looked down through the space between her legs, over her hanging booming breasts. Her wig's fake ponytails fell into her eyes. Blood rushed to her head. And here, if the mood struck her and she damn well felt like it, here, while staring at him from upside down, Cheri could make eye contact; she could bestow upon this youngish and pink-faced mark a smile of full wattage. *Imagine running into you here. Of all people.*

An easy reach. In one fluid motion, Cheri placed her G-string atop his head. She slid her thong over the crown of his skull and moved the damp parts of the fabric past the slope of his forehead, onto his quickly fogging lenses, covering his face with the crotch of her panties as if they were a surgeon's mask, so that her scent all but overpowered him, reduced him to a quivering mass, all so this guy would basically be obligated to shell out thirty bucks for a private table dance, for no other reason than to find out what *could* come next.

Cheri could do these things because she was performing not for the mark but for a movie. And in this movie she was beyond sexy. She was A STAR.

This is what she told herself.

Saturday was the busiest night of the week on Industrial, a potholed utility road that emerged from beneath several freeway underpasses and ran parallel to the busiest stretch of the Strip. The warm summer night would have made for a pleasant walk from the closest casinos, except most valets and front desk workers discouraged such strolls, as thugs were known to wait in the shadows. A cab ride cost five bucks, plus gratuity, but was worth it, the taxis bypassing the Sheetrock suppliers, tombstone wholesalers, and construction rig rental agencies, and pulling up to the street's various gentlemen's cabarets—spots like Spearmint Rhino, Cheetah's, and Little Darlings, where dancers bared their breasts and stripped to their panties, and beer and hard alcohol were served at the bar. Taxis also stopped at aptly nicknamed spread joints, such as the Can Can Room, Déjà Vu, and Crazy Horse Too (home of the world famous Las Vegas strippers), where alcohol and video poker were legally prohibited, but dancers ended up in the buff.

The Slinky Fox was smaller than the newer warehouse-size superclubs, but still more expansive than the grimy dives so often associated with strip joints. The stage was lined with footlights and strings of blinking Christmas bulbs, and was visible from almost any area inside the club. Rows of plush booths bordered the main room, carving out its space, while the booth backs created partitioned areas, smaller, more intimate playgrounds, each replete with its own series of tables and couches, as well as a side stage with some sort of fireman pole or trapeze. Frat boys clogged the aisles between the main and side rooms, watching in all directions with expressions that tried not to betray their wonder. Some off-shift dealers had pushed tables together in the central area and sat around, their starched collars unbuttoned, each man relaxing without words, absently turning over the bills he planned to leave as a tip as if flipping the hole card in a blackjack game. Cops in civvies stood in rigid bunches and focused on the stage without expression, even as they rubbed shoulders with surly union workers, beaten down from months on a picket line, who were standing in front of a few overweight immigrants, every one of them committing Cheri's curves to memory, to be recalled in an hour or so—when they'd go home and enter their wives, enter their girlfriends, enter their lonely masturbatory fantasies.

The song ended and Cheri did not respond to the scattered applause, but instead kneeled, motionless, concentrating on her breathing. Remaining perfectly still while completely naked and surrounded by a roomful of horny guys, this took a certain amount of poise. Sometimes Cheri blocked out their stares. Sometimes she feasted on them. Three sprightly piano notes echoed through the loudspeaker system, at which point remaining still was no longer her concern. She began slowly, kicking her legs out from underneath her in a fluid motion, moving them in a complete circle. Wounded innocence now, a woman's throaty voice, her lamentation: *Every night before I go to sleep, Find a ticket, win a lottery.* Cheri rose to a knee and reached toward the ceiling, stretching her arms. The piano gradually increased its pace, and a bass guitar joined in, and then drums, Patti Smith's epic moving toward its stride, with Patti wailing about buying her lover a jet plane, getting him on a higher plane, taking him up to the stratosphere and then sweeping down, *where it's hot, hot in Arabia, babia, then cool, cold fields of snow . . .*

It was an unconventional song for stripping. Usually, when a rock song got played in the Slinky Fox anymore, it was a sleazy number from the eighties, all bumps and grinds, as opposed to something from the arty side of the early New York punk scene. But Cheri had always retained a soft spot for the drama packed inside "Free Money," and when she'd been looking to expand her repertoire, by some off chance, she'd thought about the song's dark and lulling start, its epic and passionate sweep. Cheri had vision in spades, if she said so herself, and she'd recognized the potential of "Free Money," devoting a solid week to choreographing her routine, coming up with interpretive movements for every chord change, pantomimes that matched each lyric. She'd practiced trailing long see-through veils behind her, wrapping and unwrapping herself in and from those veils, beating herself down onto the stage floor. And it had paid off. The first time Cheri had performed to the song, she'd worked her entire shift doing nothing but private dances. Indeed, the routine had been so successful that other girls started putting "Free Money" onto their playlists, attempting their own clumsy interpretations, usually with feather boas. "Free Money" had been absorbed into each night's routine at the Slinky Fox for almost a year now, and of late served as nothing so much as an ironic motto for the girls to slave by, a catchphrase to tell one another as they passed in the dressing room. Which was a bummer for Cheri—she'd busted her moneymaker to come up with a distinct act, her own signature song. Heck, the soundtrack to the movie of Cheri's life came straight from the songs she stripped to, and it complicated things when she herself no longer wanted to hear her own playlist.

'Cause if like four girls in a row went on the main stage and did all three dances as a hip-hop homegirl, sure there was a chance the crowd that night would love hip-hop and all the dancers would be in the flush. But it was equally possible that twelve straight hip-hop songs would be numbing. Girl number two wouldn't make squat in stage tips, and girl three would be traveling an even harder road. Being a professional meant adjusting not only to whatever the previous girl scribbled on the DJ docket, but also to what kind of music the crowd was listening to that night. It meant keeping a notepad of which girls liked to dance to what music, what kind of songs you could dance to in any situation. Every time new meat started working the Slinky Fox, Cheri made sure to check out her routine and moves. Did this girl have anything Cheri did not? Do anything Cheri would not? Any day the Garden of Venus might call. The Garden catered to turbaned sheiks, and men in expensive ties and esteemed multinational figures. Men were not marks at the Garden, they were *clients,* and if a client phoned and reserved his favorite stripper in advance, you cleared five hundred an hour on those. The Garden had a Jacuzzi room and a waterslide, and their champagne dances were with real nonalcoholic champagne instead of apple juice like the Slinky Fox used. Cheri'd even heard that *People* magazine's sexiest man alive had recently dropped a couple of thou chasing dancers down the Garden's waterslide, and she frequently imagined the power in knowing that *People* magazine's sexiest man alive was staring, wanting nothing more than to be inside of her. Yeah, the Garden of Venus was high class, a girl had to be *asked* to audition there. And so the more distinct your personality and dance skills were, the more you could work a room and hook a customer, the better your chances of being asked to work at the Garden—which is why it was a problem when all your good shit was being absorbed. So what you ended up doing, you spent so much time checking out the other girls that some of the dykes tried to recruit you. There were misunderstandings. Uncomfortable situations. Sometimes after a shift the bouncers ended up having to walk Cheri to her Jeep as protection from men and women alike.

And the only way out was to distinguish herself.

She'd tried wigs next. A Catholic schoolgirl wig. A braided horsehair thing that went down to her ass. This sleek black silent-movie-star deal that a drag queen had received one hell of a beating over. Cheri had collagen injected into her lips every two weeks. She did five sessions a month under the lights of a rotating tanning bed. Cheri had her own nutritionist, personal trainer, and personal waxer. And back at the start of the new year, Cheri Blossom had spent five grand on new tits. Not a thing had been wrong with her God-given goodies, mind you. In actuality Cheri's breasts had been lovely. Curved little pears. They'd hung freely and pointed a bit to the sides and had lain supple beneath her T-shirts in a manner that attracted glances both discreet and unabashed. But then her boyfriend had provided her with that pamphlet. He'd explained the procedure and gone over all her questions twice. He'd told her that her worries were stupid, she was being a bitch. Her boyfriend had bugged and pestered. And on a clear February afternoon when they'd been doing shrooms for like six hours, Cheri had giggled, *What the fuck.* She'd let him drive. Just outside of the city limits. An office complex: from the outside it looked like the kind of place you'd get insurance for your car. (After-ward she realized her boyfriend must have had an arrangement, maybe had even gotten a piece of the action, to set it up so quickly.) In the time it takes to complete a load of laundry, this mulatto doctor had verified the money order. In the converted back room of his office, he'd given Cheri a sleeping gas that, when combined with the shrooms, provided Cheri with about five seconds of bliss and then somewhere around three hours of blackness. This doctor had made incisions into the hearts of Cheri's nip-ples. Stuck this weird vacuum tubing thing into precious treasures that maybe had not been the biggest in the world but that nobody had ever complained about. He'd done a bunch of other shit that Cheri did not care to know the details of, but that probably got her boyfriend off, de-mented bastard, him and his piercings and tatts and his latest ridiculous thing, wanting to shove a triple-A battery through his nose. That overcast afternoon, when Cheri Blossom had been dragged out of that storefront, she had been transformed. From a fresh-faced nymphet favored by old men and shy youths, she'd been turned into some sort of Amazon, the wet dream of all red-blooded teenagers and midlife-crisis businessmen. Two melons beneath her knit sweater. Cleavage you could land planes on. (Sil-icon Valley she later called it.) It had taken her two days to learn how to walk with the new weight. Another month to fully adjust to dancing with wet sandbags inside of her. For a week after *that,* her lower back still hurt something fierce. Even tonight, before taking to the catwalk, Cheri pow-dered her underarm scars with talcum (also giving a quick poof to her bull's-eye of pubic hair, just for luck). But meanwhile, just like her boyfriend had promised, not only had her investment been returned, but it had doubled. New stereo equipment. High-definition plasma flat screen. A significant increase in the quantity and grade of the new shit her boyfriend's connection kept bringing around. Again and again Cheri re-minded herself of this. She attempted to embrace the creature comforts.

But then it would be four in the morning and the Slinky Fox would have changed shifts. Some of the girls, a few bouncers, and the DJs would have convoyed downtown and parked their exhausted rears in the coffee shop of the Horseshoe. They'd be in their usual booth in the corner, scarfing down ninety-nine-cent night-owl specials, and Cheri would pick at the yolk of her over-easies, and she'd get all melancholy. See, she could handle that her breasts no longer bounced. Yes, her implants were so big that the skin over them was stretched and thin, they *were* too big for her body, these unnatural balloons, the left suspended a visible smidge higher than the right. Her breasts no longer gave her pleasure, *hasta la vista* to the electric tingles of joy she used to feel when her boyfriend bit down on her breast. *Sayonara* to the rush when he dug his teeth into her areolas and buried himself fully inside her and ejaculated and totally pushed her over the edge. But the thing that basically devastated her at four in the morning in a casino coffee shop was her nipples.

Because her nipples had been beautiful. Truly they had.

Thin. Long. The same chestnut shade as her natural hair. A thousand little goose-pimply protuberances appearing on her areolas when she got aroused. Her nipples used to turn thick and full, becoming a shade richer around the fifth of every month, staying that way through the tenth. They used to wrinkle in hot weather. Her nipples used to have *personality.* And now this personality had been infiltrated. Dissected. It had been taken apart and put back together, stretched and spread and all but turned to plastic. Pink antiseptic saucers with ugly little nubs. They hardly moved or got excited or did any damn thing. As much as Cheri Blossom had hate inside her loving and Christian heart, she hated her new nipples. So when her fella came up with yet another winner, it hadn't meant anything. Again, she'd said, *what the fuck.* Filled out another money order at the Western Union.

Which is why, with Patti Smith wailing and "Free Money" entering its final crescendo, as the half circle of wolves around her pinned back their ears and hooted and hollered and whooped, while her mark drooled and took deep breaths and blew the crotch of the panties out past his nose like a little pink sail—it is why Cheri could take the match that she'd had in her hand *this whole song long.*

And is why she could strike that match on the bald crown of the mark's head. Why she could move the flame to her nipples, onto her surgically hollowed-out nipple cases.

With a debutante's grace Cheri lit on fire the dyed stubs of red wax and tiny red wicks that she had packed into her surgically hollowed-out nipple casings.

Shadowy bar folk clapped and whistled and high-fived and went *Holy shit*. They threw crumpled dollar bills and fives and someone accidentally let go of a ten. They realized that they were watching magic, they were extras getting to see a stellar performance, a recital by not just any stripper, but A STAR.

And now Cheri Blossom wiggled her flaming prosthetic sandbags in the guy's face. She smothered his head with plastic and silicon and good old-fashioned fire. And lucky bastard that her client was, he got to blow out Cheri's nipples—which is what most clients did.

Or he got to extinguish them with his fingers—which some toughs did to try and impress her.

If he so chose, he could even put his lips around them and suck out the flame, like her boyfriend totally got into.

But this guy, he seemed embarrassed. Ashamed. He really didn't know what to do. And he had to get to blowing. These candles weren't even candles, just shaved candle parts that had been lumped together and topped with string. Little bitty things.

Only this guy was like, like—like the flaming nipples had interrupted him, caught him totally off guard.

Like something else was on his mind.

The extras were all around, they were yelling and laughing and howling and offering to take his place. And the flame was getting closer, flickering, burning down through the wick. Cheri was starting to wonder what would happen if the flames hit onto her plastic. Just what kind of fucked-up chemicals got involved then? She wasn't beginning to worry, not really, but something had to happen, quick. She was about to extinguish the things herself, when the prematurely balding guy returned from wherever his mind was vacationing, and the situation finally registered with him.

He took a weak breath.

Music thumped. Bass bumped. Extras laughed and high-fived and hooted.

While the wisps of smoke danced upward, behind the guy's glasses, his eyes were large and brown and apologetic. They were relieved.

He purposefully avoided looking up at her, instead staring at Cheri's smoking tits for two, three seconds. His Adam's apple bobbed. He let out another breath and for a moment seemed to concentrate. And here the level of his stare rose. Reflected neon and white ribbons of electric light danced along the lenses of his spectacles, and suddenly his face revealed itself as stony, possessed, as if he had just reached a decision.

3.3

The bill feeder unceremoniously rejected Kenny's dollar for what felt like the hundredth time. His shoulders hunched and tensed, and he curled over the front of the machine like a question mark, grabbing the bill with a defeated swipe, returning to the task of rubbing the dollar over the gleaming steel console, trying to iron out its creases. From the next machine, Newell landed an elbow into his abdomen. "This is sweet. How sweet is this?"

The boy pumped five nickels into a slot. His index finger jabbed on a square yellow button in the middle of the console. He quickly slapped a green button with his palm.

"Ooowh. Almost got me a fully loaded convertible!"

Another thrown elbow. "See. I look twenty-one. I'm always telling my dad."

A nudge now. "Damn. Two cherries that time.

"You played Tetron IV? I just rented it from Blockbuster. Those graphics are *way* better."

Rubbing his ribs, Kenny stared back. Although hair obstructed his view, and caused him to blink rapidly, he took in Newell's energy and joy, felt its contagious spread. He laughed, an awkward, donkeylike snort, and tried the dollar in front of him once more, but again the father of our country reappeared, scrolling out from the bill feeder like a mocking green tongue. "It's broke," Kenny said. "Mine's broken."

"Mine works great. See. Nothing to it."

Kenny shook his head. With hasty jerks, he began searching through his pants for another dollar, and had a fleeting thought of the Nintendo system his aunt had bought him two Christmases ago, the controlling stylus veering crazily to the right side of the screen. "So," he said. "Bing was really cool to me."

Newell continued staring into the screen, dropping coins.

"He's actually really nice."

"I still say you should have come for Byrne and them." He punched Kenny's shoulder, then made a second motion. When Kenny flinched, Newell nailed him twice more. Kenny rubbed his shoulder, although Newell's words hurt a lot more, and Kenny could not just rub away their truth. He stared for a moment at the small moth holes along his sleeve, at the curl of thinned cotton at that sleeve's end. Then he became distracted, something frilly skimming along the small of his back. And it wasn't just frilly, either—a fair amount of weight pressing at him.

A dumpy woman. Making her way between the stools and players, she filled the black leotard as if it were a sausage casing. Her arm was raised straight above her head, and she was balancing a small tray filled with neon drinks. She brushed past Kenny and looked back over her shoulder, ready to apologize. As Kenny watched her eyes narrow, a penny of doubt lodged in his chest. She kept moving, though, and squeezed past a large-boned housewife in imitation designer evening wear, navigating the narrow space of the row, eventually delivering a bottle of amber beer to a dumpy-looking grandfather, whose smile of thanks revealed a missing set of uppers.

"This is the life, huh?" Newell's elbow dug once more at Kenny's ribs. "Free and easy."

The boy pumped away, oblivious, dropping more coins into the slot machine like he couldn't get rid of his money fast enough. Kenny eyed the waitress, watching her sloppy rear shift from left to right as she continued her route. When she turned a corner, he kept staring down the row, checking to see if she—or anyone else—might be coming back. Newell said something that Kenny did not pay attention to. Still he grunted an affirmative response, and momentarily absorbed the sight of the large-boned housewife—she was gazing at the terminal in front of her with dead eyes, clutching a rosary in her large-knuckled fist, blowing a large pink bubble and then sucking it back in. Each time she pulled at the slot, she performed this little ritual, Kenny saw. Along the row, he saw baggy retirees chain-smoking and playing two machines apiece, rotely jabbing a left-right sequence of buttons on one machine, then repeating the sequence on the other. Their faces were uniformly drained from extended bouts of concentrated anticipation, yet still focused on the screens in front of them. Kenny watched a husband and wife playing their machines side by side. He watched friends wasting the night hanging out and drinking and playing. Groups of people that were ostensibly together, yet were *separate together.*

He became faintly aware of a series of electronic tones next to him, Newell removing his titanium wafer from its holster, Newell checking the number of the call, pressing a button.

The ringing ended. "That should take care of them," the boy said. He took up the drawl of a popular rapper: "Let's get this party started right."

"Once you start to play a lot," Kenny answered, "you don't really think about each spin." He recognized an urgency in his voice, a fervor whose intensity almost took him aback. Thinking over what he wanted to say now, he slowed down, took care to be precise, and repeated if not the exact words, the ideas he'd heard from his aunt through the years. "Here's the thing. The last spin was just like this one. This one is like the next. You lose and then you win and most of the times if you win it's just three coins. Even if it's a bunch more, they're only nickels."

Newell took in the wisdom. An exclamation point snorted through his nose.

"Don't you need the machine to take your money first?"

The boy grinned at his own cleverness, and now smacked the yellow button, an ecstatic punctuation. Computerized clicks sounded. Graphics simulated the acceleration of slots and then their slowing. The screen in front of Newell started blinking and flashing.

"YEAAAAH-DAAAWG." Newell pogoed on his stool. The musical notes of celebration continued. "THAT'S WHAT I'M TALKING ABOUT."

Francesca was long gone and most of the girl's friends had bailed, and what remained were friends of friends mostly, a few half friends, and a couple of kids the girl did not know, older kids, juniors and seniors, all of them scattered around the truck, resting on stolen milk crates, broken-down ice cream coolers, and a few old bar stools with torn cushions and leaky stuffing. Green Wool James was at this makeshift table. This douche bag named Piggy was next to him, nodding and using Wite-Out to paint the fingernails of her other neighbor, some zit-faced idiot with a white picket fence for a Mohawk—he kept dragging on a cigarette, then tapping its ash into a smoked green bottle. Talk about the war had died down, and attentions had turned to Sellout, this drinking game, everyone going around their little makeshift table, naming great rock songs that had been turned into commercials. The Beatles and "Revolution" for Nike got things started, although that was more a ghost story than fact, it had happened so long ago that most of the people in the truck hadn't been alive back then, nobody had even seen the actual commercial. But everyone knew about it, just like they knew "Satisfaction" by the Rolling Stones for Microsoft. And the Who got tagged for that "best I ever had" song, which had been used by Lexus automobiles. Then what all agreed was a damn fucking shame: Princess Cruises' purchase of Iggy Pop's "Lust for Life." Which was quickly topped by Black Sabbath's "Crazy Train" and its accompanying television spot for Nissan, which got tabbed as the ultimate crime against rock, until someone trotted out Zeppelin's barrage of Cadillac commercials, and Queen's "We Are the Champions" for an erectile dysfunction pill, and, oh yeah, the Ramones' atrocity (corn chips or cell phones or whatever it was). Naturalamente, Dylan came next, "The Times They Are A-Changin," the investment house of Bendem, Over, and Plunge.

From the back of the truck, the girl with the shaved head kept trying to make eye contact with Green Wool James, but he kept looking away, into his paperback, whatever. Someone said "Blowin' in the Wind" just got sold to a chili company, and laughter was everywhere, the jokes started flying. "All Along the Watchtower" for high-range sniper rifles. That "aches just like a woman" one for maxi pads. People were laughing and pounding their fists together and having a good time, and out of nowhere, Green Wool James wondered if there was a different standard for someone like Bob Dylan and like a one-hit wonder. Dylan was this icon and was recognized for a kind of integrity and already had more zillions than he'd ever know what to do with, so yeah, what's he doing, but then again, what about the band that struck it big with one song but hadn't seen any money from their music for ten years and now all of them had shitty real-life jobs. Green Wool James asked whether preserving the integrity of the best song you'd ever recorded was worth giving up whatever financial benefits and renewed exposure selling your song to a commercial might provide. He pointed out that half of the people making fun of sellouts were wearing Old Navy gear, and he pointed out that clothing companies like Independent and Vans weren't any better, they just made their fortunes by marketing directly to punks and skaters. James said he didn't see anything wrong with this. He liked it when a commercial used a song he recognized. It was a treat, just like when a television show he enjoyed watching—or a video game he enjoyed playing—used a song he liked. It put the song back into his head, which was a good thing, especially if he hadn't heard the song in a while. Green Wool James said he'd barely even heard of Zeppelin until he'd seen the Cadillac commercial, but after he'd seen the commercial, he'd downloaded their greatest hits, which he enjoyed a lot. James wondered when exactly it had become a law that where your song got played and how it got used had any bearing on whether you had integrity or what kind of person you were. He said he thought it was a lot more complicated than this, and quickly brought up the techno artist who sold a song to a commercial for a car company, then gave all the money to a group that fought pollution. Was anything wrong with that, James wanted to know. How about if your wife had cancer and the only way you could afford treatments was to sell your song to some burger barn?

I think hierarchical elitism sucks, he said. *Does that mean I shouldn't try to go to a good college?*

The girl was lit, kinda, and sitting a ways from the roundtable, and with the distance and how sound was reflecting off the hull, it was hard for her to follow just who was saying what, what was happening: there was James glancing up from his paperback to commiserate with Piggy about something or other; there was Piggy laughing—*Where the fuck did you get "hierarchical elitism"?* Half an overheard remark caused James to defect from Piggy into an impromptu threesome with the other boys, before a fragment of something else changed the pairings once more. The geometric configurations of dialogue were perpetually shifting and none of their formulations included the girl with the shaved head, which was fine with her, whatever. She was cool just sitting there, chilling out, and she stopped listening to them, gradually occupying herself with the sight of the broad wooden plank that served as their table. It was interesting to the girl that every time someone put down a beer, the plank jiggled. And it was noticeable that every time someone picked one up, the plank jiggled worse. The girl started grooving on the way the dark green bottles kept inching their way toward the far side of the plank, as if by osmosis or something, all starting in one place and creeping down like that. The plank was balanced between a pair of cinder blocks and some old telephone books and the girl with the shaved head wondered if maybe cinder blocks came in different sizes. If probably the cinder blocks and the phone books were at uneven proportions. In the hull's darkness, lit cigarette embers looked like so many fireflies to the girl, and she took a drag on her clove and decided to remember that image for a poem. She told herself that a vindictive and evil witch would not think twice about having all the bottles slide down the side of the table and dousing someone. A vindictive and evil witch just might turn your heart to stone.

Even with the windows broken and the side door open, it was like a sweatbox in the ice cream truck, and rubbing a warm bottle of piss on her neck did nothing to help. She tore a nearby flyer off the back door of a van, planning to use the limp and ancient paper for a fan. Not to be FUCKED with read the flyer, a combination of cutout fonts and scratch-off stencil patterns. **$8. 3 kegs. *10 warmup***

bands. cum *get* WASTED out in the *desert*. Off I-15 where the *pigs* **don't** cruise. In some ways it meant nothing, a paper creased into thirds and torn around the edges, a crude drawing of a skeleton with missiles for tits, some coarse advertisement for some long-ago desert bash. Only the girl with the shaved head had seen Not to Be Fucked With play live, she'd seen them like four times, actually, always at a party out in the desert, off I-15 where pigs never cruised. The girl referred to the band as the Nots and she had minor crushes on each of the band's four members and she *totally* adored their thrasher music, its hard and fast pace, power chords and violent hooks. This one song, it had this refrain; this boss *oi oi oi* thing in its chorus. Three short blurts, *oi oi oi.*

Zitty Mohawk guy lifted his beer in a toasting motion, took a dramatic swig, and sprayed beer all over Piggy, who squealed *asshole.* Glancing down at the flyer, the girl raised her hand and ran a palm over the part of her neck where her spinal cord ended and her skull took over. The follicles felt bristly and odd. Her knees jangled together and she popped her thumbs and squirmed in her seat and felt a faint urge to pee and looked down again at the flyer. Her foot tapped, *oi oi oi.* Her knees waggled, apart, together, *oi oi oi.* She kind of worried about giving the room a free show, and at the same time, it was like, fuck those fuckers, you know? *Oi oi oi.* The girl had played the song on her stereo hundreds of times, maybe thousands. Alone in her room. The girl with the shaved head had rocked out and geeked out and gotten wicked goofy to the Nots; their chorus of *oi*s had saved her soul more times than she could count. The needle of the battered record player inside the ice cream truck may have been scratching against the label of the old zydeco LP, but just then the girl with the shaved head could not have heard those *oi*s any clearer if Not to Be Fucked With had been playing right next to her. Without a doubt, she knew their demo had to be somewhere in the ice cream truck. Somewhere amid that pile of identical-sounding demo tapes and burner-produced compact discs that kids from incestuously connected local bands played late at night for one another in garages and dens and makeshift hangouts like this here ice cream truck. The possibility even existed that right then, someone might play the demo, the possibility existed that the demo *would just happen* to be cued up to the song, right at a part with the *oi oi ois*. The girl with the shaved head wondered how to figure the chances. The formula that explained how light traveled through space popped into her head. She thought of partial statistics from a math paper she'd done, which showed the world famous Las Vegas Strip was undoubtedly visible from the moon. The girl thought about wasted power and that maybe it could be used to save people in Ethiopia and then she thought that nothing said PUNK more than a big white Mohawk. She wondered if maybe a Mohawk and a three-piece suit were just costumes, both of them. She started thinking about the difference between the song with the *ois* and some song a corporation had bought for a commercial: how the song with the *ois* had struck a chord inside of her, expressed her feelings better than she ever could herself, this kind of emotional bond it made, this sort of trust. And when a corporation bought a song to use in a commercial, they were trying to take advantage of that bond, trying to take all your good and secret feelings and transfer them to their lame product.

Nobody was paying the girl a spit of attention and for the first time she was not paying attention to them either, but just sitting, shredding the edge of that flier, being alone with her aloneness. Being alone like her mother.

Wait.

No. Not like that.

See, the girl's mother, she'd come into the girl's bedroom. Two or three times a month. Usually late. Two, three in the A.M. She'd get home from another terrible date. Or maybe after the latest guy had bailed. It would be the tail end of another night at some honky-tonk or when she just could not sleep. The girl's mother would not be able to handle being alone and so she would come into her daughter's bedroom. She would slide in under the covers and wrap her arms around her daughter. Locking her bedroom door when she went to bed seemed cruel to the girl. It seemed wrong. She'd leave the door unlocked and her mother would get into the bed and would form a cocoon around the girl's body. Most of the time the girl pretended to be asleep. If she actually was asleep, then upon her mother's entrance, the girl would wake to a crush of hot breath and whiskey and perfume, and she would hear her mother weeping. She would hear how much her mother hated men. How much her mother hated her own life. The girl would lie there feeling helpless and trapped and also that her mother was kind of pathetic, and although the girl had a tender and unspeakable love for her mother, she felt distant from her mother too. The girl was strong, she was smart, she was never going to end up like her mother, no fucking way.

And this is when Ponyboy ambled to the back.

Ponyboy of the Gibraltar biceps. Ponyboy the beautiful.

He said, *"Scootover,"* and simple as that, there he was, there *they* were, scrunched together on the ice cream truck's spare tire.

He was older, she knew this much. Seventeen. Eighteen. Twenty-two, max. A college dropout finding himself. An escapee from the correction facility in Tonopah. There were all kinds of whispers. Whispers about where he slept at night. About hijacking clothes from unattended Laundromat dryers. About hustling games of speed chess and a hot stripper girlfriend, about printing fake IDs, all kindsa shit, serious shit, the kindsa shit Ponyboy didn't really like talking about, although he never did Thing Uno to dissuade the whispering.

Every time the girl had seen Ponyboy, his hair had been a different color, and on Saturday night it was black as fucking death, defying gravity in these totally amazing Vaseline spikes. His broken nose had healed pretty good, and now a new set of silver rings braided his eyebrows. There were so many barbell studs on his face that they were like pimples, and between the studs and braids, the hard ridges of his jaw and features, and the round wooden cork things that weighed down his earlobes, it was like he was bionic or something.

Oh, and that glaze to his eyes, that beautiful layer of animosity. It all but dared the girl: *Try, break through.*

Purposefully mumbling as if he were some actor from back before color films, he asked, "Wanna lager?"

She had issues with the sexual objectification of women in those beer commercials. Besides, the texture made her mouth-insides feel yucky. But thanks.

"A joint?"

The glowing ember passed across their mutual darkness. The girl told Ponyboy she was going to write a poem about firefly embers. She told him she was just thinking that maybe like the ice cream truck was its own little society. That maybe everyone in here was here because this was the place the fucked-up world wanted them to be.

Ponyboy leaned forward, not so much taking in her words as taking *her* in. "Interesting."

He stared down at his combat boots. "Kinda like being on the streets."

Now straightening, he stared at the girl, his eyes large and tender. "Days are like dog years out there," he said. "You start living with an eye over your shoulder, you know? Like, you kind of get used to not knowing where you are when you wake up, not having nothing to do with time but get through it."

He looked down now while he talked and spread his legs wide and the tip of a knee grazed against the girl's. She blushed and Ponyboy smiled, kind of shyly but also with confidence, and he started to open up, tentatively and vulnerably reciting a monologue the girl vaguely remembered hearing before: how he'd bummed and squatted his way from this Covenant House to that detention center to the friend of some relative's friend's pad. "Vegas through Hollyweird by way of Seattle. Stops along the way in Portland, the Tenderloin, and the Orange Curtain Underground."

He pulled up the bottom of his T, revealing abdomen muscles like a series of steps on a ladder. "That's a tattoo for each city, a piercing for each gig."

From the beer plank, Pretentious Superior Sellout Green Wool James was doing a terrible job of pretending not to watch her, whatever, fucker. The sound of a flooding engine carried from up front. There was cussing. A door slamming. Someone popping the hood.

Ponyboy finished with the significance of the Gothically styled stallions along his rib cage. His words were more honed now, but genuinely so, coming at a raised pitch, an excited pace. "What I really want"—he grinned, relishing the suspense—"is to shove a triple-A battery through my schnozz." He waited for the words to register on the girl. "Way I see it, every limp dick has a tatt nowadays. And even the biggest Urkel is pierced. My boy Alkaline did it and Alks told me that alls you need to do is like get your nose pierced. Then you just have to like take the stud out yourself. And then, right before the cartilage and the hole closes up and shit, right then, you have to just like take the little nub on the battery, you know that nub thing on the plus side? Well, what you have to do is jam that little nub thing into the hole in the cartilage, you got to fucking jam that bitch in there right before the hole closes up and then, right after that, you just kind of like *push,* get the rest of that battery through."

It was in the middle of the part about making sure the battery acid didn't leak in with your mucous membrane that the girl with the shaved head imagined how Ponyboy would look clean. If all the goop and dye was washed from his hair. She imagined him bathed and scrubbed. Scented with environmentally friendly soaps made by wrongfully imprisoned Tibetan monks.

Jasmine and lavender were turning pirouettes through her head when she kissed him, short and awkwardly, a forced pressing of lips, and the instant she realized what she was doing, the girl broke it up and wanted to laugh and wanted to die.

Ponyboy took a long drag of the spliff. Then he kissed her back. Opening his mouth to her, blowing a stream of sweetness into her. Ponyboy and the girl kept kissing and their kiss was soft and wet, and then it was hot and hard, and then it was over and her panties were moist, the smoke leaking out of her lips, drifting upward.

"Damn, you look sexy," Ponyboy said.

And damn, she felt sexy.

And so he kissed her again.

Shoved his tongue down her throat. Invaded her tonsils like he had a schedule to keep.

There was lurching, the van suddenly in motion, the pair sprawling onto each other. The truck made a left turn, began accelerating.

"So," Ponyboy said, once his hands were on the girl's shoulder, and had steadied her. "Why didn't you gimme the digits last time?"

"Oh. My. God."

"Oh—" Now his right hand was a blur, the scar across his wrist revealing itself as cragged and deep. "Right. What happened was, I was gonna call. Really. I meant to. See these guys at Circus Circus, it was like . . . What I mean is . . . Okay, they hired me to do this stag thing with them."

"SAY WHAT?"

"You kept having to dress and undress—"

"Owh. My. God."

"The number musta fallen outta my jeans—"

She listened with some hesitation, and took as much time as she needed, composing herself. "Then you're bi?"

Ponyboy's face turned red. Whether he was blushing or just overloading with anger, he took a moment, sucked deeply on the spliff, then exhaled white streams through his nose.

"They *buy me,* I'm *sexual.*"

3.5

Like a shot Newell was off his stool, the cartoon child who has just realized his pants are on fire, the stagecoach driver with bandits on his tail, whipping the horses, flooring it, pedal to the metal, balls to the wall, he was sprinting, pushing through any opening that might present itself, shoving to create openings. Away from the slot machine island, away from the fuzz. His arms churned and his squat little legs pumped, and his reaction time was not quite as fast as it needed to be, leaving him unable to completely avoid the exposed chest of a middle-aged man in a Hawaiian shirt.

"Scuse me," Newell yelled, and caromed off the man, bouncing with the impact, the momentum carrying him away and in a new direction. Upon reaching the mouth of the video machine bank, he shouted, *"Pardon me,"* successfully swerved around a retired farmer type whose barrel stomach hung out from the bottom of his T-shirt, and then swerved once more, this time as if his hips were on a hinge, a trick that allowed him to avoid, by fractions of an inch, what surely would have been a fatal collision, this time with the farmer's significant other, a brightly attired blue-haired woman, whose mooing face was inside a pocketbook the size of a Winnebago.

"GANGWAY, MAMA," Newell screamed.

But what was this? His legs were entangled, constricted, they weren't working properly, there was a malfunction, something was happening, his oversize jean shorts had slipped too far, gravity had betrayed him, mayday, mayday, he was going down, leading with his face, plummeting amid a group of aged tourists, taking with him a laminated name tag from a nearby breast pocket.

Jackpot nickels flew out of his fun cup and scattered all over the carpet's flourish of patterned card suits. Blood roared through Newell's ears. Before he could decode any messages or recover any nickels, a hand pulled at the back of his collar. Considerable force was yanking, bringing

Newell upright. *Busted,* he thought, and had a momentary flash of jail bars.

He almost did not recognize the face at first, for it was focused in a way that belied its usual uncertainties. Kenny's brow was tight, his eyes calm yet alive. The muscles in his jaw flared out of the sides of his face. Kenny looked at him and did not blink and then was on the move, taking the lead and pulling on Newell's collar, manhandling the boy, dragging him in the opposite direction of the table games, along a barrack of video poker machines, confidently directing their route, as if he'd already surveyed the floor and considered possible exits. Newell checked over his shoulder. He stumbled. Keeping up was a lot harder when you had to hold up your shorts.

"I think he's going for his holster," Newell said.

Kenny's hair bounced lightly on his shoulders with every step; his elbows flailed. He looked in both directions for any more security guards, saw the wall of buxom women in sequined dresses, the oily jugheads with muscles popping out of brightly colored Italian shirts. To avoid a change girl and her pushcart of racked coins, he had to let go of Newell, and now moved a bit farther ahead of the boy, veering toward a wall of partitioned fun-house mirrors.

"We're losing him," Newell said. *"Keep going."*

Bing Beiderbixxe lived in a small house in the valley with two guys he knew from college, both of whom were in the second year of business school. Most weekends, the housemates' girlfriends were around, lounging around in sweats and/or their boyfriends' boxers, halfheartedly tossing their immaculately groomed heads, watching sports with their men and passing Bing's cereal between each other, picking at it, straight from the box. Usually around nightfall, the boyfriends would rummage through the overhead cabinets, pulling out dented pots and pans that Bing's sister had long ago outgrown and passed down. The girlfriends would chop vegetables, start on a pasta sauce. Garlic would bubble on a front burner, maybe some chicken breasts lightly sautéing on the back. For his part, Bing usually stood to the side, ready to help but not exactly jumping in (he was kind of out of his element once you got beyond spreading peanut butter on bread).

Their most recent meal had been like so many others, agreeable and, for the most part, easy, the dining area busy with the small talk of people who casually knew one another, the guys discussing the securities market, a girlfriend voicing polite and good-natured jealousy about how *amazing* the sauce tasted. Bing, however, remained fairly quiet, hunched over his food. An encouraging comment floated in his direction—*been losing weight, huh, buddy?* He looked down. His silverware scraped loudly against his plate.

It was the first weekend of August and the night was enjoyably cool, with just the slightest hint of a breeze. Standing outside, on the front walkway, Bing felt a mild summer wind pass over him and stared down the street for a while, looking at the houses with their trim lawns, the homes with the front lights on, and the homes that were dark and empty. Crickets and cicadas and other bugs were doing their thing and the night sky was the gentle purple of swaddling blankets. Many were the times Bing had sat on the front steps of his house and sketched the driveway.

He used variations of this sketch whenever he needed something to take place on the street where his hero lived. That night, Bing went back inside to his room, sat at his drawing table, and looked at the mess of art books and movie stills and half-finished panel drawings on bristol board. For a time he stared at a black-and-white cityscape photo from the 1920s, which he was trying to adapt into a backdrop. Then he got up and looked for his cordless.

"Bingading! How's that deadline going? You made any progress?"

"Well, I'm gonna be hating life tomorrow—"

"Join the club, baby. I hate life every day."

"And it's not like a meal with the zombies helps any. I swear, ten minutes of their inanity, I'm all but begging for death's sweet release."

"I'm on my way down to Irvine right now for SAT boy. Figure at least a half hour."

"Cool beans."

"For you maybe. You don't have to recross the friggin' county."

"I know it's out of your way. I really appreciate it. Really, man. And like I said, I'll pay for gas."

This was the summer of shimmery cabana shirts. The high-quality ones hung loosely off the shoulders, but were form fitting around the waist, creating a slimming effect that was totally excellent—or so Bing had been told by a salesgirl in a clothing boutique on Santa Monica. Under normal conditions, Bing was allergic to salespeople, but this girl had come up to him while he was picking through a rack, she'd literally grabbed the shirt out of his hands, hunted through the rack, and pulled out a different shirt, swearing it would fit his body type better. He was in the dressing room when she'd brought him three more shirts, all similar in cut and style, but distinct in their own right, totally worth trying on, *just for variety's sake.* For the sheer hell of it, she'd also come by with a pair of what she termed *cracking* jeans—if he was buying the shirts to party in, he might as well try some jeans, see how they looked together, why not make an outfit, right? The salesgirl had been wearing a pink slip as a summer dress and its shoulder strap had been falling onto her arm in a way that had been quite charming, and when she'd left to find Bing jeans in the proper waist size, he'd watched the slip clinging around her backside. Over the store stereo, some sort of nu metal-ish band had been playing, one of those heavy, noisy messes that Bing usually dismissed, but for some reason, this time he was really able to hear and appreciate everything the band was trying to do, and when the girl returned and asked, "How you doing in there?" Bing had answered, *"Just cracking, thanks."* And when he'd exited the dressing room wearing that first outfit, she'd touched him on the arm and had smiled, and Bing had been utterly disarmed, and that day, he'd purchased every single outfit that the salesgirl recommended, putting them on the credit card that he had gotten specifically for car repairs and emergency expenses, but what the hell. The salesgirl had walked him to the register and told him her name and casually impressed upon him the importance of letting the cashier know she'd been the one who had helped him, and once his charge had been approved, she had put her arm around Bing and told him to make sure he kept in touch, and a week later, when he'd gone back into the boutique, the salesgirl had greeted him with a perky smile and a blank gaze, and for a second Bing had been unsure if she really knew who he was, at which point she'd asked how the outfits were doing, and she'd inquired whether he'd come back for more clothes, and, sure, granted, this was part of the sales world these days, you drank more often at the bar with a hot chick behind the counter smiling and flirting in a halter top, there were no virgins in a consumer world, okay. However, as Bing put on one of those hideously shimmering eighty-five-dollar cabana shirts, fished out a relatively unrumpled pair of ninety-five-dollar jeans, and readied himself for a night of getting good and crocked with his buddies, it was all but impossible for him to be reminded of anything other than his little shopping outing. Equally impossible was recalling this memory without feeling a mixture of enthusiasm and embarrassment; enthusiasm because it *was* exciting when a pretty girl was nice to you, and he *did* look smooth in those clothes; embarrassment because nobody ever goes home with that hot chick in the halter top behind the bar, because nobody likes it when they find out they've been manipulated, and it's even worse if you have been willingly manipulated, and, finally, because the reasons you allow yourself to be willingly manipulated are never easy to face. So what Bing did, he got dressed. Slapped some of his housemate's cologne on each cheek, his neck, and his underarms. He scoped out his reflection in the mirror and then rechecked the clock. Where were those fucktards, already?

They still logged in nightly to the Knitting Room, zapped e-mails back and forth with ridiculous frequency, and sometimes met in pairs for lunch or a quick drink; but it was undeniable: forces of nature and time had started pulling at their closed little chat room. 1450SAT, for example, had left an array of fellowships and graduate school offers on the table, turned his back on all subjects that involved stress or competition, and was way down in Orange County, working entry-level tech support for a medical distribution company. DOMINATR69, by contrast, was stuck in the gray town of Covina, a half hour east of Los Angeles; Bing had pulled strings and got DOM freelance work as an inker and background man with his comic book house, but the gigs were sporadic, and the comic house had neither the money nor the interest in DOM for a full-time hire, so DOM lived at home and ran the stock room in his dad's furniture shop and spent a lot of time complaining about his dead-end life. Meanwhile, nobody knew KC_FTT_B's deal, he'd been bumbling around Venice Beach for a while, flopping from one McJob to another. It was hard to keep track of him. Then again, logistically, it was difficult for all four of them to get together that much anymore, what with the Southern California freeway system being what it was. They still tried, doing what they could, meeting up to see big summer action movie blockbusters on opening day, spending designated nights in the furniture store, where they smoked fifty-cent cigars, passed around a five-dollar jug of wine, and played nickel-ante seven-card stud. And on the first Saturday night of each month, they all met up, it was set in stone, even if the back room of the store was unavailable, and they didn't do anything more than drive around and pass round an open container of alcohol and catch up on one another's problems.

The nights weren't necessarily friendly. The polemical, argumentative free-for-all nature of the chat room usually translated into a fair share of face-to-face rants. Each Knitter consistently judged his friends, weighing their respective stories and successes (and lacks thereof) as if the progress of a peer reflected on everyone else's personal well-being. At the same time, exchanges took place that were every bit as thoughtful as they were ridiculous; the Knitters still made one another laugh, still held a mutual, genuine affection for one another; the chat room was a major part of their lives and, even now, remained a refuge for them, though it was obvious that each participant felt conflicted about his involvement, felt constrained, a bit trapped. Sometimes things crossed the line, jibes became uncomfortably personal. Nonetheless, when the Knitters were like fifty and they looked back on their time in college and the years afterward, while it was true, there wouldn't be a whole lot of warm and fuzzy feelings, while a lot of their memories would be gruesome, tinged with regrets and bitterness, it would be stuff like driving around with one another and the endless hours they wasted online, crap that in another light might be seen as boring and pointless, this, each Knitter had to know, is what they'd remember. It was sappy and it wasn't the kind of thing that you could admit without getting ragged on, but this didn't make it any less true. So when that first Saturday of the month rolled around, Bing did not think twice about cutting his meal with his housemates short, found himself counting the hours until Go Time.

One week before Bing left for Vegas, after far too long a wait, the esoteric stylings of a posse of self-described old-school gangsta Negroes did indeed thump from up the road, signaling the arrival of DOMINATR69's Kia. Bing was two steps out of the door when the first wolf whistle hit. A call of *Looking smooth* served as confirmation, his clothing would be the night's prime source for humor.

The car was supposed to be *a compact hatchback,* but that was just the sadistic joke of some ambitious junior marketing exec. DOM's Kia was a tin can, cramped with bodies and an opened bottle of Jäger, with arguments and insults and rat-assing. One unseen Knitter pretended to adjust the collar of Bing's cabana shirt; another poked at the shirt's fabric and made sizzling sounds and then poured some beer on Bing to put out the imaginary fire. "Only thing missing is the cape," someone said, causing much laughter, with 1450, the asthmatic among them, breaking into a coughing fit, leaning over, taking a few deep breaths into a paper bag.

Nightclubs that advertised on the radio had too high a guy-to-girl ratio, so they were out. Franchises like Ruby Tuesday were ridiculous and not worth considering. And ixnay on the ipsterhay arsbay, because (A) the Knitters did not know how to find them and (B) even if they did, there was no way past the velvet ropes. A disagreement spread as to whether velvet ropes were even used at hipster bars, whether they were passé. Prospective destinations were shot down; arguments came and went, and it wasn't long before one of DOM and Bing's most favorite and longest-running gimmicks commenced, and the overblown language of kung fu subtitles took over. *("Foolish mortal, you have walked into my trap, prepare to be destroyed"; "Your powers are no match for me! I welcome the opportunity to squash you in my manly hands.")* This did not last long, either, for the jibes were quickly drowned out by the sound of feedback and guitars, the rest of the crew shouting lyrics—*"All I wanted was a Pepsi, just one Pepsi, AND SHE WOULDN'T GIVE IT TO ME"; "You'll take my life but I'll take yours too; You'll fire your musket but I'll run you through"; "FUCK THA POLICE. Comin' straight from the underground. Young nigga got it bad cuz I'm brown."* By the time the tape flipped to the B side, everyone was winded and a little hoarse. Bing took control, announcing, with appropriate gravity: *My brothers, the time has come to go find ourselves some poon.*

Hermosa Beach. A bar with a packed outdoor patio. The Knitters stayed in the car for a while, killing the bottle in a rising and tense silence. Among them, there were known dry spells. Bad stretches. *Streaks of involuntary celibacy.* It was more than possible that half of the members of the Knitting Room were virgins; and even if they weren't, Bing was relatively sure that the other Knitters were on streaks far longer than his, although this wasn't real consolation. Rather, it was more like winning the gold medal at the Special Olympics: you won the gold medal, fine, but then again, you were still retarded. Eventually the group could not avoid it any longer, and they paid the cover, and stumbled into the dark, packed bar, and the beer commercial that was in progress: cliques of tan and beautiful bodies grouped off with other gorgeous creatures, everyone chatting amiably, as if they all had been best friends with one another for the entirety of their beautiful lifetimes.

1450SAT immediately faded into the shadows. DOMINATR69

scowled and got intense and scary-looking. KC_FTT_B was too blitzed to do more than pinch asses. What the guy with the thunderous voice from the movie trailers would call *a time of crisis.* *"When courage was at a premium and tyranny ruled the countryside,"* he would say, *"one man would step forward: Beiderbixxe the Fearless. Beiderbixxe the Conqueror."*

Tucking in his shirt so that his flab was not so obvious, rolling up his sleeves so as to showcase his burgeoning pythons, he made his way, ever so shakily, toward a gaggle of females, each of whom possessed singularly incomparable beauty.

Intuition told Bing that women like these knew what guys were really after; that by talking to him, they'd only be humoring him, or worse, humoring *themselves.* But wholesale amounts of alcohol flooded intuition. Liquid courage was still courage, wasn't it?

"Hey? Um, excuse me."

He tried to come off as irreverent and artistic, introducing himself and explaining that he saw them all standing here and looking so stunning that he just wanted to draw them all.

He jabbed and parried and tried to look cool while he admitted that, well, that is to say, um, *comic books.* He illustrated comic books for a living.

"But, see, comics are getting much more acceptance than ever. Look at all the movies—"

"Betty and Veronica not so much," he answered, "but Jughead's kind of funny, I guess."

Throw in his daily routine of protein shakes, which gave him major league blackheads and had him farting dust. Add the vitamin supplements that fucked up his breath and turned his piss flaming yellow. What the voice-over guy from the trailers would call *a recipe for hilarity.* What the other Knitters would sensitively label, *shot down in flames.*

At two-thirty in the morning, Bing was back in his room, back at his drawing table, still buzzed but sobering up, willing his hand steady, hoping to salvage something from this wreck of a night and not screw up any of his last two days' work, all this while listening to the pounding headboards and squeaking bedsprings and grunts of monkey love that carried through the drywall from not one but *each* of the two bedrooms that bookended his. It was funny enough to make a mental note about, cruel enough to make Bing believe God was getting laughs at his expense, and he could not take too much before he slipped on his shower thongs and walked across his bedroom and rummaged through his strewn laundry. Upon finding his fifteen-pound barbells, he carried the weights into the bathroom and locked the door behind him; he sat on the toilet and busted out curls in sets, lifting and grunting until his arms burned and shook. Then Bing stayed on the can and took heavy breaths and checked out his pectorals in the mirror, kind of zoning out, just staring at the windowsill, this dead flower stem propped up in an Evian bottle.

A curvaceous, sleepy-eyed Latin woman gathered her panties from the stage and walked its perimeter. Bending quickly to pick up the few scattered bills, she waved and smiled to those who had opened their hearts and wallets. The disc jockey repeated her name, then announced which dancer needed to report to the stage. Bing watched her and continued nursing his soda, the first two of which came as part of the twenty-five-dollar cover charge. He'd moved away from the catwalk and was standing in the darkness of the main area, where black light turned T-shirts fluorescent, and disco balls cast snowflakes of light in all directions. One or two buxom women in dark leotards and fishnet stockings weaved between bystanders, delivering drinks and taking orders. Far more noticeable were the various panty sets, the teddies and dominatrix outfits and naughty teacher clothing. The black lighting electrified the lingerie, creating startlingly bright colors, you couldn't help but look at them. At the girls who filled them.

Dancers who weren't onstage worked the crowd, slinging their hips, making their smiling rounds, seeking out specific guys who'd come up during their set and given them money, as well as anyone else who purchased lap dances with any sort of regularity, and anyone who spent a lot of time talking with the other girls. Standard protocol was to ignore all lumps who nursed their cover charge drinks and stared and never gave up a friggin' buck. (Sure, you never knew who had money, who wanted to party, and who was biding his time until the right one came along; but usually, you had a pretty good idea.)

Truth be told, Bing didn't mind being passed over. The dancers *should* have been ignoring him. He wasn't a big spender, wasn't recognizable as a strip club regular. Sometimes in the dead of night, it was true, he got antsy and drove out by LAX and blew twenty bucks, slowly draining his two-drink minimum while getting up the courage to sit at the bar and maybe inch a few singles up a thigh. It also was true that, whenever Bing hit the road for a store appearance or got stuck overnight in some town, part of his routine usually involved a strip club. Small-time holes, mostly; half-empty venues where most of the customers had no intention of paying for anything more than the cover, and the only way the strippers could get through a shift without falling asleep was to stare at their own writhing reflections in the mirrored walls. When you got down to it, most of the tittie bars Bing had been in were depressing enough to make the facts of his streak of celibacy, living arrangements, and basic life history seem like Times Square on New Year's Frickin' Eve. Yeah, Bing had seen his share of tricks and special promotions. He'd watched Jell-O wrestling and hot-oil wrestling. He'd seen naked girls, kneeling inside half-filled plastic kiddy pools, doubled over, holding their ribs, looking helplessly at the disc jockey. Bing had watched more than his share of these sad spectacles and he had wanted to step in and he'd had no idea how to begin, and so he had sat, a bystander, falling in love, in his own minor fashion, with each and every tragic young woman.

Outside a near booth, a girl with straight, sandy hair and small, pointed breasts was giving a table dance to a frat type, who wore a shirt exactly like the one Bing had on. Bing watched the guy run a dollar bill up the side of the dancer's leg, saw her hold out the waistband string of her thong. The guy's hand stayed on the dancer's inner thigh, right where the waist string connected to her crotch. Unfazed, she took a step out of his reach and began a new series of rotations, such that her message— *that's not allowed*—was clearly communicated. The minor drama reminded Bing of war stories he'd heard at comic conventions—tales of different illustrators, guys who spent a lot more time in strip clubs than

Bing did, who, on occasion, offered strippers two hundred dollars to draw them; stories about strippers who took the money and told the artist to come back at the end of the shift and said *follow me,* then waited until a yellow light turned red and gunned it, leaving the poor dumb bastard stranded at the light. Bing started thinking about the flip side, too; stories involving amiable young ladies who'd followed different comic book artists to their motels and who'd sat still for the artist and bullshitted and been really cool, and then afterward, in every case, when the artist had asked if the stripper wanted to get something to eat or, you know, do something, each stripper had answered with a smile and some variation of the line, *aren't you cute,* each comic book artist reporting amusement in his stripper's voice, like there was something he wasn't getting, like he'd blown some chance without knowing he'd had a chance. The thought of paying for nookie was truly depressing to Bing Beiderbixxe. It was like admitting you had no chance whatsoever of getting some on your merits. Basically you were saying, *Yes, I am retarded but so what because I have my gold medal.* Nevertheless, the stories intrigued him. Members of his own kind had successfully broken the wall, dealt with these women in real-life situations, outside their places of employment.

Thoughts were zooming without completion, but a few decent connections were being made, and these connections distracted Bing enough that he was unprepared for the presence, now invading his personal space: an overstuffed, electric-white schoolgirl's blouse, mammaries leaping toward him, all but bursting through the fabric.

Attached to the breasts, a shapely body was stuffed into a Catholic school skirt that was so tiny, its fabric barely qualified as an afterthought. It took Bing a while before he got to her face. She did not appear to mind. Her smile was toothy, beaming in his direction, the black light making her teeth glow oddly.

Now her lips, luscious and billowy and a gloss of ruby red, formed words that were drowned out by the yelps and whistles of an excruciating pop hit.

Bing shrugged. She leaned toward him, the naughtiest and most mischievous Catholic girl there ever had been. If it was possible to shout intimately into someone's ear, she did this: *Thanks for being such a good sport about my panties.*

"Oh."

He looked down, became distracted by her breasts. "My pleasure. Heh. Put your panties on my face anytime."

A giggle. "I'm Cheri."

"Nice to meet you, Cheri. Bing."

"Bling?"

"No *L.*"

Ponytails bounced as she nodded, her smile impossibly larger and more devastating.

"That was *astounding,*" he said. "That, the way you . . ." He almost pointed to her chest, but caught himself. *"Amazing."*

"Yeah." She giggled. "I guess I am." Her hand pressed onto his shoulder, at once suggestive and soothing. "Are you just here for the weekend?"

"The night."

Between sips of his soda, leaning forward, trying to hear and be heard through the music, Bing followed her lead, answering each question, willingly proceeding into a conversation that was polite, courteous, empty, and an awful lot like talks he'd had while watching television with his housemates' girlfriends. Only where those conversations usually ended with awkward silence, presently, Bing was more than eager to participate. —*Not one of the hotels,* he answered. —*Actually it's a pretty nice motel. At the bottom of the strip. Toward the airport? —Kinda both, really, business and pleasure. —They had me come in to sign these books I draw. — Yeah, it is pretty cool, I guess . —Tonight? Awm. So far I blew forty bucks to see a pair of fags make a white tiger disappear. . . .*

When she laughed, his heart did a little jig. Emboldened, he kept talking, *About four hands of blackjack. They wiped the floor with me, I guess. But it's all good, you know. It's only money, right?*

"Just what I like to hear." Cheri giggled and leaned in closer, more affectionate now, taking his hand, squeezing with a presumptive knowingness. Did he want a refill on his drink? Did he feel like buying a lady a drink? Was he in the mood for a table dance? How about heading some-place more private?

Through his blasting goggles Bing stared into her azure eyes—or were they jade?

"Crap," she said. "Who knows what color they are tonight. I lose track. Hell, sometimes I mix up my contacts, work all night with one green eye and one blue."

"Heh."

"I'm an idiot, I know."

"Somewhere without so much music sounds nice," he said. "A room without all this commotion."

Her hips swished in a way that was worth any uncertainty Bing felt about how much money was in his wallet, and she led him by the hand across the main floor, the crowd parting for her as if she were royalty, guys gawking and staring from all over. Cheri paid them no mind, but kept her head high, the smile chiseled across her face. A nod to the steroid freak in front of the black curtain. Promptly he pulled the curtain aside.

Tasteful faux torches supplied what lighting the hallway had. Be-tween the torch lights, curtained cubicles were discreetly hidden. Small red lights flashed above the first few cubicles, and when Cheri found a green light, she opened the corresponding curtain.

"Thirty bucks a dance," she said, ushering him inside. "Half an hour for a hundred." A wink. "Or we can really get wicked and head back into the VIP room."

"Why don't we start with one. See where that goes."

The closet's walls and floors were covered in a plush black surface sim-ilar to carpet. Bing got comfortable on a padded bench against the wall. Cheri took the drink from his hand and set it down on the surface of a round table he hadn't seen.

She smiled at him and he smiled back. She played with the end of a ponytail and crossed one leg in front of the other, giving what had to be the fourth throaty giggle since she'd introduced herself. Bing gave her the benefit of the doubt. A natural tic, he decided. A means of filling silence.

When the song ended, Cheri promptly moved toward Bing, placed one hand on each of his knees, and gently eased them apart, widening his legs so they were like the foul lines of a baseball diamond. She then stepped up, between his legs and into his lap. The outside of her knees brushed against the inside of his thighs; her bloused breasts popped into his face. As she lined her pelvis up with the top of his crotch, Bing smelled the jasmine and honey oils on her skin, the sweet apple perfume on her neck. Languid, electronic beats began, filling the room, and Cheri began grinding, leisurely changing pace and direction in time to the beat, her motions fluid, wavelike. She undid the first and second buttons on her blouse, and let the fabric fall open, easily sliding off the garment, teasing him with it. Next she undid her bra, let it fall free, and was on top of Bing, straddling him, sitting on him, pressing down onto his erection, leaning forward, pushing those huge melons into his face, their heft delicious, warm on him, her nipples still smoldering, still redolent of the cinder burn.

The song hit its chanted reggae-inspired chorus and she put her hands above each side of his head, pressed the wall for leverage, and bounced on him, Bing feeling her pushing weight, her ass muscles flinching and tightening on him. The collagen of her smile betrayed a momentary pain. Just as quickly her face was blank.

She kept riding, bouncing, bringing soft groans from him. And then she withdrew, taking a step back, into the space of his opened legs. Bing watched, transfixed as she swayed back and forth, slowly wiggling her hips, and drawing out the removal of a thin, spangled string of panty.

Despite all her moves, Cheri's pubic area remained a fairly sturdy and centered sight. This allowed Bing to focus his attention.

Still, it took a moment for the sight to register.

Her mons pubis.

The damndest thing.

It wasn't pale, but a white that went beyond the limits of pale, that had nothing to do with staying out of the sun. The entirety of her body was luxurious and bronze, except for this whiteness, and this was a stunning contrast. Against this dark perfect body, the whiteness formed a heart—what looked like a heart—only there was even more to it. Because inside her white heart of skin, the stripper's pubic hair was shaped. Sculpted. *Arranged. Littler* hearts. A bull's-eye of three brightly colored hearts—green, yellow, and a small red heart at the center—the colors glowing wildly in the black light.

Whenever the stripper stayed centered long enough for Bing to really lock in, it appeared to him that each layer of hair had been cut to a different level of height. He was able to see the slight, grainy patterns of each level, as well as the thin white base of skin that separated one level of heart bull's-eye from the next. It was stunning. The white ink appeared embedded to him, sunken inside the stripper's well-tanned body. Simultaneously, the different levels of her colored hearts of pubic hair made it look as if the heart bull's-eye was jumping out from her. The harder Bing looked the more it seemed the whole design of hearts was both shrinking into and sprouting from her body.

"*Three dimensional,*" he said.

She swayed in place, expressionless.

"I mean, I thought that's what it was when I saw it onstage, but then with, with the fire . . ."

She stared blankly.

"It really looks . . . ," Bing said. "*Just unbelievable.*"

Her hands ran seductively over the skin atop his head, her pelvis rotated in a tight, circular motion.

"Ink? I can tell it's not a tan."

A giggle, a smile, half-amused, but plastic. "Some girls do the suntan trick," she admitted. "Before they go to the tanning bed, you cut out a pattern on paper, lotion it up, and press it to the area you want to cover."

"You *tattooed* your Venus mound?"

"Yeah, well, this way I can decorate."

"Decorate?"

"You know, be creative."

"So, to be *creative,* you shaved your pubes in the pattern of a bunch of bull's-eyes?"

She stepped backward. Her hands mechanically ran over her breasts, down toward her hips.

"You won't believe this," Bing said, "but a few hours ago, I got caught up in this conversation, this, I don't know . . ."

"Mmm?"

"You know how sometimes you hear an idea and even when you are talking about it, it doesn't seem real. Like it takes on its own life outside the event, you know, a mathematical problem to work through."

Cheri cleared her throat, glanced toward the door.

"But then to see you . . . I mean, to find you and the fire thing and your bull's-eye. Of all nights."

She laughed a bit, looked toward the door a second time, longer this time, swaying in place a little, but not really dancing anymore.

The song was heading into its bridge, which meant he didn't have much time left, he knew. He was so close, ready to ask why she'd done it. Exactly what went into the planning and construction of such an activity? But her unease was obvious.

In the back of his head, Bing had been thinking that she might agree to blow him, and common sense said an intimidated and scared stripper wasn't blowing squat. Bing had already dropped a hundred and fifty dollars tonight, and to be completely honest, he couldn't afford to pay for a hummer.

Then again, could he afford *not* to pay for one? And was he really about to turn his back on a chance to snap the streak, because of some tattoo?

Even more than a half-assed fifty-dollar blow job, more than the end of his streak of involuntary celibacy, what Bing Beiderbixxe really wanted in this moment were the particulars that went into keeping each bull's-eye ring trimmed at a different length. The hours this stripper devoted to the care and maintenance of her pubic hair. He wanted to hear that this woman habitually perfumed and combed, trimmed and talcumed her pubes. That she got *off* on decorating her pubic hair, and sometimes purposefully messed up, and started the lacquering process over. Indeed, though its details may have stung and further humbled Bing Beiderbixxe, he would have loved to hear Cheri Blossom tell the story of her boyfriend—Ponyboy was his name—the story of Ponyboy lathering her pubic area for the first time, then trimming it with the straight-edge razor he sometimes kept in his right boot. Bing would have enjoyed hearing how uncertain Cheri had been about that particular endeavor, but that one of the things Ponyboy was really good at was keeping his hand steady while holding that razor. The story of the sex Ponyboy and the stripper had that night undoubtedly would have gnawed at Bing and furthered his sense of personal inadequacy with regards to matters of the flesh, but he would have listened anyway, damn straight he would have. What Bing Beiderbixxe wanted right now was the sound of this stripper's voice, this woman's voice, with her guard lowered. He wanted to hear Cheri confess that she spent long stretches in front of a full-length mirror admiring the results of her and Ponyboy's diligence, and that sensitive nipples would have added greatly to the lacquering process. He wanted her to reveal. To be revealed.

His dick was a lead pipe.

He all but demanded: *What happened here?*

3.7

Every day assholes came in and leered at her body, *that's* what mother-fucking happened. Every day these would-be hotshots and millionaires-in-waiting and bald fat fucks in their cheap-ass disco shirts came in. They asked their little questions, tried to break the ice, make conversation, get her to open up. They tried to take her away from all this, to get her into a back alley, to bend her over. Twenty-dollar bills or not, this dork had followed her clam around the room the way a trained show dog follows a treat. It was one fucked proposition. She shakes her ass and makes eye contact and giggles and these mooks decide she secretly likes them, thinks they are cool, maybe she'd fall in love with them, let them rescue her from all this, if she only got to know them. These mooks literally throw money at her for table dances and lap dances and champagne dances and when it's over she puts a hand on their thighs and gives a thank-you squeeze and moves on to the next one. And like so many before and so many that would come after, this loser was trying to be nice. He was trying to be decent. Yet his question was not phrased as a question, but as if she owed him something, as if she were his property. And Cheri Blossom burned to answer with the truth: *I can buy and sell your family,* she wished she could say. *Fuck you. Fuck your pity. Do not kid yourself about who is using whom.* I was molested as an infant. I was born into poverty and know nothing better. I am a rebellious socialite sewing my wild oats. A bored middle-class girl looking for kicks. I am that misunderstood whore looking for love that you are always hearing about. All my feelings of personal worth have been sublimated into my sexual identity. All my creative instincts have been channeled into onstage performances. I am putting myself through school. I am a baaaaad puddycat. A craven abuser of pharmaceutical substances. A habitual consumer of conspicuous products. I have been betrayed by everything I have ever placed trust in. Have betrayed everyone who ever cared. I am destined for greatness. Fated to self-destruct. I do this for kicks. For money. To meet sensitive hunks like you. Why do you ask? What's it to you? You cannot have me. You cannot learn my secrets. THERE IS NO MYSTERY. THERE ARE NO SECRETS. Life throws a curveball and you swing. Sometimes you get a hit and then sometimes you miss. I swing for the fences. You take hellacious cuts, you miss sometimes. You end up with collagen injected in your lips and a bull's-eye over your privates. You end up with silicon implanted in your breasts and fake nipples that have been purposefully hollowed out, and during the third dance of each set, you set candle nubs in the hollow points so alone and horny and generally unappealing winners such as Guess Who can pay a few bucks and blow out your tits. I ended up here like you did. *EXACTLY THE SAME WAY YOU DID, BUDDY.*

Her giggle must not have done the trick this time. The balding man's face remained blank. He waited, and waited. Closing his eyes for a moment, he seemed upset with himself, and his head dropped a bit, as if in defeat. But then he opened his eyes. He looked up, back at Cheri. Mumbling to himself, he began digging through his pockets, and pulled out crumpled bills, discovering a twenty, a ten, another twenty, a five, and now a few singles, which he started counting.

INT. CLASSROOM—DAY

Dusty light pours from windows onto rows of desks, which are filled with gloomy Catholic SCHOOLGIRLS. A wimpled NUN is at the front of the room. Chalk squeaking, she writes:

"The Lord gave his only son that"

                    CHERI (V.O.)
                 (from back of room)
         I don't get it.

Giggles. Gasps. SCHOOLGIRLS look at one another knowingly.

                         NUN
        Daughter Blossom?

Cheri, a teenager, arm raised, is in the back row. One hot little
schoolgirl.

                         CHERI
                       (naughty)
              It doesn't make sense.

The other schoolgirls titter. The nun cracks her pointer on the
chalkboard, doing everything she can to remain calm.

                         NUN
        Christ died, my child, so that we might have
        cause to reflect upon that which we caused.

                         CHERI
        Right. I got that part.

                         NUN
        Then what, child, is confusing you?

                         CHERI
        Okay, if he died because we have desires, if
        he died for our wants and actions, isn't it
        kind of our duty to make sure his death is,
        you know, <u>worth it?</u>

Other schoolgirls gasp and ooh. The nun cracks her pointer on the
chalkboard.

                   CHERI (CONT'D)
        I mean, the way I see it, if Christ died for
        our sins, doesn't that make sin our duty?
        Don't we have an <u>obligation</u> to sin?

Automatic doors opened with a swoosh, and Kenny was outside, stepping into a dense warmth, with sugary yellow electricity radiating down on him from the underside of the huge cement canopy. Kenny slowed out of his sprint, checked in both directions. To be safe, he moved in the opposite direction of the large and muscular greeter—it wasn't hard, the guy was occupied with keeping foot traffic moving while simultaneously issuing salutations.

Attempting to blend in with the rest of the crowd, Kenny hugged the curb, beneath a cove of palm trees, blending in with the men in pricey outfits and women in sheer evening gowns. Slender hoses had been discreetly wrapped around the trees, their nozzles producing cascading mists, and Kenny momentarily noticed how the mists acted upon the crowd, in the manner of a soft eraser on a series of hard lines, softening their smallest defined motions (a hand to the small of a lover's back turning erotic; a playbill fanning an overheated face becoming mysterious).

The driveway was the length and width of a football field, and seemed alive, its own complex organism, a teeming digestive tract. One long line of cars was pulling up, another waiting to leave, with valets running to and fro, sweating through their color-coordinated shirts and shorts. Just to be safe, Kenny started away from them all, away from any possible suspicions, acting nonchalant, his breath coming easier now, even as he looked back and over his shoulder. . . .

Newell hadn't been that far behind him, he was sure, and was proven correct, for here was the boy now, popping from around the side of a man who wore his golf visor backward and upside down. Newell was huffing and puffing; when he saw Kenny, his face went exaggerated.

"Dude. We were fine until you spazzed."

Heat burned Kenny's cheeks. He didn't know if Newell was being serious, ironic, or sarcastic. "Me? You were the one who took off."

"Damn right. If I'da been like you and just sat there, we'd be caught right now." Newell snorted a laugh through his nose. He elbowed Kenny once more, and nodded toward the upside-down visor guy, who was passing them now, his finger knuckle deep inside his schnozz. "Pick a winner, buddy."

"*Newell.*"

"He don't care. He's digging for gold."

"Give it a break."

"What, you telling me that wouldn't be a nice little sketch. Oh—that would be *classic*. Maybe we can get him to pose. You have your pencil on you, right?"

Newell's next elbow landed deep in the soft part of Kenny's side and pain exploded in a bolt down through his legs and into his knees. He winced and found himself cursing; and more than that, he found himself stunned, betrayed, needing distance. Separating from the boy, he took off. Moving past the taxi stand and its thick bunch of yellow cars, Newell's squawks from behind—*Hey, come on, just joking, geez*—propelled him, and Kenny stared at the taxis with a feverish intensity, willfully concentrating on the fact that most of their hoods were popped, that the cabbies kept the hoods loose not only while the cars idled, but also when they pulled away from the curb.

It took a second for Kenny to figure out the air was supposed to calm the overheated motors, and for another few seconds he thought about trying the cab hood trick on his Plymouth, but decided that his hood would probably smack up into the windshield. With Kenny's luck, he'd be on the freeway and cause one of those giant pileups that back up traffic and get covered by the eye-in-the-sky news copters. It occurred to him he had never actually put his car in valet parking. He'd never been in a helicopter. Not even a plane.

"Wait up," Newell said. "Hey, what's wrong with you?"

Out from underneath the canopy of steel and cement and lights, Kenny headed onto a walkway the width of a city street, and moved alongside a row of shallow pools. Life-size marble elephants were spurting tight streams of water through their trunks and into the air. Chiseled stone acrobats were balanced precariously over wishing pools. Kenny merged amid the procession of bodies, tourists moseying at different speeds: a bacon-tan lady with dark roots jabbering agreeably with a brunette who legally should not have been allowed out in public in a sports bra and biking shorts; a retiree with a panama hat checking the time on his chunky gold watch; anorexic women toting around important-looking shopping bags, dull large men in paraphernalia that reflected a passion for auto racing; blossoming mall flirts in lovely yellow sundresses and snazzy black numbers. Different voices were talking on cellular phones, narrating each step to loved ones back home, reporting what they saw in the casino they'd just emerged from, which casino they were heading to next.

Kenny felt himself disappearing in their mass, being carried along by their collective pace. He watched a gang of Asian teenagers, all of them trapped inside shiny basketball jerseys, moving along the sidewalk as a collective group, slow and slouched, their hands in the pockets of their oversize shorts. Two of them were busy, pinching at their friends' ears, then pretending to have done nothing.

Kenny's sneaker landed on someone's toe. He was shoved in return, told *Watch it, faggot.*

From not that far behind, a voice was familiar, reaching, almost angry:

"Heads up. . . . Outta my way. . . . *I SAID GANGWAY.*"

Lorraine's hostess refilled her glass, and told her to finish her margarita. "Drinking alone makes me self-conscious."

Gail Deevers laughed. Her eyes darted. She was a generation or so older than Lorraine, of that age where her body, though well tanned and fit, had gone noticeably soft. Her perfect dye job was pulled back in a tight bun; her pin of red, white, and blue gleamed from its position over the heart of her polo shirt.

They sat on the patio in her backyard. In the distance behind them, motorized carts puttered across long, manicured greens.

Gail took a sip and started telling Lorraine about the last letter from Jimmy.

As if embarrassed by her thoughts, she leaned in and admitted that sometimes she wondered if it really was a war for oil. She conceded that she'd never wanted Jimmy to go into the reserves. He didn't need the money for college. He did it to satisfy family honor and legacy, whatever that was worth. The fourth generation of Deevers men to serve in the armed forces.

At this, Gail's laugh might have been rooted in pride, but it just as easily could have been contempt.

The mechanical squid brought ripples and bubbles from the pool's depths.

Gail was *so* pleased Lorraine had agreed to come over. It was good to talk to someone who understood.

This time it was Lorraine who smiled tightly.

They were casual acquaintances, people who were polite to each other whenever their loose web of common associates tightened, joining together for an afternoon of tennis. Lorraine's impression of Gail had always been as something of a battleship, and she remained unsure why she'd agreed to come here for lunch. But by the time their salads were ready, she understood that Gail's intentions were noble. Woman to woman, mother to mother, she sensed that Gail was truly open to what Lorraine was going through, eager to listen to anything she might have to say.

But how could Lorraine possibly respond?

Gail's son was not all that much older than Newell, and this young man, Jimmy Deevers, he'd been sent to a desert on the other side of the world. Jimmy was in the muck and hell of that godforsaken quagmire, risking his life to establish democracy, he was fighting terrorism and helping oppressed people and in all ways promoting truth, justice, and the American way, and this was entirely different from Lorraine's child, who had taken flight from these very things. So maybe it would have felt good for Lorraine to unburden herself. People you barely knew were supposed to be great for spilling your guts, cathartic and healing and no risk and all that. Maybe so. But there was no way Lorraine could share her burden with Gail Deevers. No way she could finish her drink. Rather, without making any sort of fuss or hurting Gail's feelings, she extracted herself from the situation.

Similarly, other well-meaning friends checked in on how Lorraine was doing, showed themselves to be concerned, more than ready to meet her in a restaurant if she needed to vent. They overflowed with empathetic looks and commiserative words, and Lorraine didn't hurry in getting back to them, either. She knew how they really felt, could sense their lingering discomfort, the deeper doubts that lay behind kind pretenses. In her better moments Lorraine could see her friends were trying, they wanted to help, were as sympathetic as they were capable of being. But they were human, after all. And Newell's was not the much-publicized case of a previous year, in which two preteen sisters had been strolling together, on their way back home from an afternoon of babysitting, and had never been seen again. Newell's was not the case, now commonly known throughout the valley, of a previous decade, wherein an overweight man with a dark black beard had taken a second-grader from a religious school during lunch recess.

The disappearance of a child strikes at the core of any community; innocence shattered will and must always be met with outrage and horror. But after almost five months, the police had officially categorized

Newell's case as one of voluntary flight. This was subject to change, obviously. Yet a logical mind could not help but think there must have been reasons. Reasons for the classification. Reasons why he left. Unhappy adolescents have untold ways of expressing unhappiness without leaving home, after all. Millions of them do it every day. There had to be something more here. And no matter how well meaning her friends may have been, Lorraine knew precisely where their fingers were pointed.

The outgoing message remained the same: *Hi. You have reached the Ewing home. We're not home right now but please leave a message and we'll get right back to you. Newell, honey, if this is you, we want you to come home. PLEASE leave a number where we can contact you. Please call back as soon as you can. PLEASE come home. We love you.*

She thought the whole thing would get easier and was afraid it would get easier and, no matter how much time passed, no matter how much information she gathered, it never got easier. She read advisory notices about how common it was for a friend or relative to sympathize with a boy on the lam; but Lorraine's network of contacts had been set up for so long that she no longer gained anything by checking in. The parents of her son's friends and classmates had their root canals, their bake sales, their family therapy sessions. Contacting them meant little more than coming face-to-face with the fact that her need to find her son had nothing to do with anyone else's life, a lesson that hurt no matter how many times she learned it.

If people outside the office of the Nevada Child Search could not understand what she was going through, if with each passing day, a tourniquet tightened, cutting off just a little more of the connection between Lorraine's ordeal and the world at large, then, inside that crappy storefront office, relief came in the simplest ways: wetting the backs of envelopes with a sponge, hanging out in the break room, picking the brains of other volunteers and listening in on support groups, just parking herself at an uneven table and poring through the various three-ring binders. Here, only here, did Lorraine begin to grasp the true scope of what she was up against.

The government estimated five hundred thousand to 1.5 million adolescents left or were forced out of their homes each year. At its highest end, this translated to half of 1 percent of the population, which wasn't significant enough to make teen runaways a problem worth addressing. At least, this was what other volunteers at the Nevada Child Search believed. They had long ago noticed that there were no concrete numbers, just the same estimates, rolled over, year after year. The lives of missing and runaway children didn't matter enough to the federal and local governments for it to be worth the effort to find out the difference in figures from one year to the next. This outraged Lorraine, and broke her heart.

She discovered lots of explanations, but few answers. Police reports on runaways often were incomplete or out of date. Statistics from major urban areas were often projected onto other cities. Lorraine found out that rural areas routinely got undercounted. Untold gay and lesbian teens left home and never were reported. What about the gray, small but consistent number of teenagers whose families were displaced and living in shelters, and who had struck out on their own in an effort to make a better life; did you include them? How about the inner-city and minority teenagers who never got a shred of attention for anything besides being incarcerated? How about the college students and college-aged adolescents who became enamored with Kerouac and Burroughs, and were aided by fashion and cynicism and run-of-the-mill discontent, and fell in love with the sky and wind—how many of them were grouped into this statistic? What about stoners living out of their cars, parked by some beach? What about the subculture of twentysomethings who dropped entirely from the grid of adult society and wandered the nation as what sociologists referred to as "urban nomads"?

Despite a national database and improved information-gathering networks, Lorraine learned that no small part of the problem remained the same: the impossible nature of the problem itself. The often quoted figure was that one out of every seven teenagers left his or her place of residence before the age of eighteen. But studies also showed that between 90 and 95 percent of these runaways were on temporary flights. Treks long and/or far enough to feel as if some point had been proven. They crossed some sort of private landmark: a movie theater a few miles from home, or a hangout park in a nearby city; they spent a few nights at the homes of friends with "cool" parents, drifted from the couch of one friend to another. Within a week or three, the road's mystique wore off, there were no more couches, no new crash pads. The romance ended and the reality of being out and alone in the world proved larger than whatever grudges were being nursed. Abouts got faced. Tails turned between legs. Whatever troubles that person would henceforth encounter, a life on the streets would not be one of them.

Which would have been encouraging, were it not for the stories.

This one was independently reported from five different cities. Presented as an as-told-to happening in each city, it involved a single father who worked as an airline pilot and lived with his daughter, who in most versions was sixteen. The pilot was formerly in the air force, a disciplinarian. Though he tried not to book any overnight flights (lest he be away from his daughter), he also trusted his daughter enough to know that if he had to go, she would behave herself. He never failed to call at precisely nine o'clock from the road, though these calls were made more out of love than distrust. The pilot was saving up so his daughter could spend that summer studying in Europe and this meant working lots of extra flights in order to accumulate the employee flight vouchers that would take care of the plane trip (he hoped overtime hours would pay for her hostels, Eurail, trips to the Eiffel Tower and Versailles). His daughter was an honors student, and involved in all sorts of extracurricular activities at school; she went to church and worked at soup kitchens and was a friend to geeks and jocks alike, in all ways the daughter was considered the best of eggs, and the father wanted only a golden life for her. But the pilot's daughter had a best friend, a girl she'd known from childhood. And this best friend was also sixteen, and she too lived in a single-parent household. There were issues in the best friend's home—violence and depression and the like. Well, the story got moving when some sort of terrible event happened between the best friend and her single parent, and in the best friend's mind this event cemented her need to cross the nation and visit the boy from summer camp whom she'd fallen in love with. The pilot's daughter was outraged by the incident and felt deeply for her best friend, and felt the idea of going across the country to visit the boy you loved was about the most romantic thing of all time. So the pilot's daughter went into her father's bedroom and took the flight voucher tickets from his bureau. She called the airline's reservation hotline and booked herself on a cross-country flight for that very night. Then she gave her driver's license to her best friend and helped dress her best friend in the clothes she'd worn for the license picture, and just for good measure she did her friend's hair and makeup in such a way that allowed the best friend to pass for her, the pilot's daughter. Everything went off without a hitch: the best friend made it past security, used the employee flight vouchers, no problem. Only, as it happened, a few hours later the pilot returned from a two-day trip of his own. When he went to add more vouchers to his growing collection, he made a fateful discovery. He summoned his daughter and she sat adjacent to him at their kitchen table. The pilot's daughter gave her father the director's-cut version of her poor abused friend and her horrible situation and the supreme healing power of true love. The pilot's daughter confessed everything and said that she knew stealing was wrong and knew her dad would be pissed, but she had decided it was okay to use the vouchers because her father always said you had to do the right thing not the easy thing. The pilot's daughter admitted her guilt yet again but said she hoped her dad would be proud of her, and she looked at him with genuine regret, but also with hopefulness, batting her long, beautiful lashes in a manner that she knew to be pleasing, and that she hoped would further help her cause by maybe breaking the ice. Her dad picked up the phone. He called in to work. He identified himself and said there was a problem, a runaway minor was posing as his daughter and illegally using his voucher tickets. His daughter pulled at his arm and tried to take the phone from him but the pilot was much larger and held her off. He said this runaway minor was on flight such and such heading across the nation to point X. Federal marshals were waiting when the passengers deplaned. The marshals put the sixteen-year-old best friend in cuffs. Three weeks later the pilot's daughter took off. She ended up whoring for smack. Her dad never heard from her again and killed himself in some gruesome gesture of sorrow that, in two versions of the tale, included a plea for forgiveness, spelled out in his blood on the tile of the bathroom floor.

As urban legends went, it wasn't particularly illuminating, out of the ordinary, harrowing, or even gory. When you got down to it, the story wasn't even about running away. But it cast a different pallor on traits that any parent recognized as defining the teen years—self-absorption, feelings of being unjustly persecuted when you did not get what you wanted, the twisted logic, the self-serving conclusions, the love of melodrama. Lorraine saw these traits in other stories, too, echoing and reappearing often enough to vaguely affect what sense she had of not only her child's mind-set, but also the mind-set of the reality in which he had placed himself.

And nobody could even say how many kids were out there.

So how were they going to find Newell?

Propped up against the base of the casino wall like an abandoned doll, the body was bulky in places, but still frail enough to look as if it might be carried along by a good wind. Electricity glossed over its mess of hair—kinked and matted strands of indistinct, artificial colors, clumped in all directions. Legs and shredded leggings were extended outward on a crushed cardboard box, perhaps a series of them.

Through the spaces between the people ahead of him, Kenny could see that it was hugely pregnant, stretching out and sticking out of the bottom of her tank top, her belly this mass of flesh, rubbery in appearance, the color of uncooked bird. Approaching now, maneuvering through the pedestrians, heading toward her side of the sidewalk, Kenny could see where the left side of her neck was coated with some kind of greenish slime.

Her arms reached and extended upward. Fingers danced, squalid with steel skulls and python rings. "Spare some change for some ketamine," she said. "Won't you help for some low-grade horse tranquilizer?"

And there was another ragged body. On the other side of her, he realized now. Folded up as if it were inside a small box, head in its hands, knees reaching toward its chest, heavy black clothing dripping from its spindly limbs, he—this one seemed to be a he—could have been an extra from some postapocalyptic movie, one of the decomposing undead types that come on camera to show how bad things are after the bomb. Resting against his shins was a piece of torn cardboard, its face scribbled with black marker:

I am a good person in a bad situation
Trying 2 get home 2 mom
Please help me
$30 4 a room 2nite

Now the corpse became animated, coming alive in the manner of a haunted house mechanism that pops up as children approach. A high-pitched and scornful voice screamed: *"Please, won't you help the children?"*

The pregnant girl looked at him, shook her head.

"Why you always gotta be like that, Lestat?"

Kenny could not take his eyes off them, slowing and stopping, watching the undead skeleton cackle at the pregnant girl and bare what looked to be fangs; the pregnant girl responding as if she had seen this show countless times, scratching at her distended belly. He, Kenny, was used to seeing people sleeping on park benches, homeless panhandlers, and the like. You hardly went a day in this town without seeing somebody by a freeway on-ramp, holding up a sign asking for a ride somewhere. But these two looked to be in his age range, and this was shocking, even as it sucked Kenny in further. For he saw that they were not alone.

A few yards beyond the skeleton, a large delinquent was occupying himself with a book of matches, lighting and flicking one after another at pedestrians, who were going out of their way to give him a wide berth. In fact, punkers were strewn all over the sidewalk, six, eight—Kenny tried to take in the sight of all of them without looking like he was looking at them. Their presence had him alert, defensive, but more than this, too. He began searching around in his pocket, his finger poking cleanly through a hole in the soft white lining.

"Need something there, slick?" she asked.

"Oh." Kenny started feeling around in his other pocket. "I just had it."

Preggers did not acknowledge the comment, but looked beyond him, out and down the length of the Strip. Her left hand stayed on the length of a mess of brown and gray and black fur that was curled into her side; Kenny hadn't noticed it before. This mangy, wolfish thing. Its head was nuzzled into the girl's exposed hipbone, at rest where the waist of her beaten shorts had been rolled up to form a makeshift belt. The girl stroked down the length of its back. Kenny checked his back pocket.

"DUDE."

The familiar voice, the scuffling of a compact and quickly approaching weight. "What the fuck's wrong with—"

A lack of breath ended Newell's sentence. Cradling the fun cup as if he were holding a baby to his chest, he sucked in a gust of wind, and spat onto the sidewalk. He bent over, the top of his head a bright red crayon that had been used to the point of dullness. A line of spittle hung from his hidden face, and he pulled at the end of his shorts, then reached to his stomach. When he came upright, his face was red and shimmering, and watching his struggle, Kenny immediately felt horrible about losing his temper, about having made his friend play catch-up. He had an impulse to wrap the boy in his arms.

"Dude, what are you doing? You ditching me or what?"

"I didn't— I wasn't . . . I told you to stop it."

"That's a funny way of not ditching someone."

"I got mad, Newell. When someone says—I mean—Why can't you just *stop*?"

"OKAY, *Dad*. Can I have my allowance now?"

Kenny didn't understand the last part, but figured it was some sort of slam or joke. He didn't have a response, and anyway, Newell was in the process of turning away from him, realizing they were not alone. "Whoa," the boy said, and went quiet, inspecting the scene. *"Total anarchy, man."* He took a step toward the filthy pair on the cardboard and removed a coin from his fun cup. "Want a nickel?" he asked, tossing the coin straight in the air. As it came down, his fist flashed, grabbing.

"Newell."

"Just joking." He released the nickel down into a small plastic cup, at rest on the edge of the pregnant woman's raft. "Geez."

"He didn't mean anything," Kenny told them.

"Like you know what I mean." As if mocking Kenny, Newell followed up with more dropped nickels.

"I hate taking baths, too," he volunteered. "Baths suck."

Preggers remained nonplussed, and retrieved a plastic bottle from the opened maw of her backpack. The skeleton raised his head, ignoring Newell as well, instead watching his companion unscrew the cap. Lestat's eyes narrowed at the sight of Preggers swigging, the green liquid sloshing inside transparent plastic.

"Once I didn't bathe for like a week," Newell said. "I got sent home from school. It was pretty sweet."

The skeleton's eyes shifted toward Newell. Tired, deeply set inside carved sockets, they were lined with red, but still lively. Calculating. As if sizing up what was in front of him, he said, "What's your name, li'l man?"

"Newell."

An oblique cough. A lick of chapped, blackened lips. "How do ya like that? Newell, is it?"

"That's my name, don't wear it out."

"Maybe we should—" Kenny said.

"Well, Newell, would you believe I got your name branded right here on my body."

"No *way.*"

"I swear."

"Nuh-uh."

A sickly smile, dead and yellowing teeth. "Bet on it?"

It was a dare as much as a proposition, with its own logic, some sort of hidden answer, Kenny could see that much. Exactly the kind of thing that made him nervous. He called out his friend's name. Newell stayed in place.

"Friendly wager," said the skeleton, his poker face now fully in place. "Everything in my hat against everything in your cup."

Newell willfully avoided another one of Kenny's looks, a trick that was starting to get on Kenny's nerves, to tell the truth. Kenny noticed that one end of a shoelace had been tied to the overturned baseball cap that the skeleton and the pregnant girl were using for their begging. He followed the shoelace's other end to the skeleton's far wrist, where it was tied and looped. The shoelace once had been white but now was a filthy gray, in some places black. Kenny was vaguely aware of tourists passing behind him, of the pregnant girl, bored out of her skull, staring out into the stalled parade of headlights and chrome and aerodynamic plastic. He watched the mongrel dog licking at a small open wound at the base of its tail. Watched a couple of punks on their knees, using condiments from a casino coffee shop to draw on the sidewalk.

"BULLSHIT," Newell cried.

"Read it and weep."

"Fucking BULLSHIT."

Lestat's shirt cuff was rolled up to his elbow and his hand was in the air. Just his wrist, small thin lines appeared, imprinted on the soft, stained flesh of his inner forearm:

YOUR NAME

"You know that homeless people in front of the Pick'n Save make hundreds of dollars a day asking for change," said Newell. "You know that, right? Dude. those two probably aren't even homeless. Look at them. I bet they just threw the dirt on themselves to make themselves look bad and shit. Fuck this. The whole thing's bogus."

Kenny asked if he believed what he was saying. He told Newell to look at those two, and reminded Newell that the money had been the casino's, and was just nickels anyway. "What's it matter?" Kenny asked, his voice soft but with an edge, a limit. He had a hand on each of Newell's shoulders and held the boy in place and looked deeply at Newell, locking in on Newell's eyes. It seemed to Newell that Kenny was pleading with him and at the same time telling him something warm, something intimate.

Newell's face felt hot with anger. He started to speak but quieted, and stared back at Kenny and opened his mouth just a bit. Nothing came out and consternation remained on the boy's face. But slowly, visibly, the venom dripped away. For a moment Newell seemed to consider what he'd said, and more.

"It's a pretty good trick," he admitted. "If you stop and think about it."

A step now, taken in the manner of a high chair infant trying a new food for the first time. The skeleton waited, watching, amusement smeared across each angle of his dirty face. Now he extended his hand, as if waiting for a high five. "You all right, li'l man? No hard feelings, right?"

When Newell did not meet his offering, Lestat nodded. "Tell you what, just to show my heart's in the right place, I got a good one for you. Double or nothing says you'll dig it."

"Maybe we should just—" Kenny began.

A fangy smile from Lestat. "Okay. Freebies, then."

"Not another trick."

"Tell you what, li'l man, you like the way I roll, maybe you'll hook me up, help me out with a little something. I see you're cool like that."

The boy stared at him, dubious. Both of his hands remained wrapped around the fun cup, which stayed tight, held to his stomach.

Lestat paid no attention, but coughed twice, clearing his throat. Now he wiped his nose, began rubbing at his eye with his palm. The rubbing became insistent. "Damn," he said. A forceful blink, his eye now tearing.

There had been a rumpled sweaty kid with heavy clothes and a pierced eyebrow. There had been a black girl with a prosthetic arm and large, scared eyes. Kenny used to see them, at the vocational high school. He used to see a palsied, thumb-sucking humpback—whenever they made eye contact, she'd go into a little convulsion, her smile spectacular for all its drool and spittle. Faces appeared in the hallways, showing up with enough regularity to become vaguely recognizable. Kenny always meant to approach them, but there had been complications. Never a right moment.

The filthy one with the fangs, Kenny decided, was too hard for any of this, too much of a hustler. If he ever let his guard down, it had to be to work some kind of angle. Still, there was something almost familiar about the way these homeless kids embraced their awkwardness, the way they seemed to have created personas from their outsiderness, advertising the same social deficiencies that Kenny tried to hide.

Lestat was cocking his head to one side now. His eye problems taken care of, he was settling into the cadences of ghost stories and campfires and friends confessing embarrassing things late at night, saying, "Okay, up in Hollywood? There's this place called Oki Dog—"

Kenny stepped back. Almost instinctively he looked back down the length of the row, as if searching for one particular face.

———

Because, without a doubt, he used to see the dude every once in a while. Too infrequently to put a timetable on, but amid the high school's listlessly matriculating bodies, every now and then, he'd catch a flash of colored bandana wrapped as a head scarf; that brittle body rattling around inside a T-shirt that had faded to the purple of a soft bruise. Kenny would notice that limp, so dramatic he had to stop himself from gawking, the way the right knee collapsed with each step, how the rest of the dude's body would go stilted, all of his weight transferring through his shoulder and down his arm and pouring down onto a makeshift crutch—this skateboard, a beat-up old long board, the kind you use for speed, only without wheels.

The dude would limp unassumingly through the hallways like this, pretty much staying out of everyone's way. But, as it happened, Kenny'd also seen this same dude at Amazin' Stories. Three times or so. Maybe a few more. It was a little weird, because each time Kenny'd seen him in the comic book store, this dude had been leaning against the New Arrivals bin, examining the same issues Kenny had been interested in reading. He'd be concentrating real hard, the dude—almost to the point where it looked like he was struggling with the pages, like he was trying to understand the reasoning behind the narrative, or maybe to figure where the story was going. Like this dude was unsure whether he should suspend disbelief and give in to the story and its flow, or just put the issue down, go and reap vengeance on the morons who'd perpetrated this fraud.

Not a huge deal, these crossings. A couple of ten-second intervals. A few awkward blips. Kenny might have thought about going up and finding out what was pissing the dude off so much. He might have thought about remarking in a way that showed he too recognized the numerous and fairly obvious deficiencies with the *Mutant Skinheads* artwork, the fundamentally played-out concepts in *Wendy Whitebread*. But Kenny didn't do stuff like that. He simply wasn't the type to go and interrupt some perpetually pissed-off-looking crippled dude: *Hey there! Don't you recognize me? We go to vocational high school together! Yes, not only am I unfit for standards of normalized education, I'm so dumb I'm gonna drag you straight into the moron spotlight with me. Let's talk comics!*

So Kenny stayed back and said nothing, and the dude took his issues and limped up to the register, and life went on, every bit as craptabulous as before, the whole thing a nonevent, a not-amazing nonstory. Certainly not the type of thing that stays in your mind enough to distract you from a rollicking yarn about pastrami hot dogs and sundry uses for napkins. Definitely not an incident of a heft or importance that would suck you away from the momentary particulars of the physical world. Yet in spite of a situation that had its own demands and dangers and responsibilities (Newell listening to that ongoing hot dog stand thing, a punk or two seeming to gather around as well, also being sucked in by the tale), Kenny had indeed returned, in his mind's eye, to the auditorium that passed for his second-period classroom; to the third-to-last row; an aisle seat and a swivel desk, rickety and loose, all but unhinged from its station.

It must have been right after the quarter break, because the surface of the desk had been scrubbed, the efforts of untold taggers, graffiti artists, music aficionados, and lovestruck daydreamers scoured away. What remained was a relief map, pencil indentations like zit scars on the faded, tattered wood. And three new scribblings. Two were heavy and primitive. But the third: that one had been detailed, accomplished, in its way: the face of a giant skull like an orbiting planet; braces running down its continent of teeth, acting as railroad tracks for a speeding, out-of-control train.

Kenny's aesthetic may have veered toward the intergalactic and superhuman, his sense of humor may have favored the subtle and whimsical, but it had been impossible for him not to appreciate the tiny skulls billowing from that smokestack, the bony arms flapping from the passenger cars' windows. And by the end of the period, the side of his own hand had been smeared with lead: the skull planet's orbit now broached by a space cruiser, all eight of the pilot's eyes focused, with an appreciation that bordered on glowing, upon that runaway train.

Two days later, Kenny had stared, with a dumbfounded awe, at the space cruiser's wing, and the pre-Renaissance corpse. Taking a knee, the corpse doffed its cranium. Ooze leaked from its open skull, forming the gelatinous word: *WOW.*

Half-afraid the sight would disappear if he looked up, Kenny had tried to wrap his mind around the fact: *he had been answered.*

So it began: a guarded castle stormed by zombie minions; a bikini babe wielding nunchakus to keep a shadowy dragoon cadre at bay. There were barriers, sure, there were interruptions and sabbaticals. The class didn't have a seating chart, for one thing. And the odds of Kenny getting to class in time to take that seat weren't great in the best of times. Also you had the mornings Kenny could not manage to escape from the seductive comforts of his fold-out couch. You had the times when he managed to get out and dressed, but couldn't spark the FBImobile's ignition fuse in time to make second period. And days when driving to school simply took too much energy. You had those couple of instances when Kenny had stopped at the Food King along the way to school, and had been distracted by the video poker machines. You had all those days, and you also had the fateful morning when Kenny had left his mom's place and discovered his old man, across the street, passed out, naked, in Mrs. Nguyen's year-round nativity scene, and Kenny had to get the poor sot out of there before Mom saw and lost her shit. All these distractions, and also the fact that whenever Kenny did successfully make it to second period, when he actually was fortunate enough to commandeer that seat, even then, a good half to two thirds of the time, the dumb bastard on the other side of this fun-house mirror, he'd come down with his own case of classroom attendance deficit syndrome, or himself had been unsuccessful in negotiating the politics of desk residency, which was to say, the desk would look exactly like it had the last time Kenny had left it, his most recent addition still untouched, a bride at the sacrificial altar.

It was just aggravating enough to give Kenny another excuse to stay in bed, another reason to let himself get distracted, to not try so hard, although, eventually, whether it took three days, a week, or sometimes even longer, Kenny *would* make it back to that aisle seat. And, eventually, a new series of black lines would indeed greet him there, impressed upon the wood.

Like this, slowly, gradually, with all the attention and intensity of missionaries in a new frontier, the glum confines of this physical realm had been transmogrified, turned into the expanding domain of the supernatural and otherworldly: a hobgoblin gleefully administering a super-wedgie to a superhero, who flew warp speed through the rings of hell, rushing to get Satan his pizza before the clock struck twelve; a radiation-mangled, spider-armed giant with a hockey mask and a fried-chicken bucket on his head blasting guitar at such volume that an invading army of robots was carried away (some hanging from the bottoms of the notes, others trapped inside the independent universe that each chord happened to be). Kenny'd used ripped pages from blue book test primers as his tracing paper, devoting the bulk of the period to copying out the latest skeleton and mongoloid addition. He'd spent the rest of his school day coming up with rough sketches of possible responses. Stretched out on his stomach across the floor of his dad's trailer, stretched out in his mom's living room, stretched out in front of his aunt's television, he'd recognize a few things, little quirks—which comic books might have influenced the artistic sensibilities of the other guy: those billowing clouds, for example—straight out of that *totally excellent* graphic novel *Ruthless Punishers, Dominant Visitors.* Those posed skeletons—inspired by a particularly infamous episode of *Mutant Skinheads in Love.*

Each discovered reference was simultaneously chilling and calming—this guy stealing from Kenny's favorite artists, using techniques Kenny *himself* utilized. It was more than a little odd. But more than a lot compelling, too. So Kenny would refine his artistic ideas, playing with and expanding on themes, scribbling out a mural on the surface of a pawn shop envelope, then turning over the envelope and starting over and following a different path of possibility, choosing and then honing and then perfecting an image, preparing it for the desk, all while fading away from and returning to the matter of whoever was doing the other drawings, this strange, plunging sense of inevitability taking hold—almost as if Kenny could reach out and touch the answers, as if he possessed knowledge he did not want to admit he possessed, knowledge that was not rational, but intuitive.

With a hesitant hand—a hand that Kenny eventually had to steady—he'd finally inscribed the bandana onto that desk. He'd then wrapped this drawn bandana around the bulbous head of an extraterrestrial being, whose face he'd portrayed as twisted, concentrating on the task of turning half-pike atop his airbound, rocket-powered skateboard.

Exactly twenty-four hours later, he found, carved into the wood like a series of knife thrusts, a zombie. With a mess of hair pouring down the front of its bony skull, the zombie worked feverishly at its own sketch.

In the front of the auditorium, the jayvee track coach was announcing, from his sports page, the results of the fourth race at Santa Anita. The kid in the next seat continued using a protractor to chop out a line of blow. Kenny remained in his cage, overcome with inarticulate wonder.

Thus, amid the undefined fissures that, on a daily basis, drifted through that dilapidated school, the exiguity of a rapport had blossomed. Slowly. Tenuously. Nobody else knew. If they knew, they did not care.

A private duel between anonymous gentlemen. A hothouse tango of clandestine imaginations. Floodgates opening, riptides sweeping across the woods, even the hot piece of ass who taught Dish Drying 101 made an appearance (on all fours, barking like a hound); openings created to be filled, challenges tendered to be met, with Kenny lobbing a metaphorical softball down the pike specifically so he could admire how far into the upper deck his counterpart would knock the thing, and then with the dude responding, making an entombed reference he had to know Kenny would understand; every square inch of the kidney-shaped desk being covered, a palette of squiggles and lines that every passing day was muddled further—you'd stare and see sludge, this world of shit; at last, your eyes would zero in, focusing on a specific object, that one little jewel, the key to untold dimensions.

And then there he was: waiting to go through the school metal detector, arguing with the rental cop, insisting he should not have to put his skateboard on the conveyor belt.

Kenny joined the line. Four or five people were waiting between him and the dude. Kenny shifted his weight from one worn sneaker tread to the other. He was within earshot and heard the security guard telling the dude he'd had enough, if the dude wanted to be a little shit, two could play that way.

"You know they're against school policy," the security guard said, nodding at the dude's skull.

A shift now. A sort of awareness. The dude tensed, as if he felt some-one was watching him. Responding, he turned. His eyes, large and prob-ing, stared right at Kenny. The dude did not betray recognition, but his irritation with the situation of the moment was no more. His face was delicate and slim, with blue veins visible from beneath his transparently pale skin. He did not have eyebrows, and this added to the penetrating effect of his gaze. A tardy bell rang and was ignored. The security guard repeated his order with exasperation. The dude's crystalline blue eyes stared directly at Kenny, and now he began following the security guard's order, unknotting his bandana, seeming detached from this action, his attention solely on Kenny, studying him, communicating with him, less reaching out to him than relating.

The bandana fell.

Call it gamesmanship. Etiquette. An instinctive understanding of en-gagement's rules.

Perhaps it was shock. Something as basic as freezing—choking in the moment, not knowing what to do next.

Or maybe it was as simple as fantasy's open possibilities being supe-rior to the limitations of what is real.

But in the same way a manager refuses to acknowledge a pitcher in the late innings of a perfect game, Kenny made a concerted, pained ef-fort. And *avoided* the dude's inquiring eyes. *Avoided* his clumps of hair, his patchy scalp.

And, for his part, the dude did not so much as acknowledge Kenny's snub.

Ignored Kenny right back, he did.

Kenny didn't show up for school the next day.

Friday either.

A long weekend was coming up, honoring some dead guy, and he passed the time without enthusiasm or focus, keeping to himself, not doing much of anything, really, seeing a few movies, driving around to a few familiar out-of-the-way desert roads.

When he returned to Vo Tech, a photocopied paper breezed out of his locker.

For the entirety of that school day Kenny wandered the hallways, searching.

The next day as well.

In the months since the dude had vanished, Kenny had picked up a few punk rock compilations. Each week, he'd checked out the underground comics that littered the pages of the weekly alternative giveaway newspaper. Eventually he'd flipped to the music listings, fighting his way through the paragraphs of small print that described the different bands scheduled to play at the old Huntridge Theater. He'd grown attuned to whispers about those bizarre concerts out in the desert, and had driven out there a few times, walking around in the darkness, listening to a whole lot of distorted noise.

The whole scene still remained too fast and violent for his taste, too enthusiastic about hopelessness. Yet like the shallowest of pencil imprints that remain tattooed on the surface of a recently cleaned desk, like the grainy cleansers that seep underneath your fingernails as you rub your hand over the surface, the experience had stayed with him, his failure itching at him, gnawing.

So his eyes scanned down the row of listless homeless kids on the Strip, seeking out a bandana, a skateboard, anything that might resemble a limp. Almost subconsciously, he started wandering down the stretch of the sidewalk, it was covered in mustard and ketchup, papered with small cards advertising *strippers delivered to your hotel room.* Kenny walked slowly, haphazardly, toward the far end of the group, the few faces that remained hidden there, out of view and dark.

He was still within earshot, however, and heard the first scream.

"FUCKERS!"

And the next:

"ALL RIGHT, WHO SNAKED IT?"

By the time Kenny got back to him, Newell was in the face of an over-large mongoloid. "ASSHOLES," he screamed. His eyes were bulging. The mongoloid was laughing, returning the boy's spleen with kissy faces.

Kenny pulled him away by his sleeve. Newell swung wildly into the air.
"I'M CALLING THE COPS."

"What—"

"My phone, dude. MY FUCKING PHONE."

Newell twisted in place and thrashed, patting his waist, checking his
pockets. Punks whistled, barked.

"Could you have lost it?" Kenny asked.

"*I* didn't. *They*—"

Kenny looked toward the spot where all this had begun, as if some
sort of help or answer might be found there. But all he found was the
pregnant girl's blank indignation, as if this whole thing were tiring to her.
"That's what happens." Lestat laughed, clapping, his hands creating little dust clouds. "Welch on a bet, that's what happens."

"GET OFF ME," Newell said, when Kenny reached out for him.

"Just—"

"DON'T TELL ME WHAT TO DO."

"Okay." Kenny's hands went up. He stepped back.

"I FUCKING HATE BEING TOLD WHAT TO DO."

"Okay. Just—when did you know it was gone?"

A nasal snort. "I had it. And now I *don't*."

"What about the casino?"

Another snort, more obnoxious.

"When you fell?"

"You're believing *them*?"

"I'm not believing anything, Newell. I just—"

"FUCKING BULLSHIT."

"I'm just saying. When we ran through the casino? We were moving
pretty good."

The boy felt his pockets. His mouth opened and went slack and no
sound came out. He stared through Kenny now, his eyes filling with
disbelief, with refusal, with defiance. His face was round and rigid.
Stares from people he did not know or care about, momentarily concerned as they walked along to their next entertainment. The vague
amusement of the homeless trash. Kenny saying something to him.

Every answer was not any sort of answer. Every path led down into a black hole. Dull noise lulled through his ears. His mind raced and raced and ran in place. And now Newell glanced over his shoulder, struggling for an escape hatch, some direction, a conclusion that did not end up being the obvious one, a result that left him anywhere but this place.

Chapter 4

THAT WAY, THEY'LL
KNOW I'M ALIVE

11:00 P.M.–12:30 A.M.

4.1

When the Los Angeles Dodgers used their eighth-round draft pick on a switch-hitting second baseman from a public high school in western New Mexico, Lincoln Ewing certainly did not expect that, one day, his name would be announced in the starting lineup of the All-Star game. He was not counting on having his face decorate a Wheaties box. If either of these things had happened he would have taken them, of course; any boy with a mitt who passes his afternoons throwing an old tennis ball against a brick wall has such dreams. But even as a high school senior, Lincoln was uncommonly level-headed—coaches and teammates said as much—and he was realistic enough to know the difference between dreams and fantasies. It therefore came as a surprise to people around him when Lincoln turned down scholarship offers from the University of Texas at El Paso, Cal State Northridge, and Pepperdine. Although the schools had only middling athletic programs, forsaking college for a minor league contract made little sense. After all, the pros would always be there. And it wasn't hard to imagine that a year or two of being the big fish in the proverbial small pond would improve Lincoln's draft position, signing bonus, and contract terms. All he had to do was be patient.

The morning he signed with the Dodgers, Lincoln told his old man that he didn't particularly need to be a big star. All he wanted was to give it the best ride he could. To find out how he stacked up. And this indeed is what he did: an educational and boring season of rookie ball in the metropolis of Ogden, Utah; a prolonged and confusing week when his agent kept calling, telling him to sit tight; the eventual trade and relocation to San Bernardino, the next two years of single-A ball. During all of which, the biggest thing Lincoln discovered was: *everything gets exposed.* Which is to say that if a guy steps between the foul lines each day, players, scouts, and managers will get a sense of just what he can and cannot do, not only the bubbling possibilities that exist within that player at any given moment, but also the plowlike inevitability of how he performs on a routine basis. Lincoln, well, his verdict was packed with conditionals: he was athletic, yes, but not so gifted as to differentiate himself from the general talent pool; he had the speed to steal on a pitcher who did not keep him honest, but not the wheels that stretched a defense and wreaked havoc; his glove was dependable enough to pencil in at second or short without worry, but wasn't so dazzling as to justify a place in the lineup. If you hung a curve or served up a piece of slop, Lincoln made you pay; in important at bats he could be counted on to hang in, foul off pitches, and force a pitcher to throw his best stuff. But a pitcher's best stuff *would* beat Lincoln. As scrappy and disciplined as number twenty-two may have been, Ewing didn't have the wrists to turn on a ninety-mile-an-hour fastball as it snapped and tailed nastily toward the inside black rubber of the plate. Even decent sliders blew him out of the box.

The story goes that the little engine chugged up the hill by telling himself, *I think I can;* and, certainly, there are people in every field of professional life who can will themselves to success. But force of will alone does not necessarily get a train up the hill, create a successful business, or enable an entrance into the hall of fame. Rather, will, or an unvarnished need to succeed, usually forces a person to learn his craft, to harness the talent that will guide him, rail by painful rail, down the track toward that masterpiece. This having been said, discipline and persistence also can get a person only so far. An eighteen-year-old bonus baby from the Dominican Republic was brought up from rookie ball. He spoke pidgin English, wore his stirrups unfashionably high, and routinely compensated for unforgivable mental mistakes with a fluidity that was almost leopardlike. He took Lincoln's place in the everyday lineup and not much needed to be said about why. Lincoln tried to keep his chin up, conducting himself as professionally as would be expected of someone who was hoping to be traded to a team that would give him a chance. Nevertheless, when he did get at bats, Lincoln found himself swinging from his heels, overanticipating pitches, sometimes just plain guessing. When he managed to stay focused, work the count to his advantage, then sat on a fastball and guessed right, half the time he still ended up being overpowered. Instead of the anger that he used to feel about being hung out to dry, however, Lincoln found himself feeling something else. Returning to the dugout, he'd shove his bat back into its slot on the rack, down a cup of the official athletic drink of that particular minor league park, and accept the halfhearted low fives of teammates who are obliged to console one of their own. And as he did these things, the competitive voice inside Lincoln—that same voice that propels an athlete to believe in his abilities—would be a bit more faint than on the previous day. But it was as if something else was solidifying inside of him, too, as if a suspicion that he had long harbored was now confirmed, as if a shameful secret had just been announced, for all to hear.

He was still growing into his body and would not be at his physical peak for years; he was still figuring out the mental aspects of playing professional baseball, which was the most cerebral of sports. Even so, Lincoln had the sense he was reading a lineup card that did not have his name on it, the feeling that even if he managed to rededicate himself to a daily routine of extra batting practice and weight lifting, if he shortened and compacted his stroke as hitting instructors wanted, if he followed through on his private oaths to become more thorough in charting opposing pitchers, and grew into his body, and played the game while channeling the spirits of Ty Cobb and Sandy Koufax and Secretariat, if he did all these things, Lincoln, when he checked deep in his gut, nonetheless recognized a ceiling to his potential. And from the top of this ceiling, he saw how far it was to the Show. Lincoln had the curse of being good enough to see just how much better he needed to be. He also had the ability to ask himself if he honestly wanted to work this hard, if he really wanted to spend his twenties traveling back roads on rickety buses and sleeping in motels on the side of the interstate.

Calling his dad was not one of the easier things he'd ever done, but after some silence that Lincoln had come to know meant both disappointment and understanding, his father said that all you could ask of a man was to give it his best. His dad wondered if Lincoln could stick it out until the end of the season, and he reminded Lincoln that once you quit at one thing you quit at them all. Lincoln listened, and responded with a mournful breath of his own. He told his dad that he would think about it. He told his father he loved him, and he thanked his old man, and the next day when Lincoln took the field to warm up, the smell of freshly cut grass had been about the sweetest thing in the world, and there'd been little in his life he'd ever appreciated as much as the sounds of mitts popping all around him, the protracted ease of guys loosening their bodies with a round of catch. The batboy purchased a bag of peanuts for him on the sly. The opposing pitcher was nineteen years old, threw a hundred and two miles an hour, and couldn't get a pitch over the plate with the help of a laser guided missile system. By the sixth, the game was out of hand. In the seventh, both managers were substituting freely. Lincoln fielded all three of his chances at second base cleanly and without fanfare. In the bottom of the eighth he turned on a changeup, made contact squarely on the sweet spot of his bat, and felt a continuity running deep into the marrow of his arms, grooving the ball to right for a solid single. A week earlier it would have told him there was hope, he could turn things around, a hot streak was on the way.

Instead he cleaned out his locker. His best mitts, cleats, hats, and batting gloves went into his team duffel. His game jersey, though caked with infield clay, did not go into one of the organization's large, rolling laundry bins, but headed out the door with him as well. A tag sale in front of his apartment complex freed him of his couch and dresser. What the Salvation Army did not want of his other meager furnishings, he left by the curb. Lincoln didn't have much of a plan, nothing in his life was organized to the point of thought. All he wanted was to sit by the side of a hotel pool and sip on a colorful drink with a paper umbrella in it and watch the girls unwrap themselves, just sit and dissolve underneath the sun's brightness and maybe dive in when it got too hot. He wanted to hit on girls in nightclubs and get plastered in bars, to take in glitzy shows and double down at blackjack and roll craps and go for the inside straight, anything that might distract a man who had just walked away from a good chunk of his identity.

Las Vegas had mythic status as a party town among other minor leaguers, with more than a few former teammates settling there. A catcher with arthritis in both knees offered hospitality and Lincoln accepted and drove down for a visit. At the time the Strip was still in the larval stages of its now epic transformation: financed in part by junk bonds, a maverick hotelier had constructed a pair of large five-star resort complexes a half a mile away from one another. Each resort was wildly successful, and therefore served as the forerunners in what would become a cycle of resorts that were as much city-states as they were hotels. By the time Lincoln hit town, construction had begun on a new billion-dollar MGM, whose façade and towers would be shrouded in green light in a tribute to the emerald kingdom of that studio's most famous film. Hotels with Egyptian and medieval themes were also at early stages of development. It was the ground floor of a boom time that would last more than a decade: bodies were needed to put down carpeting, wash sheets, maintain gardens, and pick up trash in parking lots. Jobs were available teaching the children of all these new hotel employees and manning the post offices that sent alimony payments back to former spouses. Since all these newly transplanted employees needed to live somewhere, even more construction jobs became available. And since there was no end to the desert, untold space existed for more master planned communities, which meant rents were pretty cheap. Topping it all off, the state had no sales tax, so a fella could make his nest egg last, were he so inclined.

The town was open all night and Lincoln made the most of every hour. Without much effort on his part, he was absorbed into the social circle of entry-level casino workers. A lifetime in locker rooms, the ease with which he deflected sarcastic jibes, the good humor he showed in handling teammates who were both joking with him and sizing him up (Lincoln gracefully giving as good as he got; though never going so far as to offend someone or leave them feeling worse about themselves), this translated well to the masculine, vaguely gangsterish backroom atmosphere of Las Vegas. At the same time, Lincoln was square-jawed and athletic and handsome in a way that was reassuring, as opposed to threatening or overtly sexual; a guy self-assured enough to know when to step back and let someone else be the star. This went over well with the corporate regimes that were coming into power. And while Lincoln still may not have been able to watch the World Series, he didn't blink when it came to telling stories about the minors, or giving the skinny on different major leaguers he'd met on their way up. This played equally well with gangsters who enjoyed pretending they were legitimate businessmen and suits who fancied themselves as modern-day Bugsy Siegels. Before Lincoln had fully accepted that Vegas was the place he wanted to settle down, he'd taken a job as a sales representative at the Kubla Khan. Thus his vacation had become something else, and though he wasn't sure what precisely that might have been, he knew the money was good, and the work wasn't too hard, and soon enough he'd spent a year there, then two, and was still enjoying his life in the manner of any twenty-two-year-old sales rep—working the barter system in which so many low-level casino residents were engaged. (On a date Lincoln and his girl might receive a night of drinks. Later the bartender would get comped at a pricey steakhouse where Lincoln brought a lot of business, and was in tight with the headwaiter, who Lincoln might then hook up with a ticket agent. . . .) He tipped big wherever he went, this was good karma, and besides he always wanted to show his appreciation for an honest effort.

He knew how to show a woman a good time. More than a few beauties were seen on his arm. Then one in particular.

They'd been going out for half a year or so when Lorraine told him she was pregnant. She hadn't returned his calls for a few days, and then she phoned him at work and said there was something they needed to talk about. She refused to answer his inquiries, but there was a hitch in her voice and she said, *See you soon, okay?* Lincoln ruminated on that hitch throughout the drive to her place, all the possibilities it contained. He was sure she was breaking up with him and his mind raced for possible reasons, and the lack of anything obvious was that much scarier. The day was a model of climate-controlled perfection, bright as a newly minted penny. Lorraine sat him down. In the manner of a kindly yet displeased schoolteacher, she first told him about her suspicions and then how they'd been confirmed, unfurling the details as if they were happening to friends of hers, as if all this had not just exploded their happy little dating adventure. She had been preparing for this all day, but her nervousness still showed, her composure wavering. She hadn't told him sooner, she said, because she'd wanted to hear first from her doctor, and because she needed to think about things before talking to him. She hadn't made any decisions, but she'd been thinking about it a lot. She went into a hard silence that lasted for an unbearable time, then said: *Oh God.*

She was all of twenty years old and her combination of looks and dancing ability had provided her with an escape from a large family and a dying small town and the smell of horseshit from a nearby industrial farm. After six months of kicking in the back line of the Rockettes traveling squad, she'd gotten an agent, and had come heartbreakingly close to making the dance squad for a professional basketball team. The chorus line of a Vegas floor show wasn't exactly Lorraine's idea of a dream job—she made no bones about her opinion of the choreography, nor the legions of self-styled cowboys, Donald Trump wannabes, and men who thought wearing loud shirts made them classy. Lincoln had had to convince her to give him her phone number, and during a week of respectful calls, she had been restrained and suspicious; although, when screening, she did pick up and talk to him, and eventually allowed him to take her to dinner after her shows, and did let him walk her to her car to make sure she was safe, and one night, after a few glasses of really good wine, she'd opened up to him enough to admit that, yes, she was learning to enjoy having money in her pocket, and that this city did indeed have its strange charms. Lorraine had let him take her to a candy factory on their first date and not long afterward she had taken two sick days and gone away with him on a camping trip to Zion, during which time they'd used the factory's chocolate syrup on each other. Lincoln and Lorraine had confided in each other, more than once broaching how they felt and agreeing there was more to what they were doing than two people just having fun, and though neither one had gone out on the ledge and used the *L* word, that ledge was not that far away, it was being approached with hopeful, toddler's steps. In light of which, her pregnancy was particularly devastating, sucking the air out of the apartment. Lorraine collapsed onto the couch, looking not at Lincoln but through him, every so often picking up on or returning to a thought, vocally unpacking the options and angles of her predicament. The obvious thing was to terminate it. She loved kids but wasn't anywhere near ready to be a mom. Nothing she knew about Lincoln remotely showed he was prepared to face fatherhood. Each possible outcome was wholly and specifically terrifying to her and a new thought crossed her eyes like a shadow and she fought back some sort of emotion and her face began to crumple. *"But then I think about it and God help me I want one."*

He would look back when things were not going well and wonder if that moment had really just been about winning, about conquering the landscape, the underdog bucking the odds and going for the hard route. After all, he had walked away from baseball because he'd thought about all the work and where it would get him, and in the end, it just hadn't been worth it. That had been the biggest decision of his life, until this point, and Lincoln had made it based on the simple thought: do I really want to do this? He remained convinced that walking away had been the right thing to do. Still, it was a lot to live with, a lot to live down. And the question welled within him again. Its implications hadn't sunk in yet, he still had no idea what the words *husband* and *father* entailed. But then again, when you got down to it, he didn't really have to be in touch with the long-term implications. Right then, he didn't need to know what he was getting into.

He picked up her phone, called the travel agent who handled all arrangements for Kubla Khan executives. Lorraine stared at him without comprehension and Lincoln waited on hold and did not tell her what this was about. He did not make a reservation for her to Tijuana, San Diego, or the Scripps Medical Center. Instead he arranged for a pair of families to be able to call the travel office. He arranged for these families to get fixed up with plane reservations for as soon as possible. Lincoln arranged for all charges to go on his own tab, and he told the reservation agent that the only thing was that neither family could know what was going on. Then he asked Lorraine for her parents' phone number, and repeated the question. Over Lorraine's protestations—*Why? What are you doing?*—Lincoln dialed the number and introduced himself to Lorraine's father. He said everything was okay, their daughter was more than fine, she was wonderful, better than that. Without so much as a ruffled feather or a hint of his larger intentions, he gave Lorraine's father the number of the ticket agent and told him to make arrangements to get here, the agent was expecting the call. Lincoln then called his own father. In the quiet voice of a grown man talking warmly to his dad, he gave a variation on this theme. Lorraine said she did not know what he was doing, that he was crazy. However, Lincoln could tell she was charmed, maybe even thrilled. *I don't know about this,* she repeated, her face flush and bright. Lincoln said they better start calling chapels. He asked did she want to go get a ring first.

It was the beginning of his adulthood.

Maybe it had to do with his own slide, entering the region between early and mid-thirties, still young enough to remember all the emotions and joys associated with teen delinquency, yet old enough now to be a little worried by the bumping bass from the car next to you. You reach a point where you look into a mirror and can't help but focus on the shining suggestions of scalp, for they are unavoidable, just beyond the front of your hairline, as if they were spots of lawn picked clean by birds. You find these hard, horizontal creases, like a series of ladder steps, down the middle of your forehead. You stare at yourself and see once-focused facial features suffering the effects of gravity, your eyes and mouth less prominent than they should be, what they once were; what, gradually, is becoming softer, a pie of a face, a face not the one you grew up with, nor the face to which you have long grown accustomed. You reach a certain age and it becomes convenient to blame the dry cleaners for the problems you have buttoning your slacks; it becomes consoling to tell yourself that, so long as you suck in your gut, you still have your ballplayer's physique. You wake up around the crack of dawn and slip into your sweats and running sneakers, and a mile or two later you are slowing to a trot, walking, placing your hands on the gray fabric at your thighs. Your knees get stiff in bad weather. You cannot sleep in the wrong position without aggravating your back. Cannot make it through the night without taking a piss. Certainly, you cannot comprehend death, the world going on, the trees and cars and life continuing onward, absent the presence of your physical and mental self. You cannot possibly fathom an end to your observations about the status of your physical decline, a final finality. Such things are beyond you, as they are beyond anyone; and yet the evidence permeates your days, unavoidably present, oozing from the southwestern décor of a master bathroom, its sandalwood and Iroquois shades, its tastefully papered walls, miniature designs of sea horses and bubble-breathing goldfish.

You stare straight into the confines of your own personal cage, it's understandable if you take consolation in a rich, fatty meal; if getting your wife into the sack constitutes a personal victory; if pounding into her until her body locks and unlocks against her will brings within you a satisfaction that is more sadistic than generous. You hit a certain point in your life, fact is, you clemently rejoice in your son's truancy, you actually *want* your child out on the town, disobeying orders, breaking his curfew, chugging a few beers—although Newell was too young for chugging, wasn't he? Well, then, out tasting his first beer. Chasing a good time. *Trying to eat the world.*

Lincoln's son was bigger than the world. The world could go to hell in comparison to his Newbie.

The ceiling fan continued its efficient hum, muting the faraway sounds that drifted through the south window—a time-activated sprinkler system in rotation, the neighbor's dog barking at an imagined intruder. Lincoln jostled his member, dislodging the last squirts, then the last drops, of a piss so satisfying as to be almost celebratory, an end-zone dance to his coital touchdown.

He lifted the cover off of the toilet's basin. His mind was happily unfocused, and he did not care that the Mexicans had never fixed the toilet like they'd promised. He jiggled the rod.

It took three steps to get to the sink. With tired yet practiced motions, he removed his contact lenses, soaked them in saline, and shut them inside their little plastic case. As soon as the lid closed, he remembered the liquid soap—usually you want to wash your hands after they're on your dick, but before they head into the eyes.

He relathered.

Welcome to your future, old man.

If death was beyond comprehension, then having a child had to be one of the more powerful ways a man came to terms with his mortality. Could there be anything more alarming than recognition of your own mannerisms in your son's movements, seeing the physical characteristics you cherished in your wife manifest in him? The seed of the father plants the stalk; every father dreams that the stalk will not linger in his shade or shadow, but will grow bigger and stronger, blooming, his roots extending into previously uncharted territory. The dream is a child who would carry on your dreams and ideals, personalizing them, meeting those new dreams and finding his own successes and happiness: at once validating and perpetuating every bit of love and attention that you had devoted. How easy it was for Lincoln to look back now and appreciate something as simple as his own father showing him the secrets of oiling and breaking in a baseball mitt—*first soak the palm and the web with oil, get it good. Okay, now put the tennis ball in there. Squeeze tight, attaboy, you're getting it. And where's the phone book?* Behind their tattered shack in Las Cruces, Lincoln's dad had taught him how to get in front of a grounder so that if the ball took a bad bounce, his body could absorb the hit. Lincoln's father also used to rear back and huck the ball up into the starry New Mexico evening, passing hours on end with his only son; handing down secrets like how to judge a ball in the soup, and how to recover when you've lost its flight, and—once young Lincoln showed he knew his fundamentals and was ready—how to look nonchalant as you made a basket catch.

There existed few words to describe what it felt like to watch his own son be just as entertained by the fancy-Dan techniques as young Lincoln had been. For more than half an hour Newell had been into it. Then he'd become antsy, twitching back and forth like a pinwheel in a spring breeze. Where each mistake that Lincoln had made as a child had spurred him to practice harder, his son was physically incapable of holding still for the time it took to learn how to properly hold his mitt: he tried but the ball bounced off the palm of his glove; he settled underneath the pop fly and got scared, at the last second ducking out of harm's way; he got frustrated and threw his glove; he put his mitt on his head and sniggered at his cleverness. During two seasons of Biddy Ball and then another season of Little League, Left Out had been the boy's unofficial position, and he had not seemed to mind, daydreaming his way through the three innings guaranteed to each player, then spending the rest of the contest at the far end of the dugout, suspiciously near the cooler of postgame soda. Each game, in his single at bat, Newell consistently unleashed lumbering, vicious cuts, and although Lincoln talked to him about being under control, waiting for the right pitch, and the victory of making contact, his words never registered for longer than the ride home. And that was fine too. Lincoln wasn't going to be one of those pathetic bastards reliving his own faded and derailed athletic glories. No, he was just going to be there, rooting through every one of those three required innings of play; supportive when a can of corn that any Nancy could have flagged shot over his son's head, then rolled into the outfield of the game on the next field; patient through every epic swing that sent his kid staggering out of the batter's box. Be it Little League or the class talent show at the end of the year, winning and losing were less important than doing your best and knowing your dad was there cheering you on. And when a departmental powwow had made him fifteen minutes late for the boy's second-grade play, had anything been so awful as Newell scanning the crowd and becoming so upset he could not go onstage? Had anything been so comforting? And when the next class play came around, who had showed up thirty minutes early, fit himself into a tiny blue chair in the back of the room, and sat through a lesson in elementary division? Who'd run onstage when the boy had slipped during his scene and bawled anew?

Your child scrapes his knee; you bleed. If he is sick, you leave early from the office. Hot Wheels racers and official casino playing cards made a flu-ridden third-grader feel better. Sci-fi action figures took care of a fourth-grader. These days, little less than an all-access pass to a Hollywood movie convention prompted a reaction. The kid had the latest computer systems and all their hardware attachments. His room was plastered with promotional posters from championship fights. He must have had five different Runnin' Rebels basketball T's (all oversize), as well as a set of UNLV team sweats (so large that Lincoln could fit into them), an official reversible game-day jersey (a goddamn tent), and each style of sneaker the Runnin' Rebels had worn during their last three seasons—the most expensive of which, naturally, the boy had immediately outgrown. Newell had an official leather basketball autographed by the members of UNLV's national championship team. He had a limited edition ball commemorating the legendary coach's final season. How the kid had turned into such a basketball fan, Lincoln had no idea. One of the neighborhood brats? Someone from school? Like getting hit by lightning in the middle of a snowstorm, it had been a shock impossible for Lincoln to prepare for, a freak of nature that provided no reason to change his daily attitude, and that also made him see things a little differently. Almost overnight, it seemed his stouthearted hotshot was leaping up, jumping to smack the top of every doorway as if it were a backboard, immersing himself in the slang and styles of a game very different from the one dear to Lincoln's heart. And again Lincoln went along. Three separate times during the previous winter, he had been larger than any tender feelings he might have nursed, and had cashed in favors at work, exchanging them for tickets his department used for entertaining prospective clients.

The University of Nevada, Las Vegas's men's basketball program had come to prominence in the seventies, thanks to a charismatic, if somewhat schlumpy, balding coach named Jerry Tarkanian. Nicknamed Tark the Shark for his habit of sucking on moistened towels during games (they kept his throat moist enough to allow him to yell at players and referees), Tarkanian was infamous for recruiting players with disreputable pasts and superhuman leaping abilities. By the late eighties UNLV had become a national powerhouse, and in 1991 destroyed Duke for the national championship. Soon after, when several of his players were photographed in a hot tub with a noted mob figure, Tarkanian came on the short end of a fight for power with university administrators, and was forced to resign. In the years since, coaches had come and gone as if they were dieting fads, and the program had never completely recovered. But if visiting celebrities no longer could be found courtside, sitting in what infamously had been called Gucci Row, Rebels basketball remained an event of local glamour. About the only way to get a pair of season tickets in nosebleed seats was to endow a chair to the school's fledgling philosophy department. Even for games against conference doormats, a pair of lower-deck seats represented something more than a coup.

"You're spoiling him," Lorraine complained. *"He needs a father, not a friend."* And: *"Why don't you ever take ME?"*

Was he supposed to disregard the joyous energy with which Newell had decked himself in scarlet and gray? Ignore the expectant banter as they'd sat in pregame traffic and listened to sports radio call-in? What was the point of connections if not to bring a father and son together? What was the point of money if not to make your child smile?

An executive order put the kid's hyperactivity diet on hold for a night. A couple of limp and steamed weenies were procured at four fifty a pop. Medium-size boxes of imitation-butter-soaked popcorn-shaped Styrofoam came at three fifty a shot. Another eight for watered-down Cokes. Ten for generic game programs with the visiting team's roster stapled inside. Before a lounge lizard had finished butchering the national anthem—in one particularly galling case, before Lincoln and Newell had successfully made it from the concession stand to their section—Newell had spotted kids from school. With a quick wave the boy had receded into the stadium crowd, disappearing as if he'd never been by his father's side. Yep, each one of those three supposed bonding experiences, those father-son outings, had ended up with Lincoln alone, near the bottom of a half-empty sold-out arena, watching with relative disinterest as UNLV phoned in the results, the Rebels registering uninspiring victories in contests that were neither as competitive nor as entertaining as trying to brush all the cat hairs off your suit jacket. Lincoln's knees would incessantly bang against the back of the seat in front of him and he'd pound more than a few ten-dollar buckets of watered-down hops, then set the empties onto the chair that his kid was supposed to be occupying. He'd apologize to the guy whose back he kept kneeing, engage in small talk with one or two others around him, and pay special attention to the players he knew to be his son's favorites. Inevitably, by the middle of the second half, the *white* Rebel players would be mopping the floor with the other team's starters. Time-out would commence on the court and the UNLV student band would strike up "Dixie" and the crowd would respond with a swelling pride, and the female cheerleaders would cartwheel from the sidelines and into the proceedings, their vented little skirts flipping up. Lincoln always stopped trading business cards for this; the horn section's brassy refrain rousing him out of conversations, thoughts about work, or flashes back to his own athletic days. A muscular male cheerleader would be at center court, waving what had to be the largest Confederate flag in the history of organized humanity; and Lincoln would slam his callused hands together, clapping loudly and roughly now, whooping it up a bit, even as his eyes scanned the aisles, checking to see if his kid was nearby.

Breaking off eye contact with his reflection in the mirror, Lincoln ran some water. Conservation regulations be damned, it took a while to get good and cold. And Lorraine always appreciated a nice glass of cold water.

Really, did life come down to more? A glass of water for the woman you love. A tub of popcorn for your kid. Was it the stronger man who ordered everyone around and in the process pleased not even himself, or the man who satisfied those around him and in the process was satisfied? The benevolent patriarch enjoys nothing so much as being able to step into responsibility and shoulder the load, making the big decisions, providing for all. Lincoln was competent and then some at his job, he didn't mind all the planning, detail work, or late nights. At the same time, no matter how hard he worked or how well a project came off, he always had a sense, basically, of how useless his job was: he did not make anything, after all, did not really provide any kind of service, but spent truly head-pounding quantities of time trying to convince corporations that having their conventions at the Kubla Khan would make for a significantly better experience than having it across the street. Any of a million people might have been able to do his job, he knew this. But the way Lincoln figured it, he might as well be the one who made use of that salary designation, the one who took care of his family in style. Thus he schmoozed the people who needed schmoozing, landed most of the new accounts that mattered, kept his customers satisfied and coming back for more. He took pride in a job well done and, a couple of times a year, he packed up his family, set their home's security system, and took off to Vail on a ski package. He headed to the Napa Valley for a weekend of wine tasting and hiking, to Puerto Vallarta and Squaw Valley, Bermuda, and Cabo. On summer mornings when Newell was just a toddler, he and Lorraine used to take him out to Lake Mead—it was about an hour-and-a-half drive and he'd keep the child entertained by pretending one of his hands was a puppet. In a high-pitched voice, Lincoln would blurt out ridiculous insults and nonsensical sentences, driving along and tickling and poking and jabbing Newell, bringing light to his kid's eyes, filling the pickup with titters, the boy laughing so hard he cramped up, *stop, Daddy, or I'm a pee.*

What could a man do but try? Try and then try harder, that was what.

Yet for all the secret time he spent trying to learn how to play the boy's video games, for all the pride Lincoln took in his son's quick wit, there were evenings when Lincoln's migraines were pounding and his stomach was upset, and about the last thing he needed was to step inside his house and hear the little bastard's sass. Even worse was when the kid pretended to be interested in his ol' man's life—buttering Lincoln up and wanting to hear the birth story again, all to mooch a few more bucks. There were evenings when the single thing on this planet that Lincoln least wanted was to step inside his house and have his wife lecture him about everything that was wrong with his kid (like he was an idiot, like he couldn't see for his own damn self). Evenings he would have given her a million dollars if she would *just let him eat in silence, okay?* When, short of taking a dinner knife and cutting out each of their rotting hearts, about the only thing he could do was get up, stand right up from the dinner table, and walk out of the dining room he had gone into debt for, wordlessly and without comment heading through the house he was still paying for, and into the clandestine tomb of his garage with all its dusty cartons and boxes of obsolete crap that he'd bought his family over the years. There were evenings when Lincoln would get inside his car and sink deflated into the driver's seat of artificial leather, and a bottle of peach schnapps would be withdrawn from the glove compartment, and Lincoln would not for one second longer be able to ignore the beast his child was turning into, and for one minute longer he would not be able to deny the shrew that his wife had become, and there would be nothing in his power that could be done to delay the inexorable destruction of his homestead, the all-but-destined dissolution of his family, and Lincoln would feel deathly afraid because the awful and cold and most assured truth was that he *welcomed* this dissolution, he *wanted* the destruction.

You bet your ass there were evenings. Evenings the clock struck six and the end of another workday had fallen upon him and he was feeling fairly on top of the world, and sure as hell he did not want to go home and have that feeling demolished. Evenings when his boss was riding him and deadlines were looming and he was too plumb worn out to deal with any more of his wife's mind games, too beaten down to give a shit about the difference between a woman who pouts and frets so that she can be consoled and one who is permanently pissed off. And so, during this past spring, sure, there had been one or two evenings when Lincoln had joined his fellow middle-management types, headed to this little dive on Industrial, and watched live lesbian sex shows. During this past spring and summer, admittedly, more than a few sunsets had been under way when Lincoln had taken a detour on his way home, heading past Vixxen's, Little Darlings, the Can Can Room, and the Crazy Horse Too.

Cars never parked in front of the small and windowless storefront, but drove around to the side. Here, a cinder block wall blocked any view from the street, and no passersby, by chance or through purposeful snooping, could identify someone's make, model, or license plate. The store's entrance was covered with black glass; a small, red lettered sign announced that all entrants had to be eighteen years of age. Inside, the store was brightly lit, with top-forty bubblegum pop piped in like Muzak, and aisles stocked with glowing cardboard boxes. In these and many other ways, the shop had a normalcy and matter-of-fact surface resemblance to thousands of stores and franchises. This always rattled Lincoln, for no small part of pornography's appeal to him was its naughty thrill, its illicit and libidinous nature, the sense that you were headed somewhere you knew better than to go. Lincoln kind of wanted his porn shop to be sleazy, a red-light-district hole in the wall, with female groans carrying from everywhere, and the smell of chemical disinfectant all but permeating the dinge.

Slowly, he'd muddle his way into the maze of aisles, wandering beneath the makeshift cardboard signs: *General. Amatoors. B&D. fetish. Man n Men. Trannies. SheMales.* Like every other guy in there, he kept his head low, avoided eye contact, and picked up various cardboard boxes, studying each brightly colored, weathered, well-handled cover, examining their nubile, scantily clad women. Sometimes he dispensed with browsing, and headed straight toward the back of the store, the rows of stalls in the style of Old West saloons. An unshaven Arab-looking guy was usually there, listlessly sloshing his mop into a half-filled bucket. Lincoln never said anything to him, but found an unoccupied booth and pushed through the two small swinging doors. He knew better than to sit on the small chair inside the stall, touch anything that did not need touching. There was a slot for coins, and an illuminated bill feeder had been embedded in the wall. Above that were two glowing yellow buttons. As soon as Lincoln put his money in the machine, the stall went dark and the television screen was activated. Lincoln used the buttons to flip through the channels, whirring amid the ungodly number of offerings, checking out what kind of women were getting it in which positions—by how many men; how many women; with what kinds of objects.

———

From a lower shelf, he grabbed the jelly glass that he normally rinsed with after brushing, and filled it with cool, refreshing water. If he saw the dripping faucet, he ignored it. Same for the black ants that marched behind Lorraine's bottles of moisturizer. His lower lumbar region was stiff, albeit in the best possible way. The stiffness was familiar to him, reassuring, an old neighborhood friend whose life had taken a different direction, but whom he still met every once in a while at a bar. So much of Lincoln's energy these days was spent at work and being a parent, it was spent trying to figure out how to maintain this lifestyle and at the same time plan for the boy's future. The stiffness reconnected him to company parties and the collective eyes of a room following Lorraine; to Lincoln next to her, smiling steadily at everyone and sneaking his hand up the back of her skirt. It connected Lincoln to Lorraine's hand *down there* during sex, to the small purple vibrator he knew she kept in her panty drawer, the handcuffs they'd once kept on the nightstand.

Between men and women there is a point where words become useless, where the physical, bestial sides of the sexes undo every knot that language can tie. A point where sex is its own language. Their most serious problems had always been solved this way, through these rhythmic dialogues.

He switched off the bathroom light and carried the jelly glass toward the bedroom. The bathroom tile was cool underfoot, and Lincoln moved down the short corridor, unencumbered testicles swinging easily between his creaking legs, confidence surging through his body. For all his fears, Lincoln felt a rightness with the world. They'd straighten everything out. Like any venture, marriages were elbow grease and overtime. At the end of the night, he had the prettiest wife in the great Silver State and the luckiest child. The funnest job and the dreamiest home. He was the goddamn camel who'd made it through the eye of that needle.

He called his wife's name. Heard the muted beeping of her activating her phone. The second time tonight she'd done this.

Moving stiffly, he reentered the bedroom.

She remained silent, sitting up in bed, luminously bare, only her raised knee shifting underneath the covers. Her head was cocked, the phone to her ear. The sweep of her bangs hid any expression, her face a polished surface of disciplined concentration. Lincoln knew her well enough to see she was trying to remain in control. He sensed her rising concern, her cold intellectual fury. He could hear the voices coming from the phone, the violent shouting. For the rest of his days, he would remember Lorraine's expression. The moment when life as he knew it ended.

Along the top of the electric canyon, the lid of sky was tinted the color of sputum. Neon drenched the girl with the shaved head and she soaked in its downpour, the neon pulsing through her like radiation, as infectious as hope or, maybe, love. She whooped and laughed, ran and then skipped, her gait unsteady, her vision blurry with dope and drink and fear and the lingering flavor of Ponyboy's kisses. In his hardened grip her fingers were brittle yet unbreakable, and with a tight squeeze he pulled her through the hot still air, and she suspended her hesitancies and followed along, peripherally aware of the half-forms running alongside, their blurred shapes and deep breaths, their screamed curses and athletic weavings. One self-styled rude boy slammed his arm against a mobile home, then limped away as if hit. Another rolled commando-style across the hood of a midsize station wagon. On the spur of the moment, the girl slapped the side mirror of a stretch limousine. From behind tinted windows, its horn bleated. She howled back "MOTHERFUCKERS." Ponyboy's grip remained firm, unaffected.

Across eight lanes, on the opposite side of the superhighway, their sprint ended where the pedestrian stream thinned. Pierced hooligans reclined against the bottom of a casino wall—some pouring condiment packages down their throats, others using the opened baggies of mustard and ketchup to make finger paint portraits on the sidewalk. A group of thugs was happily screaming obscenities into a cellular phone. Two stragglers were watching, wrenching the last scraps of humor from some earlier incident:

"Waah, who snaked my cell?"

"Waah, I'm calling the cops."

Ponyboy let go of her hand and began stepping through a circle of ghouls, accepting without notice their greetings and slaps on the back. The girl was momentarily apprehensive, and watched him approach a lanky, deeply sunburned teenager—standing at a mailbox, with his pants

around his ankles, and his hands on his crotch. In profile, half of a battery protruded out of the side of his nostril.

Ponyboy came from the rear, wrapped his biceps around his friend's
waist and lifted, an arcing golden stream spraying the crowd of passersby.

"WHAT UP, COCKSUCKER?"

The girl waited, sure Ponyboy was going to return, introduce her.
When this did not happen, she drifted, wandering absently, without direction. Green Wool James was nowhere to be found. Piggy neither—
probably home by now, she figured. Certain boys resembled various
punks she was used to, only where her friends took time to make themselves look properly disheveled, these punks *were* disheveled, their edges
harder, their seams more frayed. As the girl approached the outskirts of a
second small, disorganized circle, she felt predatory stares on her backside. A game of My Past Sucked the Worst was erupting, with tempers
flaring over the hierarchy of incest abuses, whether you got more points
for parents or grandparents, activity or grotesqueness.

"And just how do you top being jackhammered up the ass by your
dad?"

"Try having grampa's eighty-year nuts slamming against your chin,
BITCH."

"Bullshit."

"Bull*sheeyit.*"

She backpedaled, trying to get away from their vulgarity. But her legs
were suddenly rubbery, her coordination less than it should be. Her eyes
searched for some hint of Ponyboy. Battery-nose. Anyone. She settled for
a frail and enormously pregnant chick. Reclining against the bottom of
the casino wall, the pregnant chick was filthy as a mechanic's rag and just
as used, her skin bruised with dirt and grime. She was morose, and stared
blankly at this feral wolf dog next to her. The dog was ignoring the pregnant chick and scratching its ear with a hind leg, and the pregnant girl
watched for a little while, then scanned the chaos of nearby ragamuffins.
Now she chugged from a clear plastic bottle, swallowing three, four gulps,
before she gagged and then doubled over, spilling thick green liquid from
her mouth, down her chin and neck. The pregnant girl dropped her head
down between her legs, and took deep, sucking breaths, and when she

came back up, her eyes were glassy and dim, her face adrift, unfocused. She coughed up a globule, and a thin line of phlegm hung from her cracked lips, and for an instant she seemed naked in her confusion, embarrassed at her nakedness.

"You okay?" asked the girl with the shaved head.

Glassy eyes focused. The pregnant girl was impassive, suspicious. But she nodded, somewhat. She wiped her bare wrist over the bottle's lip, nudged the container forward. "Vicks?"

"Ummm . . ."

A flicker of a grin. "It's mentholated."

"Should you be doing that?"

"It's way better than drinking from any of those assholes' stash." A pointed glance. "They say they don't backwash—*yeahright*!"

"Whatever you say, *Danger-Prone Daphney*!"

The pregnant girl whirled toward the remark, "Eat me when I'm bloody, Lestat!"

"Whatever you say, *Double-Penetration Daphney*."

Somewhere in the elevated distance a digital scoreboard flashed information about a twenty-four-hour buffet. Somewhere else a man-made volcano erupted. The girl with the shaved head self-consciously applied a circle of pressure to the soft area behind the mongrel's ear.

"He's gorgeous," she said.

Then, once Daphney's attention had returned, "You sure about swigging?"

The broken smile hardened, Daphney's pie eyes going narrow.

"No disrespect or nothing," said the girl. "I just meant, with—in . . . you know, your condition and all—"

"You one of them Angels of the Streets? Damn. I sure liked you guys better when all you did was stop by with condoms and tampons. This planned pregnancy *bull*shit, it's getting to be a drag." Daphney took a swig, recoiled at the taste. "The last one said she wouldn't turn me in to social services. *Yeah, right . . . cunt.*"

Her chin raised defiantly. "Don't front on me. I been streeting so long I got my own milk carton."

The girl with the shaved head caught herself staring at Daphney's stomach, then blushed. Through the soles of her twelve-holes, it felt as if she were standing on lit matches. As she struggled to lower herself onto the sidewalk, her limbs seemed heavy and used and listless, and she noticed the corner of a denim knapsack from behind the breadth of Daphney's back. The girl's gaze was unsteady, and a bit blurred, but she was aware of the assorted leers, and she primly tucked her legs underneath her tush. She emptied her pockets, donating her remaining eight dollars into the community change pool. She scratched the bridge of the dog's nose, began to ask its name, and then, midway, stopped.

"Can I see your carton?"

Daphney spent a moment soaking in the request. Another examining the newcomer who had made it. "I used to have like nine," she answered, her voice suddenly unguarded and girlish. "It was gonna be cool as fuck, 'cause I'd be giving my baby milk from the cartons with my own face. Get it? How cool is that? Cool *as fuck,* right?"

Swollen and grime-laden hands bloomed, each steel-covered finger turning alive, adding interpretive pantomimes to the performance, becoming as agitated as Daphney's voice: "What happened was, we didn't have no place to put the milk and it went bad and so they made me throw it out. But then I kept some of the cartons, you know, stored pens and lighters and birthie stuff in some. The others I just folded up. But then, I was supposed to go base with these fuckwads right? . . . That's a total different story. Anyways, my shit got jacked."

Disco ball refractions formed a kaleidoscope across Daphney's profile, imbuing her face with a pattern of small, almost translucent snowflakes. To the girl with the shaved head she appeared beautiful and full of pain and beautiful for all her pain. The girl wanted to cover her and protect her. For an instant, she thought of taking her back home.

"I went to the stores," Daphney said, "but the cartons had all different kids."

Her voice then became quiet, cracking as she whispered, "I couldn't find me no more."

A lopsided plastic fun cup emerged from her lap. Shaking away the memory, Daphney reached for passing tourists. "Please spare some change for some low-grade ketamine."

"Punk's way over," came as one reply.

Then: "You cannot self-destruct without being complicit."

And, *"Get a fucking job."*

Daphney had been waiting for another girl for so long, and now here one was so, *Come on, let's go, yeah, no, no time for exposition, just help me up.* And Lestat saw this and went *Oooh.* And a bunch of other dickwads saw and went *Aaaawww.* And Lestat yelled *Ooh* again, and then the dickwads did the same thing, *Ahh.* Faster and faster they kept at it, *Ooh ah ooh ah,* and despite their grunts, feeling the slightest bit embold-ened, flickering with power and pride, bidding adieu with a good and proper Italian salute, Daphney and the girl with the shaved head stum-bled and leaned on each other and helped each other upright, which the mongrel dog noticed. Shedding its lackadaisical façade, the dog turned eager, bouncing alongside them, grin wide, tongue lapping. And while the dickwads called out *Where ya going ladies?* and *Munch that carpet* and *Can I watch? Come on, let me watch,* the makeshift trio turned a short corner, with Daphney's waddle strained, ginger, her every movement hampered by the backpack she insisted on lugging—a tattered and overstuffed sack, far too large and heavy for Daphney, es-pecially in her condition. They started down the alleyway and Daphney leaned into the girl with the shaved head, using the girl's body as a crutch, and insisted, with perturbed affection, *I'm fine, I got it, just slow up, please.*

The girl wondered what was she getting herself into. She had an in-stinct to confide in Daphney about not having her period for the past four months. Daphney should know about that, it seemed to the girl. She intuited there were questions she should have been asking, things she should have been saying out loud. Like about the baby's due date? And the dad? And would Daphney stay on the street when the baby was born? One by one the interrogatives trickled, a Chinese water torture through the girl's brain. She wanted to ask Daphney what sex felt like, wanted to know if it hurt. Did the baby have anything to do with the Danger-Prone Daphney nickname? Did Daphney have any idea of how they abused the cows to get the milk for those cartons? How was the girl going to get back to Ponyboy? If only she could feel her tongue.

Lordy loo, she was *soooo* drunk.

Doubling as the sides of the two casinos, the alley walls ran high and long, and were covered by shadows of varying heights and densities. All sorts of bizarre lights and colors split the shadows and bisected one another, and to the girl with the shaved head it felt a little bit like traveling down some sort of psychedelic tunnel, like she was traveling deeper into the unknown, this bizarre adventure she was on, to where, who only knew. She almost buckled under Daphney's weight, tripped over Daphney's inside leg, then was steadied by her new friend, and the pair continued, giggling and stumbling along. The girl's arm ran around Daphney's lower back and she held Daphney by the side of her stomach, and it was kind of creeping the girl out, what was in there. At the same time, it was kind of lovely, too. Only this was not the time for loveliness, no, loveliness was being preempted, canceled by deep and alarmed barking—the mongrel going berserk, chasing some unseen rat or roach. Daphney cursed the dog and yanked on the knotted jump rope she used for its leash, and now the mutt picked up some other scent, tracked some other marginal fiend.

Good shit if you get there at the right time, Daphney said, nodding toward a series of dumpsters the girl would not have otherwise noticed. *By now, though, they've been scavenged like eight zillion times.* The real place to go for leftovers was behind the groceries and restaurants, said Daphney, long as you didn't mind fighting with the bums. She leaned further onto the girl with the shaved head, relied on her more and more with every step, pawing, clawing, her backpack swinging down and banging the girl's knee. Daphney was oblivious to this, however, staggering atop a wave of cough syrup and who knew what, drifting toward then teetering on the brink of consciousness. *Too clean,* she called the girl with the shaved head, *a pavement virgin, looks like to me.* The girl was doing Daphney a big one here so Daphney was gonna help her out, let her know the way it was, out on the street, on the cold concrete, *I got your back, you got mine.*

Tit for tit, Daphney wasn't going to lie. Any chiquita getting involved with this shit had to think long and hard. It wasn't easy. Like, not only were you flying under the radar with the cops, but you're kind of alone and unprotected, too. You know, it's a man's place, the streets, and guys are always hounding. You're kinda this blank sheet to them, right? It's like they project all their shit on you, telling you their secrets. One minute you're their mother, the next you're their girlfriend, and really all they want to do is get in your pants or turn you out, you know, you're just a fucking big target. So always you have to *watch your ass.*

Night began to open, spreading beyond the center of the alleyway, a series of small circular lights coming into view, distant flashing red and blue shapes, streetlights and traffic signals, signs advertising construction rig rentals and pool decking. Soreness spread through the girl's shoulders and upper back, and alcohol and dope oozed from her every pore, and she was momentarily unable to carry Daphney's weight, she had to regroup, adjusting her body and grip. The girl almost tripped, then regained her balance, and continued onward, with Daphney leaning on her a little more, confiding in the girl with the shaved head as if she were a big sister explaining the ways of the world to her dearest younger. Really, it wasn't so bad, Daphney said. At night, all kinds of stuff was going down, what with the parties and the gigs out in the desert and all that, so really you just had to worry about getting out of the sun in the day. Like, you could cop change from inside the casino wading pools, spare a few bucks from people on the street. And the public library system had really great air-conditioning, although on Flamingo this one librarian was always looking to call juvie. And oh, there was this faggot at Underground Records who let you sleep in the storage room, long as you didn't filch the inventory. And if things got slow, needle jockeys let you hang at that twenty-four-hour piercing and tatt place.

It was a tour de force, a mixture of guerilla theater and performance art, with sprinklings of pheromonal territorialism thrown in for good measure, Daphney's every gesture simultaneously kind, combative, self-important, and self-congratulatory, her every word delivered as if she were some telemarketer needing to fill an employment quota on the last day of the month.

She told the girl she did not want word to get out, did not want it becoming trendy and what have you, but she was sort of surprised that more streeters did not end up here. *"Really,"* she said, *"when you look at it, Vegas is a good place to run to."*

A frost of solitary white light came weakly from behind a grille-covered pay window. Daphney made sure they stayed out of it, away from any potential sightings, and the small group moved in a wide arc around the side of the service station. The mongrel dog stopped every five yards to mark its territory. Wasn't cute anymore. How much piss could a dog hold, anyway?

Behind the garage, the door to a bathroom hung from thick steel hinges. A row of locks had been installed down the side, but some of the bolts had been pried from their stations. The remaining chambers were jammed with gum and clumps of once-wet toilet paper, now dried into a cementlike surface. Daphney easily pushed the door open and a bang resonated from where it hit the inside wall. Daphney took the backpack and staggered resolutely inside, disappearing into a blackness not quite the size of a prison cell, her steps audible on tile.

"Leave the door open, okay," Daphney said. "Fuck, where's that switch? I can't see shit."

The girl squinted but could not make out much, either, maybe part of a toilet; still, it was something—the night air beginning to spread, puncturing the vacuum with lesser shades of darkness.

Now the mongrel dog let out a curious whine. Concerned about its master's disappearence, it shifted its weight from one front leg to the other. It waited a few counts and then gave in, lowering its head and, with tentative, dutiful steps, following Daphney inside. The girl with the shaved head understood exactly how the dog felt. She wasn't eager to go in there, either. At the same time, the girl understood that she was a part of this, whatever this might be, and despite her better instincts, she edged forward, inside the darkness. She felt around on the wall for a few moments, the plaster warm to the touch. Then a box of sorts. A panel. Flicking the switch sent light from overhead in thick streams to reveal an empty bathroom, walls of industrial white, glowing layers of paint that, in places, still did not hide all of the graffiti beneath.

But while the girl's side of the room was well lit, the far side of the bathroom was another story—the long overhead bulb flickering for one count, then going dim for three. Amid the gloom, Daphney had reached the toilet, and was undertaking the lengthy procedure of lowering herself onto its rim. "Fuck me," she called out, laughing. "There's no seat." She gave another laugh, as if entertained by the predicament. "We'll just have to manage."

She had been waiting for this a long time, Daphney said. You don't even know.

Daphney had her knapsack between her legs and started foraging through it. The girl took a tentative step toward her, and had the tart aroma of cleaning chemicals irritate her nostrils. Reflexively, she fingered the fringe of her summer vest.

"My stepmonster had been a total bitch to me since *way* back in the day," Daphney continued, "even before I got thrown out."

From inside the backpack, Daphney pulled a can opener, then what might have been a deformed Happy Meal box, which she spent a moment examining, then put aside, reaching back inside, emerging with some sort of half-rolled tube, possibly toothpaste, who the hell knew.

"It's why they tossed me, really—I mean, things were bad enough already with my step, from when I borrowed her Mercedes and went to a rave. Anyways, with the whole pregnancy and whatnot, there was big-time tension, you know? Dad was totally flipping and pissed and bitch-cakes, he didn't want no grandkid, especially no half spook—Wait, here we go, that's right. . . . Come to mama—"

A flicking sound, a small cocoon of illumination. Inside the dimness of the far end of the room, the lighter's flame cast light upon Daphney's curled torso, as well as the knapsack balanced between her legs. A pink nightgown dangled from the sack's opening, its neckline of embroidered roses lying in a thin puddle from the last time the floor had been mopped.

"My stepmonster had scheduled the abortion with her private doctor, and everyone was trying to pretend things were normal, one big happy family and all that. We had these sit-down dinners every night, completely lame, you know, where you're supposed to be all Beaver Cleaver?"

Yellow light spun off the cover of a paperback guide to single parenting, which Daphney examined for a moment, before jamming it back in-side some compartment. A dog-grooming comb bounced politely onto the tile. With some effort, and then a relieved "Aaaah-*haaaah*," Daphney dislodged a smallish heart-shaped candy box.

"So I'd just gotten pierced, like a day before, right? And I wasn't really all that into wearing panties just then, right? Well, everyone's finished with the salad, but the pot roast isn't quite finished yet, you know how it goes, right? Blah blah, chit chat. And right when no one has no more to say, that's when I felt this little ball, you know? It sort of like clinked off my leg and like then, you know, *rolled*."

Daphney worked to undo the valentine bow. "You could hear it *ping* on the kitchen tile and like, *bounce*?" She opened the box and, without pause, continued her search. "Don'cha know my stepmonster had to go and pick it up.

"I tried to tell her it was the ball clasp for my earring—but she saw I wasn't wearing none."

The girl with the shaved head made a sound bordering on intelligible. She felt dizzy, needed a wall to lean against.

"That was the first one," Daphney added, proudly waving a black-ened diner spoon. "Base of my clit. Right where the nub splits."

"*No—*"

"I gots more now."

"*you—*"

"All labs. Majoras and minoris."

"*—don't.*"

"They do it for you at the Tatt Rack. When nobody's around and there's nothing else goin' on."

How to respond? What can you possibly say: *You must have a really strong vulva?*

"Did it hurt?" the girl came up with.

"Can you, like, ask more obvious questions?"

"*Did it?*"

For the first time since they'd entered the bathroom, Daphney's atten-tion moved away from her search, up toward the girl. She thought for a moment, and when she spoke this time, her voice turned serious. "When

I first hit here, I used to have to always defend myself about my background. Like, *because my parents have dough, I don't have problems?* Now I been out for like six months and all their money aint doin' jack for me, and whether I want it or not, it looks like I'm a have my baby on the street. Even Lestat and the others are like, 'Oh, Daphney, that's so hardcore, how can you?'"

She paused and sat forward, her forearms resting on her thighs. "Every day I sit on the street and feel my baby grow inside of me and I ask for change from people who pass by and pretend not to see me and, you know, sometimes, it makes me feel like I'm not there. Like, I kinda forget I'm alive?"

Daphney wiped her nose on her wrist. Spent a moment listening to the dog, its paws scratching against pipe fixtures.

"I mean, I know I'm alive, because feeling like that, feeling all shitty and numb and wanting to die, that's what life is, you know? *Feeling.* So I try to ask for change all nice, be polite and all to these shitkickers who totally don't want to look, they don't want to see some fucked-up pregnant chick in the middle of their vacation. They don't want to feel alive like that, right? And me, sometimes, I just want them to see me so bad, I could just fucking die; I mean, it's like *I want them to see me dying. That way, they'll know I'm alive.*"

Brushing away tears that had not yet formed, she took a deep breath. "The pain's part of it. If you're not into pain, then don't do it."

Daphney sniffled, pulling snot back into her nose. Somehow the cough syrup bottle had reappeared in her hand. She took a long swig, grimaced. "Okay. Time to jam."

Drawing from the crumpled valentine in her lap, she placed some sort of metal into the girl's hand—some kind of tool; compact, heavy. "You're gonna have to get in close," Daphney said, squirming in place, wiggling her bottom. She yanked her gym shorts down to her ankles, pushed aside the knapsack, spread her legs.

"See my body was just starting to show back then. I guess with the trimesters my lips must have become wider, something, because it's come totally unclasped."

"Just take it out then."

"I CAN'T. All the hole needs is an hour and it closes. NO WAY I give up the stud after everything that's happened. *Come on.* We *have* to get the ball back into the clasp."

Daphney paused, giggled self-consciously. "Don't be such a pussy." Her legs opened, wide and inviting. "Lestat's been begging me to let him do this. You don't even know.

"Hey," she added, almost as an afterthought, "you know how to use pliers, right?"

Not far away the door creaked on its hinges. Cars passed with airy swooshing sounds. As the girl knelt, her knee settled onto tile that was hard and smooth and uncomfortable. Overhead the lights hummed to life now, brightening the scene in front of her, but just as quickly as the moment came, and her eyes began adjusting, the bulb went dim. The girl decided to wait for her next opportunity, transferred the pliers from her weak to her strong hand, and made an uncertain, preliminary attempt at working their jaws. If she needed more light, Daphney offered her the Bic, and though the offer was made as a joke, the concern underlying it was undeniable.

The girl weakly asked Daphney to hold the lighter a little lower, please, yeah, that should do it.

She edged forward, grimacing, sober now, too sober for her own good, she did not want to be here and she did not know what she was doing and she did not know how to get out of this, and these thoughts were shattered by new sounds—to her immediate left, the mongrel dog, sniffing her face. Now the girl felt a wet brush down the side of her cheek, the dog was licking the girl with the shaved head, dabbing at her face, slobbery and affectionate strokes—an event that Daphney found *just perfect;* Daphney atop the toilet like an upended turtle, her legs spread in invitation, her pregnant belly hanging down on top of the girl's forehead; Daphney giggling in spite of herself, pulling on the dog's jump rope, the dog pulling right back, going for the girl's eyes.

The lighter's flame caromed. Daphney lurched on her throne, calling out, *"Careful now."*

Between the meat of her thighs the studs were gleaming jewels, a misshapen five-petaled flower, and as the girl with the shaved head moved in, an unfresh aroma was suddenly pungent. The girl gagged, then gave a nervous giggle, then, despite herself, continued, peeling apart the vagina's lips, feeling the steel bloom delicate on her fingertips, smooth, its appearance fascinating, alluring.

Daphney exhaled a gasp; her body stiffened. The girl felt an urge to kiss her crown jewel, to take Daphney's clitoral bolt into her mouth, suck and roll it around on her tongue.

As quickly as this instinct passed, the girl was struck by the desire to reach inside Daphney, dig her hand, her whole forearm in there, to reach inside until she got to Daphney's unborn child. She wondered if crushing the child's skull right here and now might be the best thing. Rip that little tadpole baby from Daphney's stomach. Leave that embryo floating in the toilet, but at least finished, at least that.

Withdrawing from between Daphney's legs, she sucked for air, as deep a breath as had ever been taken.

"I need the cough syrup."

Daphney laughed and seemed relieved herself. "Totally." Reaching down the side of the toilet, she found the backpack and fumbled about. "Oh," she said. "Snap. I know what we can do."

There was more rummaging, the sounds of clatter. The Happy Meal box returned to the domain of the blue-yellow flame.

Daphney liberated the burnt spoon. A small clear vial.

"Wh . . . Wha—"

Incredulous, Daphney cut her off. "Let me get this straight. I'm letting you take pliers into my cooch—*and YOU can't trust ME?*"

A collective *oooh*. Bodies spilled off the widened sidewalk, ignored traffic signals, bypassed the elevated walkways whose construction had cost taxpayers many a pretty penny. Necks craned, cameras flashed; in front of the pirate-themed hotel, the show was under way: a pair of larger-than-life-size nineteenth-century barges engaging each other: hired acrobats swinging from the airy sails. White smoke billowed, cannonballs flew.

The windshield of the FBImobile was soaked with electricity. Feedback reverberated through a crappy door speaker (the other had blown out three songs ago). In Kenny's eardrums, the speed metal and industrial noise of college radio station KUNV sounded like a whole lot of static and mess. He nodded dully along to the distortions. His fingers clung limply to the bottom rung of the steering wheel.

To his right, the boy remained slumped in the shotgun seat, eyes shut, his head resting on both the window and the bucket seat. All the running and screaming and excitement with the cell phone must have tuckered him out. All the chaos Newell caused, wasn't it something how oblivious he looked? How at peace.

Beyond the child's dormant body, above and behind the lump of his Adam's apple, a mast toppled, landing in the created lagoon with a spectacular splash. Kenny took in the choreographed effect without much interest, and looked beyond it, down the length of the Strip, taking in as much of its pulsing scale and scope as he could at once. The spectacle was too large and bright, reaching above the limits of the windshield, farther into the distance than his eyes could follow, each inch flashing, blinking. But as he stared, singular facets *were* discernible, not quite catching his eye so much as they came into focus, providing Kenny with points to concentrate on: a mammoth, postmodern take on the Egyptian pyramids that was sleek and shiny as black onyx; the glittering Eiffel Tower and the recreated laser-bright arc that acted as its hotel entranceway.

Kenny reached forward and turned the stick thing where the volume knob once had been; and as he did, the meat of the boy's neck became apparent to him. Newell's jugular predominated, appearing unnaturally thick.

Rhythms from neighboring car stereos and taxi horns merged in with what was left of the distorted radio noise. Motorcycle engines gunned unrepentantly—because if James Dean were still alive, even at a hundred and nine, that's what he'd have been doing. Traffic wasn't moving at all. For a moment Kenny stared at the big rig that was cruising solely to draw attention to the movie poster airbrushed on its flank. He noticed the small group of Hispanics, exhausted and still wearing their hotel uniforms, who had gathered underneath a bus station's covered waiting area. Someone kept their horn pressed for an extended period, and this brought a spate of other horns. Kenny adjusted himself in his seat, moving his tailbone off a crushed soda cup. He'd spent a half hour cleaning the front seats, and felt the FBImobile was looking pretty good, but oh well, no one was perfect.

His breaths were soft and he looked to his right and watched the boy sleeping. For a time Kenny invested himself in Newell's peace. His eyes moved down the boy's body now; he looked at the plastic cup balanced in Newell's crotch.

Inside the FBImobile there was a palpable inevitability, the sense of a predetermined result reaching its conclusion.

The moment was torture, for with it Kenny not only stared, but caught himself staring, and still did not stop, but for the first time was consciously aware that he was lingering on the sight—the cup perfectly at rest between the boy's thighs. Kenny felt himself flushed and tingling and very much ashamed. It was all he could do to stay inside his own skin, all he could do to force his eyes upward.

Luminescent mythologies. Blinking in montage.

A lone building seemed to call out: a darkened shell, its exoskeleton lined with scaffolds and pulley systems. Kenny swallowed dryly. A word he could not read flashed from the high-definition marquee in front of the hull, and was followed by the promise of a grand Christmas opening. Messages seemed to extend through the translucent night, stretching and dancing across the FBImobile's windshield, melding there with the residue of so many brake lights, the effluvia so much hotel glow. And beneath this unrelenting glare Kenny felt very dark. And underneath so many towers he felt so very small, so fragile and uncertain and impossibly alive.

And maybe a time would arrive when he would look back on this particular moment with some semblance of clarity. Years down the line perhaps—when his difficulties were behind him, mostly, and he no longer tossed and turned in bed, repositioning himself so often that it was as if he were wrestling a ghost; when he was emerging from his shell, stepping into a more secure, though admittedly fragile, sense of manhood; when Kenny was by no means talkative, and still could slip back into his shadow self, the haunted young man, but for the most part was making progress, and even had let his guard down somewhat.

A time of relative peace. No more created fabrications to cover for his adolescence, no more apologies about where he grew up. Even a stable, loving relationship. *Kenneth,* as friends and colleagues would refer to him, would have taken up the hobby of gardening by this time, and would be fastidious about watering the plants he kept in terra-cotta pots on the apartment windowsill. He'd attend therapy sessions twice a week, paid for through the generous benefits package he received from a North Beach–based graphic arts and design firm. There, Kenneth specialized in computer animation and did not engage in much office banter, but was a steady, dependable worker, regarded by coworkers as just about the dearest soul you could ever know.

Maybe this is when he would be able to put it all into perspective.

Equally possible was a different take on Kenny's future. A stretch on the downside of his twenties—after he had cleaned the booze and reek from his clothes, molars, and whole person; after he had bottomed out and pulled himself back up, and had some two and a half years of folding chairs and stale coffee and the dead air of church basements under his belt; when one of the Jew's twin grandsons, despite reservations galore, had hired him back at the pawn shop. A time when all the relapses and recoveries and painful brick-by-brick reconstructed temples of self, they'd led to a true yogi, not a faker this time, but a guru with the most awesome and enlightening Shakti that Kenny had ever felt. At long last, Kenny would be able to accept—truly and utterly—that it was time to get beyond his past, really this time, to let go. *Freeing himself of the sins of his youth by forgiving his youthful self.*

Or perhaps it would stop being important. After the fifteenth funeral. Once he had been the caretaker of those friends who had been closest and dearest to him. Once he had cradled their muscular bodies through painful disintegrations, watched their gregarious minds go dim. Once all the drug cocktails and protease inhibitors and radical therapies had been countered and for some reason fifteen funerals was the limit, the fifteenth being just too many for a man to feel remorse about the teenager he had been all those lifetimes ago.

One more bead in a necklace of awful memories. One more shameful moment in a lifetime spent without affection. An invisible man pushing a mop through a gray building, unable to interact with people, radiating such bitterness that even when he tried to open up, you could not help but want to shy away.

Or maybe a woman would untie this necklace—she'd enter his life and there would be a moonlit stroll and Kenny would start to tell her about his teen years, and this great burden would be removed from his shoulders, because he'd never really told anybody any of this before.

"We were just fooling around," he would say. "You know how kids goof."

Just as possible is a morning when crevices were etched into his face and his hair was thinning. A four in the morning when he lay in bed with a young man he'd eyed at a dance club in rebuilt New Orleans—a sweet muscular thing to whom Kenny had assured his negative status, then sodomized without mercy, the fifth muscle boy he would have done this to during Mardi Gras season. It is possible that a regretful and tired Kenny would lie in bed and share a glass of water with this poor doomed young fool. It is possible Kenny would stare at soft blond curls and blue eyes that were too pure to be innocent. Kenny would answer the question, then listen to a wood-chipped, honeyed response, this idiot unable to believe that *anybody* grew up in Las Vegas, let alone anybody *gay.*

Perhaps to shut the trick up, or because he himself had fallen under the ceiling fan's lullaby, this Kenny would start talking, his words redoubling on themselves, catching and pained, with disclaimers and rejoinders, an unorganized stream. Free associating and trying to figure out what to say next, by turns ironic and mocking, yet still failing to cover his deeply ingrained shyness, his fundamental embarrassment. Although, really, what was he embarrassed about, the awakening of a young man's sexuality is a beautiful thing, when you stop and think about it.

Maybe, in the New Orleans hotel room, this graying incarnation of Kenny would become reflective, and would think back to his dad's trailer. Back to magazines spread all over the floor. He would laugh at himself, telling the trick that it wasn't until years later that he realized that a big part of what he'd been looking at in those pictures involved men. Wasn't until his mom had passed away, when Kenny'd gone home to go through everything, he'd had the epiphany: flipping through those old sketches, he'd discovered a significant minority of his old drawings focused on male anatomy. Kenny the Elder would shake his head at just how clueless he had been. And then he'd start to talk about this dude, hadn't thought of him in years, but he used to see him in the hallways at his old high school—it wasn't even a high school, really, but this dude and Kenny would see each other, and they'd had a flirtation, Kenny's teenage self had been too clueless to realize that's what it was, but now it was clear. Kenny would remember other clues he had not been able to see, had been too naïve to understand, and when he was done talking about them, he would return to that long-ago Saturday night, to the fishbowl of the Strip, his swirling confusion, the sense of terror that was unleashed inside of him.

In an altogether different future, a somber man stares out of his window, taking in the distant image of the Bay Bridge.

"So many things in life seem like a big deal," he says. "But then, when you look back, it's hard to imagine what the fuss was about. You're here, right? And things are how they are. So you maybe tell yourself that it didn't matter. You convince yourself. Or try to, anyway."

A misting chill, the slightest defensiveness entering his voice. "It's natural to have excuses. Especially when you know you messed up."

From behind, his partner would wrap his arms around Ken's waist, and Ken would remember just what it felt like pulling up to the Ewings' home.

He'd been exhausted by then. He and the bald girl had searched out in the desert for what must have been an hour. Flailing around in darkness. You weren't able to see five feet in front of your face, and so all you could do was just call out the boy's name. Kenny would remember shouting until his voice was hoarse. He would remember finding sand in his hair for days afterward. They'd driven up and down I-15 and they'd fought through all the crowds at the party, and it had all been in vain. He'd pulled into the driveway. He was trying to get ready for what had to come next. You know, how am I going to do this?

The lights were on in the front window and for a few seconds it was as if everything might be fine, like maybe the boy somehow had found his way back on his own. But Newell's parents wouldn't have come out of the house like that, this rush of worry and expectations.

His mother just this stunning woman, so beautiful that she could not go inside stores. She'd always been polite to him before. But now her eyes were wild. She grabbed his arm, dug her nails into his flesh.

It was the dawn of his life as a suspect. They made him take them, show them, driving him back out into the desert, trying to draw him out on the details along the way, which had just been awful, the father controlled behind the wheel, maybe even a little kind in the way he asked his questions, though each follow-up was more specific, asking for clarifications, making adjustments to previous inquiries where maybe, Kenny figured, he hadn't answered the right way. There was a lot of silence and tension, Kenny could feel Newell's mom was ready to go off on him at any moment, and while he tried to answer as best he could, be as helpful as possible, at the same time there was a limit.

The sun had been rising over the mountains and a pale yellow light had covered the brush and weeds and vast emptiness. The stage was still out there. A couple of teens who Kenny guessed the promoters hired were straggling about, red-eyed and bagging trash. Soon enough, investigators would be there as well, taking plaster casts of different footprints, finding the remnants of treads that corresponded to the size and make of the boy's Nikes. They'd discover one trail over by the side of the interstate, exactly where Kenny said they'd been. Another trail, deep in the desert, led to a third set, harder to track and not an exact match. That one had been disrupted by other footprints and smears and scufflings. But near a collection of tire treads where most of the cars had parked—half of one heel print would match up.

That set it off. Media outlets would pay different partygoers for photos and video footage from the gigs, with the photos appearing beneath large-point headlines, the footage accompanying a special weeklong report, repeated at five, six, and eleven: *Is your child attending illicit drug and sex bacchanals? Stay tuned for what every parent ought to know.*

As Kenny remembered it, the coverage effectively put the kibosh on the parties, giving local teens one less thing to do, until the promoters found a new location. Kenny would also remember Newell's parents driving him straight from the desert to a police station, the day extending, continuous, refusing to end. Newell's dad urged his wife to have a doughnut. Haggard, frail as a dry leaf, she refused even a cup of coffee. They were filling out paperwork when someone took Kenny aside and said they needed a statement. He was guided to a small dingy room and left there, underneath lights that were hot and bright. When the officer exited, he locked the door from the outside. Most of Kenny's afternoon was spent sweating, wondering if he was under arrest. Every once in a while an investigator checked in on him, said someone would be by soon. Nobody ever brought the water he asked for.

Even after the girl backed up his version of events, a surveillance car followed Kenny, parking down the street from his dad's trailer, his mom's place, or his aunt's. The cops called him in for follow-up interviews, went over his story untold times, even asked him to take a lie detector. If the bald chick's testimony hadn't corroborated his major points, he'd still be locked up. Thank goodness for that girl. The officer in charge had been forced to admit that a couple of lie detector inconsistencies, story gaps, and some unexplained questions, all together they added up to zero tangible evidence against Kenny, certainly nothing that could hold up to a prosecutor's scrutiny. The kid's parents hadn't been happy, but what could they do? Pretty much they'd been forced to call off the dogs.

A little bit more than five months afterward, Kenny's aunt said he had a visitor. Waiting at the front door: the woman who had first provided him with a real-life notion of feminine beauty.

She wore prewashed jeans and a formless purple blouse, and seemed so very small, fiddling with the sunglasses in her hand, closing and then reopening the frames. No makeup. Complexion pale, her eyes too large in a gaunt, haunted face. When Kenny appeared, her eyes went larger. Her lips pursed and for long moments she stared at him.

She stared at him, Ken recalled, and in her stare he felt the unfathomable depth of her loss—*You are the one who did this, the one who took my child.*

She needed to know.

"About that night," she said. "About Newell."

She said this and it was as if something broke inside her, as if she had no more room for anger, no more strength for rage. On the front steps of that crappy little starter home, she shuddered and conceded defeat in her fight against tears, and Kenny did not know what to say. All he could do was take her hand, bring her inside.

Every few months afterward she stopped by. Sometimes she took him to lunch. Other times she just drove by, slowing down her sedan, letting the car idle across the street.

Kenny would come to understand that the visits coincided, more or less, with new sightings—if he remembered correctly, there was one in Tacoma, another in a small Arizona town. A call traced to a pay phone on the corner of Heart Attack and Vine. Other times the boy used one of those prepaid calling cards, or called collect and just held the phone to his ear, listening to those he'd left behind.

Lorraine told him these things. She was the one who had urged him to apply to art school, the one who had helped him fill out the financial aid forms, even putting down the deposit that secured his seat in the fall class that first term.

And he had never been able to tell her everything.

Kenneth turning to his lover: How could he?

Somewhere else, a New Age Ken sat in the lotus position and cried for all of our inner children.

Projections are endless, as innumerable as towns that may be ventured to from any specific point on a map. And there would be other formative events, other people and places to shape his identity. But no matter what life held in store for Kenny, no matter which fate he'd end up occupying, which reality he'd inhabit when he remembered this event, no matter if his eventual reality was, in fact, none of the aforementioned, whether Kenny would choose to admit the facts of his childhood, whether he chose to embellish, or fabricate, or deny the circumstances of this Saturday night, this much was true: over and over, the man he would grow into would remember certain instances exactly the same way, in the same order.

He was never good with names, but he would remember the name.

And his face. Yes.

Just a kid. Like fourteen or something.

Kenny had started off by reaching for the fun cup. Then his hand had inched upward. Along the inside seam of the boy's thigh.

As if trying to find a comfortable position to sleep in, the child's body had curled away from the attention. He'd snapped out of his drowse, his eyes uncertain and sleepy. If he was surprised he did not seem to show it, not all that much. There was murmuring, his voice garbled.

And now he sat up.

"Dude. What're you doing?"

"What?"

"That."

Underneath folds of denim, the boy's dick becoming swollen; Ken remembered it jerking.

He remembered the car silent except for the sounds of the engine's vibrations. A thin smoke drifting from underneath the FBImobile's hood.

The boy staring at him, fear growing in his eyes. "So," he asked. "You're a butt pirate?

"If you're not a butt pirate," Newell said, "why don't you get your hand off?"

"Why don't you take it off?"

In future years, when they told this story the adult Kennys would remember another spasm of life from the boy.

They would recall increasing the pace. Pressing back on the boy. Saying: "If you're not a butt pirate, why don't you stop me?"

The adult Kennys would fixate on their next question: "Do you want me to stop?"

They would recount the silence of the next seconds and the palpable terror, the feeling that the heads of their Kenny penises were going to burst. And also, they would recall a sense of calm, this placid sensation that lay underneath all the obvious errata; this thing each had discovered about himself.

For Kenny it amounted to a feeling of liberation.

But the emergence of his sexuality, the initiation of his first sexual act with another real live person, by necessity, this would forever be linked with the boy's disappearance.

And there was no language to explain how this would affect him. His adult selves could not even begin to try.

And so the Kennys would leave this story now, they'd head back to their lives, their lovers, the rest of that distant evening becoming extraneous to their purposes.

But Newell sat up. He turned in the bucket seat. More accurately, he moved away from Kenny's hand.

The boy rolled down his side window, allowing summer inside the compartment, a flooding mess of heat and noise. On the sidewalk, not too far away, a disposable camera flashed.

Purposefully avoiding Kenny's eyes, Newell chucked a nickel into the night, his sleepiness now replaced by certainty, his befuddlement by will.

"Maybe you should take me home."

Chapter 5

WHERE DO THEY GET ALL THESE GIRLS?

12:30 A.M.ish

5.1

The shirt was ragged, faded to the gray of an oncoming thunderstorm. Its trademark lightning bolts no longer jutted proudly from the first and last letters of the band's name, but had flaked and faded into a couple of scratchy lines, and the insignia itself was a ghost, just a trace of an imprint across the chest. The shirt's collar and sleeves had been cut off with a rusty pocketknife, and ventilation gashes ran down the sides in a style common to musicians who sweat a lot while they performed. A mess, all in all, bearing little resemblance to the bootleg T that Ponyboy had purchased when he was sixteen and raging with the testosterone of a changing body; when, little brother in tow, he'd attended his first ever

Metallica concert. Metallica may have gone soft and corporate, and that old shirt may have been messed up to the nines and back; even so, if Ponyboy felt like hauling it to a vintage store or posting it on some on-line auction, it would have brought him fifty bucks, easy. Vintage stores and online auctions weren't Ponyboy's style, though. He didn't make a habit of thinking about that long-ago concert, nor the demise of a once-great band, especially not about his dearly departed little bro-bro—all the tubes and wires that Ponyboy never even got to see connected to the poor kid. Fuck that. Ponyboy's style was hauling ass, blazing through smoldering afternoons, pedaling like hell over blacktop that had steam rising in waves from it. On a mountain bike whose lock he'd snapped outside the comic place where all the dorks hung out, Ponyboy's style was to arrive in different low-rent industrial neighborhoods, deliver small brown packages at different adult video stores. His style was to pick up a payment strongbox for every package he delivered. Although that wasn't style, when you got down to it. That was orders. Jabba's orders.

The sun set late in the summer, so even at seven-thirty, it was like a hundred and eight out there and, usually, by the time Ponyboy made it onto Industrial, that old concert shirt would be soaked and sticking to him like a second skin; Ponyboy's biceps and triceps and pecs would be glistening, and he'd smell like the wet cunt of this skank he used to bang back in the Tenderloin. Ponyboy kept a plastic gallon jug strung through his backpack's shoulder strap, but he wasn't so great at stopping at gas stations, refilling the thing on the free water faucet, and usually, by the end of the afternoon, if any aqua was in that jug, it was all warm and nasty. By the time he'd enter the last store, Ponyboy'd need a break.

Yo Kunjib, he'd say, pounding fists with the towelhead behind the front counter, *how's it hanging?* Heading down the aisle of transsexual videos, starting toward the stalls, Ponyboy would ask, *Asaaf, my brother, why you always gotta be mopping that spooge?* A laugh, another fist pound, then it was time to chill, flip through the channels, maybe help Asaaf with his American ("repeat after me: *Live. Long. Prosper.*"). Asaaf knew Ponyboy had shoplifted a few handcuffs (his girlfriend used the fur-lined ones in her act). Asaaf also had turned the other way when Ponyboy had lifted a pack of them vibrating brass ball things. (Cheri's exact words:

"You like them so much, stick them up *your* ass.") Seeing how Asaaf was constantly on spooge mopping detail, Ponyboy had to believe the little camel fucker was secretly happy he ripped off the place. He and Asaaf shot the shit about the various boob jobs belonging to women on the videos; they talked about the state of the National League East. When Ponyboy got bored, he tromped to the register, checked out the mad scientist lab behind the front counter, the shelves of televisions hooked up to mad crazy videotape machines, the images speeding through the screens at triple time: chicks sucking pole; dudes daisy-chaining some little spade; whatever tapes and DVDs were being duplicated right then. Kunjib—he worked up front—also kept a miniature television behind the counter, away from the duplicating equipment, and sometimes he and Ponyboy would watch part of a ball game. Ponyboy had hung out enough to know that the spooge mopper habitually used the New York Mets as the linchpin of five-team parlay bets. He'd also discovered that Kunjib was infatuated with hip-hop groups made up of preadolescent white boys. Every red-blooded American worth his dick wanted to blast himself an immigrant right about then, and Ponyboy had figured out that Asaaf and Kunjib were more than thankful to have someone acknowledge their existence as something besides *the Enemy.* Yeah, Ponyboy had gotten his master's from the school of hard knocks. He recognized that despite all the suits and weirdos who came in here, those two diaperheads were touched and moved and damn near overjoyed to have some dirty-ass white boy—some punk with spiky hair and all kinds of tatts and loads of steel—to have *this* be the sumbitch that treated them like real live human beings. Yes sir ree, Ponyboy knew all about looking in from the outside, he totally understood that Asaaf and Kunjib were omnivorous consumers of American culture. Fuckin' ay he saw why those two lapped up his tales of homelessness and degradation, his tattoo origins and piercing anecdotes. They ate that shit up. Like high school virgins who didn't know they wanted their cherries popped.

He couldn't hang for too long, though. The adult bookstore may have been taking it easy on its utility bills, but it still had its share of air-conditioning. Which was a relief to Ponyboy, age twenty, but also a hassle. A/C was partly why most bike messengers wore two T-shirts: your ratty and beloved concert T absorbed all the body's sweat and perspiration, while your second, more regular shirt acted as a sort of force field, keeping the gusting chill of ten thousand BTUs off your skin. Ponyboy, though, sometimes he didn't wear the second T because he liked his shoulders to get tan when he biked. Sometimes he didn't wear it because pimped out Jedi knights with the kung fu grip did not get colds. Sometimes he did not wear a second shirt because he did not have any clean second shirts and sometimes because he did not have any second shirts, and because did he mention second shirts were utterly and completely gay? Sometimes Ponyboy plain fucking forgot and other times his girlfriend started on him, Cheri and her shit about him being *closed,* being *blocked,* Cheri taking every opportunity she could to spew about the connections to Ponyboy's former life being as buried as his Metallica shirt, hidden underneath a protective layer, Cheri starting her crap and Ponyboy not wanting to hear. *Shows what you know,* he'd answer, *I don't even wear a second shirt on top of the Metallica—so there.* To which Cheri'd say, *I was being figurative.* To which, Ponyboy always answered with his middle figurative. But back at the start of the summer—June or so, right when the temperatures were really kicking in—at seven forty-five on this particular evening, the only things that mattered had been getting the payment strongbox, getting his docket signed, and getting back on the road. A motherfucker couldn't afford to hang around a place so much that its air-conditioning cooled his muscles. If his muscles cooled, then his body stopped sweating and then, when he got back onto his ride, he might pull something. So Ponyboy was standing around the adult bookstore, ready to hit the bricks, and he was getting antsy, wanting to get that goddamn strongbox, and meanwhile, wouldn't you know, some suit's at the front counter, waiting for his filth. Fucking Kunjib's running his turbaned ass from the register to the storage closet, all caught up in checking the number on the video box cover, then looking for the stack of black videos with the corresponding digits.

So Ponyboy, he'd leaned in, reaching over the counter. Not to steal one of them promotional tote bags with the adult film starlets on the side. Just wanted to get his strongbox back was all, just wanted to hit the road. Ponyboy'd leaned in and yeah, he'd bumped shoulders with the guy in the suit. But *accidentally*, you know? Corporate dude, he didn't so much as look at Ponyboy. Not even an *excuse me*. Like he's too high and mighty to be in a dirty bookstore. What, like a motherfucker's got steel in his face, got some ink in his skin, he can't get any respect? Like if you own a fucking suit, you're too important to have manners? Or maybe the problem was that motherfucker'd had *too many* manners. Maybe the problem was, that prick had been *too* conciliatory. Maybe Ponyboy had been in need of a fix and was at an early stage of jonesing and still had some strength in his body. Maybe he just felt ornery. He felt like trouble. He'd taken the strongbox under his arm, told himself he'd have to plagiarize Kunjib's sorry name on the docket once more. He'd shouted *Peace out Kunjiey* and exited the side door. Ponyboy had secured the strongbox in the basket of his mountain bike and he'd stood in the store's shade, appreciating the last moments of the sunlight, embracing a few precious seconds of soft, hot wind on his face.

The wind blew and slight dust specks stuck to his chin and the valley's toxins and exhaust fumes had created one of the most beautiful sunsets man had ever witnessed, and Ponyboy'd felt like he did whenever he got one of his tattoos—one of his heavy-duty multifaceted jobbers, where the work was so intricate and detailed that just the outlining took somewhere along three hours, and filling in the colors had to be divvied up into individual sections, and each part of the tatt was like its own four-hour session. Yes indeedy, standing in the miraculous sunset of that June evening had been like a moment in the middle of the third hour of his fourth tatt session, a moment that always came when the Chink finished messing with his protective latex gloves, fiddled with the angle on the lamp for like the millionth time, and told Ponyboy to hold still, his L's sounding like R's—*hord stirr, hord stirr;* it was like the moment when the drill's electric whine was the equivalent to the feeling of a battery's copper ends against Ponyboy's tongue, and electricity lit up Ponyboy's skeletal structure as if it were a pinball machine on a multi-ball extravaganza, and the mingling odors of brimstone and sulfur and sweat and burning skin filled Ponyboy's nostrils, and the Chink like pulled away the needle and swabbed at Ponyboy's flesh, and that little cotton poof soaked up Ponyboy's blood and, as with the man who swears he still feels the presence of his amputated arm, Ponyboy *continued* feeling the small sharp jolts, thousands of pinpricks through pressure-pointed parts of his body that Ponyboy did not even know were connected, and once again the Chink fiddled with the lamp angle and once again he told Ponyboy to *hord stirr,* and every second of successfully hording stirr made Ponyboy want to leap, shout, bark, dance, and the Chink reapplied the needle and the pinball machine lit back up, triple f'in bonus jackpot points this time, and Ponyboy couldn't think about how much time was left or how many more sessions he needed to fill the tattoo, he was physically unable to look at the nearby countertop—at the tackle box filled with paint tubes, at the anatomically correct blow-up doll covered from head to toe with lewdly drawn images, at the small shelf of reference and art books; no, the only thing Ponyboy could do in a situation such as this would be to chew his bubble gum, get lost in the chewing, his attention centering not on the objects and world around him, but on something else—this faraway point, in the distance, on the horizon.

Outside that adult bookstore on that June night, the darkness was solidifying and some of the passing cars were turning on their headlights. Ponyboy flamed up a Marlboro. He toed at the pebbles beneath his combat boots, then checked his beeper. He took a long moment and meditated on that faraway point on the horizon. The prick in the suit exited out of the side door and Ponyboy rammed a knee through his crotch. Ponyboy followed through, thrusting his knee in an angled blow that had a chance at propelling that motherfucker's nose bone into his sorry excuse for a pea brain. *Yeah, motherfucker,* Ponyboy shouted. *Ain't so big now.* The motherfucker flopped onto his back and covered his nose with his hands and curled into a fetal ball and made gurgling sounds. Now it was a fast and easy move into that *tool's* back pocket. Maybe Ponyboy stomped the guy once more, *asswipe,* before he got onto his mountain bike and hightailed it back into the summer heat. With his heart still beating out a fret board guitar solo, Ponyboy pedaled directly to a flower store and charged a dozen long-stemmed white roses on the guy's AmEx. *Darling sweet baby Cheri,* he wrote on the little gift card thing. *I know we're going threw tuff timez but I ♡ U so much UR the best thing in my miserable fucking life.* Ponyboy scribbled a reminder on the palm of his hand, so that when he got to Cheri's place, he'd call this hacker, sell off them credit card numbers. He started to write something else, then figured the credit card one would remind him to fence the ID, so that did not need its own note. When deliveries were slow, it was not uncommon for Ponyboy to earn a few bucks as a day laborer at nonunion construction sites. He had an on and off gig that involved roaming the streets at night, duct-taping flyers for cut-rate moving services. Cheri also had rigged it so when the Slinky Fox was in a pinch, he could man the door. There were a bunch of other piddling errands. There was some other shit he was less proud of and didn't like thinking about. He pedaled onward, crouching low to reduce the wind resistance, churning his legs and cranking his pace another notch, the extra perspiration pouring into his old Metallica shirt.

By an airport terminal for privately owned planes, billboards alerted visitors to *NUDES ON ICE AT THE UNION PLAZA, HOT GIRLS: ONLY AT THE RIVIERA,* and the *THUNDER FROM DOWN UNDER MALE EROTIC REVIEW.* There were a few split-level motor inns, a couple of office complexes, buildings so generic you could look right at them without noting their existence. This meant they were perfect for wandering. You curled up beneath their stairwells, cracked open a can of tuna, unrolled the sheet of eggshell foam that served as your makeshift bed—although that could get risky too. Nobody wants to get their sleeping ass woken by some outraged business dude at nine in the morning. Straights like that always call the cops.

The middle complex was Ponyboy's destination, and he rode around its side, away from the roads and parking lots. Then he walked the bike down a long corridor with a bunch of different doors with company names on them, to the last door, a corner suite with no name on it, no suite number, no identifying marks. Yellowed blinds were down in the window and if someone didn't know what he was looking for, basically, the place was unfindable. Taking the ice pick from his boot, Ponyboy got ready to jimmy the window, climb inside. Then he remembered what

Jabba had told him and checked through the blinds. The back of a mammoth head was visible—a balding crown, a ponytail of long gray wires, the big bastard sitting in his leather swivel chair, a phone jammed between Jabba's skull and a ring of neck flab.

Life just got a lot harder for the self-anointed Jedi knight, smooch to the booch, it did. But Ponyboy mentally prepared himself. Then he nudged open the door with his mountain bike's front wheel, and guided the bike inside, into a dingy but large office, air stultifying and smelling of mold; barren walls the color of dental plaque. Immediately Ponyboy placed the strongbox and docket on the desk, right in front of Jabba. The big bastard hardly glanced up from his conversation, his face remaining as expressive as a manhole cover.

The rotations of a small desk fan kept blowing up the corners of the magazines and yellowed papers that sat within range of its oscillations. Ponyboy would have loved to raise the fan to his face, maybe air out his pits. He would have killed to grab a tall-boy from the miniature fridge, press the chilled aluminum against the back of his neck. Jabba grunted into the receiver, nodded at Ponyboy, his heavy lidded eyes radiating all the grace and warmth of a dock worker.

Ponyboy took his time in returning the gesture—even in front of Jabba the Hutt, Jedi knights knew to be cool. Beyond that, it was hard to figure what came next. Jabba could be on the phone for a while, but he also could hang up with a bang. He could chill or he could blow up like napalm. Ponyboy called him Jabba like the guy was all blubber, but even a cursory look showed a packed, huge mass, nothing any sane person wanted to fuck with. Meanwhile Ponyboy still had to straighten the desk and empty the trash. He had to separate the week's metered mail from the order catalogues. He had to weed out all the overdue bills, then make a special pile of the warrants and IRS notices. Ponyboy'd never seen anyone besides Jabba in here, and little about the place suggested anyone else ever came in.

"They're saying I WHAT?"

Jabba's voice was raspy with outrage, and Ponyboy knew better than to go near him when he was like this. So he ducked his head and started into the office. Footprints, cigarette butts, whiskey stains, and other unidentified mishaps had bludgeoned the shag's normal shade into puddle water. Different-colored videotapes—green, blue, red, yellow—were stacked at the same knee-high levels where Ponyboy'd finished stacking them last time. A few large cardboard boxes had been sliced open, with glossy magazine spreads unfolding onto the carpet, lying right where they'd been when Ponyboy'd last finished with them. Ponyboy cut a diagonal path toward the far wall, and a sofa sectional, this huge three-unit couch of impenetrable black leather—Jabba let him curl up on it whenever Cheri was pissed. Like, for a week after Cheri'd got her rack done, Ponyboy'd slept on that couch—including one wild night with this skank from the Olympic Garden, which wasn't cheating, technically, since Cheri'd been the one who'd thrown him out.

"A hundred and fifty-eight?"

Forcing himself not to check over his shoulder, Ponyboy made a quick turn into an open-air bathroom vestibule. He splashed cold water on his face and head, put his mouth below the tap, swallowing some water, letting the rest strike his neck and spray onto his ripped T. The carrying remnants of Jabba's voice were drowned out by the sound of the water, and Ponyboy dipped two fingers into the nearest jar of petroleum jelly. He took his time, re-spiked his damp and tangled hair, and stared at his body, all sunburned and glistening. His shoulder tatt *majorly* needed touching up.

"Come on. Ninety percent of the vice cops on the West Coast are breaking down my doors to get into the industry. And a community standards rap? It's VEGAS, for Christsakes."

The trick here—any streeter knew—was to eavesdrop while looking like you weren't eavesdropping. Stay out of the way and at the same time stay right in sight. Look like the dumbest fucker in the world and learn whatever there is to learn. The trick is, was, and always would be to take whatever wasn't nailed down, and then it was to get a hammer and start yanking on them nails. Loyalty went as far as the end of your fucking nose ring, especially when some motherfucker was riding your ass around in volcano weather.

Ponyboy left the water running and reentered the suite's main area. He sat on the section of the couch farthest away from Jabba and felt the rush of a day of fighting and biking and fuck knew what . . .

"She signs a *contract*," Jabba said.

Ponyboy ducked his head low between his legs; sucking for air, deep breaths . . .

"Her driver's license says she's *eighteen*."

Ponyboy concentrated on Jabba's screams, returning to the world.

"Explain to me—her lie is *MY* fault?"

He kept his head low and his body poised on the edge of the couch, and deliberately used the top of his pupils to check across the room, watching Jabba: the big man starting to speak into the phone, then stopping, listening, his face dumb with concern. "Right," Jabba said. "Maybe our lobbyists . . . I mean, *a hundred and fifty-eight?*"

"Right." Jabba sank into his chair. "Yeah. Okay. Get back to me."

Less hanging up than simply letting go, Jabba stared out and into nothing. Ponyboy watched him pull invisible hairs from his skull by their imaginary roots. Watched him look up to the ceiling, rub the three-day beard on the underside of his neck.

"Lemme ask you."

Fucker. How'd he know?

"Say a kid's . . . what, fourteen." Jabba's hands made a rolling motion. "It's three in the afternoon. Zero on the tube. His older brother's at football practice. Bedroom's unlocked. Kid goes in. Looks around. It's natural, right?"

"I guess."

"Okay. Right. He's not supposed to go in, he does. He has a chance, he takes it. A barrier goes up. You want to see behind it."

Overhead a commercial airliner passed, shaking the matchstick walls. Jabba waited it out.

"Now, throw in the beauty and mysteries of the female form."

The fat man paused, looking at the strongbox in front of him. He spent a moment with the docket. Another with his own thoughts. "Different example. Your girlfriend."

Ponyboy's head rose.

"Let's say she likes making a scene."

"Can you not say shit about Cheri."

"What? I like her. She's a talented individual."

Ponyboy popped his thumbs. He kept his eyes level and rocked slightly in place.

Jabba gave a quick grin. "Some generic girlfriend, then. A girlfriend that doesn't exist."

"Just don't be saying shit about Cheri."

Jabba's palms spread in front of him. *"A make-believe girlfriend."* He smiled. "Let's see. Let's . . . how about . . . make believe *she's an actress.*"

Without waiting for a reaction, Jabba swiveled in his chair. He reached down. There was the muted sound of a door opening; a tiny, metallic popping sound; air releasing.

"So it's Friday night," Jabba said, swiveled back toward Ponyboy, an aluminum can now in his fist. "Date night. You go to rent movies. She drags you to the adult section in back. Like I said she's an *actress.* One of them extroverts. She shouts out the dirtiest titles. Wants the whole video store to hear—it makes her hot or something."

"Where you going with this, biggie?"

"Imaginary, remember?"

"Something you want maybe?"

"You rent a dirty movie with yer *imaginary girlfriend.*"

Jabba's tone let Ponyboy know the big man's patience had run out. Ponyboy felt violence simmering in his gaze. He thought of saying something, thought better of it.

"Back at her place. She wants to imitate all the positions. Fucks you till your eyes *bleed.* Tell me, tough guy—anything detrimental to the common good in *that*?"

Jabba cackled, leaned forward, and slammed the opened can of beer down onto the desk. Foam came in rivers from the can, like a miniature volcano eruption. Jabba unleashed a shit-eating grin and shook his soaked hand, obviously pleased with himself.

"How about this?" He wiped his hand on his pants. "You're just out of a long-term deal, into the idea of meeting new people. You wish you were sexually active. But what can you do? You're just not in a place where you can put yourself at risk. Not yet.

"Could be you're an average guy who just finished a third date with a girl he's really into, the festivities having gone far, but not far enough.

"You're a fifty-one-year-old widower. A middle manager. You got this meager, settled life. No foreseeable prospects.

"Maybe your wife's ass keeps getting fatter and her breasts are sagging toward the floor. She's looking more and more like a tub of lard, and you're no bargain, either, but hey, why shouldn't you be able to look at young pretty bodies?"

Jabba paused, caught his breath. Now he offered Ponyboy the beer.

"Viewing pornography is NOT a crime," he said. "Every member of the male species who whacks off to an explicit prompt is *not necessarily* going to rape the little girl next door. A seventeen-year-old clicks onto an adult website, he's not gonna stalk your sister or instigate an abusive relationship. It's horseshit. Why not say every person who's ever told an offensive joke is a racist? Anyone whose lips touch beer is alcoholic?"

Pushing off the desk, Jabba rose. "We got all these political opportunists, all the right-wing God squadders, bunch of tight-ass virgins. Throw in a bunch of hairy-lip feminist dissertation grad school dogshit. Now the terms get skewed. Anyone who willingly makes a living from their body is exploited. Who cares if the girls sign papers? If they choose this life? If they make good money. God forbid they actually *enjoy* sex."

Ponyboy relaxed, kicked back. He'd seen the Pacing Defense Attorney routine before, heard the arguments more than a few times. The rants were a relief, actually; their familiarity gave Ponyboy a path to follow. He listened, allowing himself to get caught up in Jabba's excitement, to remember how fascinating this shit was.

"A rational mind, a *thinking* mind—you and me, brah—we accept masturbation as universal, as natural. You keep too much inside, you bust. Cleopatra, she used to have slaves rub their semen into her skin as beauty ointment. Didn't know that, didja? I collect shit and you bet I'm gonna whip it out. I got a Sears catalogue from the 1890s. They got a listing for clitoral stimulators. Know what it says? *'Relieves tension. Allows a woman to concentrate on her housework.'* "

Ponyboy chuckled along.

"Here's the nut," Jabba said. "All these years later people are the same, only now the world's different. Women got the pill and vibrators now, they want their orgasm just like men. I got all these lezzies, more than happy to yell how their films 'reclaim pornography for the clit.' I got fags, they luuuv their fag porn and don't care who knows it. I say God bless them. Because porn's not just a guilty pleasure for the raincoat crowd, not no more. These days you got teenagers flipping Mommy and Daddy the bird, buying a Porn Star brand T-shirt from the clothing company that Mommy and Daddy own stock in. You got porn jokes in talk show monologues. Paris designers using adult stars in fashion shows. You got professional power women heading to the gym after work, taking classes in aerobic pole dancing."

Jabba took a moment, caught his breath, his face alive now.

"Now. Does this necessarily mean porn should be celebrated?

"That there's no exploitation? No objectification?

"Does it mean that prolonged, sustained viewing of this shit has no long-term effects?"

5.2

Following Daphney's directions the girl slowly rotated the powder-filled spoon above the blue and orange sections of the cigarette lighter's flame. Her jitters and contrary instincts were like so many years of public service warnings, acknowledged for the precise reason of opposing, and the girl lifted the spoon to her nose, she closed her eyes and tilted her head backward. A long inhalation, a deep snort; the jagged edges and larger rocks aggravated her interior nasal passages, felt rough along the fleshy and sensitive tissues. *There you go,* Danger-Prone Daphney said. *Nice and easy, right?* The girl with the shaved head swayed, then stayed still, half-expecting butterflies that morphed into sky rockets, afraid of tentacles leaping out from the middle of a blue forehead, all that weird Goth zombie shit that the girl imagined came from taking hard drugs. Suddenly she did not want to open her eyes, was afraid to give in to what was waiting for her. She realized there was no turning back. She also thought how cool it would be if there were like a menu of hallucinations, like if she could order her hallucination from one of the fast-food places she abhorred and boycotted and yet sometimes still craved. The girl with the shaved head wanted to ride on a butterfly and kiss the stars. She opened her eyes and looked around and there weren't any butterflies, no stars, just Daphney squirming on the toilet seat, the mongrel dog licking up water from the floor. The girl did not feel the drug inside her lungs, she was not aware of her body's carbolic acids doing their assigned work— breaking down the different hallucinogens that were inside the basement-made methamphetamine, allowing each to make its way into her bloodstream. The girl's heart pumped with goodwill for all of the childhood friends whose names she no longer remembered—boys who used to catch lizards and frogs near the boat basin, a freckled happy girl with pigtails whose bladder problem had been in direct conflict with her affinity for playing jump rope at recess. Hydrochloride salt is the glue agent that holds together many inhaled drugs; it is used as glue specifically because the chloride is water soluble, and because blood is mostly water. The girl's heart beat generously, with each pulse helping to further separate the inhaled drug's essential ingredients. The drug's glue atoms further dissolved and the essential agents of each hallucinogen were further absorbed into and carried along the girl's bloodstream, and she was oblivious. Complained, in fact, wanting to know where her hallucination meal was. Said she might as well have been waiting in line behind some old lady. The girl with the shaved head said waiting for the drug to kick in was like having that old lady search through her purse for the nickels and quarters. It was like you waited and after all that waiting the old lady had counted out the exact amount for her gas, but then all of a sudden remembered that she needed to buy milk, too. Danger-Prone Daphney half-listened. Pulling some sort of vial out from her tampon applicator, Daphney laughed and snorted in a kind of knowing way that, to the girl, sounded like a walrus. Now Daphney uncorked the vial, and took a long hit, snorting that whole stash, and now lurching backward, slipping without warning, skidding backward, and there was some sort of significant and definite sound, splashing, something was going on, but it was impossible for the girl with the shaved head to know what, impossible for her to see, for the girl was occupied, she was being bathed in a celestial light, a brightness that was infinite and immaculate. The girl with the shaved head felt loose and limpid, her every pore simultaneously opening and being filled with the energy of truth, with the charge of young love in bloom, with all events turning into echoes of one singular and primordial event. Suddenly time was outside of the confines of linear temporality for the girl, substance existed outside of dimensions that defined all notions of substance. Every action, every event, every sound and energy and transference, they were ripples in the cosmic continuum, dust in the fucking wind; the high was the girl's end and the high was her means, the high was her word, and this word was good. And as for all of the other words, the girl was a part of them as well. Her esophagus was the source of Daphney's newest cry, the girl's ecstasy an extension of Daphney's sudden shock, Daphney now calling out, *It's not funny,* Daphney embarrassed, laughing at herself; wiggling in place some more and saying, *Yeah, I guess it kinda is funny, isn't it?* The girl with the shaved head laughed along, although she did not know why she was laughing, but at the same time, she could see it all: reality was this large lake of gravy, the girl was a buttermilk biscuit. The girl had to sop up all of reality, take it in and absorb everything she could, she had to savor each image—the sight of Daphney's hands on the toilet lip, the spectacle of Daphney pushing, making those splashing noises and stomping her feet, Daphney saying *I'm stuck,* and *Can you believe this shit?* And now the girl understood, and she celebrated, bending down, laughing and bleating, singsonging, *Daphney got stuck in the toilet, Daphney got stuck in the toilet.* The girl laughed harder, so hard that she had to stop singing, for she was suddenly aware of her own realization of this ridiculousness. The girl laughed because she had not been able to see the obvious sight of Daphney's ass lodged in the toilet, and she laughed because she had been laughing for so long. *God, this is so funny. The universe is so absurd.* And now, as if all this were not enough, now the girl caught a glimpse of something else: running between Daphney's thighs, Daphney's underwear strung like a washing line between tenements. *What?* Daphney wanted to know, rocking to the left, snorting herself, her giggles like the moans of an embarrassed walrus. Her face shining with tears, Daphney looked down, trying to see. *What's so funny? I can't see around my belly. Tell me.*

Of the estimated million teenagers who left home each year, as many as two hundred thousand did not turn around and return home, but kept on running, their wounds too deep, their worlds simply too fucked up to inhabit any longer. At least 60 percent of these cases, Lorraine learned, involved sexual abuse, assault, and other unholy acts that by all rights should have been run away from. Which was terrifying. The day before Newell had disappeared, if you had suggested that Newell had been abused, the idea would have been too ridiculous to consider. But Lorraine no longer knew what to think, what to believe.

She had to know more. Whether it was watching as many movie adaptations of *Tom Sawyer* as she could get her hands on, listening to an audio book of *On the Road* while driving, or spending hours at a time behind the locked door of her bedroom, running through the missing person's webpages of different sheriff's departments, Lorraine searched for answers, for explanations. For anything she could grasp on to.

With regards to the high rate of abuse, experts uniformly agreed: flight from home most often was an act of self-preservation. A declaration of life. This was the bottom line, a reality that also extended to cases that did not necessarily involve abuse, where assignments of blame were not so cut and dried, flawed situations that the teenager's decisions had both contributed to and exacerbated; cases where revenge, anger, shame, fear, parents, teachers, lovers, crushes, and friends all gave way to what, in the end, had to be seen as a high-stakes game of self-discovery.

Thus, read Lorraine, there was no quote unquote *point* to running away. Or, if there was a point, then that point was, there was no point; flight from home was the inevitable choice, simply because a young man or woman could not run away from his or her own body.

Denial is the natural instinct, Lorraine read, turning the page in some stupid manual. *No parent or guardian can be faulted for their disbelief. However, be advised that denial solves nothing. Acceptance of larger problems is the first and most necessary step in moving forward.*

And then there were the first-person accounts. The tales from the front.

Indeed, Lorraine had a collection of them by now, duplicates that she'd taken home from the center. Inspirational letters, mostly, their happy endings providing Lorraine with strength, giving her tangible proof that her time was being well spent, her hope well placed. But there were others, too. A few of them. Undated. Unsigned. This one, Lorraine found amid the stacks: a loose sheet that had been placed inside a binder and then forgotten. She'd flattened it out, but its creases remained prominent, dividing the paper into sections reminiscent of a tic-tac-toe board.

She envisioned the page folded up inside the back pocket of a pair of grimy jeans, carried around for so long that its corrugations had become part of its structure. She stared at the frazzled stick letters, wild scratches that progressively had more trouble staying grounded within the notebook's light blue guidelines. She started reading and the words slapped her across the face, leaving her shocked, half-numb, and frightened, as if she suddenly had been granted access to the secret correspondence of the wartime enemy.

Still, she could not help but read. She could not help but add the document to her collection.

Dear Hot line fucks,

Until I trusted you and your treachorous hotline I was doing aces. I had me a job working a piercing gun in this tent on Venice Beach, and even arranged to move in with this rasta chick who works at the next tent braiding hair with beads and sea shells. The history with my dad is still there but I wanted him to know that after all the hell I been through, I'm doing okay and there's some light. Since calls to the house still get tracked I used the hotline. It was good too, until your helping hand cownseler checks on dad's name. Turns out pop left a message. Maybe it makes me a pussy that after hearing about my brother I wanted to go home, but I'll be that kind of pussy any day, and anyone who has a problem with it is going to get their ass handed to them. So the next thing I know, I am talking to the phone cownseler about that Greyhound thing. The operater keeps me on the line while he verifys my runway status with the police. Then he tells me he has to make sure I am going to go home to my legal gardean, it's the rules. I was real nervous but I held on and after a while there is a clicking sound. I have to admit it kind of got me to hear the old man's voice, and I could tell he was releived to here from me too. We arranged everything and I got off the phone. The rule is, I have to be at the bus station a hour early to get my ticket, so Mase and me hauled ass to his van. I gathered up my shit but was getting kind of nervous because nine months is a long time. It took a while to get to the station cuz the traffic was a big pile of ass. It is total

BULLSHIT that the driver does not want to let me on—
I wasn't doing nothing, and even showed him my ticket too.
But that FUCKER radios and gets the COPS involved.
I kepped screaming how I was trying to go home to my dad
but they cuffed me anyways. Now I am in the Tonapah
Juvenille Youth Detention Agency. Days we wear orange
jumpsuits and go out to the middle of the desert and
pickaxe rocks. They got this bigass chain around our legs
and it is hot as shit. There aint no shade and we only get two
water breaks, and this huge nigger keeps blowing kisses at
me. I hate you do gooder bleeding heart phone bastards.
You ruined my miserable fucking life.

People want to talk. They want to give you the combination to their hearts. That's where your smart motherfucker gets the advantage. Like with Jabba. The fat bastard's delivered his defense argument, what, a hundred times? Ponyboy listened to every one. The more familiar Ponyboy became with Jabba's main points, the more accustomed he became to Jabba's digressions, the more that number leapt out at him. Jabba would say *one hundred and fifty-eight,* and it was like one of them little triangle things from the marching band sounded. *A hundred and fifty-eight concurrent state and federal charges,* DING. Ponyboy got to thinking that the feds were firing a lot of ammunition. He began to recognize the prohibitive fear that oozed through Jabba's bravado. Your smart motherfucker, that's what he waits for. What he lives for.

July's rolling around, mad patriot fever's everywhere, flags on lawns and in store windows, all the little civic groups got their homogay little fireworks stands outside the shopping centers. Ponyboy's in the office, stacking videotapes. The red pile. The blue pile. All the colors got their own piles. Jabba's busy with his phone calls, and Ponyboy gets to wondering: what's up with all the different colors? Ponyboy shoved his finger up his schnozz and made himself look especially bright. "Yo, Jabba. We should mix the red tapes with the blue ones. Get a little flag working. It'd be patriotic."

Jabba covered the mouthpiece with his paw. "Don't fuck with my inventory."

Well, now you know, when the fat bastard wasn't looking, Ponyboy had to pick up a red videotape. Check out the little peel-off label, the ink-jet printing:

AMATEUR FIRST TIME DEBUTANTES #25.

NOTICE: THE ENCLOSED CASSETTE IS RED. IF IT IS NOT RED, IT IS AN ILLEGAL, INFERIOR COPY. $500.00 REWARD FOR ARREST AND CONVICTION OF ANY COPYRIGHT INFRINGEMENT. *All models appearing in the visual depiction of actual sexual conduct displayed on this box or in this video are over 18 years. All records comply with government-mandated record keeping and labeling requirements and are kept in the office of the manufacturer/ distributor at the following location:*

A bunch of legal mumbo jumbo, right? Nothing to think twice about. Not unless you've been hauling them little delivery packages for like eight months. You been hauling them delivery packages, though, it's possible you've noticed a few things. For instance, it's possible you've watched Kunjib tear open the brown paper on the packages you deliver. Like eight million times you've observed Kunjib counting out ten cardboard videotape boxes—each one glossy, with girls positioned all around. You've also watched Kunjib open them cardboard boxes and take out what Stevie Wonder could see were not colored videotapes, but black ones. Always they were black.

And now it's like in them late-show movies, your detective with the trench coat and the brim hat finds his ass in the middle of something that doesn't look kosher. He has to stay cool, right? Camera shows Sam Spade all stone-faced. He's thinking, only he can't rub his jaw. If he rubs his jaw, the dragon lady knows something's up, she's gonna double-cross him. She and the little major are gonna betray Sam Spade. Gonna kill his little brother and go to the smoky airport and fly that propeller plane straight out of Chinatown. And where's Sam Spade then? Bent over the piano, is where. Taking it up the rear from a Bojangles. Sam taking it from the motherfucking spade.

Everyone's ready to fuck everyone, was Ponyboy's gist. So if you discover a piece of information, a smart motherfucker zips his lip. No point in Jabba knowing you saw the difference in the videotape colors.

'Cause there'd been a time when this motherfucker hadn't been so smart. A time when Ponyboy'd first started working for Jabba. The fat man had put him on strongbox fetching detail, and naturally, Ponyboy'd jimmied open one of those bad boys. Jabba'd seen the lock all busted open, resealed with Krazy Glue. Jabba had played it cool, though, sucking on one of them cigars he loved so much. Out of nowhere, he'd lifted the strongbox. Said Ponyboy wouldn't be human if he hadn't taken his shot. Then he'd removed a big-ass hunting knife from the desk.

"You got two choices," Jabba had told him, fingering that blade, its edges so jagged the elephants screamed when you castrated them.

"Blood on this knife is behind curtain number one," Jabba'd said.

The fat bastard had pushed himself up from the chair. Unzipped his slacks.

"Curtain two, there's gonna be some shit on this dick."

Ponyboy'd stared at Jabba and that fat bastard had smiled this twisted-ass smile, and his eyes had been black and lusterless, and right there Ponyboy'd known that Jabba had seen straight and deep into his soul—everything that Ponyboy tried so hard to forget about late at night, the memories that sometimes still hit Ponyboy in the middle of the day, sensations that were activated by the angle of sunlight hitting a car window. Jabba saw Ponyboy's life on the streets and what Ponyboy had done to stay alive—all them old men in their long cars idling slowly on the corners, that moment when them jailhouse bastards came to the lockup and gave him the note that the most beautiful little brother that ever walked this earth was fucking dead in his sleep in a hospital bed, his big brother wouldn't even get a chance to see him, didn't even get a chance to say goodbye.

In the office out by the airport, Jabba had stared at Ponyboy and Ponyboy had known this motherfucker had his number, and for the first time in fuck knows how long he'd felt fear, true and immaculate.

So a lot was at stake now, even if Ponyboy couldn't let anybody know. The next day, he chilled at the counter of the video store. Taking out one of the sparklers that he'd strong-armed from a troupe of Cub Scouts, Ponyboy dug for ear wax, whistled himself a happy little tune, and watched Kunjib take out a notebook with a professional wrestler on its cover. Kunjib marked the ledger with inventory numbers for each box, and moseyed over to the back shelves. When he got to the rows of televisions and video machines, Kunjib then loaded each delivered cassette into a different videotape machine. Cracking open a set of blank videotapes from Price Club, he began loading them into the machines too.

A suit was approaching the counter with one of the cardboard box covers, and Ponyboy smiled and entertained thoughts of making a necklace from the guy's teeth. Then he got out of the dude's way, watching the sale. Just like Ponyboy guessed, Kunjib came back from the inventory closet, bringing the suit what Stevie Wonder could see was one of them black Price Club videotapes.

Ponyboy leaned over for a peek at its little dot matrix printer label.

1st Tyme AMATeur debuatants.

NOTICE: THIS VIDEO MAY INSITE BOUTS OF FRENZIED MASTURBATION. The producer assumes no liability for low sperm count, chafeing, or an abnormally muscular right arm. VIEW AT YOUR OWN RISK

Peace out, Ponyboy told Kunjib. *Keep on mopping,* he shouted to Asaaf.

The sun beat down on Ponyboy like he was its favorite thing in all creation, and he saddled back up onto the bike and cruised down Tropicana Avenue. Ponyboy lifted his hands from his handlebars and navigated with his knees. He held a bottle rocket close to his body, lit the fuse, and shot the rocket into the open partition of a nearby fireworks stand. Someone yelled *Fire in the hole* and, immediately, a whole bunch of 4-H'ers came running out then and the place exploded.

Ponyboy's mind churned faster than his legs, and he joyously trekked toward his next drop-off. He had all kinds of time for ruminating now.

The way he figured it, Jabba had a hundred and fifty-eight concurrent jail sentences breathing down his fat neck, but still was shrewd enough to double-dip, ordering a small number of colored videotapes from his bosses, then selling black duplicates to all the Asaafs and Kunjibs out there. Dude's that smart, wouldn't be anything to do away with a curious little shit like Ponyboy. Nothing but a chicken wing on a yo-yo string.

Ponyboy was riding like a motherfucker now, his legs pumping themselves to butter. He's thinking how every porn store he delivers to is in a fucked-up neighborhood—low-ass rents, a bunch of Asaafs for employees, always looking over their shoulders to see if immigration or whoever is on their tail. Ponyboy, he's Sam Spade meets Oliver Goddamn Stoner, connecting dots left and right. And them Price Club videotapes got to cost lots less than if you bought the real movies from Jabba, correct? Makes sense for the Asaafs to order less videos from Jabba than *they* needed, pay Jabba enough so that he's satisfied, and make their real money from the bootlegs they print behind the front counter. Jabba don't notice because he's too busy pulling the same duplication scam with whoever he's working for, who's probably screwing over someone else. Bottom line, everyone's filling their own pocket. So long as one of them glossy cardboard boxes is on the shelf, the suit picking through them, he doesn't give a shit. Only thing the suit cares about is, the chick on the box cover bears some resemblance to his wife from back when they started dating, that plus she takes it in her ear.

A beautiful scam. Just beautiful.

Two days later, Ponyboy cut side deals with Asaaf and Kunjib and Mujibar and all the other glottal clusterfucks on his route. In exchange for a small fee, he agreed to haul videotapes in bulk over from the Price Club. But goodness gracious, wasn't it a coincidence: each porn store *just happened* to order one extra pack of clearance-price generic low-end videotapes?

Now he was rolling. The Chink tattoo artist was more than agreeable, for a small cut, to peddle videos from his cubicle. Where all the stores charged thirty, Pony and the Chink would charge fifteen. The Chink didn't even need that much convincing to volunteer his videotape machine.

The same afternoon, he gets back to Cheri's place. She's recovering from her shift, wrapped in silk sheets, snoring like a twin cam engine. Ponyboy hooked up the Chink's videotape machine to hers. Cheri's VCR was programmed to tape the morning show with the rich white bitch who made quilts so your home looked all homey. 'It was also programmed for the one with that black whore who got all meaningful and sensitive-looking while she explained why every trouble in a relationship was the man's fault. Well, Cheri'd have to live without her shows for a day. She was a big girl; she'd be fine.

Cheri's living room carpet was plush and white, so snowlike in appearance that Ponyboy fought the urge to whip out his dick and write his name on it. He disengaged his ammo belt of interlocked backpacks, unlinking their straps from across his chest. The packs landed with a thud and dust went everywhere and Ponyboy dumped out the contents of the nearest sack. A whole stash of them different-colored videotapes from Jabba's office fell out and now Ponyboy dumped another bag, this one full of generic black videotapes. Walking around in a circle, Ponyboy checked to make sure Cheri's bedroom door was shut, then he cranked speed metal on her stereo and swallowed fistfuls of cheese crackers. Ponyboy plopped down with his back against the bottom of the couch Cheri had dragged his ass to the furniture store to see. He banged his head to the beat and hit PLAY on one VCR. He found the remote control for the second machine, then depressed > and REC simultaneously. Ponyboy stretched and took a long breath.

Instinctively his weaker hand reached for the opposite tricep, and a tattoo—his fingers running along smooth warm stretches, raised indentations, ink over flesh over bone. From the point of his elbow to the bottom of his armpit—a tattoo of a long, opened zipper. Four hours of detail work had been devoted to making it look like the teeth of the zipper were open, as if exposing the flesh of Ponyboy's body, revealing the thick scar from where Jabba had cut him.

After Jabba had sliced Ponyboy, he'd let Ponyboy use the phone. Cheri was supposed to be back on the stage in five minutes, but when she'd gotten that call, she'd driven like the proverbial bat out of hell. Ponyboy told her no hospitals, he did not want those fuckers to kill him like they'd killed his brother. Cheri had not known what to do, right in front of her eyes, her boyfriend was bleeding like a stuck pig. But her disconnect gimmick must have kicked in, because later she told Ponyboy that she'd seen herself watching him bleed. She'd watched herself help Ponyboy into a seat belt, and then seen herself get into her Jeep and floor the gas, eighty miles an hour back to the apartment. Ponyboy had been mumbling words that Cheri could not understand, and she'd propped his weakened and bloodied body up on her toilet and spoken patiently to him, like she was guiding a first-timer through the patter of a lap dance: *Just reach up, okay baby? For the shower rod, okay?*

Her hands had been shaking and she had fumbled through the medicine cabinet and found the blue painkillers she used whenever her muscles hurt from squatting over the clothed dicks of men she didn't give a fuck about. Putting the little blue doodads in her boyfriend's mouth, she'd tilted his head back and told him *swallow, swallow,* and when he'd finally swallowed, she'd run and gotten the sewing kit she always meant to use for making quilts like on the WASP woman's show. Then she'd folded up one of the bathroom towels and put it in between her boyfriend's teeth and told him to bite down.

Like Cheri was in a movie about Mother Teresa, she had saved him, sewing his body back together, bearing his flinches and convulsions, laying him down in her marble tub and running warm water over him and scrubbing. Later, she told Ponyboy that in this scene of the movie of her life, there was a part where the camera pulled up and back, into a wide shot, and from the corners of the screen darkness began creeping in, until the lighting around the two of them was like this fuzzy little cave, and the image of the movie star Cheri bathing her battered Ponyboy was like this small and almost holy moment.

Yes sir ree bob, his girlfriend had sewed him up and spoon-fed him and pampered him. She'd put on her Horny Stripper Nurse costume and checked his fever and, *oopsie,* flashed him all the way up the length of her leg, to a high-cut panty. On an individual and regular basis Cheri had made Ponyboy feel like his health and welfare actually mattered—made him feel like he was worth something. Cheri Blossom was a lifesaver, a fucking miracle, this angel from the goddamn sky. Ponyboy knew it was true in that moment of crisis and he knew it was true now, in this moment of decision. He ran a callused palm over the raised stitch indentations of his scar, felt the hot pinching sensation of electric needle drilling into the skin of his mind.

All the cool shit that Cheri's fake tits had purchased weren't enough for her to forgive Ponyboy for talking her into getting them done, he knew this. But he was equally sure there was money to be shaken from the tree of pornography. Ponyboy would have rather died than lose Cheri and he would have rather killed himself than gone back to peddling his ass on street corners to a bunch of old pervs. The bass from the stereo system was making Cheri's porcelain clown figures vibrate on their mantel, and Ponyboy was staring into the seventy-eight-inch high-definition flat screen that Cheri had purchased right after her tits had paid for themselves. He was shoving another fist of baked cheese crackers into his mouth and now he was fiddling with a fourth of July sparkler. And a plan was slowly starting to form, its barest and most scant beginnings. Not for a second would Ponyboy consider the strain this plan would bring into his relationship with the woman he loved. He would not think about how wrong things can go between two people, or how desperate he soon would be to make things right. Ponyboy rose off the carpet and made sure the second videotape machine was recording. He watched the wide and wondrous screen.

5.4

During that first fall, in the fallout of the boy's disappearance, Lincoln Ewing remained clean-shaven. His collared shirts remained pressed. He asked no quarter from his superiors at the Kubla Khan; neither did he try to lock his suffering away from the people he worked with. Quieter in meetings, he became less of a textbook alpha male, though not to the extent where he retreated behind any kind of granitelike exterior, the way loss seems to harden so many men. Rather, Lincoln considered more options than he ever had, took more input, and delegated more, all without abdicating his responsibilities, or foisting his duties onto others. In this way he empowered members of his staff, placing them in situations where each could carry out those functions for which he/she was best suited. Consensus in the office held that Lincoln's newfound openness added to the poignancy, made the whole thing sadder. His department flourished and his staff quietly set up a fund to help find Newell and, in short order, other divisions at the Kubla Khan contributed to the fund. Lincoln would stop in the middle of a hallway and quietly thank a coworker for their concern and contributions. He'd return the hugs of secretaries, exchange kind and hopeful words with anyone who was kind enough to be hopeful. And then he would retreat to his office and tell his assistant he needed a minute.

Closing the flimsy door behind him, Lincoln would switch off the Nokia wireless he used for personal calls, and the BlackBerry that his office had him carry, and he'd sit and stare—gazing at the parking lot below him, or perhaps the rotating triangles on his screen saver. He played computer solitaire until the game's tracking meter could document a physical day of his life that had been wasted, at which point, disgusted with his inertia, Lincoln dragged the program into the trash. Although he did not care about his stocks, Lincoln fell into the habit of refreshing the webpage that tracked their progress so often that it became a nervous tic. He would return messages from his dad, compose loving and supportive

e-mails to Lorraine, and receive updates from whichever private investigator he had on the case at that moment, all this while wrangling with
law enforcement and missing-child agency staffers, politely handling
their bureaucratic idiocies, smooth talking whoever he needed to ap-
prove his latest request, even as he secretly wished he could ram a cluster
bomb up all of their asinine asses.

The air had cooled noticeably, and the days were starting to get dark
earlier, with people breaking out Windbreakers, and the first pumpkins
appearing on windows and stoops. It was pitch-black outside, the dead
of night, and Lincoln came home to the usual locked bedroom. He
headed to the guest room and tucked himself underneath the covers,
and, beneath him, he felt . . . these . . . these . . . *things,* all this fur moving, slinky and squirming. There was hissing. Lashing. Must have been,
Jesus, twenty cats in there. *"Fuck."* Lincoln leapt off the bed pronto. He
went banging on the door of the bedroom he'd paid for. He demanded
to know what the sam hell was going on. After a time the door opened.
Lorraine was groggy; but even newly awake, she was matter-of-fact. She
told him about the animal refuge. Saving all the poor stray kitties.

His wife was hurting real bad, anyone could see this; even in his rage
and his own grief Lincoln felt for her. She needed to cry? He gave her his
shoulder. Needed space? He gave her space. Needed to lock him out of
his bed and then transform the room where he slept into a wildlife pre-
serve? Needed to watch that morbid video from the pizza party until she
wore its film into mulch? Needed to turn what was already a nightmare
into this living goddamn horror that Lincoln could not even begin to figure out how to address? He sludged downstairs. He tried to get comfortable on the couch in the living room. The truly ridiculous thing, he told
himself, was this was the closest he'd been to pussy in quite some time.

Didn't he have needs? It wasn't anything he could talk about; there
wasn't anything to say, really. Lincoln shut up and went to work and
went through the motions of his life. He lost five and ten and fifteen
minutes at a time, slipping into fugues for which there was no account-
ing or explanation. A good chunk of one afternoon got wasted typing the
names of former teammates into a search engine. The rest of that afternoon was spent doing the same thing with former girlfriends. Every sin-

gle day he emptied his mailbox of electronic solicitations and just about every day, he quote unquote *accidentally* clicked on one, and then, each and every day, his next half hour was devoted to disentangling himself from the loops of interconnected pop-up advertisements. One moment Lincoln would be constructing a point-by-point response to some preliminary draft; in the blink of an eye he'd be registering for a three-day trial membership to an adult website, clicking the button that confirmed the discreetly billed charge of four dollars and ninety-five cents on his Bank One Platinum MasterCard. He'd be entering a six-letter password that started with N; opening the photo sections, perusing thumbnail galleries, and clicking on pictures he wanted to magnify to full screen size. Since the Khan had one of those networks where its computers were always online, Lincoln could just click back and forth between his reports and the photos. Blondes were his thing, mostly. Strong-legged blondes. Full round breasts. Childbearing hips. Lincoln wasn't so far gone that he was about to masturbate in his office in the middle of the workday. Basically he ogled, spending less time at his voyeurism than McKagan down the hall devoted to finding weekend police auctions to attend. Moreover, Lincoln made sure to cancel his trial memberships before their regular costs—thirty dollars a month—kicked in. He made sure to download the most attractive photos into the ACCNTNGMEM.EXE file of his hard drive. And then Lincoln would turn his attention back to his memoranda, to preparations for his next meeting, to revisions of that Power-Point presentation, to piles of never-ending, unfinished bullshit.

Toward the end of October, at the end of an unnecessarily tense day, a few of the guys from the department were on their way out for a few beers, heading to this little dive. Lincoln offered to tag along. It was a short drive. A dark hole in the wall: mostly empty, a television above the bar switched to a fishing show on one of ESPN's lesser channels; a half-naked woman on a raised platform, swinging upside down from a pole. She seemed bored, maybe because there wasn't much of a crowd to dance for, and her movements were careless. Even so, there was a certain adjustment to having a live topless woman that was not your wife of twelve and a half years pole dance in front of you. A guy might sneak peeks at nakedness on the Web, but live nakedness was a different story. Lincoln bought the first round. Table conversation quickly turned to the stripper's breasts, a scale of one to ten. By the next round, talk centered on whether the stripper was worth taking home. Two of the men at the table were in their twenties, divorced, and if Lincoln remembered correctly, had kids. One guy wasn't thirty-five and was on his third marriage. Lincoln's coworkers loosened their ties. Lincoln sunk into his chair. He brought the screwdriver toward his mouth and tried not to be too obvious about staring at the stripper. Apparently he didn't succeed at this, because the stripper stopped dancing and came over. Putting her arm around Lincoln's shoulders, she asked if he liked what he saw. She mussed Lincoln's hair and said he was sweet and blew into his ear. Her body was warm against his and oh mercy was she built. *Have a little fun,* his coworkers urged, and sweet chariot mercy, could Lincoln have used a little fun just about then.

But the boy was going to be found. His marriage was going to recover. There was work to be done, yes, and it wasn't going to be easy, no, but the work *would* get done, Newell *would* be found, and then this here situation, it was going to normalize. Lincoln had faith. Addressing the stripper by her first name, he bid her good night and thanked her for her attention. He purchased a round for the road for his coworkers and signed off on the entire bill, leaving instructions with the waitress for a gratuity that was generous indeed. Lincoln Ewing knew how to take care of people, yes sir. Sometimes, though, he wondered if the people who were supposed to take care of Lincoln Ewing did not know how to take care of him. If maybe they did not know how to take care of themselves. Maybe Lincoln had to take care of someone by going and finding his missing little pubescent ass himself and dragging it back home. Lincoln maybe had to take care of someone else by giving up his bedroom and giving her enough space so she could grow into an understanding of his devotion. However you wanted to cut it, a man did not bitch or make a production of his suffering or take the easy way out. A man did what he was supposed to do. In this case he left the Paradise Club, drove down Industrial a bit, and then made a turn and pulled his sedan in behind that cinder block wall. He entered the store through its side entrance and thought that by now the immigrant behind the counter must know his face.

He settled above a particular box cover that had been handled more than a few times. Its cardboard was thin and indented along the bottom, where thumbprints smudged the blue backdrop. Lincoln grabbed those same areas. He paid cursory attention to the title—*Temporary Positions,* screaming across the top of the box. Rather, the platinum blonde was his focal point. Shapely. Lithe. Visibly young, yet old enough to know what she was doing, this particular young woman looked like she *really* knew: her lips moist and cherry-red, parted *just so,* the temple of her eyeglasses sitting suggestively between her biting teeth. She wore a business-woman's blouse, which was opened at the throat, its gap trailing downward, revealing just enough of what seemed to be two lovely handfuls, the outlines of nipples suggesting a chilly day. One eyebrow was cocked, and she was staring at whoever thought he was man enough to pick up her box, defiant, daring that unknown person: take her on, be man enough to watch.

Lincoln felt a sense of growing anticipation as he turned the box over and began examining the cluster of small pictures, still shots that had been taken from the movie using the same process that had put Newell's stare from that pizza party on hundreds of lamppost fliers. Did the blonde look appropriately excited about being bent over the copy machine? What was the deal with the little redhead spreading her legs atop the file cabinet? Lincoln started to read the summary—*When sexy computer programmer Prada Nightingale takes a temp assignment at industry-leading Byte Software . . .* —then just took the thing up to the counter.

On the drive he called Lorraine—*Yeah, honey, McKagan screwed everything up. I've got a shitload of stuff to fix.* Unless of course he did not call home, but just headed back to his office and pressed a button and closed the blinds on his windows. The Khan's administrative level was high enough that nobody could see inside, but Lincoln closed the windows anyway. Maybe five or six times Lincoln also watched in the dark stillness of his own living room. He could not help himself, those times, and Lorraine was barricaded in her cave, and he would load a newly purchased black videotape into the machine. Admittedly, those were always uncomfortable experiences—in each case, Lincoln's conscience would disturb him and he'd lay off for a while afterward. Far easier, far *safer,* was to head back to work, shut the door to his office, and close the blinds. It still felt dirty, but in a way that was acceptable to Lincoln, a way he could live with. He fired up the machine he used for reviewing promotional materials and ad agency stuff. He hit the PLAY button on the remote and then manipulated the dial thingy to adjust the tracking. Then, always, Lincoln turned down the volume so nobody from the next office could overhear. He performed this small and secretive ritual and the television screen went from blue to black and, inevitably, a blonde in a pink negligé began fellating an earpiece; an olive-skinned brunette put the receiver between her obviously inflated breasts. She said, *Pick up the phone and make me moan,* and a 976 number flashed on the screen. Lincoln would learn to fast-forward through the commercials, as well as the public service announcements about free speech, and the WARNING disclaimer things, the bright orange counter speeding ahead.

Of course, part of the goof was how dead-on the jokes and stereotypes turned out to be—all the nonsensical blue-collar fantasies, clumsy takeoffs of popular movies, and plot machinations that were nothing more than the flimsiest of excuses to mix and match fornicators; the acting beyond even the most patronizing expectations, portrayals of seduction and attempts at erotica that were nothing less than embarrassing, and background soundtracks so bereft of even vaguely redeeming qualities that they hardly qualified as music. In *Temporary Positions,* the software office was barren of computers. The programmers wrote their codes on paper, stored their files in cabinets. The hackers held up pliers and power tools before announcing a system was easy to crash. Mistakes someone *had* to know better than to make, and yet there they were, so numerous and unrelenting and varied as to guarantee that, sorry, no one knew better. But did it matter? The blonde from the cover sashayed onto the screen at double-time. Lincoln hit PLAY.

A stunning woman. Really. In a world where children did not disappear, she would have been a model. A starlet. Perhaps even a showgirl in a Las Vegas review. And it wasn't only her. The executive's personal assistant was breathtaking in a particularly devilish and filthy way. The mousy programmer was a find. The women whose presences never got explained nonetheless were hot. Lincoln Ewing's life was a functioning state of purgatory, a daily walk amid incomprehensible circumstances. He loosened his belt and remained in his seat. He pushed at the carpet with his feet and rolled his chair back and provided himself a little more room to, ah, operate. Lincoln watched *Temporary Positions.* He watched *Executive Privilege.* He watched *Going Down in Suburbia.* One scene at a time, one tape at a time, a collection accumulating in the bottom right drawer of his desk at work, Lincoln Ewing entered a parallel dimension, where every woman was as beautiful as a medicated dream, eager as a honeymoon bride: leggy drinks of water who had not yet grown into their bodies; statuesque, hourglass-figured veterans with eye-popping, scientifically supplied cleavage; God-fearing corn-fed daughters; black chicks; Asians; ones who had heavy European accents; ones who had long Slavic faces; Mexicans; mulattos; white trash; each and every single one of them beyond the pale and orbit of mere mortals: with all-body tans or sexy bikini lines; with dragon lady fingernails painted in metallic colors and gold bands around index fingers and turquoise bands around manicured toes; women with visible rib cages and tummy chains and sexy tattoos on the lower part of the smalls of their backs; with nipples that were dark and pointed as chocolate kisses, with tongue studs and nipple rings; women with the glowing skin of youth and the slightest thickening to their tummies; with bruises on their legs from pole dancing mishaps; with teething marks; with pregnancy scars. Women varied and distinct and similar as the sunsets. Women young and no longer young, some as old as thirty. Lincoln did not know their names and did not want to know their names, and despite himself he would come to recognize a few: the Honey Linguses, the Chastity Cleavages. He would come to recognize more as well; hairstyles that defied both logic and gravity, dyes and streaks that had been done to match the style of popular Hollywood celebrities, but that had turned out like something more suited to Long Island drag queens. The sky would be black and Lincoln would be sitting in his ergonomically adjustable executive roller chair and his erection would be protruding through the flap in his silk boxers, and on the screen, three semi-beautiful idiots would be in varying states of undress, and all of a sudden Lincoln would find himself processing some woman's collagen pout and concave cheeks, her unnaturally wide nostrils, the wrinkles at the corners of her eyes and the bags beneath them and that flat, uncaring stare. . . .

Some things must be learned over and over, and with every tape, with almost every scene, Lincoln witnessed firsthand that nothing can live up to what a mind imagines, that the idea of porn is far more erotic than its reality. This wasn't the kind of realization that blows your mind; at the same time it wasn't necessarily easy to accept. Lincoln had participated in more than his share of freaky shit back during his skirt-chasing days. Absolutely he had. But as he sped through one mechanical plow after another, it became impossible to deny the hard kernel inside of him that held the act of sex to be intimate—even the sport fucks and hogging and beer-goggle bangs of his youth, even the most impersonal lays, the bootie calls where he'd gotten caught up in his own pleasure and the chick had become amorphous, yes, even the dead fish, the one-night stands that Lincoln had fantasized through and forgotten and been razzed over. The intimacy may have been limited, varied in intensity and degree. But for some scant shred of time, without a doubt, some form of intimacy *had* existed. And it seemed to Lincoln there was a definitive, canyon-size difference between the privacy that formed between two people as they engaged in the most intimate act in which two people can engage, and the reality of a woman having to constantly brush hair out of her face while she performs fellatio on a guy, between the act of *sex,* or the activity of *making love,* or even the physical process of *fucking,* between any of these and the sequence wherein a woman is getting pounded from behind, and she looks straight ahead at the camera and deliberately brushes the hair out of her eyes, and then makes a face—pretending not only that she is having the time of her life, but that the jackass watching the tape is providing it.

This was at odds with all that was truly sexual and erotic to Lincoln. This was the opposite of sexy, something of a totally separate phylum, and without looking away or reducing the pace with which he was stroking himself, he would use his free hand and press a button on the right side of his remote, sending the forms on his screen forward in double-time.

Watching made Lincoln a tacit participant, and so he did not watch. Even if he did not stop.

A scene was boring. Did that mean he should give up his hard-on and go home?

He'd paid for this tape, right? This tape was *his*.

Because every once in a great while a sequence would arrive.

A threesome. The copy repairman and the starlet temp and the curvy redheaded programmer. The copy repair guy had the redhead on the table, and was working on her back door. He was covered with sweat, really pounding into the redhead, who had stopped eating out the blonde and was lying on her side. The redhead's face was toward the camera and her eyes were closed, and she was grunting with each stroke and her face was contorting. She was just lying there and taking it up the ass and keeping her eyes shut and her mouth open, simply waiting it out, waiting for it to be over and to have survived, and here, now, for the shortest of snippets, one and two and out, the camera captured the blond woman leaning over, gently stroking the side of the redhead's brow.

Lincoln would watch this and he would have to turn away. He'd have to turn off the videotape. He'd go back to his life and his wife, carrying on like normal, until the next time he needed to view such a spectacle.

At which juncture the tape was cued right up to where he'd left it.

Over and over he watched, until the genuine moment lost its freshness, until the accidentally captured seconds of humanity were devoid of their luster.

Then he purchased a new tape.

He also liked when the guy had the woman's panties hanging from his cock.

And the squishy sounds. A bed's rattle and thump. Balls smacking against a woman's ass.

All sorts of playful things, Lincoln appreciated: frilly G-strings and crotchless panties; a pink nipple at attention, peeking out from the cup of a cheesy bra. A woman driving her female partner crazy, teasing her lips with the humming vibrator. *Do you want me? Beg for me. . . .*

Or if she stared deeply into the guy's eyes while he was in her mouth, her attention entirely on him—yeah, Lincoln was totally into that.

What was it like for your partner when you pulled lightly on her clitoral stud with your teeth?

What would it be like to be blown by a woman with a steel barbell through her tongue?

Frank moments, *that's* what he wanted: fleshy boomers jiggling as they were squashed together, putting pressure on the penis head, turning its cover purple. . . .

The woman on top, lowering herself onto him, wiggling and shaking and grinding into him, her breasts full and bouncing up and down while he slapped her ass and spanked her and she screamed—*Harder, yeah, fuck my pussy, oh yeah, right there, fuck my pussy right there, HARDER*—and he began slapping her right tit and pulling and twisting the long and erect nipple, and the veins in her neck got tense and her eyes rolled back into her head . . .

There. *That's* what he was after. Not close-ups of methodical phone-it-in plodding. Not desensitized sex. Certainly not the politically correct wuss-outs where condoms were used—as if anyone wanted to see porn with wrappers, as if anyone watching a porno wanted to be reminded of all the real-world garbage that went with sex.

Not real sex.

Not fake sex.

The way sex *should be.*

There were carryovers, however. More than once he caught himself staring at how the lace pattern of his assistant's brassiere disrupted the flow of her blouse.

At the panty outlined beneath the skirts and slacks of passing teenage girls.

At belly shirts and exposed navels; the diagonal strings of thong underwear tucking into the low-cut waistline of hipster jeans.

Shorts that bunched up too tightly around some tourist's thighs.

The crease of fabric stuck in a cocktail waitress's ass crack.

The holidays looming. The static cling of cat hair still a reminder of the rescue shelter debacle. Lorraine had moved on to some other sort of volunteer binge. Lincoln arrived home with a few cartons of Chinese, and found a black videocassette waiting for him on the dinner table. The sight knocked the wind from him. Immediately he thought of the video he and his wife had separately watched over and over, only that was impossible. That tape had been eaten by the spools of the machine. The possibility still froze him. A duplicate? A new videotape that captured Newell and provided clues to his whereabouts? He got close enough to read the label and immediately called out his wife's name. Lincoln marched upstairs and the knob on the bedroom door did not give and he repeated Lorraine's name, in a rational voice this time, and tried to explain through the door and almost started pounding. He turned around and walked back downstairs and sat down on the couch and turned the videotape over and over in his hands. He cursed himself for bringing the damn thing home and doubly cursed himself for forgetting it in the machine. The next morning when Lorraine came down she looked as perfect and delectable as she had in Lincoln did not know how long. She moved right to him and put a finger in his chest. It was bad enough he had to go and destroy that video of their son, she said, but if *this* was what he'd sunk to, he should at least have the good sense to do his dirty business in private. That or the balls not to skulk around and hide like some sort of pervert. Either way he was disgusting. He was weak. The blood drained from Lincoln's face. His jaw clenched and the veins in his neck pulsed. The kitchen was gleamingly clean, the day's promise shining brightly through the bay window. Lincoln answered sincerely and somberly and his words carried the weight of the world. He was at the end of his rope. He was sorry. She locked the door, every night she locked it, and he hadn't known what to do. A man has needs. Lorraine was an icy exterior in response. She was a wall. What had happened, Lincoln continued, what was happening, what *they* were going through, it was awful, Lor, there was no sense, no reason. But Newell was coming back. They had to believe. And when he came back, Lincoln wanted him to come back to parents who were united and together. They had to stay together, Lor, they had to stay strong. Lincoln put his hands on her upper arms and held her. He talked softly. Maybe it wasn't a bad idea to think about a fresh start, he said. Another kid, maybe? They had to do something. They couldn't let themselves be ruined. Couldn't give up on everything, could they?

How the garbage on that tape represented any kind of act of faith, Lorraine wanted to know.

"Jesus Fucking Christ—"

"Explain that one to me."

"I'm talking about our lives here and you're fixated on masturbation?"

"Explain that to me, Link."

"Isn't watching the same goddamn sequence from that pizza party just as pornographic?"

"You fucking bastard."

"Isn't going and beating yourself over the head with all the missing kids on this earth—"

"You slashed it. I KNOW YOU DID."

"—isn't that just as obscene?"

"GODDAMN BASTARD."

"ISN'T THAT JUST AS OBSCENE, LOR?"

Temperatures did not cool down, not exactly. Rather, the heat was channeled in specific, separate directions. Neither party wanted to address what had happened, nor were they willing to apologize, or let it go. They kept their respectful distances and at the same time made sure to keep from making things worse. The Nevada Child Search was trying to raise funds to buy a property, which would become its headquarters. A support center. Beds and laundry facilities and computers for job training. They didn't have a property in mind, nor did they have money, but Lorraine was devoting her energies toward these things. For his part Lincoln found more reasons to stay at work. And then out of nowhere, he came home with news of a few overtures he'd made to get the Khan's banquet room, if Lorraine ever needed it for anything. She was speechless. Hadn't even known he was aware of her activities. She thanked him and the next day when he got home, a roast was in the oven, a plate of veggies and potatoes were in the microwave, and instructions for reheating were on the table.

It wasn't the easiest truce, it was awkward, and more than a little forced, but their ship was momentarily righted. They were in this together, more or less, and so Lorraine did not tell Lincoln that it had been the *third* videotape he'd forgotten in the machine. Nor did she tell Lincoln that she'd been a little curious about these tapes, that the thought of them had turned her on more than a little. She did not tell him that she had watched his smut, or that some of the rough stuff had awakened certain urges. Nor was there any need for Lincoln to know that, sometimes, in the middle of the afternoon, when everybody else was in organizational meetings, and stuffing envelopes had her bored out of her skull, just every once in a while, she cruised dirty chat rooms.

But everyone in those things was a boy. What she needed was a man.

And your smart motherfucker, he thought it was *hilarious.*

The glorious awfulness of it all. Pounds of pancake and yards of fake lashes. Times where the carpet didn't come close to matching the drapes. Dumb fuckers who had no discernible involvement in a plot, but just sort of magically showed up and started fucking. Five-second close-ups of a single pelvic thrust that got looped so they played for like two minutes straight. The gonzo stuff, shot with shaky, handheld retail cameras, so it looked like home-movie footage: two hours of coeds in the shower, as taken from the partially blocked perspective of an air duct; four hours of skirted women being followed up stairwells and escalators; scene after scene where some overtanned asshole went through the motions of pretending to pick up a college student, and you the viewer were supposed to believe that this hard-looking chick with Russian satellites for breasts, heavy metal hair, and a *Computers for Dummies* manual (which she held upside down), you were supposed to believe she actually was in college, and truly didn't have a problem with a camera filming her being picked up, and was completely cool with a camera taping her having sex with some graceless, charmless asshole, who, oh yeah by the way, she'd just met. Right. Totally. Absolutely. *Excellent.* Ponyboy watched the same supposed amateur chicks get nailed in like eight or nine different gonzo amateur series. Regular as clockwork, he watched sequences when all of a sudden the director's hand reached into the shot and he grabbed himself some ass. Moans from closed throats. Dubbed squeals that made kung fu voice-overs sound authentic. How almost anytime you wanted to see a woman's face, the camera was on her body. How anytime you wanted to see her body, it was on her face. How when the unthinkable happened and a chick had a climax that *wasn't faked,* guess how many of those the camera missed? Fucking *classic*! All the cutaways they made to the *guy's* reaction instead! Like that wasn't the least important thing in the world?

To Ponyboy, it was funnier than that soap opera hag who got nominated for best actress for like nineteen years in a row and kept getting dressed up and going to the awards show—*nineteen straight years* they announce someone else's name and she's sitting there knowing she's a schmuck and a laughingstock and just ate shit *yet again.* Ponyboy watched. He duplicated those videotapes. His pile of bootlegged stock increased and the bloopers and discrepancies swelled toward infinity. And as he became more and more accustomed to the possibility, this festering new idea, simultaneously, Ponyboy began to appreciate how the soap opera bitch and the people making those pornos, how they were alike in one other important area, too—because that soap opera hag had gotten more famous for losing than she ever would have for a win. And as for the porno biz . . . um . . . well, maybe they hadn't gotten famous off them discrepancies or nothing, but . . . okay maybe the comparison didn't technically work. But fuck it. Yeah. *That's* what he was getting at. What your smart motherfucker found so wonderful. So long as they had the desks and chairs to fuck on, who cared if the office didn't have computers? Why worry about a plot when the mook's just gonna fast-forward through the talking anyway? *Fuck it. They're fucking fuck films.*

You look at this shit right, it's liberation.

So Ponyboy sat tight on his girlfriend's carpet and he made his duplicates and he passed the point where he knew the names of the major actors and minor actresses, where he not only had favorite porn stars, but also favorite *parts* of those stars. Your smart motherfucker got used to damaged dental work. Smiles whose imperfections had been accentuated by the business's necessarily oral nature. He became accustomed to skin that hung wearily around gravity-defying silicon. To soft and scarred and loose buttocks, needle marks and bruises. Your smart motherfucker, he watched so much porn that straight up normal fucks no longer cranked his motor.

Two months ago he had not been able to understand how the guys could be staying flaccid while going down on the women. A month ago he had mocked how much effort some of those jackasses put into erection maintenance, calling them retards for the way they choked up on their bats. Now Ponyboy made sure Cheri was asleep and he loaded the machines and watched hot scorching anal scenes, he watched double penetrations and gang bangs, he watched bukkakae and fat chicks in bondage and sexy seniors delivering golden showers. Ponyboy watched truly obscene shit. Still it was a chore to prompt life from his woebegone, scabrous dick.

He couldn't say when he'd started concentrating on the male bodies. The camera's priority always had to be the act of penetration, Ponyboy knew, so the rest of the male body had to stay out of the shot. This resulted in the guys performing calisthenic routines, doing the deed in positions that seemed like stunt work as much as anything. Guys in porn were in unbelievable shape, yet to a man they were so plastic, so empty of personality, that it was difficult to envision any of them being able to get laid on their own—yet another tidbit that Ponyboy found hilarious, perfect as an egg, right up to the moment he worried that paying so much attention to the men meant he was a fag.

His dreams became twisted, sexual mutations, until he stopped dreaming, began waking up flaccid, his morning hard-ons—once mammoth and regular as tax time—now gone like the fucking wind.

Honestly, about the only thing that got Ponyboy excited anymore were the red videotapes from Jabba's office.

Each started the same way: with an unfocused, shaky shot from a handheld video camera.

Low-resolution focus. A cheap motel room. A dim and scantily furnished apartment. Half-barren, badly lit. A woman lounging on a couch. Sitting on the edge of a bed.

After a second or two, the picture was honed, and came in with a fine-tuned clarity that allowed the viewer to make out the types of flowers on the bedsheet print.

She was in or around or just leaving the flower of her youth.

She had the fresh face and tight bod of a high school student.

The dumb unworldliness that showed no awareness whatsoever of her sexual power.

The enhancements and lingerie and crucifix tattoos that certified her as a stripper.

The razor scars that documented all the nights she had not brought back enough money to her pimp.

The gleam of someone dangerously unstable.

Most seemed nervous, at least a bit uncertain. A good amount glanced toward someone out of the camera's view, which was a minor distraction.

A voice from behind the camera. Throaty. Deep timbered:

We have some new talent here today.

The beautiful and lovely Appolonia.

Nice to meet you, Silky.

Mei-Ling, is that how you pronounce it?

You're how old?

And you're a dancer, correct?

Tell me, what do you like most about dancing?

Why are you trying out for us today?

Great. Great. What's your favorite part of sex?

What's the biggest dick you've ever had?

What's the craziest sex thing you've done?

Craziest place you've done it?

That's cool. Let's see your tits.

Wow. Real tits are taboo in this biz. Like how kinky is doing it on a bed.

Ponyboy kept waiting for one to show some personality, shed some insight into her life. Nothing doing. The interviews were wheels spinning in mud: too basic to have been scripted, too pat for epiphanies. The young women waved their hair back and out of their faces and twirled loose ends around their fingers. They smiled big and pretty and uncertainly, playing along as best they could, trying to get through the butterflies, doing their best to vamp and sass and be flirty, drawing out their answers as if to tease. —*Twenty-three years old.* —*Twenty-uhm-five.* —*I turned eighteen three weeks ago.* —*I'm good at being bad.* —*I'm a nasty girl.* —*I'm an exhibitionist, so what that means is I like being naked in front of lots of guys for money.*

Mid-answer, the sound could disappear. Some words were purposefully overdubbed, replaced by static, probably to protect those who might have needed protection. Sometimes the girl just stared through the questions.

Eight and ten years, she answered.

Three mont. Three mont in America.

No in school.

No in job.

That's some pooper you've got there, went the director.

Stick it out.

Bend over and stick it out for the camera.

Yeah. Give us a little show.

Take it off, yeah all of it, slow and sexy, yeah, like you're on stage, give us a good look.

Don't be embarrassed—what, him? Our photog. For the magazines. Don't worry about him. He's seen bush before.

The lens zooming in for an absurdly close close-up: a pubic mound that had been shaved bald. Shaved to look like a heart. The rare holdout, thick and curling and wild.

There you go. Beautiful. You, my dear, have a beautiful pussy. Now play with your pretty pussy. Go ahead. Just like you do at home.

If she liked that, asked the interview voice. How that felt.

The talent giggled, or smirked, or ignored him. She kept her eyes shut and strummed and the screen flashed white from the bulb of the still camera guy. For a count the camcorder shook and was out of focus, then everything was back and clear, coming from a medium distance now.

An overtanned, unshaven man stood by the side of the bed. The musculature of his upper body was beginning to sag and he was naked, except for a pair of blue braces on his knees. He was stroking himself.

Ready for your woodman? the interviewer asked.

A coy smile, maybe a pleasantry. The woodman lurched and shoved his tongue down her throat. He put his hand up her crotch. Whenever he grabbed the top of the woman's head and started guiding her face downward, Ponyboy noticed, the streetwalkers and porno vets did not protest, but went with it, spitting on their hands, smoothly widening their jaws so that their teeth did not scrape the skin. They bobbed their skulls, jacked their hands up and down. Pros knew how to pitch a man's tent, as well as how to override the gag reflex. Also they had a trick where their fist pumped up and down and it looked like they were deep-throating, but in reality only the head was in their mouth. In this and many other respects, watching a seasoned veteran try out was exactly like watching a regular porno; which is to say that Ponyboy was not the least bit interested.

The sections that held Ponyboy's interest, that had him forgetting about his plans and his girlfriend and what was going to happen next, that sprung him to life, those were the truly amateur ones: the girls who gagged and threw coughing fits and looked dumbly to the camera for help and guidance, the strippers and party gals and dead-enders and nymphomaniacs who figured they'd had plenty of sex before, and so of course they could manage this. Ponyboy liked watching the ones who understood this was not going to be the same kind of night they'd spend with a boyfriend, who knew this was not going to be a session of gentle and sweet lovemaking, and yet still remained clueless as to the significant differences between uncaring and promiscuous and even quid pro quo sex, and just what they had signed on for here. How could they know? They were desperate creatures. They had their own concrete reasons for arriving in front of those cameras. How the fuck could they know?

And it was when the blood had accumulated in the base of the wood-man's penis, and his wood had revealed itself to be a full-grown sequoia; when, without compunction or pause, the woodman was pounding the girl through the gamut of positions inherent to a porn scene; when the director was calling out, *You like that, baby,* and *Let me hear you scream,* and *Fuck her like a jailhouse boy;* it was when the woodman increased his pace and the director shouted *Fuck her like her daddy used to,* and the woodman slapped her ass and spread her cheeks and laughed directly into the camera and plunged into her as deeply as he could, and the di-rector screamed *Break that colt* and *Who's your daddy now?* when this hap-pened, what always got Ponyboy was the face of the girl. The pulse of worry as she realized she was in too deep. The pain. The abject terror. What Ponyboy got off on were the girls who grabbed the bedsheet and held on for dear life. Who tried not to look as if they were being split apart. Whose legs buckled and gave way. The girls who had to lie down and fan themselves with a hand, then had to search to find which side of the bed the camera was shooting from so they could start staring at the lens again. The girls who gasped and winced and curled their upper lip and gnashed their teeth and shut their eyes. Who checked out and shut down, their faces freezing with distance and shock, and who then were told, *Hair, hair, hair.* It was the girls who ignored the welling tears and, through their shocked, victimized stares, compliantly looked at the camera. Who grunted from the force of the next thrust and wiped away the strands of hair and forced their tightly shut lips into a smile.

Your high-end garbage, your fake amateurs, even them tryout videos, in all of them, the money shot was as the name implied, the most important part, the payoff for all the guys, both on and off camera. Porno women never swallowed for this reason, because lots of your suits and mooks needed an on-camera money shot to trigger their own orgasms. The woodman would make eye contact with the chick. He'd warn *I'm gonna pop.* He'd pull out and quick like a rabbit she'd be off her back, on her knees, making sure to face that camera. Cut to the dude's head all jerking back. Now cut again, that first hard burst and the overflow, thick white drops scattering into her hair and her eyes. Smart motherfuckers delayed their own burst. Waited until after that first on-screen gush. You make it to those precious seconds *after* the girl's tonsils are splattered; now she's regurgitating the money shot and letting it gurgle all over her lips and down her chin, she's sucking that cock with a sexy laziness, draining its last drops and looking up at her partner. Your smart motherfucker he's pumping and holding and ready to burst. That whore on the screen is nowhere near as pretty as Cheri, nowhere near close to being as good in the sack as Cheri, and all of a sudden this plan seems possible to Ponyboy, an event that *might actually happen.*

A rustle from the next office.

The cleaning staff doing its thing a ways down the hallway.

Lincoln Ewing shut his eyes and shuddered and then slumped forward. He took a breath and his heart fluttered like a baby hummingbird's wings, and he felt the same depression he always felt immediately after an orgasm, this intense sense of deflation. The smell of ejaculate strong and embarrassing. From the periphery of the hallway, the vacuum cleaner moving closer. He just sat there with his pants around his ankles, an excess of sperm sticky down the side of his fist and along his wedding ring. He was in no great hurry to hit the remote or grab a Kleenex from off his desk. In no hurry whatsoever to proceed with the rest of the night, let alone with the rest of his life.

Those girls, Lincoln would find himself thinking.

Where do they get all those girls?

PART THREE

Chapter 6

NEWELL   12:50–2:15 A.M.

6.1

Ghostly light filtered from the streetlamps in diffuse pockets, giving the parking lot a desolate, almost virginal glow. The Plymouth plunged into an opening in the sidewalk, its front bumper scraping against the pavement, its trunk flying open and slamming back down. A harsh squeak rose from the chassis, as if someone were torturing a cat, and the Plymouth came out of the bounce, riding the dregs of its momentum. White smoke came from beneath the hood and the junker eased its way toward the rows of unoccupied gas pumps.

Newell remained jammed against the passenger door, as far from Kenny as the vehicle's confines would allow. A sound like the blast of a twelve-gauge came from deep inside the engine. The car stopped rolling; immediately Newell pushed open the door. He stumbled out of the shaking hull and his shorts slipped and Newell jerked the waistline upward. Heat rushed to his face; he had to control himself to keep from looking backward, checking to see if Kenny had seen his underwear. He left the door open behind him and hurried away from the car.

Whatever the time, it was way, *way* past his curfew. Beyond this, Newell wasn't sure. He wished he were in bed, although the moment he opened the front door to his home, a thunderstorm was surely awaiting. About the last thing Newell wanted to deal with was Hurricane Lorraine. Not that he wanted to be stranded with Chester the Molester, either.

He felt a taut line aimed his way, a concentrated focus that tugged at the back of his neck, warm there, and he increased his pace—away from the car, from the watching eyes, from anything the Molester might have to say.

He rushed past the side-by-side phone booths without noticing them. Pressing his palm on the glass, Newell pushed on the door. An electronic chime accompanied his entrance and overhead fluorescence stung his eyes. He'd believed getting inside would make him feel better; but the store came off as too clean and cold for comfort. A few stragglers mulled without enthusiasm: two crones in the closest aisle, grimly sitting on stools and pumping coins into video poker terminals; a scruffy guy in a John Deere baseball cap doing something over by the hot dog rotisserie; some frat boys noisily opening cooler doors and arguing about imported beers.

Newell was approaching the register counter when his eyes caught sight of the midget—or maybe it was a hobbit, but some sort of fully formed miniature type person was sitting on the counter, his tan slacks dangling halfway to the ground, his muddy hunting boots swinging forward and back. Newell could not help but gawk. The dwarf paid no attention, he was leafing through a biker magazine, pointing out something to the counter worker, a tub of goo in an orange smock.

There was no better destination for a troubled boy than the candy aisle, no place offering a larger measure of safety: the triple deck of bins; the inviting colors and shiny wrappers; chocolate bars; chocolate bars with peanuts; white chocolate with peanut butter and real peanuts; chocolate bars with nougat caramel centers surrounded by white cream filling . . .

He had not made it a quarter of the way down the aisle when the entrance chimed again.

"Just an overheating engine. Should be back on the road in no time."

Newell froze and stared at a bin of chocolate dollops, each one wrapped in shiny foil. Distaste spread through his mouth; the chiming remained in his ears, extending, repeating.

A voice from the kiosk interrupted: "In or out, buddy."

Kenny quickly stepped into the store and the chime stilled. Looking slightly embarrassed, he slunk to the opening of the candy aisle. Now Newell's former friend shifted his gaze; the boy felt Kenny's palpable dismay, his unspoken desperation: *How bad is what happened? How mad are you?*

The thing about being hyperactive, doctor's orders turned candy aisles into a giant tease. You could look and you could even touch, but tasting was off-limits. You had to settle for an apple. You couldn't have soda. Even the joys of orange concentrate were off-limits. *Orange concentrate isn't orange juice, Newell, and even if it was, that's still too sweet.* When you'd been officially diagnosed as hyperactive you were placed in the same category as the kids with their own sets of holidays and students whose breathing problems kept them inside at recess. By all accounts, you weren't normal. You were a *spaz.* And the king commandment of the playground was that protesting your spazziness only proved how irredeemable a spaz you were. So on the one hand there was no arguing against your spazziness, while on the other, attempt to prove that your body was fine and dandy and *just like everybody else's*—if, for example, at lunch, you found someone willing to take your weekly allowance in exchange for some chocolate chip cookies—well, then, ten minutes later, turns out, you could not sit in place without thrumming your fingers. You *were* jumpy, you *were* abrasive, you *did* stand up in class and babble and wave your arms, reaffirming to the teacher and your fellow students and yes, even yourself—*you really were a spaz.* So there wasn't any way out. You were either a spaz or you were Lord God King Spaz.

Pretty much the only thing that made sense, if you could, was not to go in either direction.

Newell kept his head down and trained all his attention on the middle and bottom bins. His hands stayed in his pockets, and he pulled up his shorts, fighting against the gravitational effect of all those nickels. Kenny's eyes were still on him, Newell could feel them. But with his head down and low, the boy was able to look up, through the top of his eyes, at the elevated glass-circle thing—that reflective oval they hide the video cameras behind. In this way, Newell, without seeming like he was looking, successfully snagged a peek at the thin young man who brought up so many strange emotions inside of him: Kenny, blurred and gray and sticklike.

In the small featureless gaze from the mirrored oval ahead of him, Newell felt the looming worry, the concentrated focus—Kenny's need to be acknowledged, unavoidable, inescapable.

And implicit within that need, something else.

If a classmate wronged him, when that kid's birthday came around, Newell crossed his arms atop his desk and buried his head and refused to sing along with the song (not that he got to eat the stupid cake, but at least he showed them). In first grade, Newell had done a show-and-tell about the merits of grapes and cherries, as opposed to the impact of sugar on your teeth. His back rigid as a yardstick, he'd stood at the front of the class and delivered his report, swelling with an odd pride, because his condition made him special. It was nice to feel that way, even if he'd secretly remained envious toward the other kids for the way they got to devour candy without limits. Though Newell had acted proprietary about the taste of skim milk and walnuts, it had been just that, an act; the sugar-coated cereals still called to him, the forbidden appeal of caffeine magnified in his psyche.

Newell does not apply himself consistently appeared in the handwritten comments on his take-home report cards. *Newell has trouble respecting other people's personal space,* explained the apologetic and encouraging young teacher. *Newell is uninterested in any conversation or subject that he is not the center of or expert at,* said the jarhead disciplinarian at St. Andrews. *If such a conversation occurs, he frequently makes a point of disrupting it.*

Again, no matter how things played out, which direction he chose, the boy was screwed. Ergo, it was only natural to play both sides. Grab as much as he could.

By the same token, Kenny was waiting, seeking some sort of acknowledgment from Newell, searching for what might even have been forgiveness.

But *not* giving someone what he wanted, that came with its own charge. And not giving it to him *precisely because he wanted that thing,* this had its own propulsion. Spite came with the taste of your own blood.

A taste to which Newell was not accustomed.

But maybe could grow into.

He leaned down to the bottom troughs, where all the loose treats were—gum squares wrapped in the colors of the American flag, gelatinous animals sealed in plastic. Newell pretended to examine a few small, dense cubes of chocolate, then put them back down in the wrong bins. Discreetly, he checked different areas of the store. Moving so as to be out of view of the counter dorks, he positioned his back to shield his actions from the overhead glass mirror. In one fluid motion, Newell reached into a bin and scarfed up a handful of Old Glory gum singles. A deft move deposited them into his front pocket.

Newell waited for something to happen but nothing did: the scruffy guy was still loitering by the microwave; the frat guys were shouting about one another's tastes in brewski; and the dwarf was on that counter, kicking his legs and showing his biker magazine to the register blob.

Kenny's chest, narrow and blurred, rose and fell in the elevated mirror. Virtual Kenny rubbed the back of his neck, stared down like he was gathering his thoughts. Like he was gathering himself. Which was *bogus,* Kenny of all people rendering judgment, feeling disappointed, neglected, whatever the fuck, just total and utter *bullshit*—especially when *Kenny* had been the one who had ruined it all, *Kenny* had been the one who'd grabbed a place that friends were not supposed to grab. Only now it was Newell who wasn't able to share in the victory of his little gum-square caper, Newell who wasn't even able to look at Kenny, *Newell* feeling all guilty and bad, hurting *Kenny's feelings*?

And how much more fucked was it when that sulking molester bastard walked right past the candy aisle?

Kenny picked up a clear snub-nosed bottle of water from a promotional display. He examined the label and took the bottle with him toward the fountain drink station. He ignored Newell and the whole deal messed with Newell's head, messed with it bad, and he looked at the bins and candies, and every single item was stupid and made him want to retch, and at the same time, each candy looked hellsa lots better than what he had in his pocket. Newell picked up a Charms Blow Pop and examined it and put it down. He did the same thing with one of those jewel candy necklaces. Now Newell sneaked a glance at the clerk and the midget. A kid just standing there in the candy aisle all this time and not choosing anything? If Newell was behind the counter, he'd be suspicious. Then again, if he was an adult, he wouldn't be working the midnight shift at the 7-Eleven.

Right now his mom was bent out of shape and coming up with plans involving some sort of military school. His dad was playing down his mom's concern, making excuses, responding to her in a way that straddled the border between condescension and insult.

From one side of the store a cooler door slammed. From another, the microwave screeched, the high beep that means it's done.

If right after losing his cell phone, Newell had called its phone number, he could have tracked the thing down. Why hadn't he thought of calling sooner? He wouldn't have this problem. Wouldn't even be in this situation.

Then again, if he somehow slipped away from Kenny right now and called, even if the person on the other end was willing to give his phone back, he'd still have to go and get it, and how was he supposed to do that?

Newell was thinking about the possibility of calling his cellular phone tomorrow, and whether he could somehow recover the phone without his parents ever knowing, when he heard a familiar voice, matter-of-fact: "You charged me for the water too, right?"

The boy's head jerked as if on a swivel, toward the sight at the register kiosk, and who was standing to the side of the dwarf, positioned politely, so as not to get in the way of those swinging little legs. A cold chill ran down the back of Newell's neck. He watched Kenny receive his change. "Great," Kenny said. "You have a nice night, too."

From the counter, Kenny picked up a large red cardboard cup, and took a sip out of the zany straw. Now he wearily turned so Newell saw his profile, long tangles in front of Kenny's face as always.

From where Newell was standing it was impossible that Kenny couldn't see him right back. But Kenny did not address Newell in any fashion. Rather, he bypassed the candy aisle completely for a second time. He headed toward the mart's front door.

The prospect of abandonment burgeoned. Newell's fear was delicious, tingling. *He was going to be left here.*

But no. Kenny idled in front of an unoccupied video poker machine. He placed his soda cup upright in the crook between his chest and his upper arm, began sifting through his change, then moved a hand into his right pocket, his elbows beginning a slow, played-out version of the bizarre chickenlike flailing routine that Newell had seen so many times. This time it ended with Kenny scavenging a dollar from his pocket, then stopping, picking at his chin.

Now his former friend looked up from the terminal and toward the boy at the mouth of the candy aisle.

"I'll be outside. Whenever you're ready. Don't take forever."

And then the laser chime system; the door closing behind Kenny; the night curling around the back side of posters for twenty-four packs of cola, appearing in the wall of Plexiglas windows with all the color and depth of a vacant television screen. An uneventful, almost disappointing normalcy rushed into whatever space had been created by Kenny's absence. Newell became aware of the scruffy guy unwrapping his burrito to find a steaming mess; the indignant and contrary voices of the dwarf and the counter guy; the frat boys making their way to the register.

If Newell wanted, this was his chance. All he had to do was go to any of them and say that he'd been touched in a bad place by the bad man.

Candy bars were stacked inside flimsy cardboard boxes. Significantly more bars remained in the box with Hershey's milk chocolate with almonds than in the neighboring box (Hershey's milk chocolate). Next to these, Newell saw, were Nestlés. From what Newell could see, a lot more Nestlé chocolate bars were left than Hershey's bars. Probably this meant Hershey's bars were a lot more popular than Nestlés; although it occurred to Newell that it was equally possible that Nestlé candy bars were *way* better; anyone who paid attention to chocolates knew how much better a Nestlé bar was, *everybody* loved Nestlé bars, they were flying off the racks, every day they had to be replaced. Newell was not allowed to have chocolate, though, so he couldn't speak to the accuracy of this hypothesis.

When your formative years had been spent with you not being allowed to partake in eating chocolate, you ended up with an exaggerated interest in matters such as this. Although, actually, such an interest might turn out to be useful, especially when you got caught in a no-win situation. For example the one Newell was in.

With what Newell's father would have called *an excess of sass,* a case of beer was set down on the counter. One of the frat guys reacted to something with a comedic double take, smearing laughter over his buddies. This distracted Newell. His attention turned to the sight of the frat guys taking out wallets and pooling their money and showing proper identification. Newell noticed the scruffy guy was among them. He also saw that the dwarf had stopped kicking his legs, and sat motionless, his face crimson.

The leader of the frat guys told the dwarf it was cool. Suppressing another laugh, he took the alcohol in his arms. His friends followed, heading toward the door and making no attempts whatsoever to contain their amusement. The laser chime rang and someone shouted, *"Damn, dude, you know you're fucked up when you start seeing trolls."*

Back at the counter the tub of goo tried to rub the dwarf's head in consolation but the dwarf jerked from under the massive hand and knocked it away. Twin lights flared from outside, reflecting off and spreading along the wall of glass, as if someone were shining a pair of searchlights into the store. For an instant, Newell felt as alive as he ever had. *Yes,* he thought, and stared into the glare, watching as the late model sports car backed out of its spot, starting its turn, its metallic grille visible.

The sports car screeched and peeled out and disappeared, revealing in the far background, underneath the metal canopy, the FBImobile, dormant amid the gas pumps. Newell could see the solitary body in front of the opened car hood, Kenny looking down, going through the motions of wrapping the tail of his shirt around his hand, readying himself to duck underneath the hood.

The thought of biting into chocolate conjured sensations of the film that—those few times Newell had actually tried chocolate—had felt totally gross on his teeth, and now his prime opportunity for chocolate consumption did not seem so prime. It made more sense for him to just get out of the store, and he was on his way when, by chance, he laid eyes on the smallish box. It was a minty green and had a sophisticated script across its face. Looked a little fun, kinda.

A digital clock and lighted advertisements for cigarettes hung above the store kiosk and its full circle of angled corner surfaces and counter space. Connected to its ceiling by a series of vertical support beams, the kiosk looked like a cross between a control center and an open-air cage, its design allowing for an unencumbered view of any area in the store. Newell stopped in front of the register. The midget murmured thoughts that did not sound charitable. Newell acknowledged him and set down the single pack of candy cigarettes. *Ho hum. Just your average kid buying your average piece of sweets.*

The blob's face was cartoonishly oversize. His large almond eyes showed neither kindness nor malice.

"What about in your pocket?"

A wisp of hair marred the blob's lip like a bad milk stain. "Come on, li'l man," he said.

"Dude, what are you talking about?"

"All you fuckers," the dwarf hissed. "Think you can get away with whatever you want."

The blob cast a stern look. "Easy there, Raoul," he said.

Newell looked at them as if they were speaking a language he did not understand. The blob's attention returned to him. "You can pay for it," he said, patiently, not unkindly, "or you can put it back—"

The dwarf broke in: "I say we string him by his—"

"Or we can call your folks. Or we can call juvie." The blob waited. "Up to you, li'l man."

On the support beam nearest to the cash register, cheap metal racks were stocked with the latest tabloids. Directly above the top rack, a fire extinguisher hung from a nail. Newell eyed the red hanging canister.

If the cops called his parents, they'd find out he'd not only been eating banned sugar products, but he'd been *stealing* banned sugar products.

This on top of losing his phone.

And breaking curfew.

And then if his mom and dad found out about in the car . . .

Newell felt around in his pocket. The gum squares were immediately identifiable—fatter than the nickels, just as solid and hard, but with a different density, the layer of sugary dust on the wrappers immediately recognizable on his fingertips.

"There you go," the blob said. "What are those, six cents each? Definitely not worth juvie. Not for, for—how many do you got there?"

"Eight."

"Nine," the dwarf interjected. "That's nine."

"*Eight.*"

"Count them again," the blob said. "Just for the safe side."

Through the glass door Newell could see the FBImobile still in the parking lot, its hood still up. From this angle it looked like the engine had swallowed Kenny's upper body.

"Hey there," the dwarf said. "Today?"

"Give him a break, Raoul."

"Plus sales tax," the dwarf said.

"Stop it, Raoul. There's no sales tax in Nevada."

"Food products *are so* taxed."

"It's gum."

"What the sweet hell do you think gum is?"

"I got six this time," Newell said.

"Try again," said blob. "But out loud."

"You put gum in your mouth," the dwarf spat. "You fucking chew on it."

"You put tobacco in your mouth. You chew tobacco. But tobacco's not a food, is it, Raoul?"

"That's cuz you don't *swallow* tobacco."

"Five," Newell whined. "Six."

"You don't swallow gum."

"You never swallow your gum?" The dwarf considered this with a rub of his jaw. He gave a low whistle. "You're a better man than I am."

When or how Newell's right hand ended up back in his pocket, he didn't know. But without the gum inside the cloth pouch, he could feel a fair amount of nickels. He was aware of Raoul making dusty sounds, like he was clearing his throat, only with a nasty satisfaction. And the blob was chuckling, too; Newell could see his man-breasts jiggling beneath his orange convenience store blouse. Newell's hand gathered around a group of nickels. Now it closed into a ball. As with a child who pantomimes the actions of a game where there is no ball to play with, his arm became a whip of motion; the air suddenly sparkled; and while the blob had enough time to determine that something was happening— enough time to register the movement of Newell's arm—he could not do more than flinch, putting his hands up, calling out *hey.* But by then two hard *pings* were sounding off the back safe; by then Newell was releasing some sort of defiant sound.

Stepping backward and to his left, he avoided the hobbit's grasp. A second helping came up from his pocket, *thwack-thwack,* nailing that little midget hobbit guy *square on,* and WHAM the hobbit lost his balance, he had to grip the counter to keep from falling. But there was a slipping and a huge *CRASH* and now all these glass jars and displays of baseball cards and sugar bomberinos were on the floor, spiraling in all directions.

"Fuck," went the blob. *"My eye."* Half-bent, he was covering his face with his shirt, and just as the crones at the video poker machines finally figured out that something might be happening on this earth besides a straight beating two pair, here came the dwarf, getting his balance back, cursing up a storm. "LITTLESHITCOCKSUCKER."

Newell took the first of the steps necessary to *get the hell out of there.* And again he saw the red canister. Hanging right in front of him.

From underneath the raised hood Kenny's head jerked. He saw the boy, coming out of the convenience store. Something was cradled in his arms. Newell looked like a running back, he was moving at high speed, pushing through the door and into the hot air; a leap; he was off the sidewalk; on asphalt, his shorts falling down beneath his hips, the denim getting in the way . . .

"DUDE!"

The Big Gulp cup tilted too far and Kenny double clutched and water sloshed all over the engine and made sizzling noises.

Newell straightened and accelerated into a full sprint. "GO!" The red canister dangling from his front hand as if it were a loaf of bread.

"LET'S *GO.*"

The hood slammed. Newell reached the car and jumped on board and his breath was deep and Kenny was in the driver's seat and asking, *what's going on,* and now he was looking back at the dashboard and the car was not, not, not turning over.

"DUDE. DUDE! He's fucking coming! *Fucking go.*"

"I'm trying," Kenny said.

Another turn of the key; a whinnying. Then a roar. Newell said *"Holy shit"* and Kenny shifted into reverse and floored it and kept looking over his shoulder. Liquid was spilling all over Kenny and noise was cranking, the stupid radio must have been on when the car had been turned off. Newell rolled down his window and there was the shifting of gears, the screeching of tires, the smell of burnt rubber, *"holy fuck holy shit"*; there was a child's gleeful scream and a sudden, unexpected expulsion—white smoke streaming from the car window as if from a dragon's nostrils, the sound of a monstrous exhalation.

Pale smoke plumed into the night and spread over the parking space like a cancerous cloud. Newell cackled and screamed and a second burst of white smoke streamed through the window.

They were accelerating through a yellow light, speeding down a straightaway, carried along by a second wind now, one point five liters of adrenaline and testosterone and undistilled mayhem and pure, unregulated whup-ass.

"*What did you do?*" Kenny asked. "*What were you doing?*"

Dude, it was fucked up back there, Newell admitted it was.

But knowledge did not stop him from doing a series of break-dance moves and swaying along to that *classic* Run DMC song. Knowledge did not stop Newell from tapping his fingers atop the long metal canister. Knowledge did not do one thing to stop him from nailing one of those sidewalk news boxes where six quarters got you a listing of hookers. Newell talked smack about how cool it would be to drive out to those Indian reservations in Pahrump and buy fireworks and fucking bomb people. He cooked up mad schemes for next Fourth of July. Apprehensive laughter came from the driver's side, and Newell said it must be rad to do a drive-by shooting. Turning up the radio, he shouted along at the top of his young lungs:

I'm the king of rock, there is none higher
Sucka MCs should call me Sire.

6.2

During the Fourth of July weekend, inspired by the men who had given their lives that freedom might flourish, and at the urging of her foul-mouthed boyfriend, Cheri Blossom, exchanging her usual candle stubs for sparkler wicks, appeared on the catwalk of the Slinky Fox with sparks of crimson and silver frothing out of her breasts. Throughout the crowd, eyes popped, presidents were released from billfolds, patriots of all stripes climbed over one another, buying Cheri drinks, paying for lap dances, private dances, and extended private sessions in the VIP room. Dawn had taken the horizon when Ponyboy finally swung by in Cheri's Jeep. Amplifier reverb was a constant echo through her eardrums by then, and a red-hot wire of pain was sharp through her lower back, and except for recurring spasms in her thighs, her legs were numb. But Cheri kissed Ponyboy on the cheek with a giddy, girlish excitement and busted out an oily wad, denominations packed atop one another until they'd strained the limitations of the hair scrunchy.

Ponyboy carried her athletic bag and unlocked the door to the apartment. He let Cheri enter first and watched her take in the sight that awaited—for not only had Ponyboy picked all of his knapsacks and chess sets and videotapes and dildos from off her carpet, not only had he vacuumed up all his potato chip remains and removed the wads of crumpled Kleenex, but he'd gone and *washed the carpet,* cleaned it of his bootprints and scuffs. A bouquet of freshly cut flowers sat on the coffee table in a glass vase. A dozen white, long-stemmed roses lay across the pillows of Cheri's bed. Ponyboy offered to make breakfast if she was hungry. He volunteered to run a bath if she wanted. Cheri thanked him with a soft kiss on the cheek and a warm hug, fell onto her bed, and moaned how good it felt to just lie there.

Too wired to sleep, Cheri said. *Too tired for anything else.*

Ponyboy offered supportive murmurs and took away the roses and filled a spare pitcher with water and put the flowers in it. He kneeled down and unzipped each of her thigh-high boots and helped them off. He rubbed Cheri's feet for an undetermined but blissful period of time, taking care to avoid the blisters, kneading through the knots beneath the calluses. She purred thanks and shut her eyes and enjoyed every second and felt a soft kiss on her cheek. Pulling a baggie from his pocket, Pony-boy asked if she wanted some of Jamaica's highest quality cess.

For as long as she'd been going out with Ponyboy, he'd never paid for anything, and of all the things he never paid for, drugs was number one with a bullet. She looked at him and realized that he had dyed his hair midnight black, which he knew to be her favorite color. He'd even trimmed his fingernails.

"What is it this time?"

Ponyboy grinned, continued rolling a meticulous fattie inside the casing of a dollar cigar.

"Actually, I *was* kind of hoping to talk with you."

He would not ever do anything to hurt her. And if she told him no, that was fine.

And of course she told him no. Absolutely not. Sleazy guys were paid to scour strip clubs and escort services. If she had a nickel for every jerk who'd approached her to do something like this—

"No," she said. "No Fucking Way. I can't believe you. What do you think I am?"

He licked the rolling paper, joined the ends together. "Fine. Totally copacetic. The answer is no," he said. "This matter's settled. . . . So you might as well listen to me, right?

"Baby, see the thing about getting involved with the industry is that if you do it right, you're set. *Set.* Like, the dynamics, they totally depend on where you are on the food chain. Once you make it onto the cover of a videotape box, you've got the whole enchilada, the guacamole, the salsa on the side."

He sat on the edge of the bed, moved toward her, offered the spliff.

"It's all marketing, see. When a guy goes to get a porno, only thing he knows about the film is what's on the box. Hard-core pervs may get to where they know directors and who's who in the cast, but they're pervs so who cares. The stuff you really choose a tape on, what really matters—is how bad you want to nail the girl on the box cover.

"I've been researching like no tomorrow, Cheri, baby girl, sweetie pie. . . . Right now the adult film industry's like got this glut of European babes. They got third worlders, all kinds of chinks and spics and jungle bunny bullshit. But let me ask. Who's watching porn? The guys in your strip bar, that's who. They leave the Slinky Fox and at the next light they make a quick turn and some of them get a mag, but most of them watch a video. I seen it. You and me, we both know that your customers want to watch a white girl. They want the prettiest white girl with the blond-est hair and the biggest tits. They want to watch Catholic schoolgirl cheerleader prom queen Miss America get thirteen inches of wood put to her. Baby, you look American like Chevrolet. That's a big plus right there. And, sweet sugar doll, from experience, I can guar-an-tee there's no problems in the fucking department."

How Ponyboy knew so much about this?

"I told you already."

He stared at her like the cat with the feathers of Grandma's canary hanging from his mouth. Cheri blew smoke into his face. He coughed, blinked violently, forced out another of those shit-eating grins.

"Research."

She blew another stream.

"Baby, *I'm telling you.* You make it onto the covers of the videotape box, you gots it made in the everglade shade. Getting paid, getting laid, drinking king-size lemonade. All it takes is a demo. One demo and your future is locked up. Cover girls are famous. They get their own 976 lines and fan clubs and personalized websites. What do you think makes the Internet run, baby? It's horny guys—they love your movies, right? They pay twenty, thirty bucks a month for clips of you. They like go into spe-cial chat rooms with other fans, argue about which one of your scenes made them come the hardest. Swear to Christ. Box cover girls get on *Howard Stern.*"

From outside came a compact discharge, a low-level explosive being detonated, the drunken cheering of overgrown boys with nothing else to do. For a moment, Cheri wasn't sure whether some jerks were playing with fireworks, if her mind was exploding. She grabbed a throw pillow, held it in front of her chest. Her brow furrowed.

"Howard Stern?"

"That's just the beginning, baby. Did you know that Paris designers put porn stars in their fashion campaigns? Sweetie, do this right, you get your own personalized blow-up dolls. You won't believe this, but there's this company? They do the dolls with a customized version of your mouth, plastic vag, plastic anuses. I know it's trippy but they do. For reals. I guess you like sit and they make a mold from off you and when it dries it's got all the contours and whatnot. You get a fifteen percent slice—heh—from all sales of the plastic version of your vagina. How awesome would it be to have a doll of you with like the bull's-eye and the light-up tits and everything? Right, I'm getting ahead of myself. But I see the world here."

His eyes were ablaze, the cords in his neck tense.

"It's a breeze, baby. I already talked to Jabba."

She smacked him with the pillow. "You got this from him?"

"He's totally willing to help."

"I bet."

"You just got to go in there, do a interview. Q and A stuff. One interview scene, baby, that's all. Hell, you could do it with me."

"It doesn't matter to you that the whole world's gonna think I'm a slut?"

"It's not like that. You do it one time. All anyone sees is the video."

"Yeah—a video of me fucking somebody."

"You do it with me." Ponyboy rocked in place and he looked down and his cheeks ballooned and he rubbed his hair and tried to rein in his temper. "I mean, shit, Cheri, you're already lighting your fucking tits on fire."

"THAT'S NOT FAIR."

A few silent seconds. Ponyboy looked at Cheri with pleading, lost-puppy eyes. When his apology was successfully communicated, he eased the pillow from her grasp. "I swear to you," he said, "all it is is one time. You do this, we'll find out where we stand. Either you get into an agency or they put you on the B-girl heap. If it's a B-girl, forget it, we're out. No discussion. Goodbye, thanks for playing. But if we get you to the right agency, baby, you're on the fast track. Hell, cover girls don't even *do* porn. Maybe a flick a month. *Maybe.* Two scenes a month, tops."

"I don't know."

"You bang your boyfriend ten times a year in front of a camera. Lick a girlie maybe ten more."

A smirk. "What's a B-girl?"

"Huh?"

"What's a B-girl?"

"Don't worry about it. It's just a name."

She pulled on his sleeve. "Why are they called B-girls, then?"

Ponyboy did not react, then seemed to concentrate, his face becoming vague, almost childlike. "Don't you worry about them, baby. You're cover girl material no problem-o. Guaran-fucking-teed."

"That's not an answer."

"Baby. You just worked the longest shift of your life, right? Made more money in one night than in what, a week? I mean, let's look at things. Flaming nipples are a great trick. But they're a trick all the same. You been doing it how many times a night now for what—five months. And the Garden, they just don't seem to have your number."

Ponyboy rubbed his jaw. "I'm sorry, honey, I hate to say it, but they don't. And the way things are going, if nothing changes, I mean, if you don't get your shit in gear, you're going to be stuck in the Slinky Fox, on your knees in the back room, sucking some loser's crank for a hundred dollars a pop."

Cheri did not try to hide how each word made her feel, she had to shut her eyes, shielding herself.

"All I'm saying," Ponyboy continued, "one way or another, it seems like this is where you're headed. But we do this right, Cheri, honey, sweetie, listen to me, we get you on the box covers, then you're a name, you get to say who you work with, you get to say when and you get to say where. One week a month, you're making a movie. The other three weeks you travel to the best strip clubs in the country."

She opened her eyes; he was still there.

"Better than the Garden of Venus. I promise. I promise you. The big time, baby."

She swallowed slightly. "Suki and Jane *have* been telling me about Guam."

It was a fragile statement, one that wasn't easy to make. Afterward, Cheri waited for Ponyboy's reaction. When there was none, she hesitated, then continued. "They say it's this really beautiful island. White sandy beaches. Waterfalls. Even a real volcano."

"Yeah?"

"It's supposed to be a like eighteen-hour flight from America, but people from Japan vacation there all the time. I guess the army's got all these naval bases, for refueling and stuff, so there's all these clubs. It's really hard to get hired. If they sign you, it's for two months. Suki worked there and she bought an Escalade when she came back.

"We could go off to Guam together," Cheri continued. "Take a vacation."

"That's what I'm talking about," Ponyboy answered.

"Go snorkeling. Fall asleep in a hammock at sunset."

Ponyboy scooted toward her, took her hand, and kissed it. "Baby, we do this right, we'll be living the high life. You'll see. Rock and roll all night. Party every day. I promise. I promise you."

A crescent of blue light shone upon a limited, triangular swatch of the alley, illuminating the outline of a rat running along the top of an opened dumpster. The blue light vanished, and when it lit up the same specific area a second time, the rat had disappeared. Watching the blinking pattern from a spot three steps inside the alley, Ponyboy was vaguely reminded of his promise. It seemed like years ago to him now instead of a few weeks.

He was using his back as a protective shield against the noise of the Strip, and had his head tilted to the side, his free hand cupped against his ear. But the carrying hum of neon still was too loud. The foot traffic from the walkway behind him was disruptive as fuck. Ponyboy jammed the cellular phone to his ear canal. Through the waves of radiated heat—pulsing from the metal phone into his eardrum, down the side of his face—he heard enough for this to be clear: for the first time since the tryout, his perpetually frustrated girlfriend possessed hope.

"So the tattoo would jump out from the skin, I guess. I don't know, it seems kind of funky to me. It *is* crazy. He wanted me to do it, but I don't know. I told him it sounded more like your thing."

Ponyboy turned in place, looking into the alley, and let the wall support his weight. He thought about responding and bit his lip. Simultaneously, as if someone had pushed a lever, Cheri switched back into the mood he knew all too well of late: *Okay, you tell me, just why the hell is it that every single guy I meet has a ridiculous scheme? And how come when YOU want to exploit ME, everything's hunky fucking dory, party all night sleep all day, whatever I have to do is no problem. But if I learn about a get-rich scheme, you get all—*

Her reference to the tryout stunned him. The way everything had gone down was still prominent, obviously, in each of their minds, and this left Ponyboy especially vulnerable. What Cheri was saying was like a punch to his solar plexus. He had no response, not even a way to respond, he didn't even know how to try. But as for three-dimensional tattoos—well, what did Cheri want him to say? That in all the times he'd gone under the tattoo needle he *could* come up with a single instance where the ink had accumulated like some sort of fucking laundry pile? That the idea *wasn't* bizarre? *Didn't* sound like the kind of shit a twelve-year-old comes up with when he gets stoned for the first time? That tonight, sitting in a junked-out ice cream truck with a bunch of teenagers, Ponyboy *hadn't* heard plots for world domination, ideas about witchery, and a whole bunch of other garbage, any or each of which *hadn't* sounded a whole lot more plausible?

"Baby, it's not a stupid idea," he said.

She softened and at the same time became excited, her voice speeding up. "Do you want to talk to the comic guy? He's right here and he's *really* sweet, he'll explain it *lots* better."

Fumbling sounds were accompanied by a high-pitched electric whine, and a crackling fragment of some song, the Fox's sound system going good and strong. Ponyboy could almost make out an exchange: some guy saying *you probably tell all your customers they're sweet;* Cheri laughing out her response, answering—*But you are*—in that paralyzing way of hers, sounding erotic and smart and sexy and cynical, all rolled into a fine line of cocaine.

"HEY, COMIC BOOK GUY?"

More fumbling and then the guy's voice was uncertain, a little high-pitched and whiny. "Um, hey—"

"I want you to listen to me." Ponyboy didn't wait for a response. "You touch my girlfriend, I will personally hunt you down, got me? First I will find you. Second I will slit your throat. And then my friend, then I will fuck the wound."

Tension through the other end of the phone, silence.

"You understand me?" Ponyboy asked.

More silence.

"As long as we're clear on that, mama's little angel. Put Cheri back on."

Why did Ponyboy have to be such a *cock*, Cheri demanded. And where the hell had he been all night? How hard was it to answer a god-damn beeper? Wasn't that the whole purpose of having a beeper, so that you would get in contact with the person trying to reach you?

"This is me calling you back, babe."

The last word wasn't out of his mouth before Cheri wanted to know whose phone he was on. Before Ponyboy could begin to address *that,* another question piled on top. Ponyboy felt as if his legs were going to buckle beneath their weight. He felt wrung out and worn down, as if he could sleep for a thousand years. For a moment he actually thought of waking up in a new world. Then he realized that what he wanted was his old world back. A world where Cheri wasn't hostile. Or at least where her hostility wasn't directed at him.

He tried to say something along those lines, only the battery was beginning to go, the connection was getting fuzzy. And down the length of the alley, too, he could see some sort of vague shape, maybe shapes, Ponyboy couldn't tell, he actually wasn't looking that hard. But the shape or shapes were approaching, coming his way, and whatever it was, it was bringing these giggles with it, competing and high pitched and echoing off the casino walls. And different sorts of dragging sounds were coming too, the scrapes of unsteady footsteps, the murmurs of a conversation.

"I've always thought of myself as romantic," Cheri was saying. *"But maybe romantic is just another word for sucker?"*

Her agitated breathing emanated through the receiver, but was drowned out by a high-pitched cackle—the fat shadow on the alley wall spreading and larger, the shapes nearing the dumpster, moving into the crescent-shaped swatch of light. Soft hues distinguished two separate bodies; Ponyboy zeroed in on the thin, tight figure draped along Danger-Prone Daphney's side. He tasted a kiss from earlier in the night. Its tang. Its ripeness.

There were only so many ways he could apologize and only so many things he could do, but Ponyboy was willing to do anything for forgiveness from Cheri, anything to make things better.

If things weren't going to get better, though, he could not help but want to be with someone who trusted him, someone who looked at him and believed he could do no wrong.

He slid down the wall, into a crouch, and kept staring down the alley, listening to Cheri talk about the plan for three-dimensional tattoos—how they hadn't done them yet but there was big money to be made.

Momentarily, Ponyboy had to shut his eyes, he had to lose himself in the oncoming laughter, the whimsy of teenage girls.

His mouth felt parched, his tongue heavy and thick. He tilted his head backward, looked to the sky, swallowed. "Okay," he told Cheri. "I might have something. For this plan. I don't know but—"

And now a shriek of high-pitched recognition. Heavy hurried steps coming his way. Ponyboy heard his name and before he could fully straighten, stringy arms were wrapping around him, embracing him, and these were followed by a light weight, colliding with, flopping onto him. Lips that were feathery and sloppy and perfect pressed against his cheek. The girl with the shaved head fell into his arms. She tipped her lips to his ear, breathless and joyful, slurring and melodic: *"Hey there, beautiful."*

———

And then his tongue was swirling in her throat and a molten sensation was flowing through the girl with the shaved head, this concentrated sense of warmth, building in momentum, thickening, accumulating its own density. And the practice sessions she'd performed on her stuffed animals would never be recalled the same way, for now there was the comparison of this kiss. That time in the fourth grade when she had chased the towheaded boy around the swing set; the birthday party games in which the girl with the shaved head had nervously participated—heading into a darkened closet with some boy she barely knew, surviving the first awkward seconds, then struggling to find the proper approach angle (clicking her front teeth against his) . . . ; these, as well as the day when between third and fourth period, in the far right stall of the girls lav, she and Francesca had been dared for ten dollars to French for thirty seconds; plus the fumbling make-out sessions that had distracted her through so many empty afternoons: Duff, T.J., T-Bone, Mohammed, Javier, then Duff again. Every experience, fulfilling or not, in one way or another had contributed to her idea of what a kiss should be. From this point forward, she would see them only through the tinted lens of this kiss.

Beads of perspiration had formed on her forehead and were gaining enough mass to run down the side of her face, but she did not feel their trickle. She was vaguely aware of a warm wind whipping onto her upper back and neck, a breeze that bordered on hot, but that provided relief anyway. She possessed the knowledge that she was in motion, that the ice cream truck was moving and she was inside the truck once again, although how she'd physically gotten back inside the truck, the girl did not know. Nor was she aware where the truck was going. The girl discovered that she could not remember how to get her body to move in such a manner as to get Ponyboy's hand off of her knee. And, almost instinctively, she was okay with her limitations. Her disconnect felt unique to her, it felt delicious and pleasing. Somehow, she understood that the nebulous sounds and sensations were caused by Ponyboy's kisses. She knew that the gap between what was going on in her head and what was going on in the truck had been forged on the strength of Ponyboy's kisses. Ponyboy's kisses overloaded power grids throughout the South-west and were the guiding light through the blackouts they'd caused. His kisses parched rivers until they were dry beds, and they were the water that would save her from the thirst of his kisses as she wandered through the desert that also was his kisses. And if the girl with the shaved head wanted to survive, she needed to be kissing Ponyboy, *she needed to be kissing Ponyboy more.*

Her tongue pressed into his, circling, moving faster, her kisses turning urgent, powerful, they took control of her breathing, left her short of air. Her body was just alert enough to break the embrace, and Ponyboy bit lightly down onto her lower lip, and more of the world started filling in around her now, each sensation like a section from a color-by-numbers drawing: first the separate and contrary noise of two bottles rolling across the floor in different directions; then the crimson flicker of a lava lamp with draining batteries; and then the lights of a passing semi, a neon motel vacancy sign, both coming in through an open space.

The ice cream truck kept barreling down the open road, and in the mouth of the truck's opened door, she saw the shadowed bodies of different punks pushing at one another, jostling and cursing, most of it good-naturedly, everyone packed pretty tightly back there. In the darkness, a lot of the punkers had the appearance of parachuters bunched into the back of a World War II bomber, and the stench of their unwashed, baking bodies was worse than the smell of rotting garbage when the girl forgot to take out the trash. She remained unconcerned, kept staring at Ponyboy, at how the incoming breeze was playing lightly with his wilting spikes of hair, at the quarter moon of sweat knifing the side of his face. Although she could not read his expression, he was staring back at her, the whites of his eyes shimmering, his irises glowing with dazzling delicacy. And staring at him, watching him stare right back, the girl knew Ponyboy was examining something inside her. Studying the girl in a way that made her know that, for the first time in her life, someone understood the crucial details of her being.

But something else was happening, too, the larger atmosphere becoming charged, voices were rising, centered around what sounded like whelping, a happy animal, shouts and jibes and gleeful barks. Ponyboy's pupils flickered in response, drifting off center. And even as a pit opened inside the girl, she also did a half turn on the old tire, attempting to see between the blurring bodies, to the source of the commotion.

It was some sort of bizarre dance: this brownish animal in the door well. First the girl thought it might be a horse, but it was too small for that, so maybe like a dog. It was trying to get a sniff of wind, but someone was flicking its ears, play-slapping at its nose. The girl couldn't entirely make out who kept bothering the dog. Like some kind of walrus, only with this massive, bulbous stomach. The bulbous walrus was swaying and unsteady, but kept teasing the animal, feinting at it like a shadow boxer, and the animal was following along, tracking the hands, measuring their movements, making small lunges and then unleashing these rich, happy whelps.

In the recesses of the overstuffed closet that was the girl's mind, it seemed she had intimate knowledge of the walrus. If she had been lucid, the girl was sure she'd recognize its laughing sounds. Only now something else was intruding. Thin like a blade. But covered in black. A vampire.

"JESUS, DAPHNEY," the vampire screamed, as he jumped between the dog and the walrus. Jerking on the mongrel's rope leash, he pulled the dog away from the ledge, back into the van. *"Nice fucking mom there."*

The wheels of the girl's mind, rusty though they may have been, ground forward.

"Can't even take care of a fucking mutt," Lestat continued.

The girl tried to get up, only to have her lack of dexterity reaffirmed. She tried again, barely getting to her feet and then plopping back down. Slurring, she yelled. "FUCKER. DON'T YOU TOUCH HER."

Then became aware of the hand lingering on the edge of the broken hem of her thrift-store skirt; aware of Ponyboy's touch—calm, practiced, firm. The girl discovered she liked being touched by someone who knew what he was doing.

"Don't worry about them," Ponyboy said. "Those two pull this shit all the time. Like some old married couple."

"That vampire's lucky. If I had some protein in me, he wouldn't be picking on no dogs."

Daphney's laughing protests were loud, as were Lestat's insults. The girl stumbled over a syllable, paused. "I'm not scared of nothing. Can magic like you don't know. All kinds of witchy shit. Gimme some protein, I'm castin' spells."

Her eyes welled. She managed to get her palm up to the side of Ponyboy's face. "I can't explain it to you," she slurred. "I can, but I can't, you know?"

Maybe there was something better he and the girl could be doing, Ponyboy replied.

"People act like they're so bad," she said.

A bump. The ice cream truck over some sort of pothole.

"Hurting each other, takin' advantage for no reason. It just makes me, like I want to . . ."

Her hand fluttered in front of his face now, casting an enchantment.

"Destroy them motherfuckers."

As if her words truly carried the power to perform the act, the ice cream truck turned gravely quiet, its bustling and barking giving way to the flapping of the trash bag over the hole where the rear window should have been, the lulling consistency of tires speeding down a straightaway. Ponyboy looked at her with an intense defensiveness, a fierce disbelief. The truck momentarily drifted atop those raised lane marker bumps. The night whistled by, roadside mile markers and sagebrush and cacti and tumbleweeds in a piecemeal montage. Ponyboy kept staring at the girl, and the lava lamp's flickering crimson gleamed against the small balls of surgical steel on his brow. His mouth was half-illuminated, tightly shut. Stoic and intense, he seemed to consider what the girl had just said, a cover of clouds passing over him now, his eyes turning small and hard, the light inside of him seeming to extinguish, or rather, withdrawing, turning inward, like a movie theater going dark before the images begin to flicker and roll.

6.3

A long block with a twenty-four-hour sports club. Shrubbery, a parking lot.

"Over there," Newell said.

"What?"

"Dude, you see?"

"Yeah, but—"

"Slow down."

"What's going on?"

"Just pull up to her, okay?" His voice was authoritative and dismissive at once. Kenny wasn't sure what to do, but followed orders, and slowed the FBImobile to ten miles an hour, approaching the bicyclist. Midway down the block, slowly pedaling.

Down went the passenger window. "Hello?" said Newell. "Hey?"

As the car pulled up, she remained curled on her perch, her T-shirt loose and drenched with sweat, her shorts made of the form-fitting Lycra of a serious cyclist.

"Ma'am?" asked Newell.

"What are—" Kenny asked, softly.

"Please?" begged Newell.

She finally gave in and looked. The boy paused, triumphant, trying to keep a straight face. "Do you know where the nearest gym is?"

There was a long second between the end of the question and the extinguisher's appearance, just enough time for the bicyclist's expression to change, her puzzlement twisting into the tangibly awful sense that she'd been taken. But by then it was too late: white smoke was hissing outward from the compression nozzle; she was being engulfed; she was flailing; slow, exaggerated motions; leaning one way; tilting the bike and capsizing into one of the prickly, decorative ferns.

The FBImobile screeched and its transmission didn't labor while jumping into third. Between wheezing laughs Newell called it *a brutal facial,* and let loose with a honking snort, the chlorine mist drifting from the extinguisher nozzle having little to do with his tears. *Classic,* he said, just about wetting himself. *"What the fuck was that?"* Kenny answered. *"What the fuck are you doing?"* Kenny's foot stayed on the gas and he shifted his eyes from the empty road to the rearview, and saw a guy running over from his car, vaulting the parking lot's miniature containing wall. In the rearview, the bright colors of the guy's workout clothes were shrinking into the darkness, but the guy kept sprinting—toward the dissipating white cloud; the guy crouching, taking the fallen woman into his arms.

"Her own fault." Newell looked back over his shoulder. A guilty cackle. "What's she doing *EXERCISING* so late?"

By the end of the next block, Kenny finally was able to breathe, and had stopped looking into the rearview. Perched on the edge of the ripped upholstery, Newell appeared thrilled, absorbed, hunting for another target. His body language encouraged Kenny. He wasn't at all happy about what Newell had just done, what *they'd* just done. But it looked like the boy was in a better mood. So maybe everything was going to be all right after all. If a little mayhem was what it took to get things back to normal between them, Kenny was up for it.

Maintaining a steady pace of thirty miles an hour and keeping in syncopation with the city's computerized traffic signals, the FBImobile eased through one green light after another, moving though empty intersections. Each new block was burdened with competing shopping plazas and chain stores, every one of them as large as a palace, anchored by twenty-four-hour supermarkets and wide-acred lots. Strip malls were dappled with neighborhood watering holes and their accompanying clusters of parked cars. Fast-food joints infected everywhere you looked. Attacking a drunk or someone in a car was too big a risk, it seemed to Kenny. Even on a major road like this, finding someone else to nail wasn't going to be a piece of cake.

He kept driving and glanced out of the corner of his eye, and saw the boy poised, willfully focused. It seemed to Kenny that Newell's adrenaline rush had given way to a state of perpetual anticipation. Then again, Newell had his own reasons to be searching out there.

Pier 1 Imports and Pottery Barn, Bank of America and Olive Garden, Supercuts and Blockbuster and Kinko's, the stores progressed and repeated, the blocks melded together, kind of like those cartoons where the same rock formations continually looped through the backdrop, but the coyote and roadrunner stayed in their stationary poses. Kenny pointed this out to Newell and received a halfhearted snort in reply. He kept heading north, crossing the two of them over some sort of unofficial line, into a new neighborhood, one of wholesale liquidators, cell phone and beeper emporiums. An all-night laundry center advertised its ten-cent slot machines. A lonely Elks lodge was sandwiched between competing shops that issued payday, title, and signature loans. Some stores, Kenny couldn't tell what they were, since their managers switched off the marquee lights at night, to save on the utility bill. Without all the residual neon, the sky was noticeably darker, giving storefronts the foreboding feel of a run-down warehouse district.

On one lonesome corner, they found a Latino guy entertaining himself with slight, fluid hip-hop movements. "Mofo's packing," Newell said, waving off the possibility. A block or so later, in front of a Western Union, a grizzled Asian man listlessly pushed a broom over the sidewalk. "Let him alone," Kenny warned. "He has enough problems."

Ignoring Newell's cold shoulder and implied disapproval, Kenny guided the steering wheel with one hand, starting the FBImobile into the curving *S* of a road where every third streetlamp had burned out, been shot out, or had its fuse box gutted—a road whose navigation was second nature to Kenny, its pull all but tangible for him. He passed the exterminator office with the giant plaster cockroach fixed atop its roof, then the Salvation Army clothing store. He noticed Newell was rigid, the extinguisher positioned just beneath the passenger window. The FBImobile accelerated through a yellow light, and now the thoroughfare opened onto the clearing of eight-dollar-a-night parking lots. Looking up and ahead, Kenny took in the long dome covering Fremont Street, downtown's few casino towers gathered above the animated rainbow glow.

Temporary shelters of cardboard and plywood were visible in the doorway of a liquor shop. Around the side of a bail bonds place, slumped bodies were covered by giveaway blankets. Here was a three-hundred-pound black woman falling out of a pair of tiny jean shorts. Moving unsteadily on silver high heels, she sauntered in front of a motel office, where three thugs were loitering. Pulling her shorts from her butt, she promptly whirled and flipped off the hooting men.

She would have made a perfect target, could have been the opening Newell had been looking for. Instead the boy tightened in his seat. He brought the canister closer in to his body, an action that reminded Kenny of his aunt years ago—all the times the bus had moved into this territory, the countless times she'd clutched her purse just a little tighter.

"I never come down here," Newell said.

How to respond? What could Kenny really say, other than, *Yeah, you're right*?

For how long now had Kenny himself been put off by downtown's squalor? How many times had he been repulsed by the prospect of coming down here to get his aunt, vaguely afraid, insulted even—as if he were a cut better than this neighborhood, as if life had something better in store for him? How many times had Kenny seen similar things and wanted to disappear?

As he struggled for an answer, Kenny felt more than this, too.

Newell's distaste, his unpleasant manner and assumption of privilege, everything that lay beneath the boy's short declaration and slight motion. It made Kenny defensive, turned him territorial.

Not long ago, Kenny's father had spent a week in one of the motels up ahead. Right after a stint in a halfway house, the old man had gotten himself cleaned up pretty good. Each day, when the pawn shop opened, he made sure he was waiting for Kenny's aunt, hoping to convince her to get Kenny's mom to take him back. Hit by the memory now, Kenny found the story entertaining. With more than a little nostalgia, he recalled how furious the Jew's Daughter had been with Kenny's dad, she already had more than enough bums hanging around. The Jew's Daughter repeatedly ordered him out of the pawn shop, but Kenny's dad wouldn't leave, not without Kenny's aunt agreeing to help with his marital distress, which his aunt most certainly would not do. The whole thing turned into a real mess. Kenny's dad even ended up working at the pawn shop for a little while, sweeping the floor at the end of the day, wiping down the displays, and hosing off the sidewalk—activities that usually were done by a homeless black guy, Loveless, in exchange for five dollars. Of course, when Loveless showed up and saw Kenny's dad doing the tasks that he relied on—*five bucks a day* going right out the window— the two had almost come to blows, separating only when the Jew's Daughter took out a shotgun. In the end, Kenny's father and Loveless had compromised, splitting the responsibilities. They actually got along pretty well for a while—until the police rounded up all the homeless people and Loveless disappeared, which was a different story.

It would not have been difficult for Kenny to tell Newell about this minor comic nightmare. The stories he had forgotten about the pawn shop would have entertained Newell until puberty kicked in.

But it occurred to Kenny that when Newell said, *I never come down here,* what he'd really meant to do was ask, *Why are we down here?*

He'd wanted to know: *What are we doing?*

What are you going to do to me now?

Downtown was upon them, hotels and towers packed into that dense square district, tour buses parked like gigantic, end-to-end dominos along the right side of the street. A bombastic patriotic jingle blared through the overhead speakers, emanating from the open-air mall of Fremont Street, where the animation loop was running—red and white stars flowing down a sky-blue backdrop, cartoon fighter jets traversing the length of the street. Not too many people were beneath the dome to watch—a lone woman, elderly and stooped, had put down her overstuffed shopping bags and was looking up; a pair of undefined gambling fiends were making their way around a shut-down souvenir cart. A few other miscreants were out there, too, swerving and staggering, the drunken dregs, the losers and the lost and those who knew they would keep on losing, yet were powerless to stop themselves. Newell was watching it all without betraying the slightest emotion, at least he was putting up a good front—Kenny knew him well enough to recognize that's what it was: the boy tightly constricted, visibly failing in his efforts to keep his fears at bay. He was so obviously susceptible, so tangibly vulnerable. Kenny was overcome with how young Newell actually was. His throat caught and he swallowed dryly.

If he made an immediate right turn and went down the short alleyway, the car would emerge on the other side of the pawn shop. But unlike hundreds and maybe thousands of times before this, he drove past the turn, did not so much as look in the direction of the shop.

Newell's chin rose. His head turned a degree or two, and he stayed with the sight above the entrance to a sports-themed casino. A huge bronze statue, posed like the centerpiece of an oversize trophy. A baseball player, front knee forward, arms extended, following through on his perfect home run swing.

"This one time, the mayor wanted to make more tourists come down here?" Kenny started unsteadily. "The cops got ordered to round up all the homeless people from Fremont Street. I don't know if you remember this. I guess the cops went through downtown and loaded all the bums onto police buses and gave them like a sack lunch. They dropped everyone off outside city limits. My aunt was thrilled. But the lady who runs the pawn shop? She got concerned. Turns out Loveless had already told her—word about the round-up was already out on the streets. When Loveless didn't show up to clean the windows for a week, the pawn shop lady complained."

In accordance with the flow of traffic Kenny eased off the accelerator. Two or three traffic signals ahead, large sand dunes and round cement pillars supported a system of ramps for an elevated series of freeways.

"Well, the cops just laughed, like: *What are you complaining about?* But tell you what, when the *Review-Journal* did the big story, who was laughing then? Even that didn't matter though. Turns out, the cops still clear Fremont all the time, and the bums keep coming back anyway."

Newell was finally looking at him.

"I'm not making sense," Kenny admitted.

A yellow light. The Reliant stopped short. "What I'm saying—wait. Okay, here, when I was little . . ." He paused again, concentrating now, his bottom lip pinching over the top.

"Okay, like my dad. He used to tell me they purposefully built those freeways to surround the Strip and Fremont. If the race riots came, the army'd put tanks on top of the freeway. I guess they were supposed to fence off the black section of town from the casinos. My dad told me that this way, the tourists would be safe to gamble."

A passing beat. Kenny added: "You can't really believe anything he says when he's drunk, though."

"This is all I mean." He paused once more. "My dad. He's like everyone else, you know? Like the police and the mayor and all the plans people make.' Or, or—like driving around with the extinguisher. How people say stuff. Or when I . . . I mean." Kenny grimaced. He took a long breath. "You do something. And maybe it feels right just then. Or you just do something to, you know, just to do it. Don't mean you want it to come out like it does. You can't know how it's gonna come out. You don't really think about it, you know?"

He glanced over, waiting for an answer.

6.4

Ponyboy always thought of it as a crutch, to be honest. A defense mechanism, only with more self-promotion. Cheri would harp on the redemptive powers of the imaginative act, saying *Really,* and *I'm serious,* and *Fine, fuckhead, be condescending.* A million times, Ponyboy had heard the lecture: how imagining the worst moments of her life being projected onto the silver screen was the very thing that allowed Cheri to survive those moments; how envisioning herself as a character in that movie created the distance that was so key to calming her. She'd go on about *character arcs* and *emotional journeys* until the friggin' cows came home. Only, this one time, about a week after everything between them and Jabba went down, Cheri hadn't lectured Ponyboy. She'd merely looked at him with all this pity and sadness, and said she'd been thinking. "My character's getting to the point where she should be learning from her mistakes, you know? I think maybe I should be acting like that in real life, too."

Didn't need to be Sherlock f'in Clouseau to decipher the undertone there. Didn't need to be some nautical engineer to understand rough waves were ahead. Although, even without the trouble in their relationship, even if the movie of Cheri's life *hadn't* included cryptic jibes, Ponyboy would have been distrustful of the whole device. Why? He couldn't say. Maybe it was as simple as someone getting turned off by qualities in other people that they can't stand in themselves. It could have been that Ponyboy shunned Cheri's movie fantasies as a reaction to his own inclination for drama. Maybe since Ponyboy's life *already* involved an act of flight, one that was particularly real and gritty and physical, he saw something plastic in the notion of mentally depositing himself in a theater's back row, using the dispassionate eye of a surgeon to consider the gamut of reactions at his disposal. It was too desperate. Too pathetic.

Except now he was in back of that ice cream truck and the girl with the shaved head kept looking at him and her eyes were deep and doelike and smudged black with kohl, so very resolute in her belief in him—almost as if she were willing Ponyboy to be worth her belief. And in her gaze, Ponyboy felt exposed. Her remark about *people hurting people for no reason* had nailed him in a particularly sensitive area, and while he could tell her comment hadn't been specifically pointed toward him; while he could see the girl didn't know what she was saying, was buzzing too hard to have a clue about the gravity of, well, *anything,* still, Ponyboy felt all sorts of intense and contrary emotions. Whether he should keep making moves on the girl with the shaved head? If he should try to keep her on the hook like he had promised Cheri? The thing about the tattoos sounded like the direct opposite of what the girl had said about unnecessary cruelty. But then again, her remark pretty much applied to every fucking single thing that Ponyboy had gotten Cheri involved with. Trying to juggle all these thoughts just about had Ponyboy's head exploding.

So then, a world premiere. The first-look sneak preview.

A gradual fade, an edit that properly conveyed the distance of Ponyboy's thoughts at the current moment, the viewer transported away from the darkening and blurry events in the ice cream truck, and toward a newly forming scene. The entrance of the Slinky Fox. Cheri Blossom emerging from the padded doors, Cheri moving at a hurried clip, having changed from her work clothes into her current fave outfit: satiny canary-yellow sweatpants with the word JUICY on the ass and a coordinated tank top. Her dominatrix boots had given way to flip-flops, which were making scratchy sounds, as they weren't built for fast walking. Cheri passed the bouncer and told him she was in a hurry and was sorry, she would settle up with him tomorrow, and as she kept on going, she cursed under her breath because leaving early had not excused her from tipping out everyone, and these finances were only furthering her doubts concerning the wisdom of what she was doing. In this scene, the strap of Cheri's gym bag was digging into her shoulder, and the bag was open, and some of her work supplies (a sports bra, a box of tampons with all their strings cut off, a backup pack of fake nails) were jostling. When something fell out, Cheri didn't notice.

Which was an opportunity.

In his imagined movie, Ponyboy's vision of the comic book guy took the form of a thirty-year-old five-hundred-pound virgin. It was a foregone conclusion that this tub of lard didn't have the cojones to venture within a pissing tit of Cheri, especially after Ponyboy had talked with him. Even if Comic Guy went and rented himself some courage, Cheri had to know better than to hook up with him, because that would be signing the guy's death certificate. Nonetheless, Ponyboy found himself concerned about the notion of his girlfriend listening to some jackass she'd met while stripping. Ponyboy assumed that three-dimensional tattoos were impossible, but with supercomputers and fiber optic lasers and all that shit, who knew. To Ponyboy it sounded like the Comic Guy had captured Cheri's ear with a plan that maybe was out there and sci-fi, but that also sounded cool and interesting, the type of shit Ponyboy might want on his body.

So the jackoff's plan might actually happen, while on the other hand, Ponyboy never failed to have plans blow up in his grille.

In the movie of Ponyboy's life, the comic book guy may have been obese, slovenly, and physically inferior to Ponyboy, but he was superior to Ponyboy in every other way. And he was outside the Slinky Fox, picking up whatever had fallen out of Cheri's workout bag. He was catching up with Cheri, handing her that stupid thing.

And here, in a trick borrowed from ye olden days of filmmaking, Vaseline would get dabbed around the camera lens. Blurring would occur, the scene slowly dissolving.

No longer Ponyboy's movie of Cheri's life, but now a flashback.

Fringed and overstuffed pillows abounding. The teasing sounds of laughter like the best kind of music.

Cheri had done laundry, and was wearing one of Ponyboy's freshly clean concert T's as a bed shirt, its faded cloth hanging comfortably to the middle of her thighs. She was lying on her canopy bed and her legs were jutting out from beyond the end of the shirt, appearing as smooth and golden as anything that had ever existed.

In the flashback, Cheri knew how good she looked, and she was a little frisky, and laughed, playfully slapping Ponyboy's shoulder, telling him to be serious.

He held up three videotapes. The green tape was directed by a former box cover starlet—Ponyboy said it was from a series that catered to a couple's sensual needs. "Might be good for syncopation or, you know, whatever."

She said she had not gone seven straight days without sex since, shit . . .

The yellow one, Ponyboy continued, was from a "best of" series—maybe there were moves he and Cheri could steal.

And the thought of Ponyboy being Mr. Abstinence was even more absurd, Cheri said. No way he was going to make it through a week without some of her home cooking, she said.

She thrust her boobs underneath his nose. *Look at these.* Her voice went intentionally high, played for comic effect: *Tell me Papi no like.*

"As for the red . . . Well, forget about that one."

"Pony."

"If we wait, we'll get more into it. We'll have all these techniques and pent-up energy."

Ponyboy had note cards. He already had some thoughts about stuff she should remember for the camera.

"Gee, Professor Hard-on, I didn't know there was going to be a test. Too bad it's not going to be a hands-on exam."

She razzed and teased and Ponyboy jammed the yellow tape into the VCR and halfway through scene one, abstinence be damned. That easily, the week that was supposed to be devoted to preparation turned into a continuous bout of on-the-job training. Brute and primal at moments, their sex leapt beyond the parameters of simple physicality, combusting into something ludicrous and funny, like the time they went into Cheri's walk-in closet and tried to use the metal clothes rack to replicate something on a trapeze, and Ponyboy kept checking to see what was happening on the television, and finally Cheri was laughing so hard she lost her grip on the bar and the two of them went crashing down. Just as easily their sex would turn tender and wonderful—they'd be covered with sweat and tired and at the same time wired like General Electric, screwing like maniacs, and shabazz, for no real reason, she would stare into Ponyboy's eyes, and he would stare back, and then they were together in their own private universe. And if Cheri never quite understood why it was so important that she be the one to remember all the technical jazz (*You have to remember*, Ponyboy'd say, getting weird), if every few hours or so, Ponyboy called and updated her on how the contracts were progressing (*All systems full ahead*), or reported nothing but his own excitement (*I love you so much, baby*), the weird thing was, not for a fraction of a millisecond did she actually believe it was going to take place. In six days, in four days, in three hours, she'd be copulating in front of a room full of people, and the preparations and the progression and, yes, the event to which all this was leading, the whole caboodle seemed unreal to her. Sure, duh, Cheri understood that a camera was going to tape her getting nailed, that these images were going to be reproduced and mass-produced, that lonely men would be in their lonely little homes jacking off to a taped clip of her. She understood that if her mom and grandma and kindergarten teacher knew about her stripping career, they would have declared her damned, so, boy howdy, would she be going to hell for this. It *was* sleazy. *Was* slutty. While doing her daily routine of stomach crunches, Cheri would be taking care to keep her legs elevated and together, and she'd momentarily think about just how slutty it was, and she'd lose count of reps. And yet Cheri would recover and continue with her crunches, getting back to the business at hand. Because, in the parlance of her boyfriend, when the grease left the grill and the burger hit the bun, only one part of this little scheme impacted her immediate and daily life, only one part of it felt real. This was corny, Cheri admitted it was. As much as she wanted to shout her news down onto the valley, what she wanted to scream was too cheesy for words; she could never have possibly explained it.

The one thing about this scheme that felt real to Cheri, the single thing she could literally roll around in her mouth as if it were a marble, was her belief in her man. Sure he didn't brush his teeth more than once every four days, and when he did, he scrubbed so hard that white drool ended up on the bathroom walls, in his hair, and, yes, once or twice, on his ass. How you brushed your teeth and got toothpaste on your *ass*, Cheri never could figure, but her man did it. And okay it was true, he used her purse as his personal ATM. And whenever she took him to the movies, he crunched food through all the previews. And one time when the preview came on for the animated movie about a horse that could never be tamed, at the part where the sunset was glowing and the little girl was hugging her horsie around its neck, and the cute animated child said, *Spirit, you'll always be in my heart,* admittedly, Ponyboy had cupped his hands around his mouth and screamed *BOOOOO*. Her boyfriend was indeed The Smelly Musclebound Asshole Who Heckled Little Girls and Their Cartoon Horsies. The man she loved had spent a full, uninterrupted month trying to embed cordless phones into vibrators, to this day insisting that, done correctly, Hands On Phone Sex was a surefire gold mine. Ponyboy was constantly dumping his shit all over the floor, peeing on the toilet seat, blasting the abomination he called music at a volume that caused the neighbor's plants to wither and go brown. He was preternaturally absent whenever it came time to pay his share of the utilities, prepare a meal, or wash one goddamn dish, although if Jasmine, Rain, or any of Cheri's other friends from work were over, wasn't it something how Ponyboy *just happened* to be hanging out? Too many times Cheri had caught him staring at Jasmine's big round caboose, and whenever she called him on it, he got angry—*What, how'm I not going to look at that?*— like it was *her* fault for catching him. Cheri would bet her tits that Ponyboy had cheated on her, at least three specific women she could think of, and she had suspicions about more. This was off the top of her head. Without even getting into the breast implant thing, her boyfriend's desire to have her do hard-core porn notwithstanding, it wasn't real hard to see the scales of justice tilting heavily on one side. In the hard cold light of truth Cheri definitely could see the verdict, she could ask herself, just what the hell she was doing with Ponyboy.

But what was funny was how easily the light of truth could change, how the correct verdict wasn't necessarily the obvious one. Some boyfriends, you came to them with your problem and they said, *What have you done now.* Some said, *Don't worry, it will be all right.* Legend had it, there were boyfriends who responded: *What can I do to help?* But with Ponyboy, you shared your problem and, right off the bat, he laughed. Then he said your problem wasn't even a problem, you should hear what's happening to his friend, this guy who had a f'in BATTERY shoved through his nose. Ponyboy would get to talking, and while he talked, he'd raid your fridge, because he'd been smoking your dope all night, he had the munchies, and so now, while he was playing down your troubles and topping them, he also was spitting chunks of your food all over, going on and on about the guy with a battery in his nose, and maybe you hadn't been listening correctly, because somehow the story had morphed, it had turned into something involving Ponyboy being camped out in this drainage pipe, Ponyboy trying to sleep while just down the way from him, this fucking space alien was boning some chick. A story about rain coming down and tons of water flowing through the drainage pipe and the space alien didn't have a penis, it had like these big long tentacles, so *boning* maybe wasn't the right word, and it's raining so bad that Ponyboy couldn't stay in the pipe, but at the same time, he's got to stay in there, cuz how many times do you get to see a space alien bang some chick? And Cheri, in her kitchen, listening to this, Cheri would find the scales of justice tipping even further, because none of her problems were being solved. In fact, thinking about it, she had all her old problems, plus her fridge was empty, and her stash was gone, and now, in addition to being filthy and obnoxious, in addition to lying, mooching, and philandering, in addition to being an opportunist and an egomaniac and just a fucking *dick,* there was the very real and disturbing possibility that Ponyboy was a full-on, batteries included, no assembly required, *MORON.*

An insatiable lightness took her. A gust of uneasy delight. She sat and laughed and finally could not take it anymore. "Stop shitting me. Was there really an alien?"

Ponyboy gave her this constipated look. *"Haven't you been listening? I'm not talking about an alien here. I'm fucking talking about SURVIVAL."*

And well, how was she supposed to keep a straight face? It was like watching your dog shit on some lady's lawn right when that woman's coming out of her house. It was like walking down the street and seeing a little kitten, so happy and perfect and cute that it was all you could do not to kick that little fucker. It was the moment when you saw something that you knew was fucked up and wrong, but still could not help yourself; when you could not control your actions and were going on autopilot, and maybe later you would feel bad about it and pledge to be a better person, but right now, oh well. The wrongness was the endearing part. Wrongness was the bond. The turn-on. And yeah, Ponyboy may have very well been a filthy obnoxious lying mooching philandering opportunist. Probably he was a moron to boot. But he was Cheri's moron. Whatever problems the two of them had in an empty kitchen, they had together. Whatever bullshit they had to face, they would survive together. And so what if Cheri could not sit still for ten seconds, think about the idea of a video camera capturing her naked body, and feel anything except a desire to run for the hills. So the hell what. Because the idea of getting filmed with *her man,* the thought of all those lonely people cueing up the videotape and watching *her and Ponyboy*—well, that was a lemur of a whole other stripe.

So Cheri watched his pornos and even studied his stupid-ass note cards. She got more turned on and the sex between them got filthier, and she shouted the nastiest names she could think of, the ones that hurt him worse than anything. Cheri told him, *You don't deserve this pussy, you piece of shit, you fucking cocksucker,* and she felt more powerful, more excited, closer to him than ever before. Their plan moved forward and Cheri followed his leads, and when the big day had arrived, she'd been full of nervous energy, and it was as if the two of them were embarking on a weekend trip up to Mount Charleston, something they'd always talked about.

Ponyboy drove. Let Cheri listen to whatever music she wanted—a first for him. He kept to himself, quiet, watching the road. They bypassed the route to the Strip, which surprised Cheri. "I guess I figured we'd be booked into a room at the Palms," she said. "Somewhere classy."

Ponyboy took her hand and wouldn't let go, which was sweet and assuring, but also kind of strange.

They passed the batting cages of a softball complex, and the long flat greens of a public park, and then made a right on Tropicana. Cheri checked the mirror attached to the back of the sun visor, and made sure her mascara was fine. Ponyboy roused from his thoughts long enough to stare at her. He said that right now she had to be the most lovely person on the planet, and he squeezed her hand, and they idled, waiting to make a left turn. Ponyboy was unlike his normal self in that he did not chance it and try to zip through some minor opening; rather, he waited for the coast to clear, then made the turn, and started the Jeep down a wide road busy with billboards for weekend room rates and flashing ads for cabaret shows. He pointed out a series of buildings where he used to crash when he first came to the city, which Cheri already knew about, but smiled at anyway. Her hand caressed his. Just ahead, distinct blue and maroon parking structures stood out against a wide backdrop of jagged, purple mountains. The sky was spacious and calm, off-white and thin, like a weak tea, maybe.

The small, toylike shell of a jumbo jet flashed its landing lights in tandem, leveled with the horizon, and gradually started its descent. A plain and everyday sight, it seemed to Cheri to contain an elegance that was just as regular, and she stared at it for a time. Immediately ahead of the Jeep, colored signs were hanging above the road, each sign above a different lane: ARRIVING FLIGHTS, DEPARTURES, LONG-TERM PARKING. Taxicab traffic was thick. Ponyboy got into the through lane. Cheri felt a rush of love for her boyfriend that was so ferocious as to throb. She leaned over and pressed her lips into his cheek with all the force in her body.

And so it had come to this: an office structure that looked like you'd visit for tax help, a maze of unlit corridors with cement floors, a black metal door without a company name or logo. Standing at the threshold, Cheri flashed back to another crappy office complex and that skeezey doctor—his pathetic comb-over, his patient leer. She reminded herself of all the money her new breasts had brought, told herself things had turned out more than okay. "Guess I'm nervous," she said.

Ponyboy seemed to be looking at the window, those grimy blinds of faded yellow plastic, pulled all the way down. For a horrific instant Cheri worried he was going to go in through the window.

Thank goodness he went to the door.

Cheri smoothed out her outfit. Once more she asked about logistics, the order of how things were going to go, just to make sure she had things right, just so she could hear, yet again, that everything would turn out okay.

"Hey, hey there's that smokin' body!"

The deep voice came as the door swung open. And just like that, this huge hulk of a man was in front of her. No neck, just a wide, flat head that seemed to have been screwed into his massive body.

"Hey, Jabba."

Ponyboy stepped inside, eagerly taking one of the man's hands. "We made it. Right on time."

Jabba's monstrously large forehead made an easy transition into a huge, bald dome, both of which were tanned to a char, the gray hair above his ears slick with styling gel, his smile revealing deeply grooved wrinkles around his eyes. Patting Ponyboy's shoulder, Jabba moved straight toward Cheri, opening his arms, his shirt almost blinding her: bright oranges and flaming yellows, unbuttoned to the middle of his stomach. He kissed her on each cheek; she smelled coconut oil, and a tart cologne, and beneath their layers, Jabba's natural body odor like the stench of sardines.

"Caught your set the other night." His eyes drifted toward her chest. "Sensational."

Cheri did exactly what she was supposed to—first giving her brightest, fakest smile, then straightening her back so Jabba had a better view. Leaning forward and returning his peck on the cheek, she gave him a better angle to stare down her blouse.

"You're sweet," she said.

Jabba showed her in and she latched on to Ponyboy's hand, squeezing so hard that the blood left her fingers. The office was gloomy, its walls the color of dried vanilla pudding, its ceiling panels stained with nicotine soot. A crappy desk was covered in dirty magazines, littered with a few large, opened plastic containers of coleslaw. A revolving fan blew on one of the magazines, threatening to flip the foldout.

In the middle of the room, a skinny Japanese guy was figuring out the right height for a lighting apparatus. A man in coaching shorts was sitting on a sofa sectional whose dark leather remined Cheri of bitter chocolate. The guy was older, some, a bit thick in the stomach, his golfing shirt tight and short in the sleeves. He was patiently unpacking his bag, removing a flesh-colored dildo, a syringe kit, and a blue Velcro-looking sleeve of some sort.

Both men stopped what they were doing and watched Cheri's entrance, and the feeling was something she well knew. Putting some oomph into her hips, she sashayed into the room, graceful on four-inch heels, deftly avoiding a stack of videotapes, making herself the show, letting their eyes linger on her body. She pretended to examine the lone wall hanging, a poster of the Las Vegas Strip at night, black velvet inside a flimsy metal frame, and it was impossible not to feel something of a letdown, being in this office for what she was about to do.

Just as hard was faking that she did not recognize the colored videotapes as ones Ponyboy had her watch.

But she betrayed nothing. A quick pirouette gave the techies a nice view of her backside, and she made her way back toward the desk now. The increasing attention of the men behind her was palpitant, and Jabba's leer had her on edge. But at the same time, in a different way, it gave her more confidence. Nervous as these guys had her, their looks had her understanding the potential of this idea; and suddenly the blooms of love Cheri felt for Ponyboy flowered; suddenly she was on top of the world, horny as a fucking toad. Man oh man was she looking forward to giving Ponyboy some horny toad love in front of all these exploiter pervs.

She took the cigar from Jabba's mouth, put it in her own, blew smoke in his face.

"Real first-class operation you got here."

Jabba coughed. "We're renovating." He cleared his throat. "Your tests came back. Everything's great. All we need now is a picture of your ID."

"Got it," Ponyboy interjected. "Right here."

Jabba took the card without looking, his attention staying with Cheri. "Hiro!"

Halfway across the room, the guy stopped fiddling with the portable lights. Cheri noticed a large camera around his neck, an even more imposing telephoto lens.

"You need anything?" Jabba asked. "A few drinks to loosen you up?"

"Thanks," Cheri said.

"Amyl nitrate? Poppers? Blow?"

Again Cheri reached for Ponyboy's hand. "I'm good."

"Great. You sure I can't convince you to show us those flaming nipples today?"

Ponyboy took an uncertain step forward. "Yeah, Jabba, about that." His hesitance surprised Cheri. She wasn't used to him being deferential. Not to another man, that was for sure. "We just think it would be better if we saved it," he said, and smiled apologetically. "I mean, why give away a gold mine, right?" A shrug now. "Let's keep it for the box covers, is what I'm saying."

Jabba grunted, turned into the room. "How we doing over there? Rod, all systems go, or what?"

On the sofa sectional, the overtanned and unshaven guy continued working a blue sleeve up his leg. With painstakingly slow and almost ritualistically distant movements, he fit the metal construct of his knee brace around the sleeve. Cheri could see a doughnut of flab pouring over the waist of his coaching shorts. He might have been handsome a long time ago.

"Wow," said Ponyboy. "That really him?"

"Live and in the flesh," Jabba answered. "Five-pound cock and all."

"I love his work."

"You're lucky. Normally he won't travel for these. But Vegas is Rod's kind of town."

Cheri pulled on Ponyboy's shirt, whispered into his ear: "Who's that?"

Newell had completed the first of his three guaranteed innings when the coach had moved him over from left field to right. The move had dropped Newell's place in the batting order as well; and instead of being the second batter in the upcoming inning, he missed out on getting to the plate entirely. Newell reacted with shouts as to the bogusness of the switch; he called the coach *completely bogus* and refused to participate in the traditional postgame handshakes with the other team. His folks watched in silent horror in a row near the top of the bleachers, but Newell did not care, and chucked his mitt into a trash can. Ignoring the coach, who shouted *"Get back here,"* Newell removed his jersey and stalked away. Thoughts of walking home entertained him, but he stopped at the back of his dad's Suburban, his face flushed now, his body sweating. Kids from both teams were gathering around the ice cream shack; his mom and his coach were standing in the middle of the diamond, colluding against him, he was sure.

Newell had a good sweet while to sit and sulk and think about what he'd done, before Lincoln arrived at the Suburban. He was alone, had recovered Newell's baseball glove, and was hiding it (sticky with soda and smelling of refuse) out of Newell's line of sight. He also had a Bomb Pop. Lincoln said *Hey* in the low small voice that adults talked to one another in when they were serious, and asked if Newell was all right. Newell kept looking down, the wall of defiance inside him suddenly becoming that much thicker. Lincoln did not seem to mind. "We don't need to talk about what happened," he said. "There's time for that later. And we'll get to punishment, too."

Patiently unpeeling the wrapper of his confection, revealing its hard, fluorescent colors, Lincoln began telling his son about a phone call he'd once made, and the night he had told his father he'd had enough of minor league baseball. "It was an important moment for me. But my dad, he didn't take it so well. He was sure I could make it to the show, you know, because parents love you, they believe in you. He was sure I could do anything. But it wasn't going to happen, and I could see it, and, well, I don't know how long we talked. Felt like forever. But by the time it was over, I could tell I'd made my point, the old man understood where I was coming from, not that he could do much about it anyway."

Lincoln passed the Bomb Pop to Newell, who took it with a soberness that matched the mood. Then Lincoln put his hand around his son's wrist, held it there. "But my dad told me some other things that day, and they've stayed with me a long time now." A hard squeeze; he looked his son in the eye. "Newell, all anyone can ask a man is to do his best. When he does his best, he doesn't look back and wonder. He knows."

Waiting, Lincoln let his point sink in. "Dad also told me, you quit one thing, it gets easier. Soon you're quitting everything. Giving up before you even started."

Inside the FBImobile, all of Kenny's sidelong glances, mannerisms, and fumbling silences registered with Newell. Instinctively, subconsciously. The way Kenny started over on his little lecture and talked all low and serious, the effort Kenny was making; the gravity with which he was trying to address his mistake; the logic of his words and the palpable want behind them.

Newell felt the same repulsion that hit him whenever his father tried to buy his friendship, or just tried too damn hard.

He turned away. He looked out the window.

The coach was dragging a bag with the team bats and helmets back to his car when Newell went up and, using the exact words his father told him to say, apologized. The coach offered his own in return, saying he had not meant for Newell to miss his at bat, and asking Newell no hard feelings, right? They shook on it, and the coach said, a good thing about pencils, they have erasers. The coach followed this by informing Newell that he could not have any more tantrums and stay on the team. He asked if Newell understood, and when Newell nodded, the coach said

Newell would have to work off his mistake at the next practice. Newell had accepted his punishment, running two laps around the playing field with only a minimum of grousing, and though the tantrum had caused further rifts between him and the more gung ho players, and had caused Newell to be ostracized even more by the core of popular teammates, Newell had not missed another practice or game. And after the pizza party at the end of the season, his dad had proudly placed his trophy on the mantel in the living room, next to the framed copy of Lincoln's first and only professional baseball contract. It was something that still made Newell proud, whenever he saw it.

Probably it was every two weeks or so that Kenny got up his courage and said he'd be there this time. He promised and Newell tried not to get excited, because he'd sworn he wouldn't get burnt anymore, but the boy always ended up thinking this time was the time, for reals. Lorraine would tilt her head in that way she did, tut-tutting because she did not want Newell to be let down again, and this would get Newell mad and he would defend his friend, and that Saturday, Newell would be at the comic book shop half an hour before the guest artist was scheduled to start signing books, and two hours later he would still be waiting, listening to older kids make their sex jokes, acting like he understood what they were talking about, resenting Kenny for not being there to explain the jokes to him, for not being there to tell him not to worry about it in a way that always made Newell feel better. Newell would feel the absence and empty space that came with getting let down, and he'd feel the rancid humiliation of getting burnt the same way over and over. He'd be angry at Kenny for being such a coward, and he'd be furious with his mom because she'd known better than him after all, and he would resent her for trying to be nice to him and saying she was sorry, and would resent her even more when she got upset at him, and sniped that she did not understand why he'd thought it would be different this time.

But today it *had* been different, Kenny had shown his drawings, and the comic book guy *had* liked them. But then Newell's mom had forced him to leave before the good stuff happened. Newell always got shafted.

If he wanted a measly twenty bucks Newell had to listen to his dad's boring stories; he had to be back home by ten o'clock on what was supposed to be the funnest night of the week, only even when Newell stayed out way past his curfew, the night wasn't so great. Gambling didn't turn out to be such a big deal, and he ended up chased out of the casino, and the vampire guy had tricked him on that bet, and those homeless pieces of shit had stolen his phone. Newell couldn't even grab candy from a 7-Eleven without having a midget threaten him. Every shell Newell insisted the marble was under was empty, every turn he made led to a dead end. Time after time Newell was let down, deceived, corrected, Newell was swindled, scolded, taken for a ride. All the times Newell's mom had bugged and warned Newell, all the times she had worried that something was wrong with Kenny, and it turns out she was right, Newell was wrong. Wrong for all the times he had defended his friend. Wrong for getting touched in a bad place. Wrong for how the touch made him feel.

Throughout the FBImobile the rattle and grind of the working engine was the only audible sound. The car stopped at a red light.

Then an ocean. Cascading breaks. Froth lapping at her arms and legs. Half-submerged, the girl with the shaved head floated, supported by tides, rocking in their swell and ebb, the waves caressing and enveloping: purple the color of blood before it hit the atmosphere, crimson the color of blood in broad daylight. The lull in her ears was calming, and now was joined: by an amplifier fizzing in the not too distance, the incremental sounds of a guitar being tuned. Then the indistinct noise of multiple conversations, a small crowd buzzing from somewhere beyond the girl's reach. Now there were more voices, closer to her, over her, someone expressing joy that the opening acts must have run late. She heard heavy clomping sounds and when the girl opened her eyes, she saw lumpish forms jumping out of the ice cream truck, bodies abandoning the vehicle before it had lurched and stopped. For a few bizarre seconds the girl did not understand how a truck could be in the middle of the ocean. She could not determine whether her eyes were playing tricks on her, if her senses were off track, or what. She started to rise and even this was curious because she definitely was in the breadth of something warm, the hold of something strong, which suggested a body of water—only this thing wasn't wet, but solid, pulling on her arm, though gently. The girl recognized the voice.

"Let them go," Ponyboy said.

She gave herself to his arms and he brought her toward his musky chest and his hand was alive on her knee once more. The girl opened her mouth and pressed it to his, and each following sensation was a miracle and a revelation, the prayer and its answer. They slipped down onto the floor and the rush made her head spin, and when the girl closed her eyes the ocean returned and spun around inside her eyelids, and when she opened her eyes, the waves receded and the world returned, but spinning at an even faster pace. Shag follicles and the crumbs of all kinds of snack foods dug into her back and the girl was aware of the scratching sensations, but felt removed from their irritation. She was lucid enough, barely, to know she was drifting between hallucinations and lucidity, but not together to the extent where she could differentiate between what was real and what was imagined. The associative leaps blurred: the girl was on the cordless with Francesca, complaining that her mom could not seem to grasp the concept that a dress wasn't old, it was *vintage;* she felt her skirt bunching up, warm air around her hips. There was an instant when a hand came to rest on the outer lining of her panties and there was the eternal second when the girl decided to let it linger on the elastic band.

Drool had accumulated in the corner of her mouth but she was too disassociated from her body to do anything about it. She was barely able to raise her head from the carpet. The absence of all other sound in the truck sounded very much like joy and she marshaled all of her strength to experience the sensation of that hand and she was eight years old and had straight golden tresses down to the middle of her back and was dressed up like a cheerleader for Halloween. The boats were lined up and sitting quietly in the boat basin and the girl smelled the muskiness and salt in the air and the ocean washed up onto the shore and her mom told her not to think of dinner as leftovers but as *vintage casserole.* The girl turned the stereo up and juggled the cordless and said, *I'm such a martyr I should get my palms pierced.*

Was she swapping spit with Ponyboy or was she flashing back to kissing Ponyboy, or was the whole night a hallucination? How long had passed between that moment and this one, between that first hallucinated kiss and the hallucination of her confusion?

The back of his hand traced lightly over her mons.

This, her last sensation.

"How do I get back to your house again?"

Newell stiffened in response to the question; he remained covered in shadows, kept looking out the window.

Kenny's hand left the steering wheel; he wearily rubbed his eyes. "I can take Maryland Parkway, right? That'll cross with Sahara."

Newell snorted, as if he could not believe what he'd heard. For the first time in a while, he turned and fixed a hard look at Kenny. "This is bullshit."

"We've had enough fun tonight, don't you think?"

"Yeah. You had fun."

"I'm trying to talk to you here."

Newell answered over Kenny, drowning his words: "Yeah, you try all your fag bullshit on me. You get all *oh, you do something cuz you just feel like doing it.*" The boy's voice turned mocking now, vicious: *"That don't mean you know how it's gonna come out—"*

"Great. Have another tantrum, Newell. Make sure everyone's kissing your selfish little ass."

"BULLSHIT—"

"Really cool there, *dude.*"

Newell's eyes bulged, hatred consuming his ability to think, his ability to speak, his stare burning. "Fuck you, Kenny," he said.

"Yeah, fuck you, too."

"I know you want to. We both know you want to."

Kenny pushed against the steering wheel, releasing and opening his hands. "I was trying to talk to you. Can't you hold on with your little spoiled routine just for five seconds?" Kenny's voice wavered, but he controlled it, and released each word with an icy calmness. "Be a fucking human being for five seconds, okay?" His hands closed around the wheel once more. He took three hard breaths now, leaving his chest hollow. "I said I was sorry, Newell. I am sorry. I didn't mean . . . I didn't mean to—"

"So it's *my fault!*"

Kenny bit his lip. "It was just a couple of seconds. I couldn't . . ." His next words, *help* and *myself,* twisted, fading before they could form. There was silence, the low constant rattle of the FBImobile, the darkness shifting to cover Kenny, Newell, the seats they sat on, the trash around them. The sound of a gunned engine rose from the opposite side of the street, where a tricked-out flatbed was waiting for the light to change.

As if released from a straitjacket, Newell suddenly jerked back against the bucket seat. He moved the canister to his side and crossed his arms. He looked past Kenny now, into the intersection, and Kenny did the same, the pair of them staring anywhere but at each other, the light remaining red.

"The longest light ever," Kenny said.

Newell turned, staring out the window, the back of his head facing Kenny.

"I'm your friend," Kenny said.

"You lie."

"Maybe," Kenny grunted. "But I am."

"I don't believe you." Newell kept looking out the window. "I don't believe anything you have to say."

Kenny took in the boy's words, waited, and finally responded with a low exasperation, almost as if he were arguing with himself. "Well, fuck if I know what to do, then."

"You lie just like everyone," Newell spat.

"You don't want to go home. And you sure don't want to be in this car with me. So you tell me: what do you want to do? Fucking tell me, Newell."

Chapter 7

DESERT 1:15–2:15 A.M.

7.1

It sounded like a train wreck, feedback overwhelming the piles of home stereo speakers, distortion blasting through the amplifiers, coming out like revving lawn mower engines, aluminum bats pounding on sheet metal. Only there wasn't any edge. The sound wasn't dirty and driving, wasn't muddy and sleazy in the worst way, which is the best way. It wasn't an *evil* train wreck.

Way back in a previous lifetime, Lestat had been a stereo junkie. Even now his favorite way of scrounging bread was to work as a cut-rate sound tech at shows and ragtag gigs like this one in the desert. Sometimes bar managers gave him a job sweeping up afterward, and once in Austin—at least Lestat thought it was Austin—a band had let him sleep in their rental van. If Lestat had been the tech guy tonight, no way he would have put up with this droning bullshit, especially not out here where sound carried so well.

Emerging from a whirl of elbows and purple dreadlocks and kicked-up dust, he headed away from the mosh pit, unable to see for shit, the night filling in almost everything, the headlights of a few cars barely outlining the congestion in front of him—fans bouncing up and down like human bingo balls in a popper, punks holding their cell phones toward the stage. Lestat twisted in between a pair of skinheads; his knee felt stiff; he started favoring his right leg. But he survived the thickest part of the crowd and passed some dweeb stupid enough to be wearing a green wool stretch cap in the middle of August. Then he passed a stacked blonde too awesome-looking to ever talk to—alone, she had a camcorder pointed more or less toward the stage. The blonde had pink streaks in her hair, and she was swaying from side to side with a lazy sexuality that reminded Lestat of a similarly amazing brunette he'd hopped trains with before he had started rolling with Danger-Prone Daphney. Raven was her name. New Mexico and Arizona they'd traveled together, and she'd never let Lestat touch her. She'd had wild green eyes, Raven, and a penchant for mysticism. More than a few times Raven had explained to Lestat that she came from a lineage of important figures in the federal government. Lestat never found out that her real name was April Wiss, that she was seventeen years old, or that her government lineage was a third cousin who worked nights sorting mail. Lestat never knew that April Wiss had last been seen at her residence in Wichita, Kansas, on January 11 at approximately ten P.M. He never knew that April had not told anyone where she was going or when she would return. When they were riding on steamer trains in the black of night, April Wiss, aka Raven, used to put her head on Lestat's shoulder and nod off, and Lestat would feel her breath on his neck. April Wiss had three dots tattooed on her right hand, behind her thumb. She was supposed to take medication for mental illness but when Lestat and she used to ride trains, she took no medicine, just smoked bushels of weed. Frequently April became depressed and violent for reasons Lestat could not understand, and nothing he did helped. April had not taken any clothing or personal belongings when she left home, and her mother had not seen nor heard from her since that evening. When she needed money real bad, Raven disappeared. The next morning or sometimes even three days later Lestat would meet her at some predetermined coffee shop, she'd be sitting at the counter, all quiet and nonresponsive. They'd been in Scottsdale together and Lestat had gotten himself a job as a dishwasher and he'd given his first week's salary to Raven and still she'd refused to fuck him. Said it would have meant too much.

The cellular phone they'd gotten off that kid earlier in the night. Lestat wondered if the tip he'd been given about who had it was true.

The incline became steeper over the next twenty yards, and as Lestat's combat boots sank into the soft sand, he began the gradual climb, heading toward the interstate. Out here the crowd had fanned out, populating the desert basin in the manner of the stars in the constellations, and a few camping flashlights and lighters were floating around, which made the analogy especially accurate, Lestat thought. He approached a circle of pierced kids. They had a small flare lit at their feet, and were passing a bottle around, and as Lestat drew close, he saw that some were wearing concert shirts from hard rock bands that had broken up before their occupants were born. Lestat then noticed the insignias on some of the shirts weren't actually for real bands, but brand names. The fad shocked Lestat, and his irritation must have shown, because the pierced kids vibed him pretty good in return, and he veered sharply, avoiding the group entirely. He climbed a bit more, his legs heavy now, his lungs feeling a smoggy burn. But the music sounded cleaner out here, crisper; the band had settled down, found themselves a rhythm and stride, and Lestat could hear the hook—it was kind of catchy, actually. Lestat paused and looked back, taking in the scene: the crescent moon on a high perch in the clouded charcoal sky; the mountain ranges crossing the horizon in jagged, looming shadows; the rim of civilization shimmering to the east and giving way to darkness. Amid the field of blackness, a horseshoe of truck headlights were focused on the party, and from this height and distance, the band almost seemed to him to be a set of action figures in motion atop a cardboard box. A few idiots were climbing onto the stage and dancing around with disjunctive energy, they were turning and running, leaping off the edge of the stage, into the mêlée of slam dancers and raised hands. But all this chaos was neutered by distance. The whole scene seemed insignificant from here, an excuse that allowed everyone to congregate and party, be they scruffy and goateed Hackey Sackers, ravers in bright oversize shirts, lotharios chatting up jailbait, or runaways. Yeah, they were out here, too.

Like maybe this guy he used to see on the street every now and then. Lestat never knew his name but the guy was funny as shit, just had a great sense of humor. Three or four times Lestat had landed in some new city with a decent runaway population and was trying to figure out the lay of the land, and wouldn't you know it, he'd run into that guy. Each time the guy had shouted Lestat's name and wrapped Lestat inside a bear hug and they'd spent the night laughing and catching up, like they were college roomies at the alumni club or something, and by then it was too late to ask the guy's name. Tall and yoked with muscles, the guy had a strawberry birthmark on the tip of his right ear. His right nostril and right ear were pierced, and he had three studs on his right eyebrow. He had a steel barbell in his tongue and a messy black cross on his right shoulder. Back when the ink of the guy's cross was still fresh and glowing, Lestat had teamed up with him for a while. They were both in the Northeast and it was one of those relentless winters, too cold to be out on the street. Lestat and the guy went halfsies on thirty-dollar flop rooms each night. Sometimes they ran shoplifting scams and split the take, but more often, at the crack of noon, each went his own way, out to panhandle, steal, and hustle up the bucks for a room. In addition to his backpack, the guy carried around a pool stick inside a thin black case. He also had a small set of Craftsman work tools. He'd find abandoned televisions and videocassette players on the street and spend hours dismantling and putting them back together. Lestat and the guy spent a fair amount of their time talking about gearhead stuff, it was yet another bonding point between them, finishing their hustles for the day and meeting up to gab and—if they had the cash—drink themselves insaner. Once when they were blasted out of their minds, the big lug might or might not have told Lestat his real name was Jeromy Dernay. Lestat only heard part of what he was saying, so he wasn't sure. Lestat had ended up blacking out and when he'd awakened, all the information from his previous eight hours had disappeared, so he continued referring to him by nodding and going *Hey.* The missing person's report on Jeromy Dernay, originally filed in Newton, Mass, related that Jeromy was six feet two inches, 210 pounds, with black hair, and a date of birth of May 19. On June 22 of some two years ago, following a fight with his parents, Jeromy left a note stating that he wanted to be on his own. Jeromy took clothing and personal belongings, as well as jewelry belonging to his stepmother. He was known to be proficient at the sport of billiards and had been sighted at pool halls throughout the Midwest, although each of those sightings would now have been more than six months old. The police's last reported sightings for Jeromy had indeed been in the city of Las Vegas, Nevada. More than once Jeromy had been spotted at or around the WestCare health facility, whose officials did not report their clients' comings and goings to authorities. One of the last times Lestat had taken Daphne to get checked out there, Jeromy had been in the waiting room. He'd given Lestat one of his sun-blinding smiles and had crushed Lestat's spleen with his hug and they had exchanged a number of sincere and heartfelt pleasantries, and Lestat hadn't said anything about the sarcoma lesion on Jeromy's chin. Lestat had remembered that the big galoot was in town because one of the pierced guys in the group with all the faux heavy metal T-shirts had the build and mannerisms of Jeromy. But Lestat wasn't about to go back and confirm, either way.

Deblinda Big Black was out there, too, although she may have been calling herself Rosa, Heather, or Whisper. She was sitting on the arm of a long-discarded couch that sagged in the dirt and was bereft of its cushions. A bunch of younger types were also there, pubescents and adolescents, eyes closed, knees pulled to their chests, talking low and passing a pipe. Deblinda was five feet five inches, 116 pounds, with a birthmark under her right eye, and was known in her conservative hometown of Troutdale, Oregon, for the outrageous act of piling on the black eyeliner. Deblinda had attended Turtledove Catholic High School, where teachers described her as sullen, and students referred to her as a freak. On May 18 of this year, at approximately three fifteen P.M., Deblinda had called her mom to let her know she would be home after drama tryouts. However, Deblinda had neither come home nor returned to school. The last time Deblinda had run away, she'd been missing for two months before authorities discovered her in an apartment complex in Medford, Oregon. She'd been found in the company of a thirty-one-year-old Caucasian male, who at the time was in possession of a .45 caliber automatic pistol, a weapons permit, five sheets of homemade acid, and materials that might be helpful in manufacturing crystal meth. Deblinda's purse was found to contain matchbooks from bars in Sheridan, Wyoming, as well as a blank postcard from Devil's Canyon—which, Lestat guessed, was where she'd met Danger-Prone Daphney, their friendship catching fire in a manner not all that different from the way Daphney had taken to that little bald girl tonight. Deblinda, or Whisper, or whatever she called herself, looked the worse for wear on that couch, Lestat thought. She had lost a disturbing amount of weight, and her pallor was sickly, a pale bluish green. Plus something had happened to her jaw; it was no longer properly aligned, but veered dramatically to the right side. Just moving her mouth looked like it caused her a great deal of pain. Maybe that was why everyone called her Whisper.

Lestat continued his quest, heading up the sandy incline, not thinking so much about the call he was going to make now, but remembering, getting lost in the experience of moving and being transitory, making his way through winding and graveled and mud-filled roads, looking out for the nearest gas station hoses, for back alley spigots, for the flashing lights of a speeding police car. Lestat had waited out thunderstorms in the dim game rooms of rural bowling alleys, and he'd trembled in the wake of semis going so fast they made the ground vibrate, shook the morning dew from the grass. One night that seemed not all that long ago, Lestat had found shelter in an abandoned shanty of a farmhouse that was situated right beneath a bunch of power lines. Another time he'd picked grapes with illegal aliens in a field for sixteen hours, receiving twenty bucks for his efforts. Lestat regularly followed delivery trucks at five in the morning, stealing newspapers the minute they'd been laid down on lawns; he stood on thoroughfare medians and sold those papers to morning commuters. Just about anywhere you went, the grocery stores left stacks of folded-up cardboard boxes right behind the trucker ramps, and if you made sure to have a box or two with you, then when you took a break and sat on the sidewalk, your ass would not get sore. Lestat kept a ninety-nine-cent black marker on hand so he could turn that supermarket cardboard into a sign that might help get him a ride, traveling on whims, traveling with specific purpose; staring out through a bus window at desolate landscapes, balling himself up in the back of pickup trucks and turning up the collar on his heavy peacoat. One memorable afternoon, Lestat had wandered a hiking trail in some unnamed forest, and the shafts of sunlight had poured down through the spaces between the leaves and branches, and the rustling wind had been loud enough to make him think a plane was taking off. Birds that he could not see had had some sort of careless dialogue among themselves, and as Lestat had listened to them, he'd stared contemplatively at how moss was growing along the barks of fallen trees, and for a time, he'd felt a deep and abiding tranquility, a peace whose very idea under normal circumstances he would have denied and ridiculed; and the beauty of this peace had about justified everything Lestat had been through.

But moments where the solitude actually worked for you, these were few and far between. When you were alone as much as a runaway was, you lived beneath the crushing weight and breadth of a freedom where there was nowhere specific to go, no one to turn to or rely on; a freedom without restraint or responsibility, that was both empowered and burdened by the realization that you did not matter. If you didn't keep yourself collected, something as random as the bright red innards of roadkill could send you spiraling. It got so bad that even with the day's paper right in front of him, Lestat still couldn't keep track of the day of the week. Meanwhile, there was no such thing as a fast-food assistant manager who was comfortable with a runaway stinking up his booth (no matter how many apple pies you bought, they didn't want you). Clerks shooed you out of quick marts; rental cops pulled you from department stores. The real pigs rousted you from park benches. You had to avoid the social workers, the Jesus freaks, and most important, the shelters for runaway teens—rumors circulated of girls raped, of brutal beatings, and on top of that, the guys who ran the place were inevitably pervs, *they fondled boys.* Arrest and juvenile detention centers were constant threats. Deportation loomed at the end of every distant siren. Time and all its emptiness worked against you, simultaneously propelling and chasing you. The best antidote Lestat had come up with, the only way to prevent all the threats from swallowing him, the only way to stop his experiences from fusing together, was to try to fully involve himself, to engage, utterly and completely, with whatever came his way. As Lestat humped and hitched rides and sat in doorways; as he waited for some guy to get back from someplace, to meet up with him, to direct him to some other guy who might put him up for a while (so long as he didn't mind sleeping on a floor); as he waited for the solution of his next meal or just for the rain to ease up, there was always the odd detail, the memory poem, not necessarily exciting, but involving: the next sentence of the letter he was composing in his head (to each parent, to every single one of his unrequited loves), the knot where a scam or swindle hadn't worked out so well, ins and outs, new twists and options and things he could have done differently.

He could close his eyes right now and recall the great Victorian mansion. Most of New Orleans still was a wreck, but the garden district had remained untouched, and the French Quarter, too, and the gated home had appeared so stately and ominous to Lestat. Lestat hadn't talked to another human being for three consecutive days at this point, and something like eleven of his previous fifteen had been without significant human contact, but his three-state journey had been completed, and he'd buzzed and buzzed. And hadn't it been a thrill when a voice answered him? Hadn't it been a moment to remember? Through the speakerphone, Lestat had learned that *Anne Rice does not live here anymore. She has sold the house and moved to California.* These were the things that stayed with you, you didn't even have to try to remember. On a bench in Jackson Square park, with the rest of a long and humid day ahead of him, Lestat had slowly eaten through a dozen crawfish served in a paper basket, and he'd thought about the recklessness and foolishness of hiking halfway across the country to meet Anne Rice. He'd thought about the things he'd wanted to ask her and then he'd seriously considered whether, in all honesty, Anne Rice would have been able to help him, even if she hadn't moved across the country. Lestat had started to worry about where things were going for him and what he was going to do next, and then a wailing had surprised him, the shock being that the cries were not coming out of his own throat, but from another bench. This chubby chick. Bawling up a storm. People were turning their heads to watch, but Lestat was the only person to go up to her. He approached with the intention of telling her to shut the hell up, but they'd stolen her dog, was the thing. Those bastards had cut her dog's leash from off her wrist while she was sleeping. Lestat had calmed her as best he could, but this chick was a life force, loud and manic and in no condition to figure out what she had to do next. It had been easier for Lestat to concern himself with her problems. It allowed him to delay his own. Lestat had tracked down the nearest police station, and he'd learned that this crazy chick's hound had indeed been found. Whoever had stolen the dog must have had more on their hands than they could deal with because they'd abandoned the dog. A morning jogger had come across it, but by that time the animal was scared and distrustful. It had taken good chunks out of the jogger, and put up quite a struggle when the humane society arrived. The upshot being the chick's dog was scheduled for destruction. The chick had the dog's papers, its registration, and its record of vaccinations, but policy was policy. Even when Lestat used his emergency quarters and tracked down a public advocate who would listen, there weren't a lot of legal options. In the end, all the advocate had been able to do was help register a new dog from the pound—a playful brownish-gray mutt. Which is how Lestat had met Danger-Prone Daphney. Lestat remembered the whole thing like it was still happening.

Problem was, Danger-Prone Daphney swore she'd never been to New Orleans, Daphney was a West Coast gal; Lestat must have mistaken her for some other pregnant goddess. Moreover, the time frame of Daphney's pregnancy didn't jibe with when Lestat had supposedly helped her, and neither did her dog's age. All facts and evidence pointed to the impossibility of Daphney being in New Orleans at that time, and Daphney enjoyed lording this over Lestat, using it as a trump card in their arguments, or when she was simply pissed at the world. The alcohol had affected Lestat's brain, Daphney would say. *He* was the one with the memory problems. Lestat had no answers for this, so he would put up a stoic front, admitting that he was wrong, ha ha, it was kind of funny, wasn't it. Meanwhile, Lestat's memory was one of the few things he believed in, and it embarrassed him to no end that he'd juxtaposed Daphney's hair and body onto another experience. In a million years Lestat never would have admitted that when he focused, he saw he had not helped Daphney in the French Quarter; but a pockmarked and thin-waisted wild child, who, in the end, also had not returned Lestat's affections. Lestat was painfully aware of his habit of attaching himself to chicks who wanted only platonic friendships from him; and while he wished he could change what had—and hadn't—taken place with these women, he was basically resigned to bad endings, accepting of what he thought of as his fate. Throw in his sense of duty toward a damsel in distress. You start to understand why he'd saddled up alongside Daphney for so long, why he sometimes called home and asked his mom for help with Danger-Prone Daphney. The nursing supervisor at County General, Lestat's mom always asked how Daphney was doing, and told Lestat to get that girl to a hospital. Then his mom always caved and helped with whatever situation Daphney had gotten herself into. His mom accepted the charges whether Lestat called from the middle of a self-pitying drunk, whether he felt lonely and worn down, when he called to tell his mom lies about how he was doing or just to get medical advice. The sound of his mom's voice never failed to bring Lestat to the brink of tears. However, if Lestat's dad answered the phone, the charges would not be accepted. Lestat's father felt it was his son's decision to leave, it would be his decision to come back, and until then, he would not get on the phone with Lestat. Whenever Lestat's call home started winding down, the firm hard silences of Lestat and his mother trying to find something to talk about were resonant, and lots of times, Lestat got real quiet and started sputtering, not because he didn't know how to talk, but because this wasn't one of his fleece jobs or shell games; because too much had happened for him to put into words to someone who meant this much to him. It was impossible to figure out where to start.

So the dial tone broke; the pay phone receiver went back into the cradle, the phone slammed back into its station, it dropped and hung and was suspended from its steel cord. Lestat left the booth and headed toward the corner where the big Mexican wasted time by doing chin-ups on a construction stanchion. He walked away from the stanchion and past the bench with the old toothless lady and the old crippled man and their plastic bags of glass and aluminum. Lestat walked down the street and toward the bevy of transvestite hookers who occasionally treated him to Hostess CupCakes. He crossed the street to get away from the crazy blind man defecating on the sidewalk. The black guy trying to sell a new Rolex ignored Lestat. The incense salesman trained his narrow eyes and, in a heavy Caribbean accent, whispered, *You in a dark place now, lad.* Lestat wore two pairs of socks at all times to try to cut down on his blisters. He cobbled the rubber soles of his boots, layering them with Super Glue, running a Zippo lighter up and down the soles. His feet still cramped and grew swollen. His blisters ballooned and popped and became infected. No matter how hard Lestat tried to stay on the shaded parts of the street, he attracted killer sunburns. No matter how many times he told himself he was going to stop sniffing glue, he sniffed, leaving the lid off the glue, the cap off the marker, drying out both items, rendering them useless. Lots more grocery dumpsters had padlocks nowadays, and this gave Lestat an excuse to be lazy, and he'd pretty much given up on dumpster diving. Necessity *had* made him a student of the protocols of toilet paper acquisition, though, and he'd accumulated a stash of standardized mini-napkins that were rough on his ass but still did the trick, pocketing napkins from each trip he made to Mickey Dees, rummaging through public garbage cans for paper bags with coffee cups or sandwich wrappers (sometimes napkins had been left in there). Lestat worried about toilet paper more than food or even where to crap— hunger wasn't novel anymore, and finding a public restroom wasn't usually so difficult; but clean underwear was another matter. Clean underwear was one of the things that tangibly separated Lestat from the bums. Bums were hopeless, in Lestat's eyes—they were lost causes. And any blurring of the line between Lestat and a lost cause was of no small concern to him. Which is why, when Lestat didn't have napkins, he used old newspapers. He used paper bags. He used his right sock one time when he had the runs; afterward he turned the sock inside out and was about to put it back on and then thought about it, good and hard.

Out here you found yourself in situations where there was no right answer, where you didn't want to live like this but here you were and now something had to be done, a decision had to be made. Large, rectangular cars slowed as they approached Lestat on the corner, the windows rolling down with an automatic hum, revealing middle-aged men, elderly men, one at a time, alone in a prehistoric car that slowed and pulled up. The small talk would be awkward and finally Lestat decided to forgo small talk, he just threw himself into the passenger seat and named his price. When Lestat fell to his knees he felt like he was betraying everything he knew about himself, and at the same time it was a very logical decision. Lestat needed money to eat. He needed money to live. There was a chance he'd get taken to an apartment where he could get a shower. There was a chance an old guy would give him jackets he hadn't worn in years. There was a chance Lestat could empty the fridge and a chance that he could stuff his pockets the moment his trick's back was turned. The stink of an aged scrotum after it had been cooped up inside ancient jockey shorts was the most vile thing ever known. The taste of powder-dry semen was three times worse. Lestat went into long quiet sulks. He lost his appetite for weeks at a time. He gave up fast food entirely and used his money for tuna fish tins and went back to diving in dumpsters for scraps, and occasionally still broke down, springing for a gooey slice. Lestat often got abdominal cramps that doubled him over. He was always starving. He was severely constipated, then had bouts of diarrhea like nobody's business. He drank sodas for energy and the carbonation and caffeine made him dehydrated. He became jittery, anxious, paranoid, jumpy and bitter, cynical and nonresponsive. In the middle of talking about one thing, he'd get lost and drift away. Never one to put on weight, Lestat grew more and more gaunt, the sockets of his eyes sinking into his head, his collar gaping from off his neck. When it got hot, Lestat itched; when it was cold, he itched worse, constantly, everywhere, weird-ass rashes, underneath his thermals, kind of like bedsores, only Lestat rarely slept in a bed, so it wasn't that. His fingers were so caked in dirt that he had to stop brushing his teeth with them. He had lice. He had ticks. Lestat got chills, he got the shakes, he coughed and coughed, for like six months now he'd been coughing. When Lestat got out into the country he'd try to find one of those supersize gas stations that catered primarily to truckers. Most had shower stalls in their bathrooms and Lestat used them whenever possible, letting the warm water pour over him, watching the river of black go down the drain. He'd scrub the nicotine and grime off his hands, and it wasn't until after the first twenty showers that he realized the pink liquid soap only made his rash itch worse. Old acquaintances frequently commented on how shitty he looked. They said it was *like staring at a fucking ghost, dude.* Lestat would look back at them, a silence in his face, a distant light in his eyes.

No longer could he articulate a particular reason to stay on the streets, yet going home was not an option, not really, and so he passed long stretches in hiding, shuffling along, dragging his feet, trying to get to the next thing to get through, waiting for the day to be over, for the night to be over, bouncing between people who wanted as much from him as he needed from them, asking passersby for a few extra bucks, for spare change, for money to help get a room, could they spare some change for bus fare, a slice of pizza, could they spare a cigarette, a working pen. When Danger-Prone Daphney hadn't started showing yet, the two of them targeted rocker dudes who thought they could make Daphney. They targeted old people and hippy-looking college chicks with leather sandals and anyone else who looked like they'd be soft marks. Lestat would park himself right in the middle of an upscale shopping area with heavy foot traffic. He'd lean against a wall and watch the beautiful people toting their shopping bags and talking on their cell phones. Only instead of slinging his rap, Lestat would stare at the flow of lives he would never lead, whose comfort he would never know. People walked past and ignored Lestat and he resented them. Their eyes glanced over him and he despised them. Whenever pedestrians slowed down and reached for the places they kept their currency, wanting to know if he was okay, what Daphney's story was, whenever that happened, Lestat wished those fuckers were dead. Sitting on the curb out along Hollywood's hipster mecca of Melrose Avenue, the pointy bones of his ass would be sore, and Daphney would be rambling about this and that, and Lestat would look up at the palm trees that lined the sides of the street, and the way their clusters of leaves slumped toward the centers of the traffic median would have Lestat seeing the bowed, furry heads of repentant children. Would have him seeing hands clasped in prayer.

The sane sober businessman does not walk down the street talking out loud to himself, but the crazy homeless man does. And this, Lestat understood, was one of the fundamental differences between the two. Over time Lestat had also grown to understand how the former becomes the latter. How all your thoughts and frustrations can inch closer and closer toward one uninterrupted rant. How the chasm between a person and the world around him can grow, a shell forming between the life you once had and the life you are living.

Lestat had been out on the streets for fuck knew how long, and as he ran along the edge of this stupid-ass punk gig out in the Nevada desert, bulling through brush, he did not try to pick out the faces of people he knew. Lestat didn't want to see those ugly mugs, yet they were unavoidable all the same, fighting in the mosh pit, standing in the crowd, sitting on abandoned couches, wandering aimlessly, passing around bottles and joints, exchanging war stories—the stragglers, the outsiders, the dirty smelly weirdos who showed up at the party with no real connection and were always the last to leave, the forlorn ones who walked on the railroad tracks on the edge of the night and stood in the middle of moving traffic and tried to rinse a few more drops from the sadness that was their joy. Lestat recognized the faded gleam of their smiles. He remembered their smells. It was as if he had some kind of inbred detection system. He did not need to feel connected to them to be connected with them. He did not need to see their faces to know their stories, he knew them anyway, whether he wanted to or not:

The classically trained pianist and standout gymnast who was suicidal because he was in love with his older sister—he had been out on his own for five days now.

The college underclassman who went hitchhiking for the summer and took a bad hit of the wrong drug and since then had wandered aimlessly, half-witted.

The rambunctious daughter rebelling against her father's hypocritical religious doctrine.

The young woman who'd kicked her habits and gotten a grip on her inner pain to a point where she'd obtained a GED, a farty little paper-hat job, and what had seemed like a new lease on life, until familiar demons took hold.

When Lestat hadn't been on the road for too long, a freak snowstorm had hit the Windy City. It was supposed to be spring, but a cold front had blown in from the Great Lakes and the heavens had opened up. On that night the snow had been truly fearsome, and Lestat had been on the south side. The snow was coming down in thick sheets, swirling in the cross drafts and winds so it looked like flakes were arriving from three and five directions at once, glistening in the streetlamped light, wondrous against the grand and imposing backdrop of housing projects and brownstones and dim gray subway cars roaring by on elevated tracks. It had been the kind of cold that set a brutal numbness through your fingers and toes, too cold even for delivery boys to salt the sidewalks or shovel snow. Parked cars were covered in drifts so perfect as to be chaste. The pigs were searching for homeless people to get off the streets, into shelters and hospitals. Whether the bums wanted to or not, they had to go. Lestat was on his way to an all-night pool hall when he came upon an ambulance, pulled up to the sidewalk, its sirens whirling, its back doors flung open. A pair of paramedics in black parkas were trying to get someone onto the stretcher—trying to work with whoever was wrapped inside that battered trench coat, one of those obviously insane people who was constantly jabbering and screaming. It took Lestat a moment to recognize the person. This woman—she was forever collapsed in the corners of delivery ramps and storefronts, withdrawn from the foot traffic as if it were lethal, bunched up in a ball, beer cans strewn around her, maybe the remains of a take-out tray. Lestat was the kind of guy that most people crossed the street to avoid coming into contact with, but this old woman looked so demented that, usually, she was too much even for him. Only, the thing was, every once in a while she'd looked at Lestat and her eyes had contained a lucidity that was frightening. Lestat did not know this woman's name, he did not believe that nine out of ten times she would have been capable of responding to it. But the tenth time, the lucidity in her eyes made him sure this woman had moments sane enough for her to know what was happening to her, what her life was becoming. Lestat could not see her face on that winter night. He'd been standing down the street a bit, but was close enough to witness the black parkas of the paramedics, their wet vinyl sheen. The two men were bent over the woman's huddled body and she had the shakes real bad. While the paramedic on the left shone a pen flashlight into her eyes, the woman held still as best she could. She looked into the light and in Lestat's memory, her profile was bluish and pale, and she answered their questions as best she could, her tone acquiescent, that of a child who knows how important it is to obey orders. She could not stand on her own and the paramedics helped her up and moved her toward the back of the ambulance. She whimpered and they nodded and one strapped her into the stretcher and jacked it up so she was sitting in a diagonal position. The other took out a stethoscope and started into her layers of clothes. It was possible that the homeless woman had been through this many times, that the paramedics who covered this stretch of the city knew her name, that this was all routine, but it seemed unlikely to Lestat. What was happening was serious. The paramedics were either going to save the woman, or she was going to die, or maybe they would save her but she would have to have like her foot amputated. It was possible they would treat her and then would have to let her go and she would continue toward her inevitable death. Like how a family of grown children flies in from all over the country, coming together at their parents' home for Thanksgiving dinner, and this gathering of all grown children happens only once every few years, and so is an event of paramount importance, with days' worth of cooking, bottles of wine get emptied, hours of fun and goodwill and best behaviors, even when the pumpkin pie comes, everyone still talking and catching up and reminiscing and joking. So no one pays attention when Mom takes a tray into the kitchen. Sister begins clearing plates. Grandpa and Dad are still talking, discussing politics or what have you, but the oldest brother wanders off to check on the score of the game; the middle brother heads into the backyard where he lights a cigarette and calls his girlfriend to see how her dinner went. Cousin

Ned has to change the baby, maybe check his e-mail. Gradually the table empties and the participants disperse to different parts of the house, and the dinner is over. One way or another that crazy homeless woman on the stretcher had reached what Lestat felt to be a moment of gravity. A Thanksgiving dinner of sorts was at hand. But after it was finished, instead of flying back to whatever neat little life the woman had for herself, she was going to have lost a leg to frostbite, or she was going to be right back on the streets, getting drunk and scaring the normals and on occasions more and more rare, suffering a twinkle of sanity.

Things ended. They had to, moving toward termination from the moment they started. And when friendships, when relationships, when *people* were involved, it was Lestat's experience that things ended badly. You woke up one morning and found out that your unrequited love had rifled through your pack and taken all of your valuables and disappeared without so much as a goodbye note. You discovered that your pool hustling compadre was a profligate tweaker and when he got wired on crystal meth, he picked fights and attacked you with a pool cue. You traveled in the same circles as an irritating and crazy and completely enchanting pregnant girl and as much as you wanted to save something, to take care of someone, nothing you did could stop her from destroying herself, from retarding or destroying the life inside of her, you couldn't stop her any more than you'd been able to stop another unrequited love from toting her wares under an on-the-fritz streetlamp and, late one night, getting into the wrong car. Any more than you could stop any number of friends from accidentally filling a main vein with some bad shit. Any more than you could do anything about your own disintegration. Your own destruction.

A valley gust blew sand into his eyes and set his shirtsleeves whispering. He completed his route, and arrived at the dormant rows of cars, the small group of people gathered at its head, grouping around a pickup truck. Lestat glanced at the truck where three boisterous yahoos were standing—one taking money from a heavy-legged woman, another guy pouring beers from one of the kegs. The third yahoo tried a pickup line on the girl. As Letsat ran, he noticed the plastic of different cups shining atop the sand, and though he would not have minded a beer, he passed the plastic cups by. The bass line did not match the tempo of the rest of the song; the lead singer's voice had turned scratchy and off-key. Lestat wanted to be someplace safe and warm where he could write down everything he had ever seen. He wanted to write a book that would change the world.

He paid no attention to the popped hood on the station wagon, or the rat-tailed delinquent fucking with its distributor cap. Lestat's destination was just ahead: the ancient pink ice cream truck. It was shaking in place. Rocking to and fro.

Lincoln removed the videotape from the kitchen pantry, carefully wrapping its broken ribbon around the casing. If all went well, barely a blink would be lost, not even a handful of the twenty-four frames that filled a viewing second. But if the film had been crumpled or shredded, who could say how many images would need to be cut.

The editing geeks couldn't guarantee how things would play out with Lincoln's tape, not by just looking at it, which complicated things. For Lincoln, the possibility of having one more second of his son taken away was a gratuitous and keenly pointed insult, a lit cigarette to a wound that refused to heal. But really, what choice did he have?

He paid the fifty bucks to get the tape spliced back together, the twenty to transfer the contents onto a DVD, and the piddling surcharge to rush the job. If this went well, he had untold videotapes to convert. He had a short lifetime of material. Precisely at three-fifteen, the air-sealed package arrived and Lincoln closed the door to his office and felt his pulse in his throat. The disc he had been waiting all day for slid into the machine, and in short order, images Lincoln had not seen in months began as plainly as they ever had, the sequence tattooed on his brain: the lens zooming in, then drawing back; the children in bright orange jerseys, the matching baseball caps worn backward, the chins shining with grease.

The break came just before where Lincoln—and Lorraine, he guessed—always stopped watching and hit rewind. Newell was being ignored at the pizza party, growing frustrated, giving up and beginning to sink into his chair. A count later, the flesh of his cheeks would go slack, small eyes would cloud and turn dark. But no. A boy and girl in the team jerseys, busy playing rock-paper-scissors.

For Lincoln, watching the jump was akin to taking a step and discovering there was no ground beneath him, as if he had been sent aimlessly through space. The missing frames captured Newell slouching and unexpressive. They provided a clear glimpse of the trouble that Lincoln had refused to acknowledge before his son had disappeared, the unhappiness that, long after his son went missing, Lincoln still hadn't wanted to face, yet had forced himself to confront, studying the still image that stared back at him from thousands of those flyers, going over that video sequence as if it would provide him with the secret behind those blank eyes. Lincoln loathed those images. Lorraine always accused him of cutting the tape, and the truth was that if the idea had ever occurred to him, he well might have done it. But now he'd never have the chance to watch that sequence again. Those brief seconds no longer existed.

He zoned out through his four o'clock, settling on thoughts of Newell and Lorraine together in the living room, sitting on the couch and passing a box of cookies between them. Newell caustically dismissing a situation comedy or telling his mom to switch back to a summer blockbuster, Lorraine sticking to the classics channel, answering the boy in a pleased voice, *just because the film's in black and white doesn't mean it's not any good.* Their running commentary would continue throughout the prime-time schedule, and Lincoln thought about the regular occurrence of coming home to find the two of them on the couch, laughing at a clever bit from one of their favorite programs. He thought about all the nights when they were deep in some show and too absorbed to fill him in on what he'd missed. All the nights he was too tired to concentrate, but pretended to follow what was going on, and was just happy to sit there.

And, too, there was the brilliant summer day when Lorraine had put floaties on Newell's arms and taught him to swim. There was the time when Newell had given her the huge wax candle he'd made in art class for her Mother's Day present. And some random time when Lorraine tried to help him with homework, and she didn't know how the hell to figure out the questions, either, and they called Lincoln to come down from upstairs, just so the whole family could be utterly confused by this stupid assignment.

He would have sacrificed a limb to be able to watch any of it.

———

We have the lovely and talented Cheri Blossom here tonight.

Focusing, the camera panned in. A dry white wall, a woman seated in the center of a brown sofa.

She was preoccupied, motioning toward someone just out of viewing range, but this did not stop the camera. Rather, its leer continued, documenting her blond, luxurious hair, her long-limbed body.

Skin seemingly carved from a deeply tan bar of soap glowed against her pink camisole of mesh fishnet, packed breasts all but bursting through the tight, sheer fabric. The gemstone in her navel appeared to posterity as a discolored flash. Where her waist tapered, and the swell of her hips began, black strings traced toward a thin panty. But her legs were crossed, so the view was blocked.

Life's hard when everyone wants you, right, baby?

As if caught passing notes by a teacher, Cheri stopped gesturing. Her face froze. If someone had adjusted the tracking on their VCR—and also had been staring above her neck—that viewer would have seen how unsettled she was.

Well. This is going to be a real treat. We are lucky enough to have Cheri Blossom with us. Cheri is like the hottest dancer in Las Vegas right now. And she's decided to get into the industry.

Her eyes settled on the camera. Blood-red lipstick stretched into a plastic smile.

How are you doing tonight, Cheri?

"Oh, I'm just ducky."

Heh. I like that. You're just ducky and tonight you're going to get fucky.

Lashes batted defensively. The smile stayed frozen.

What? I'm a poet. You just didn't know it. . . . Wow. Tough room. So tell me, Cheri. What made you decide to get involved with adult films.

The camera was still and it was silent for a moment and it did not seem she was going to respond. Then she said, "My boyfriend."

Wow. No kidding? He must be a great guy. Gruff laughter. *Remind me to thank him later.*

She shot a look toward the side of the screen.

FORGET ABOUT HIM.

The lens shook with the order, then settled and calmed. *Just worry about the camera, okay, honey?*

A pan now, forward, until the camera was a yard or so away from Cheri, right above her, looking down from a point of dominance, the shot capturing the liquid of her eyes, their terror, and their quick change under way—Cheri's trapped fury, her outrage, and then her cool distance. A woman taking in exactly what had been said to her, precisely what was happening, not only the ridiculousness, but how scary the vibe was, how predatory.

The uncomfortable sound of a smoker's cough emerged from the other side of the camera. But the shot remained focused on Cheri, and the longer it stayed on her, the more ornamental her layers of makeup appeared. Beneath her attitude and glamorous stylings, beyond her body glitter and sparkling tan, the truth was strikingly obvious. A face that was nothing special, as plain and midwestern as the upbringing she was trying to hide.

Tell you what, went the voice. *Why don't we get started? Let's take a look at you.*

It seemed she was calculating, reaching some sort of decision. For more than a second, it appeared possible she was going to leave.

"So this is what you want?" she asked, looking toward the left side of the shot.

We'll get it in editing, the voice told someone at his side.

Rising, she stood with her legs a shoulder width apart, her movements sharp now, but exaggeratedly so—an angry slinging of weight onto one hip, a defiant push of her chest. Cheri tossed her hair so it fell in front of her face and she pouted and, in an obvious *fuck you,* put her middle finger into her mouth, sucking on it.

Oh, you're a horny little thing, aren't you. How about you give us a— turn around. Let's see that butt.

Was it possible these people were too stupid to recognize that she was mocking them? The thought entertained her. She snarled over her shoulder.

Yeah. That's it. The feisty ones are always the best, aren't they? Now bend over for all the people out there at home. Give us a sexy little show, baby.

Maybe she followed orders because the voice was so stupid, so unbelievably cheesy; or maybe because each of her slights was ignored, every jab and haymaker she threw was rolled with; because she got to display her power and get out her aggressions and put these nimrods in their place; because the whole scene plugged into her own natural desire for attention, and the pent-up colt released from the gate finally had something to do with all this nervous energy. The red light stayed on, the film kept rolling, the voice, grainy and businesslike, kept egging—*Into the camera. That's right.* And although the woman in the lens was not giving the guy behind the camera exactly what he asked for, neither was she telling him to fuck off. Indeed, with each move— a strap of the camisole falling over one of her wriggling shoulders, her hand covering a breast—the natural give-and-take of a working relationship seemed to form, its movements incrementally becoming more professional.

There you go, baby.

Hooking a finger into each string of her thong she slowly began its descent. The camcorder closed in, too fast, blurring the bull's-eye. Just as quickly the video pulled back, regained focus.

Very impressive. I'm sure our millions and millions of viewers out there would love to hit that bull's-eye.

Quickly she opened her legs, spread eagle, then snapped her knees shut. A camera flashbulb exploded, the screen filling momentarily with white light.

Make sure you get the bull's-eye, ordered Smoke Voice.

Murmured assent. The flashbulb popped again, creating a strobe effect.

Now a jiggle. From the right side of the screen someone entering the shot, a middle-aged beach bum. He had complex braces on each knee and was otherwise nude, his tan line the width of dental floss. Far more body hair than any sane person wants to see on a naked man.

Well, well, well, here's a welcome surprise. I guess it's time to meet your woodman, Cheri. Couldn't wait for her, I guess, could you, Rod?

The guy continued limping as quickly as he could, his legs rotating in wide half circles, accommodating the Erector set constructions. Even half-hard he was humongous.

Cheri's instinct was to look away, but she fought through her embarrassment and nerves. He reached the couch and looked at her and his eyes were small and dark and droopy.

Here he is, you know him, I know you'll love him—the one and only Rod Erectile.

He smiled. Deep grooves appeared down the sides of his face. "Hey," he said, and for the briefest of moments, Cheri thought she recognized a resignation in him, an apology. But before she could process this thought, he was putting his mouth on hers, forceful, pressing, his thick cow tongue was pushing down her throat, too much for her to defend against.

"CUT."

Now something impacted her, someone shoved her. She wanted it to be Ponyboy, saving her, beating the hell out of everything in sight. But when she opened her eyes, it was the guy with the cow tongue, Rod Erectile, flinging her body away from him. "FUCK," he was yelling. "CUT."

Rod.

"God DAMN!"

Stepping away from the couch, Rod turned his back to everyone and seemed to shake his head and look down. He put his hands on his hips. His face was that of a boy watching his birthday balloon trail toward telephone wires. "I'm sorry, Al. Her dance—"

I know. I know.

"I was feeling it. I went for it. I just—"

This shit always happens with you, man.

"I just lost it, I don't—" Rod turned to her. "I'm really sorry about this."

You're just lucky I know you so well. Hiro, you got the instant wood?

The camera continued taping, and in the next moments captured Cheri's ashen face. Unsure of where she was, she collapsed backward, reclining fully against the couch, feeling its back with her hand to make sure it was there. Rod Erectile, looking pissed at himself, grabbed the loaded syrette away from the slim Asian.

"Why you don't just take a Viagra?" asked the Asian. "Eat a bunch of celery like the old-school days?"

Don't kid yourself, kid. An entertained snort from the director. *Ol' Hot Rod lives for that needle.*

To Cheri he said, *Stay ready. But don't masturbate, we want that for the take.*

Once again Cheri looked to the left side of the screen, searching. Fixing on him, she all but implored: take control, protect me, *do something.*

Ponyboy chomped rigidly on an unlit cigar and looked as if he were about to be sick. His eyes met Cheri's, then broke contact, instead watching the syringe; it was moving toward Rod's penis.

A groan. Rod's musculature went tense. His hand balled into a fist.

Whenever Lincoln neared a convenience store, fast-food joint, or anywhere else a twelve-year-old boy might be found, he slowed down just a bit more. His contacts weren't in, and even with the high beams blaring it was hard to make out objects and shapes. Still, strangely enough, he felt contented.

He believed he was wasting his time, that his kid was already home. He imagined Newell inching the front door open, relieved that his parents had left it unlocked. Newell had to have liquor on his breath, Lincoln figured, and the stench would be masked in a cursory way, grape bubble gum was what he'd used, back in the day. Lincoln imagined Newell's eyes were dilated, too, red from a little weed, maybe some eyedrops. The instant that front door budged, Lorraine would pounce, rushing over from the kitchen, where she'd been in her bathrobe, on the phone with her mom, probably brewing a pot of that green tea crap. Or maybe she'd give the kid a break, let him make it upstairs on the balls of his feet. Could be that she'd wait until the boy had changed into his pajamas and tucked himself underneath the sheets, until he was thinking that maybe he'd gotten away with it.

The streets all looked the same at this time of night, and as Lincoln made a turn, he was unable to come up with a reasonable explanation for the voice screaming obscenities that had come from the other end of

Newell's cell phone. Lincoln was wearing one of his suit jackets and a pair of old sweatpants. His feet were smashed into an ancient pair of dock sneakers, their backs crushed down by the weight. He'd staggered out to the car in this haphazard outfit and Lorraine had followed, gripping her bathrobe tightly around the waist and nagging him, complaining about driving safety and the kind of people who were out on the road at this time of night. She'd double-checked to make sure he had his wireless, then worried because he did not know what kind of car Newell was in, did not even know where to *begin* looking. Lorraine had made him promise to check in, and she'd assured Lincoln that she would call if there were any updates, and if she had not kissed him before he got into the car, Lincoln nonetheless felt she was back on his side, that their dinner and evening together, and yes even this little mini-crisis, had thawed her frost for him.

Kids were going to be kids, Lincoln knew that much. They were going to inhale substances that by all rights no sensible person would imagine inhaling. They were going to put their private parts in all sorts of bizarre places. And they were going to lie, telling you they were going to be home by a certain time and then showing up a lot later. Newell's lie was just another link in the chain, part of the nature of being a son, just like fathers had to look into their children's eyes, sometimes, and tell them untruths right back.

In Newell's case, the time had come to take control. Get the kid some discipline. Some therapy. Some shit. Lincoln thought of his son in platitudes. The boy just needed a little straightening, was all. If he and Lorraine handled it all the right way, this was a chance to really do something, help the kid and get him on track. A deep sense of satisfaction took Lincoln with this admission, and it was as if he'd taken care of one of the important steps in a long, detailed project, a step that didn't necessarily ensure the project's success, but ensured that the project *could* be completed. Lincoln felt glad to be at this point in his life, happy to have his wife and son, his family, even with all their problems and bitching. He even was okay with driving around in circles at one in the morning, bleary-eyed, waiting for the phone to bleat and inform him he should come home, all was right in the world. He thought about stopping for some coffee and a doughnut, reminded himself about calorie intake.

Hell, pretty soon it was going to be time to tell the kid about the birds and the bees.

The roar of an overhead plane shook the office to its structurally flimsy foundations. The crew was huddled, Rod Erectile swabbing his dick with a cotton ball; Jabba and the camera guy going back and forth about which lighting angle would best hide the injection mark.

On the far end of the couch, Cheri sat, quietly still in shock. Beside her, Ponyboy had his hands in his pockets, and was looking sheepish. "Apparently," he started, "there's been, I guess, this backlash against fake breasts."

He looked down at the carpet as he spoke. "Yeah. Looks like they only want all natural girls now."

His hand left his pocket, scratched his ear; he still couldn't meet her eyes. "I had to cut a deal," he said.

Silence.

"It's the only way they'd do it, baby."

Cheri forced herself to her feet. Nothing about one second of what was happening felt unusual to her, the events unfolding as they did during any other day: Ponyboy calling her *baby* and reaching out; Jabba's voice directed her way as well now, asking if there was some sort of problem, which Ponyboy answered by saying he was handling it.

Cheri continued toward the little alcove outside the bathroom.

"He told me you'd gone over the details," Jabba said.

"I'm handling it, Jabba—"

"I DO NOT WANT TO FUCK ANOTHER GUY."

Her words echoed, faded, were replaced by the sounds of moths and flies circling the light fixture. Cheri remained rooted in place. Jabba waited, then matter-of-factly said, "It's the standard deal. We supply the cock. All the regulars: Oral. Vag. Anal—"

Cheri's mouth parted. She crossed her arms, felt her skin cold against her hand.

Jabba was still talking: "—then the money shot and good night."

Now Ponyboy was back, out from whatever rock. "See, um, that's the other thing."

Cheri could not look at him, could not bear what she knew would be in his face, the shame and helplessness, his apology smoothly mixing in with whatever the next thing was that he had in mind for her. She held back. Did not call him a jackoff, an asshole, a betrayer, or a Judas. She could not do these things. She was too busy letting the back wall of the vestibule support her, was too busy shutting her eyes, leaning back, resting against the wall.

"Any schlub with a video camera and a website can screw in front of the world nowadays," Jabba continued.

"It's the only way they do tryouts anymore," Ponyboy added, as if this were helpful.

And if her life had been a movie—not this kind of movie, but a real film, with creative, artistic and even moral value—then at this point the voices would turn garbled and fade.

On the silver screen, Cheri would not be paying attention to the Asian photographer's venom. *(It's called being a professional, you fucking twat.)* Instead, she would be opening her eyes. The bathroom vestibule would have a mirror on the wall and Cheri would be looking past all of the men who also had jammed themselves into this alcove. She would be looking at the mirror, noticing herself: a woman who at once looked stunning, and sexy, and—in this outfit and makeup—ridiculous.

Now a voice-over would begin, the disembodied voice of Cheri's mind, calm and smart, saying this was the last place in the world that she wanted to be.

INTERIOR. LARGE CLASSROOM OF CATHOLIC SCHOOL.

The classroom alive with laughter and jeers. Wimpled NUN stands over the child version of CHERI BLOSSOM. NUN curls lip, removes glasses. Her eyes are soft and liquidy.

NUN

To be human is to sin, my children. Perhaps
you cannot understand because you are
small and your lives are not hard, and perhaps you can understand because you are
small and blessed are the children.

But you do need to know that Jesus or Bud-
dha or Muhammad or Vishnu or Jehovah or
the Hebrew God Yahweh, all forms of God
love all forms of his children.

It is important to know this.

And so I say it again. My children, you are
human for your sins and God loves you for
your humanity.

It is your sins that make you beautiful.
But this does not necessarily give us license to do whatever we wish.

And here I want you to listen carefully.
What I am about to say is very important.

Kenny's hand remained easy on the bottom of the steering wheel, and kept the car steady along the gradually curving road. It didn't take much effort for him to see the passing streetlamps as a succession of lit matches, as burning skulls atop long, thin steel pikes. Newell was numb in the passenger seat, his face glowering, unable to hide its resentment. *Tell me what you want to do now,* Kenny had said, issuing a challenge as much as a question. Newell had not answered, and had no idea what he was supposed to do, what was coming next. The whipping wind through the open passenger window smashed onto his face and neck. The night kept expanding around him.

Kenny took his silence as permission. For a moment he let himself wander, was distracted by the light reflecting off the asphalt ahead, all the revealed scars where tar had been poured to fix cracks.

"It'll be cool," Kenny said, as if reassuring himself. "Just wait. You'll see."

Newell kept decomposing in his seat. If Kenny tried any more pervy stuff, he was going to get a full-on blast of fire extinguisher. Newell would do it, too. He wasn't going to put up with any more bull, and that included the party Kenny was talking about. Newell didn't know whether to believe there even was a rock show, and was worried about being taken out to the boonies for another kind of party, one inside Kenny's pants. Out in the middle of nowhere Kenny would be able to do anything he wanted, Newell thought. Then he remembered Kenny's apology, Kenny promising that he was Newell's friend. This statement held true with everything Newell knew about Kenny. Everything, that is, except one thing.

Newell didn't know what to think. This was new territory, and it had him dizzy.

"I don't have to do more gay shit?"

He meant to protect himself by taking the offensive. But his voice caught. The sentence came out without any spine or certainty. Even so, it hit home. The bad energy inside the car metastasized. Kenny felt the blood leave his face, he worked like hell to keep silent. The Reliant wheezed, lumbering as best its four cylinders would allow: through a yellow light, heading south, in pretty much the opposite direction they had been driving not that long ago.

Whatever response Newell was expecting, it was not coming. The little lesson at the end of the mistake. The attempt to right the ship and get back on course. No assurances from Kenny. No apologies. No arguments. Just Kenny, seething in his seat, not even trying anymore. It was another shattered border between them, one whose dissolution shocked Newell. For an instant he felt responsible, both dumb and chastised. He started to get pissed at Kenny for giving up on him, then made a tremendous discovery: he did not care, either. *If you want to shut up,* Newell thought, *it's not like I give a shit.* If he felt bad about anything, it was the hitch that had marred his question. Helpless was the last thing Newell was. *Just try me and see.*

Dirt and dead bugs splotched the windshield. Strip malls passed at something less than an antiseptic blur, including the cell phone place that used to be a video store, and then the supermarket belonging to the chain Kenny had worked for last summer—for like a week he'd chased down shopping carts, until he'd gotten heat exhaustion and thrown up all over the parking lot.

Kenny's recognition of these places did not go so far as to be recognition, but was just a low hue, a tint in the background of his thoughts.

Everything is fucked, he was thinking.

It seemed to him that he and Newell had been in this car forever; that he'd shown his drawings to Bing Beiderbixxe during a different century. The smell of sweaty clothes wafted momentarily to his nostrils. He tried to rally, reminding himself that Bing Beiderbixxe would not have shown him that pencil grip just to be nice, pros like that just don't give away their secrets, not if they don't think you have something going for you.

It took a Herculean effort for him not to look over at Newell. Kenny felt as if his body were held together by a framework of chicken wire, as if his bones and organs would collapse at any moment. Newell would tell someone what he'd done. It would happen sooner instead of later.

Kenny ignored the goose bumps that came with this realization, and kept trying not to freak. One thing at a time. Let's just get this party thing over with.

In the mob they took people out to the desert and dealt with them.

Yeah. Right.

Then another thought: it would be the boy's word against his.

And Newell wasn't the most believable person, was he.

Extending through the darkness, all the high walls and gated communities joined together, shimmering as if they were the surface of a translucent ocean. Through the passenger window, the colored towers of the Strip appeared to Newell as a distant row of glowing toys. When they'd gotten so far away, he did not know. But the distance felt appropriate. The hotels could catch on fire and crumble into dust for all he cared.

On the playground in grade school, once in a while, he and the other kids talked about what they would do when they grew up. Teachers, too, asked Newell what he wanted to do with his life. And his mom, approaching her breaking point, would challenge him, asking if Newell wanted to spend the entirety of his adulthood digging ditches, because if he didn't, he better get his little rear in gear. More than once Newell answered that he actually *did* want to dig ditches. In fact, he'd tell his mom, just now he'd started on a ditch to China that would get him the hell away from her. Newell would tell his teacher that he had his future all figured out. He was going to be a mattress tester, that way he could sleep all day. Actually—serious though—he hadn't decided yet. He was torn, policeman or astronaut? Right now, he'd said, his plan was to combine them and fight crime in outer space. *First priority,* he said, *is getting rid of the Klingons around Uranus.* The class had roared, and their laughter had been more than worth the trip to the principal's office, and afterward, Newell had added the possibility of being a comedian to his list.

His other possible careers included: jet-setting billionaire secret agent with a heart of stone; superhero who sneaks around in darkness and comes up behind terrorists and slits their throats; international jewel thief on a Harley with mounted laser guns. Newell was going to climb the highest mountain on earth in his special mountain-climbing submarine, and he was going to vomit down on a passing troop as they sold Girl Scout cookies, and if anyone fucked with him, they'd pay, oh yeah, you best believe his enemies would be punished like nobody had been punished before.

Only there was something else, too. Loosely connected but still coming to mind.

When his father would take him to Rebels games at the Thomas & Mack. The part Newell always looked forward to the most. It came after Newell had abandoned his dad in section 119 (*See you at ten,* his father'd say, meaning that Newell should be back when the game had ten minutes left), and after Newell had met up with a couple of jackasses from school, kids who didn't pick on him that much while he tagged along with them. When it got to be too much work for Newell to wedge a word into their conversations, he'd mumble an excuse and give a half-hearted wave. Dropping from the end of their pack, he'd then wander the loop around the arena's mezzanine. It was pretty excellent: except for the vendors going back and forth to refill their trays, and dudes heading to the bathrooms to whiz out their beer, Newell pretty much had the whole mezzanine to himself. He could listen to his own footsteps echo off the concrete, and at the same time, was able to hear the roar of the crowd. Sometimes Newell would sneak peeks inside the tinted windows of the luxury boxes, just to see what things looked like when you were living large. Sometimes he went to a concession stand and pretended he was mute and mimed out his order for a medium popcorn or hot dog. The loge level was rarely more than half-filled, and it wouldn't have been too difficult for him to sneak down and snag himself an excellent seat, but Newell never did. Instead he stayed out of sight of his parental unit, away from the bullying reach of any jerks from school. Upper deck was where all the fun was. Some bereft section. Away from the blocks of underprivileged and sick kids here through charity programs. Newell would kick back in an empty seat and take in the spectacle below him, the game and the dynamics of the crowd. Idly picking at his stale popcorn even after he was full, he might get some peanuts from a passing vendor for good measure. Once settled, Newell would rip pages out of his official game program and take the glossy sheets and fold them into paper airplanes and try to float them down. The best got some air under their makeshift wings and rode in delicate, arcing paths. A chosen few even caught a second gust and kept going, beyond the rim of the upper deck, over the plastic red seats of the mezzanine, the politely attired season-ticket holders, the corporate bigwigs. It became a game for Newell, watching his planes glide deliciously toward the edges of the basketball court. Seeing just how far they could go. Old farts sometimes tossed uneasy looks his way, or warned him to cut it out. Newell ignored them, or stared lasers in return. Gathering his stuff, it would be time to get moving, to climb higher, into the nosebleed seats and rafters, continuing his exploration, his adventure.

The void was no longer foreign, no longer a fresh sensation, but constant, second nature to the point of becoming unnoticed in their lives, the axis for all their comings and goings. Lincoln still returned home each night—it was a matter of personal pride—but he often stumbled in around or past midnight, with one or two drinks under his belt. For her part, Lorraine was gone with the dawn, out at yoga, or at the local coffee nook, poring over her notebooks and papers, throwing herself into her project of raising money for the Child Search. Their daily lives were almost wholly separate now; and even when they found themselves under the same roof, the house had more than enough space and freedom for each. And though the air between them was stale, without the slightest charge or energy, the signs of effort and consideration were still there, numerous, if you wanted to see them. Lincoln made sure to pick up towels and keep things neat in his bathroom. He clipped articles he thought would interest Lorraine, leaving them on the kitchen table, or e-mailing her the links. Lorraine returned the considerations, taking care of his dry cleaning, making sure the fridge was stocked with his favorite comfort foods.

They ran into each other, obviously, they had to—on the stairs, or when the television was on and each happened to be nearby. Thankfully, their exchanges featured little drama or strain. Lorraine might ask, with the utmost sympathy, about the extra pounds that the cut of Lincoln's suit could not hide. Lincoln might walk behind her, put his hands on her shoulders, and try to massage away some of her tension. They'd talk about small things—payment schedules for the pool cleaners, or someone wanted to pass on a greeting. Now and then Lincoln and Lorraine even managed the courage to look into each other's eyes. Sustaining their gazes, they'd transcend their fragile truce, moving beyond the polite balance of all the responsibilities expected of each of them, beyond the toil necessary to fulfill those responsibilities and the exhaustion they felt through their bones. Holding the marriage together took so much time and energy. Keeping things from not getting any worse took every bit of emotional strength either one of them had, and more than that. But Lincoln and Lorraine would look into each other's eyes and all of the pain and the wear and the fear would be there, all the stuff there were no words for, the stuff they just felt, which made them keep looking, afraid to blink, even as they knew someone had to, something had to happen.

7.5

The ice cream truck stopped rocking with an abruptness that suggested its plug had been pulled from a socket. The back doors creaked open and a figure stumbled into the opening—a shadow of broad shoulders against the dark night air; a chest bare and gleaming with sweat. One arm, thick and raised, showed a musculature as pronounced as the cords on dock rope. Facial studs glistened then disappeared.

Ponyboy rubbed his eyes and ran his hand back over his forehead, up through thorns of matted hair. His opposite hand remained on a flimsy set of cutoff sweatpants, making sure they didn't fall below his waist. From a middle distance, instruments were being played without syncopation. A stench reached him: like being downwind from the worst fart in the world. From the same direction came the uneven sound of footsteps, someone favoring a bad leg.

"Pony?" the newcomer's voice showed surprise. "Yo man, I don't want to disturb nothing. I didn't know you was in there."

Ponyboy calmly closed the door behind him and hopped down from the rim of the ice cream truck, landing with a soft thud.

"Ain't got time for your shit right now, El."

Lestat's hands rose as if to show he was not armed. "Bro, I'm just looking for that cell? From earlier tonight?"

Ponyboy scanned the immediate distance—over the little vampire's right shoulder, toward the direction of the show. "Phone's not in there, El."

"Right. Just thought, maybe I saw it in there on the way over, was all."

Ponyboy's head tilted to the side, he started tying the drawstring of his sweats. "What, you gonna cry to your folks some more."

"Yo, Pony, I said I don't want any trouble."

"I ain't got time for you right now, El. Go check with your old lady if you need something to do. Last I saw, she had it."

"Daphney?"

"Borrowed it when we got here."

"Daphney has the phone?"

"Word as bond, man. I guess she wasn't feeling so good. She needed to make a call. Go spec her out."

Lestat tried to measure if anything Ponyboy was saying was straight. His experience was that the guy was so full of shit that it usually came straight out of his throat. At the same time, Ponyboy was vibrating with menace, bearing down on Lestat, not warning him, but trying to convince him through sheer force of will. Whatever was happening in that truck, Lestat understood it was heavy enough that Ponyboy would do anything to keep him out of there. Even maybe tell the truth about Daphney.

Lestat nodded and kept his eyes trained on Ponyboy and back-pedaled, taking two careful steps. When he started back down into the desert, a hand grabbed his neck. "Good luck with that," Ponyboy said, shoving him. "Make sure you let me know how everything turns out."

Ponyboy kept his eyes on Lestat all the way to the outskirts of the quad. And when that little bastard was basically out of the picture, and Ponyboy was satisfied that all was copacetic, then it was time for him to start hauling ass: sinking ankle deep into the sand and kicking up explosions of dirt, beginning a sprint down the length of parked cars. The pungency of sex still lingered in Ponyboy's nostrils and tasted acidic on his tongue, and although Lestat's appearance had been a little too close for comfort, and their conversation had sapped some lead from Ponyboy's pencil, he was still hard enough, his dick slapping between the fabric of his cutoffs and his thigh, the physical activity of running providing his body with a release that was satisfying, but not what he needed.

Sand burned beneath his feet like he fucking cared how it felt, and Ponyboy veered near an abandoned old couch, where he bulled through a bunch of nimrods, spilling their paper cups. Without saying thing fucking one, he continued, scoping shit out Terminator-style, eight directions at once. A grim clarity had Ponyboy now. Each second the ice cream truck remained unattended was a second his new plan could fall apart. Countdown was at T minus hurry the fuck up. All kinds of reasons for him to give up the fucking ghost on this one, just head back to the ice cream truck, cover his tracks as best he could, and get the hell out of Dodge.

All sorts of warning signs. Any rational idiot would stop here.

Motherfuckers yap about the moment of truth, but what happens when there's all kinds of truths in the moment? Door number one, door number two, door number three—and every door has its own merits, right? But at the same time, the merits of each door affect the bearings of the next.

At the tryout, Ponyboy and Jabba had been in this little alcove by the bathroom, trying to get everything back under control: Jabba was talking to Cheri, explaining the way the porn business works. And at first glance Cheri looked like she was following every word; but really, Ponyboy could tell she was somewhere else. In fact, ever so slowly, Cheri was, like, *inching* down the wall, her skin making this sick sound against the wallpaper. Finally she sank onto her ass and sat in a messy heap on the industrial carpet. Her legs were spread and her hands were on the floor between her knees and she was looking out at nothing, her eyes all glassy and distant. And then, like she was talking to herself, she whispered something, one word. Again and again Cheri said it, each time more softly. *No.*

In the doorway: Rod Erectile had been wild-eyed and jittery and stiff as a diving board. He had come a long way just for this shoot, and he had a plane back to the valley in four hours, and he didn't give a flying FUCK what the holdup was. *It's not like this broad's a virgin, right?*

Jabba rubbed the back of his neck, studied the fixture above them. "Hiro. This light's strong enough to shoot in?"

The Jap sneaked into the doorway, checked a viewfinder. "Maybe. Probably."

"Set up a pod, just to be safe." Turning to Rod now, Jabba said, "Put her on the counter if you need to. That's always hot."

They moved equipment and reblocked the shoot, acting like nothing unusual was happening, like Cheri was an obstacle they had to work around. A yellow, bilious taste crawled from the bottom of Ponyboy's stomach. If there were ever a time in his life to grab his light saber and adjust the kung fu grip, he knew this was it.

And he did it. He said, "Don't think so, Jab," and felt his stomach hardening, the bile in his throat turning dry.

His first step wasn't the steadiest step he'd ever taken but it did the trick. His next step was not a lick easier. *Just what the fuck are you doing,* Jabba wanted to know. Ponyboy answered by reaching for the woman he loved, getting close enough to her cheek to smell her perfume. He whispered her name and kissed her forehead. He was going to take care of everything, he said. On the count of three she should try and get up. ·

His arms went underneath hers and he counted one and Jabba repeated his desire to know what was going on. A contract was a contract, Jabba said.

From over his shoulder, he heard Rod Erectile cuss and snort. He heard Jabba rustling. Cheri's body was warm, responsive and pliant. Ponyboy lifted her, and she followed his guidance once more, into the open main area of the vestibule, where a human wall had formed: the Jap dead of expression; Rod Erectile, his eyes buggy, all twitching and tweaking. A moth flew down from the lighting fixture. Jabba was behind his goons, waiting.

"You sure you want to cross me, boy? All that's going to happen is that we snap every bone in your body, she ends up getting fucked anyway."

The guy was as close to a fucking dad as Ponyboy'd had since he'd been out on his own, and he was grinning. "Maybe when I'm done with her, I'll take care of you next. Way I remember it, you don't exactly mind having my dick in your mouth."

Ponyboy kept staring straight ahead. He clenched his fists, waiting for shit to go down, for the beginning of the end of life as he knew it.

And so occupied, he wasn't exactly tuned in when Cheri's hand lifted from his shoulder.

Indeed, it wasn't until she took that first tentative step toward the sink counter that Ponyboy recognized she was moving.

Motherfuckers talk about the moment of truth and they think they fucking know, and the truth is, they don't know dick. Meanwhile, when all the fucking chips had been on the table and Ponyboy had been staring into the face of the devil, what had happened?

What had happened was that Cheri had gathered up her blouse, and then her silky sweatpants.

She was wobbly, composing herself, holding her shit in this messy bundle in front of her chest, with her hair falling down in front of her face.

Turning toward the exit, she ducked her head, and started forward. She looked small, damaged, catatonic, teetering on her high heels, her steps uneven and slight.

Jabba's eyes stayed trained on Ponyboy. Ponyboy stayed focused right back, at the same time very much aware of his girl.

And what happened was, Cheri kept walking.

Right past Jabba. Through the henchmen, who all made a point of looking fierce and leering at her chest and shoving out their bellies so they rubbed against her. She walked right out of the office and Ponyboy followed behind and turned back to watch them to see they didn't follow.

The Jeep was right where they'd left it. The compact disc player started up at the same point in the song where it had been when the engine shut down.

Look, a man fucks up, there's a price. Anyone worth a piss understands as much. This price gets paid in the airy static of an expensive stereo system through a wordless drive home. It gets paid in the slamming of doors. Or it's worse: not one door gets slammed; her voice doesn't raise so much as an octave; she does not utter one word in anger, or spite, or anything except a tight, controlled politeness; the door to her bedroom behind her shuts gently and then there is no sound, no response. You put your woman in a situation the way Ponyboy did, you deserve what you get, and he could accept that much. Ponyboy took responsibility. He slept on the couch without complaint, telling Cheri that if she wanted him out, that was cool, only could he borrow a few bucks to get a room? Cheri did not so much as crack a smile. Which was understandable. She'd been through the wringer. There had to be some kind of decompression period.

When Ponyboy had been planning the tryout, he'd told himself that the difference between him and Jabba—between him and *anyone* involved in the porn industry—was that they were the products of what a life without love did to you, whereas he had his Cheri girl. Even when the shit had gone down, when Ponyboy had faced his moment of truth, he'd picked the right door. Using the kung fu grip, he'd drawn an inside straight on the devil and triumphed over Darth Fucking Vader. Ponyboy had rescued his lady from the insurmountable clutches of evil. Only, now it turned out, there wasn't no ride off into the Technicolor sunset while the credits rolled. He didn't get no big fucking party with Ewoks waving into the camera and licensed movie underwear. No. His big moment of truth and he'd done the right thing, and after it all was said and done, his Cheri girl had not decompressed, his Cheri girl had closed down to him. Something inside the woman Ponyboy loved was shut off, locked away, and meanwhile here he was, running through the middle of the desert, into the crowd, wading through waves of people who had come out here looking for, maybe even finding, some kind of salvation; yeah, that's what they wanted, that's why these motherfuckers were out here, the pretty girls basking in their own beauty and the attention it brought; the nonentities finding something in the scene that brought out the kind of person that maybe they thought they wanted to be; the skinheads finding some sort of salvation through hatred and confrontation and the violence of the pit. But something, some damn thing, whether temporary or permanent. Every one of these sinners, out here in the night, standing in Ponyboy's way, talking, watching the band, tripping out, zoning, whatever the fuck, all of them looking for something that might sustain them, that might keep them going the way that a cold hard motherfucker was sustained by the voice of the girl he loves, by the feeling that he was the most special and important person in the world to her. This is what any strong relationship provides, allowing a human being to survive in this miserable and fucked-up world.

You fuck that up, all bets are off.

Ponyboy's dick was in a medium state of hardness, not raging or anything, but still in working shape. Toward the side of the stage he plowed through some scrawny fuck, knocking the green wool cap from his head, leaving the guy in a puddle of pain. Ponyboy looked in all directions, hurried now, a bit of panic setting in. Then he saw the blonde with pink streaks in her hair. Swaying side to side, she had a deadly rack. Best of all she was carrying a digital camera. Just what he was looking for.

Consciousness announced itself with pressure. Throbbing, from behind her eye sockets, worked outward. Keeping her eyes closed allowed her to block out the pain, almost, and the girl with the shaved head kept her eyes shut. She tried to give herself to the blackness, letting go until the borders of her physical form no longer existed. The blackness tempted her, flirting; she felt solitary, disembodied. Then the pressure came back, pounding with more intensity.

She became aware of a muted warmth down the breadth of her back, of heat, thick and heavy in the air around her. For the first time she noticed the droning sound, carrying through the space above her, from someplace far behind her. The girl lay in the darkness and listened for a time, but time did not prepare her for even more blackness when she opened her eyes, a darkness so complete that she could not tell if her eyes indeed had opened. The girl became confused as to whether her body could even follow basic commands. Panic garbled any logical counters, any answers. But soon a thaw began as well; her eyes adjusted a bit, differentiating shapes—the impenetrable roof and walls that framed her confines, the shade of what might have been the evening sky, apparent now through what must have been some sort of window.

Looking beyond the length of her body, she successfully made out more shapes—the outlines of a number of short square objects, and then the table around which those crates were positioned. Pressure crawled to her temples and bore outward and she was sure it would emerge from the front of her skull. Instinctively, the girl started her hand toward the pain. But was restrained—around the wrist. She pulled a second time, confused now, her eyes following the roll of her shoulder, her head turning.

Suspended in a dim, flickering crimson light, she saw her arm hanging limply behind her, connected to a long crate, attached to some sort of handle. Metallic heat, like a thin bracelet, ran across her wrist. The rest of her hand tingled, was numb, and looked to be smothered inside a folded black cloth.

Panic rushed her. She pulled at the restraint again and the fabric stretched and the knot slipped, then held. The girl tried once more and failed—but wait, something jiggled that time, atop the crate, the red light toppling now, landing with a sick thud.

It wasn't much—maybe twenty watts, flickering from a lava lamp with drained batteries, but the light flickered along her right like an asp, allowing the girl to see more of her predicament: her summer vest unbuttoned, its left flap folded on itself, its stitching apparent. The cup of her bra was misaligned and mangled, she saw, and a swell of her flesh was peeking out from the mashed wire edge. She saw the hollow of her belly, slick with sweat. And her skin. It was smeared with crimson that had nothing to do with illumination.

Percussions continued through the background. Outside the nearest wall, two guys were talking. The girl did not cry out to them. The light dimmed around the area where her hips began—right where her skirt was bunched, askew, turned half backward. The girl kept staring at her body. Moving her left hand, she discovered it was not bound. She found that her feet and legs were also free. The girl tentatively started to sit up. And felt a spasm of pain, sharp and white, in her core.

And then a great wail cleaved the night, piercing at first, fanning out from the stage in all directions like beams of the sun through a downtown skyline. The tones and feedback altered as they carried, creating their own effects and grades. Sweaty strands fell in front of the guitarist's face and he addressed his strings and frets and whammy bar, *wailing*, keeping his pick against the uncoated third string, extending and then bending each played chord, repeating the song's central riff, but changing it for his own purposes, easing from it a vulnerability, the fragility that by nature must lie beneath so much bombast—this exquisite sense of despair.

Flickers now: a few thumbs pressing down onto plastic ignition wheels, flames dancing atop disposable plastic, hands rising into the night, the time-honored arena rock tradition that borders on a parody of itself, the virtuoso getting his props from the appreciative and the knowing and the poseurs who wanted to look like they also were in the know—as many as ten lighters flaming up. Maybe twice as many people had their eyes closed, were giving themselves to the groove.

Chewing the end of his swizzle stick, Bing Beiderbixxe did not acknowledge the waitress's impatient posture, nor her withering glare. Instead he looked toward the mouth of the small booth, and the black curtain at the entranceway.

Just wait here, the stripper had said, three ten-dollar Pepsis ago. *I'll be right back.*

The Library strip club came and went, as did the Gambler's Book Shop, the Liberace Museum, the Pinball Hall of Fame, and that indoor shooting range where a hundred bucks got you a half hour with an automatic rifle. Places Newell had never been and places he did not recognize and places that passed without thought or notice. His attention was occupied by a peculiar kind of righteousness: the angry certainty that comes from basking in the knowledge that you have been wronged; the cynical defiance of a person who finds his pain to be an excuse, whether he knows this or not. A damaged person intent on ignoring his own mistakes, refusing to examine anything he's said, anything he'd done. (Why should I? Why?) Newell's thoughts were soupy, numb. But something else was stirring within him. Growing out of the muck, it was the smallest of sensations, but was quickly increasing in intensity, this molten warmth.

Cheri blinked, pulled on her closed lid, and rolled her eyeball—a childhood trick to get out sand. Rubbing her tearing eyes, she used the break to catch her breath a bit. Nearby some obnoxious idiot kept screaming for the band to play "Free Bird," and enough people were laughing to egg him on, and Cheri stumbled away from that area as best she could, her vision returning now, enough to where she could get back to her search, her attention shifting toward any flash that might have been promising—the parent grabbing his daughter by the ear and screaming that if she ever took the Escalade again, he was calling the police, *understand;* the shiny surface of plastic backpacks gleaming; a pair of girls dragging a third out of their clique, and into a private consultation. Now someone zagged, sprinting as best he could. But his gait was all wrong, Cheri decided. He was too slow. Too scrawny.

She paged Ponyboy and got jack shit in response. Cheri checked her phone's digital log for the umpteenth time, then dialed the number that, earlier in the night, Ponyboy had called from. A voice mail started; Cheri had grown familiar with the message by now—it was really funny, a boy, probably nine years old.

It seemed fantastic to Cheri that she'd believed she'd find Ponyboy out here. Just deciding where to look next was almost too much.

Ever since that nightmare of a tryout, Cheri had been committed to watering her plants. She'd entertained unfocused thoughts about getting a kitten and returning to school. Certain emotional complications had been too tangled for her to take on, she just hadn't had the inner strength to face them. Nonetheless, personal growth had been a definitive and predominant aspect of Cheri's thinking. And even more resonant was a single carved truth: she would never be put through anything like that again. If Cheri had to be as ruthless as the people in Jabba's office had been to her, so be it. If she had to treat anyone in her path as the slice of meat she herself had been treated as, this was the way of the world.

Was that why she'd given the comic book guy's idea to the one person whose schemes routinely bested themselves as the worst things that ever happened to her?

Was that a good enough excuse?

Her ears, still ringing from the strip club's sound system, were full of drone and fuzz, and the earth was consistently presenting itself at lower plateaus than Cheri's feet were ready for. Cheri didn't pause for a second, but kept stumbling down that small dune, moving as best she could in her flip-flops. Because whether she told herself she would be ruthless or not, the truth was, Cheri couldn't ignore the other side of ruthlessness,

the people who were put upon, the price of suffering. It wasn't something she could just turn off. She'd tried to do so tonight, but her conscience wouldn't let her. And now, heading down into the desert, Cheri
kept seeing how young all these partiers were. Even the ones who were
her age looked infinitely younger than Cheri felt. All too well Cheri understood the way these anarchist chicks would titter and coo when Ponyboy showed them the slightest bit of attention—how their gangly bodies
would wave in place, their eyes going bright and dreamy.

Cheri wasn't equipped to know if three-dimensional tattoos could be
taken out of the realm of the hypothetical, but with a chilling clarity, she
remembered the electric buzz of that needle as it shot ink into the skin
on her pubis. Remembered the sudden pinch that turned into fire.

Through the jutting heads and limbs, the stage looked pretty far
away, like some sort of demented puppet theater. The crowd at the front
was surging toward the bass player—he had wandered to the edge of the
stage, and was sprinkling water from a plastic bottle down onto the overheated moshers. On that far side, Cheri also saw heads as they turned in
one direction, people looking toward some sort of disruption, this
dervish, cutting through people and heading away from the stage, arms
churning, his legs fluid.

Cheri called his name and there was no response.

Stumbling on the sand, she hooked between a pair of goateed kids
tossing a Frisbee. The Frisbee almost hit her and she flinched and ignored the apologies, heading around a small group of squatters and
buskers who were sitting around in a semicircle, one of them strumming
a battered six-string.

Cheri cupped her hands and shouted. Ponyboy did not completely
break stride. But he slowed, seeming a bit confused, looking in her
direction.

His hair was slick with sweat, she saw, his chest aglow.

"Hey," she said, finally catching up, grabbing the moist skin along his
upper arm.

Ponyboy's eyes blazed, and he took her in as if he did not recognize
her.

"So," she continued, "I'm here."

The breadth of his massive chest rose and fell, and she could see he was struggling to control himself, to stand in front of her. He tensed now and, without betraying the slightest emotion, said, "Great." His eyes began drifting toward something in the direction Cheri had come from, his right arm started behind his back.

She'd always teased that he was like some sort of indestructible mutant cockroach, that terrorists could set off dirty bombs and it wouldn't matter, Ponyboy would be the only thing left on the face of the earth, he'd be going through the pockets of the corpses or whatever. But the ultimate survivor was in front of her now, half-naked, sweaty, Cheri could smell the sex all over him. She looked at him trying to hide the camcorder in his hand, trapped, obviously struggling to figure out his next move. Tattoos and her plan were the last thing on his mind, she saw.

He was making one of those tapes.

Trying like hell to control her repulsion, Cheri planted her feet and forced herself to stay in front of him, to look right back at him.

The way Ponyboy was staring at her made it apparent to Cheri for the first time that she'd been wrong about the cockroach thing, too.

He would try anything to survive, she could taste that. But even more certain was that he was going to destroy himself. Whatever had happened between Ponyboy and his parents, whatever he had suffered through on the streets, the accumulated damage was simply too much to overcome. Cheri saw that now. She saw his destruction would happen despite his better instincts and nature. It would happen against his own wishes. But all the mistakes and miscues and hardships were going to inspire more schemes, each more desperate and ugly and convoluted and far-reaching than its predecessors. Ponyboy was headed for a crash. And whether it was her or some poor little girl, anyone unlucky enough to be within his reach, they were going down with him.

In the final scene before the screenplay of the movie of Cheri's life was put away, the nun stood at the front of the schoolroom and announced that God's obligation was his presence within us.

The nun said this presence was nothing so much as a person questioning how they might be more than they are.

In the screenplay of Cheri's life it said that for God to have mercy on our souls, we must have mercy upon one another.

It said Cheri had to do better than this.

A delicate and loving sadness filled her as she reached out now, her fingertips lightly rubbing the width of Ponyboy's shoulder.

He flinched, as if tensing for a fight, but Cheri continued, pressing her palm down onto him.

"Don't you want to see the band?" she asked. "Come on, honey. Let's check out the band."

A sideways glance confirmed Newell's profile would be perfect for one of those portrait sketches, the kind where you use fancy pencils with fine points. Kenny envisioned a scant amount of light down the middle of Newell's face. He wanted the effect of a boy in the dark with a candle. Soft, wispish lines would recapture the angle of Newell's head, raised just a bit, his snubbed nose slightly turned upward, as if the boy were posing, pretending he did not smell something foul. A scribbled brow, thickish and clouded. Then Newell's eyelid, heavy and long, but also done in soft strokes—maybe this would make the boy's gaze properly haggard. The visible half of his pupil would be solid but flat, his iris gray and dull. The white of the paper would also be the white of Newell's eye, and this would tap into his intensity, and still show the boy looking outward, without betraying the slightest sense of emotion on his face. It seemed to Kenny that Newell's expression had solidified into armor, and the boy Kenny knew was hiding behind that armor, and Kenny wanted to capture this. He wanted to hint at freckles, maybe by going darker inside the shades along his cheeks. He wanted baby fat whose suppleness would accentuate just how weary Newell looked. Newell's mouth parted just a bit now, and this seemed to be important—the way the nearest side of his upper lip turned upward, forming what looked like a smirk. As if Newell could not care less what was out there. Bravado was the wrong word for what Kenny was seeing. But what about disdain?

Spring was a gift: deep shades of green and vibrant blooms. Neighbor-hoods had an idyllic feel that almost seemed too good to be true. Despite a few scorchers, the mercury still hadn't broken ninety when May ar-rived. People were especially encouraged. Could be, summer would be mild this year.

On Lorraine's birthday the phone rang during the noon hour. No-body was home to answer it, and no message was left, but Caller ID reg-istered the source: *out of area*. Newell remained outside the realm of the law—never getting arrested, never turning up in a juvenile center, hospi-tal, or morgue. Every so often the case officer or a hired detective checked in, bringing details of a discovered body, a boy with some pre-liminary similarities to Newell. Lincoln and Lorraine would be electri-fied, each of them on edge through the next days, praying for their child to be alive, while at the same time desiring some sort of positive, conclu-sive identification, hating themselves for this, but wanting to know, fi-nally, one way or another, what had happened to their son.

The failure to discover a body, for so long a source of hope that Newell was still alive, had started turning on itself. It was natural: how could you help but stop putting so much of your soul into each update? It was understandable: how could you keep jumping up in response when logic told you it was another dead end?

Neither Lincoln nor Lorraine could admit, even to their private selves, that after so many months, the odds of Newell being alive were al-most nil. Nor could they accept the growing likelihood that they would never know why he had left, what kind of life he had found, what kind of end he had come to.

Still, there was that phone call. The hopeful weather. Lorraine's dis-covery of the converted DVDs, stacked and waiting for her in the kitchen pantry, also had an effect, further spurring something like a rebirth for the couple. That first night they sat on the couch together and watched memories of him until they both fell asleep. Two nights later, Lorraine found herself trusting Lincoln enough to show what she had of her fundraising proposal. He read carefully, went to lengths to praise what he saw, and pointed out potential sticking points. They stayed up late once again, this time brainstorming possible solutions. The next day they text messaged each other with the frequency of teen lovers, met at home at a prearranged time, and coordinated the proposal to varying degrees of mutual satisfaction. The result: a fourteen-page PowerPoint document, which quickly made its way to key personnel within the upper echelon of the Kubla Khan's community outreach and marketing departments.

"Score one for the good guys," Lincoln said, calling from outside his office. Not only was the banquet on, but thanks to the Khan's largesse, every red cent that was raised would go directly toward the construction of a support center for homeless, runaway, and at-risk teenagers. Lorraine, for the first time in who knew how long, heard a hint of enthusiasm in her husband's voice. As if saying the details out loud confirmed them, as if sharing made each victory even more true, he went over the laundry list of what was being comped: the two-hundred-and-fifty-seat Oasis Banquet Hall, the four different types of appetizers for the reception, soup or salad at dinner, as well as a choice of three entrées, dessert, and coffee, all from the Khan's seventy-five-dollar-a-plate banquet menu, which wasn't the highest-end menu, Lincoln explained, but wasn't cheap, and certainly was more than they had any right to expect. *"Catering staff. Even floral!"*

The only problems were minor. Mainly, it was impossible to have the event on the one-year anniversary of the night Newell had not come home. That date was booked.

He said this knowing that when the proposal had been notecards and Post-it notes, Lorraine's primary organizing principle had been having the banquet on the one-year anniversary. He talked plainly, in that troubleshooting, preemptive way of his, moving smoothly into the list of perfectly agreeable days the Khan had offered. Lorraine said nothing. He moved to the next sticking point.

She listened, then repeated the next problem—*"Cash bar?"*—with a disbelief that suggested they might as well cancel the event. "Jesus Christ,

Link, for five hundred dollars, people expect an open bar. You go help and get sloshed. That's the whole idea."

His silence was every bit as loud as her rejoinder, and just like that, in the course of discussing the basic date and price of this fund-raiser, it was obvious that their relationship was not about to be repaired, but was at a much deeper impasse. In the following days, the price of the tickets became a wedge issue and a symbol and a Ping-Pong ball, volleyed and smashed back and forth, Lincoln arguing they should knock down the price a hundred or even two, maybe have the guests pay for their own booze. He had no problem asking clients to buy tickets, getting them to go to bat for the cause with their superiors, or even purchase corporate tables, he was just a little reluctant to look like he was putting the screws to anyone, especially anyone who had placed their trust in him. See, unlike in this house, at work there were actually people who *cared* what he said. To which Lorraine answered *Mmm-hmm*. With an exaggerated slowness, as if the person she was addressing were mildly retarded, she'd explained that the elite nature of their fund-raiser mattered at least as much as the goodness of the cause being championed. "Part of the way you make something elite is to charge a lot of money for it," she said. "You get celebrities to endorse a good cause and then set a ridiculous price to get in. Anybody who's anyone in this town will want to be there, and anyone who thinks of themselves as on their way to being somebodies will be right behind, clamoring for a better view."

It was one thing to be civil when you were polishing an outline. Quite another when you had a whole evening to put together. All of a sudden, Lincoln and Lorraine actually had tickets to sell, an entire banquet to plan, and all the problems this entailed. If Lorraine wasn't coming up with options for dealing with the cash bar, she was drawing up new schemes to maximize revenue, getting competitive estimates on invitations, playing phone tag with the Khan's banquet planner, going back and forth about just what the hotel florist was or was not capable of doing. After untold requests, she received a bunch of faxes with the floor plans of the Oasis Hall, as well as the dimensions of the different sizes of the various shapes of banquet tables. Calculating how many round tables could fit in the room, as compared to square or rectangular tables, Lorraine did more math than she'd imagined her brain could handle, and came up with a plan that would squeeze in twelve more tables of eight into the room, which would allow them to cut down on the ticket price and end up with the same take, or maybe keep tickets at their present cost and add fifty grand to the night's gross. The banquet planner left a perky answer on the machine, in which she explained that Lorraine also had to calculate chairs and bodies into the equation. Usually this added a ring of eighteen inches or so around each table. "But it was a *super* idea," said the planner, her voice so insincere it was nauseating.

Time was a whip, lashing down, and meanwhile the tasks did not end. A connection in the Khan's community outreach department forwarded Lincoln the corporate mailing list for fund-raising/charitable activities. Soon, Lorraine had volunteers from the Nevada Child Search making calls and stuffing scented envelopes of heavy cardstock. A booking agency returned her call about a possible celebrity spokesman, informing Lorraine that the star of a highly rated prime-time family drama was a dream to work with, so long as he had an unlimited amount of methadone and hookers. Lorraine rolled with the punches and took her lumps. Every day stretched with dead space when nobody was calling her back and she was on hold with someone's secretary, and she filled the time by clicking back and forth between files and windows, making notes on stalled projects, revising lists with days of unreturned phone calls, and organizing priorities for things that, dammit, *had* to move forward. She could recite any of these lists by memory, explaining how things were progressing with ticket sales, which people she was still waiting on, and the history of negotiations with each of them. She clicked back and forth chronically, habitually. Getting things right meant more to her than to anyone else, so why should she delegate? Nobody else could do anything, least of all Lincoln. So what if he'd transferred a bunch of tapes onto discs? *She* had been the one who had been against Newell going out. From the beginning, *she* had known something was wrong with that Kenny. Newell had told her Kenny was a *mutant sewer dweller*, he'd told her that Kenny was a *total perv*. *Cheeseburgers and then anal sodomy* had been the plan for that night, and Lorraine had warned her husband that Newell would end up buried in the desert with Hoffa and then, against her gut instincts, she'd caved, agreed to let her son go out with his friend. And for what? So she could have an expensive dinner. So she could lie still while her husband fucked her. Lincoln was the one who had let her son go away and he could claim this was revisionist history until the sun jumped over the moon for all Lorraine cared. She had listened to him on that fateful Saturday night but she would not be so foolish again. Thus, she made sure the caterer understood there would be no ham on the menu. (*"Ham at a fund-raiser? Haven't you ever heard of Jews?"*) She engaged the banquet planner in deep, meaningful discussions as to whether white orchid centerpieces took up too much table space. Lorraine redrew the seating chart and put all the volunteers from Nevada Child Search near the doors to the kitchen; she knew she was being a ruthless bitch, but the fact remained, they would be getting their tickets for free; meanwhile some corporation shelling out five grand for a table couldn't be sitting in the back.

And still there was the nagging matter of putting fannies in the seats. Husbands who had long flirted with Lorraine at cocktails under the guise of social levity were more than happy to hear from her. Men she had condescended to, politely ignored, or otherwise considered out of her league, for the most part they took her calls as well. Lorraine listened patiently as Gail Deevers told her about her son's heroic return from overseas, and then the orders for his second deployment. She called friends whose lunch appointments she hadn't been strong enough to keep, this time offering to take *them* for a bite. Local politicians received visits, as did the rivals who Lorraine knew coveted their city council seats. She cajoled and schmoozed. When it became necessary, she even hounded Lincoln. Lorraine did not particularly care if he felt she had taken this over and turned it into another one of her crusades. She did not give a crap about all the time it took to get appointments with the different resorts up and down the Strip, did not believe him when he said the wheels were in motion, people were talking to people, he was just waiting on them to get back to him. Lorraine recognized there was truth in what he was saying, but time's lash was cracking down, taking big chunks out of her psyche, and no matter how much Lincoln explained that you had to know the way things worked, Lorraine could not *just let everything take its course.* Instead she placed calls to the few choreographers who were still around from back in the day, as well as girlfriends that, during the past year, she had fallen out of touch with.

The scene: Lorraine rising neatly from a waiting room chair, smoothing out her little gray business skirt, approaching on her three-inch heels; Lorraine smiling wide, maintaining eye contact—be it with the oversize gray and wheezing executive vice president in the cheap suit, the slick-haired associate with the pockmarked skin and nicotine fingers, or the friend of a friend whose laser-white teeth gleamed even brighter than his pinky ring. They never resembled anything close to what she expected power brokers to look like, yet Lorraine effusively thanked one man after another, saying *I can't tell you how much I appreciate you taking the time from your busy schedule to meet with me on short notice.* She was equally businesslike in acknowledging each apology for having kept her waiting so long, brushing aside the delays as if forty-five minutes were nothing more than an overheard sneeze. Chuckling at anything resembling a joke, throwing tasteful compliments around as if they were pennies, Lorraine made the requisite amount of small talk and headed into each man's office, all the while waiting for that telltale sigh, *Okay,* her signal to get down to business. More than half the meetings took place around one P.M., because the guy she was meeting with had a full schedule. Instead of leading her back into an office, he'd want to know if they could do this over lunch. On a crowded elevator she'd receive her signal—*So, Miss, ah, Mrs. Ewing, what can I do you for?* And then, while trailing the huffing fat man—who himself was negotiating his way through slot players—Lorraine would start talking. Yes, she thought it was unusual for power brokers to act this way, but Lorraine did not ask questions. Rather, she put up with their idiosyncrasies, even the buffets, those god-awful things, Lorraine following her erstwhile dining partner while he flashed his VIP employee card to the hostess and bypassed the line of waiting tourists, Lorraine sliding her tray down the long metal rows as if she were back in a grade-school cafeteria, doing her best not to gag when steam rose from the mounds of glazed food.

Her dining partners filled out keno slips for a dollar, *Just to have some action going.* They kept an eye out for the ticket girl. They called Lorraine and the ticket girl and the waitress *darling*. Still, Lorraine didn't lose her cool. Not when she got asked to stop her presentation so they could take phone calls. Not when they kept jabbering and she could feel her own phone in her purse, vibrating with the announcement of what could only be the return call of someone she'd been trying to reach for a week. Lorraine stayed controlled and picked at her salad and waited patiently. At the proper moment, with a grace that seemed offhanded, she resumed her pitch, picking up with exactly what needed to be known about her son.

These men had gold watchbands thick as bicycle chains. They had hairpieces that looked like roadkill, tie clips with boyhood vulgarities engraved into them, manners that would make inbreds blush. However, it also must be said that these men were shrewd enough to notice the undercurrents of discomfort that rippled from Lorraine when a guiding hand was placed on the small of her back. Her dining companions inevitably would look across the table and see the damage the year had done to her. Without question she remained in the higher echelon of females. She wore expensive lines of makeup that accentuated every drop of the beauty that for so long she had taken for granted. Nevertheless, the signs were there, appearing at select moments—as she was listening to reasons it was tough for that particular resort to commit revenue for the banquet, for example: or, right when the executive was shoveling another spoon of macaroni and cheese into his mouth, and kept talking, exposing a mouth of yellow goop. The days of slights would take their mounting toll, and it would become impossible for Lorraine to contemplate a next step, and if her dining companion happened to look up from his trough, he would see sockets hollow and deep in her face, cheeks no longer carrying a downy blush of life: he would see slight creases carved into the corners of her mouth, her face hard and rigid, its skin stretching tightly like a thin spray of paint. He would see Lorraine's determination flagging, her beauty fading. Composure that was an imitation of composure. Revealed in her eyes, a pain that would not end.

With less than three weeks before the event, Lorraine received a call from one of the city's beloved figures, an elderly man reputed to have been a minor member of the Rat Pack. His impish grin commonly popped up on television whenever a news magazine needed a quote about the Vegas of old. One of Lincoln's contacts had put Lorraine in touch with the guy, and though Lincoln had been dubious—*I don't know how much pull that old man has anymore, I mean, does he even have a job?*—nonetheless, Lorraine met with him, twice, both times at one of the oldest casinos on the Strip, a resort that was perpetually switching owners and being renovated. In a wood-paneled steak house overlooking the breadth of the Strip, Lorraine, each time, was taken to the same table—a corner in the back, next to a massive window where you could look down at the neon marquees. There, the old man was entrenched, his table a bevy of activity: waiters and medium-level hotel employees delivering hushed messages, his bookie dropping off handfuls of betting slips. Throughout the meal, diners left other tables to stop by and glad-hand. The old man thanked them and made sure to introduce Lorraine, saying that she was having a banquet for what was it—right, kids that run away. He told the visitors they should call her and get involved. He chewed on his dentures and followed Lorraine's talking points, at key moments putting his hand on her wrist and letting it sit there, as if to say *I am with you.* His wrist had a jewel-encrusted Rolex around it. His fingers were thick with chunky gold. Long after her presentation, the old man kept Lorraine at the table, entertaining her with ribald stories— about walking into his office one day to find Dean Martin taking Lola Falana from behind; about Sinatra ordering him to steal Sammy Davis Jr.'s glass eye and the subsequent hijinks. Lorraine laughed hard enough that she became embarrassed. During their second meeting, the old man re- peated each story, verbatim, and Lorraine giggled anyway. They sat and talked well beyond the lunch hour and deep into the afternoon, until the restaurant was empty of customers and the waiters were eating their own meals, and each time Lorraine had left the steak house feeling a bit sorry for the sweet lonely man. At the same time, memos from the department of self-interest said this was a good development, if he was going to add his clout, the banquet could really take off.

For a week she did not hear from him, and her calls consistently ended up routed to an answering machine, where she had to wait through a backlog of beeps. Lorraine didn't hold it against him, as she didn't exactly have time for his dissembling, anyway. Charity fund-raisers weren't like baseball games or movie theaters, you didn't have walk-up crowds lining up at a ticket booth. According to the latest figures, it was going to take a minor miracle to get the room beyond 60 percent capacity. Lorraine hustled to come up with ways to sell seats at discount prices, even as she worked to reel in corporate clients, while at the same time feuding with the Banquet Bitch over appetizers. The head chef was after her to turn in a final menu and a definite number for the dinners. There also were brush fires with the florist, with a pair of rival politicians, even the valet parking union, which Lorraine did not even understand because why should parking a car for the banquet be different from parking any other car? Lorraine had to get fitted for her gown. She had to come up with matching shoes. There were complimentary goodie bags to assemble for the celebrities, and she hadn't thought about how to get whatever was supposed to go in them, wasn't even sure what she'd promised the booking agency anymore. Her plate was overflowing and the old guy was about last in the line of her priorities, and so when the call came in the middle of a Wednesday afternoon, it took Lorraine a few moments to realize whose squeaky voice was asking her to stop by his office. It took a few more seconds to make the connection between *his office* and the restaurant table, and when Lorraine did this, she felt a spasm of hope. "Give me a half hour," she told the old man.

Busboys, adults every one of them, were gathered around a pair of tables near the kitchen's double doors, busily rolling silverware inside cloth napkins. The waitstaff lounged on bar stools, taking notes while the head chef explained the night's specials. Propped in his usual booth, the old man looked small and pudgy behind a large clothed table, like a rumpled puppet. He did not get up when Lorraine greeted him with kisses on each cheek, and his smell was not fresh, but that's how it was when you got old, Lorraine figured. Placing her purse on the table, she said how much she'd missed him, she was thrilled to see him again, and what do you know, she really meant it. She reached for the water pitcher that was always on the table, and grabbed it before she saw it was empty, and she laughed casually, a bit embarrassed, but happily so.

The old man's face was not unkind. Neither was it friendly. He thought he had something for her. Lorraine answered okay. She could see the small pattern of liver spots atop his temple, a sight she had grown accustomed to during their previous meetings.

He then inquired as to what Lorraine would do in exchange for his support.

"A table cost what?" he said. "Five grand? That's a lot of dough for a gal with mileage on her tires."

The skin beneath his eyes had weathered to a soft purple. His shirt had thin tan epaulets, loopy strips of fabric, and as Lorraine stared at him, she could not help but notice that the far right epaulet had come loose, was hanging in the air like a twig. The old man remarked about the specific carnal acts that would make this worth his while, and Lorraine rose from her chair. She wished him well. Her legs were jelly beneath her as she turned, and she'd taken three steps when there was a sound. Looking over her shoulder was a mistake, but she could not help herself, and saw that he, too, had risen from his cushioned spot, he was moving out from behind the table. And he was not wearing pants. The makings of an erection might have been visible, denting the dingy fabric of boxer shorts. Lorraine didn't stay long enough for confirmation.

This hadn't been the first time someone in an official capacity had hit on her. Certainly not. Since she'd started taking meetings—"taking meetings," geez, even that had a filthy edge—Lorraine had learned to control herself when her dining companion lowered his gaze toward her chest. There had been leers that bordered on vulgar. Double entendres delivered with all the suavity and confidence of a junior high school student asking out a girl for the first time. A good part of the rest of Lorraine's afternoon was occupied by such recollections. And though she had tons of work to do, she did not—as she'd promised she would—head back to the offices of the Nevada Child Search. Instead she drove. Randomly, just to get her bearings, adrenaline surging through her, a meaty, almost lusty want tingeing her mouth. Any idea that came into her head was plausible: she might head to Newell's old comic book shop and purchase all his favorites and then go out to the desert and set fire to them. Just as likely she would race the sunset and outrun memories and lose herself in a seedy roadside bar with a grizzled man who had his own past to forget. All sorts of sexual energy had been channeled into her causes and her missions; all sorts of desires and needs had been subli-mated, transformed into aggressiveness. She dialed Lincoln in spasms, five- or ten-minute intervals, hitting the END key before completing any of the calls. On the fourth try, Lorraine hung in there, punching all of the necessary pulse tones. Two rings later, she learned that Lincoln Ewing was in a meeting or away from his desk right now, but if she left her number and a brief message, he would call back as soon as he could. Lorraine transferred into the turn lane leading into the Kubla Khan's parking lot, and was looking at the hotel spread out before her. The thought of being inside a casino gave her vertigo. Moreover, as much as she needed a friendly ear right then, as much as she and Lincoln had been each other's bedrocks over the years, the thought of needing com-fort from Lincoln now was deeply upsetting to Lorraine. About the last thing she wanted was for him to know he had been right.

It wasn't just Lincoln, though. And it wasn't being hit on, necessarily. It wasn't even that she had trusted the old guy and been betrayed. These were jags of a much deeper iceberg, Lorraine could admit that much. From proposal to meetings to fund-raising, she had taken the banquet by the force of her personality, and through every step had demanded things be done her way. When all evidence suggested the contrary, she'd held on to the belief that her connections had gotten her meetings with execu-tives of true influence. While stuck watching half-wits fixate on dollar keno, she'd convinced herself those mongoloids actually had some juice, could indeed do something for her. Lorraine had come up with trap-doors that waylaid all the facts that she was too smart to completely ig-nore, she'd used a prod and a chair to hold her worst suspicions at bay, even going so far as to believe that a sad and lonely old man who sat in a restaurant all day with nowhere else to go, he was going to turn things around for her—although that wasn't completely fair, maybe the old man could have helped, if he'd wanted to help, if he'd really been worth a damn.

That she'd been so transparent. So *susceptible.* Trotting her need around, naked, displayed in a cage for moron after moron, letting them ogle it, letting them prod it with sticks. Lorraine's shame was pink and withering. How she must have looked! How willfully blind she had been! No way around what she had done. No excuses. This was not one of those situations where you looked back at the person you had been years ago and the stupid things you'd done and felt embarrassed, but also were able to tell yourself that the thing had happened a long time ago. This was recent enough that Lorraine felt it was possible to reach back into those lunches and jostle herself to alertness, and this feeling was not the least bit helpful. Because there wasn't any good reason she should not have known better. There had been only her need.

She drove, north and west, heading into the dying sun, long thin diagonals of yellow and white spilling across the left side of the windshield. Large empty circles of light seemed to jump out at her, and in spite of the tinted windshield, it was difficult to see. But not being able to see traffic fully, not being able to discern a road signal, these things really didn't distract Lorraine. The silence that occurs when you are alone with your thoughts was not so bad for her, either. Time was progressing as emptily as it always had, but now, oddly enough, she no longer felt its meaty anxiousness. After swimming upstream for so long, fighting against the strong tide and harsh current, Lorraine now felt as if she finally understood the error of her direction, and she proceeded to lay herself upon the water, to float.

When she arrived home, her voice mail system was jammed. The banquet planner asking if Lorraine could give her a call when she got in. Molly from Nevada Child Search wondering if Lorraine was going to be in this afternoon. The case officer thanking her for the tickets (he'd received them today). A ramble from her mom, which Lorraine forwarded through.

And then Lincoln: "Hey. It's me. Caller ID says you've been calling. Okay."

The house was crisp and chilly that day, the cleaning lady must have forgotten to turn the air conditioner to a low setting before she took off for the bus. A thought about the guaranteed spike in the utilities bill was fleeting, unimportant. Lorraine headed upstairs, without much in her mind. Goose pimples had broken out along her upper arms and shoulders.

Once you got to the second floor, a banister ran behind the stairwell. When they'd been house hunting, Lorraine had learned the logic behind this contraption: you did not want someone—say a child—to be running around upstairs, slip, and then fall down the stairs. The banister not only prevented this, but also created a small upstairs corridor. Lorraine had developed the habit of hooking tightly around the rail and heading left, into the master bedroom. Presently, however, she broke to her right, the first time in quite a while she'd taken this direction.

She hadn't intentionally stopped visiting her son's room, no more than she'd meant for Lincoln to stop sleeping in their bed, for the boy to disappear, or for any part of this snowballing hell that was their lives to get rolling the way it had. As with so many things, there had been reasons for it and then there had been the happenstance of how it all panned out. Part of it was logistical. By holing herself up in the master bedroom, Lorraine had, in effect, ceded the rest of upstairs to her husband. It just didn't feel right to venture inside the guest room, where her husband was sleeping in exile. Same for the hall bathroom, where he showered and shaved. It was improper. Disrespectful in some way. But to get to the boy's room you had to pass the guest room, then make a right turn before the door to the guest bathroom. In short, Newell's bedroom was deep inside Lincoln's domain. In the months following her son's disappearance, this hadn't stopped Lorraine; indeed, she'd sought out the pain of that empty room—approaching the door that Lincoln left closed, consistently feeling a flash of belief as she turned the handle, suddenly sure that her son would be safely inside, sprawled on the floor, having his action figures perform wrestling holds on one another. But the pain had become too much, and the turf war had taken its own toll, and eventually the door had stayed closed, the room drifting that much deeper into enemy territory.

She eased the door open and found the room as she'd grown to dread it: the bed made and neat, the carpet barren of the strewn clothes and toys that used to frustrate her. A residue of dust swirled in the half-light of the space where the window curtains did not quite meet. Lorraine walked the perimeter of the room, looking absently at toys, at mementos, finally, at nothing. She sat on the edge of the bed, and soon enough was remembering: moments when she'd come to tuck in her son, talk about his homework, or make peace with him after some sort of problem, mornings when he had to be up early and knocking brought no answer so she'd eased the door open and watched her son sleeping and peaceful, and she had been filled with love for him, so much love for this beautiful fucking child of hers, even when she could see he was faking and just did not want to get up to go to school; even when she had places to go and people to see, and did not have the time or energy for his crap, her love for him still could come out from hiding and just about make her heart burst. But these were the easy memories. The convenient ones. Truth was, when Newell had first turned up missing, these were the memories she'd willed into being whenever she used to come in here. They'd been a comfort, a natural defense mechanism. Today, however, these memories had accumulated almost mystifying levels of complexity. It was almost impossible for Lorraine to make sense of them, to feel anything beyond wear.

The bedspread. A cluttered goulash of red and gray images promoting the university basketball team. Lorraine straightened it a little, then stopped and let herself go beyond the easy memories. She recalled looking through a catalogue with her husband, how Lincoln had wished the boy wanted something with the logo of a Major League Baseball team. She lingered on her husband's ability to give in on that matter. After everything she'd been through with Link, Lorraine remained impressed at his ability to distance his preferences from those of his son's.

This afternoon she let her mind wander, gave herself to the poltergeists. A pillowcase looked clean unless you were the child's mother, in which case you could still make out the outline from the night when you had gone upstairs to ask about a school bake sale, and had surprised your child in his bed, causing him to spill the soda that house rules prohibited him from bringing upstairs, and that he should not have had anyway. Lorraine walked around inside the memories; even as their details rushed her, she lingered on every single one—the boy's pajamas getting soaked; the fantasy book he had been reading.

And the sports posters, curling at their edges, straining against the tape and wall tacks that held them in place. The pool of nickels and quarters and matchbooks that had accumulated on the boy's bureau—those, Lorraine steered herself away from, willfully directing her attention from Lincoln's belongings, toward the bookshelf: the comic books and school primers, the arrangement of die-cast figures. The room was pregnant with memories. An imagination unfurling; Newell explaining, from the sedan's rear seat, how he had set up this particular battle, and then the conflict's root. Lorraine saw herself pretending to listen, saw her son behind her, his mouth moving, forming unheard words. A different drive home now; Newell not responding to her inquiries, sullen, his one-word answers, his head in a comic.

At a hobby store she had examined all sorts of paints and tubes and thin brushes and flagged down a passing salesman and voiced her concerns about the model paint, making sure it was not lead-based and would not be harmful, and the child got impatient, he already was upset that she wanted to buy the cheaper kind of paint and not the officially sponsored brand of the National Association for Fantasy Figures, and he pointed to words on the label that said SAFE FOR KIDS, and Lorraine remembered this even as she looked at the grand total, those three figures that had ended up getting painted.

With no small amount of love, she could not help but remember the boy complaining that he was bored, and there was nothing to do. She'd respond with, *Why don't you paint some of your action men,* and he'd look at her as if she were insane. Maybe so. Maybe she was.

When she had been that age she had loved ballet and used to practice the drills in her room for hours on end. With each plié there was the possibility for physical perfection. Lorraine had tried to work toward that perfection, focusing on each movement, getting each part of the whole correct.

But then you couldn't get life correct, could you?

You look back and see clues everywhere, but how were you supposed to know? A twelve-year-old boy is attracted to darkness. To special effects and sarcasm. Saying no when any idiot could see the answer was yes. If every boy with a short attention span and a propensity for smart remarks abandoned his life, who would be left? In her weaker moments she could blame Lincoln for coddling the child, for being the one who got to spoil him, for forcing her to be the disciplinarian and watchdog she'd never wanted to be; but at the end of the day, her anger was pointless, the strap of ribbon that swirls from a maypole in a hurricane. It was easy to say that Newell spent too much time watching television or playing video games; the truth is that there are times when you have to cook or clean or need a moment to yourself and a television or game gets him out of your hair. That was not an indication of their abilities as parents.

They had tried to give Newell everything he had wanted. Where was the crime in that? They had poured their best wishes and hopes for the world into their son; what more could you ask for? And their boy knew he was loved. They had made sure of this much.

But Lorraine could repeat these sentences to herself so many times. She could console herself with a million fund-raisers, immerse herself in untold lost causes. In the end all she was left with were clichés. A pristine room of reminders. Everything waiting for the boy to return, waiting to pick up exactly where things had left off. He would be preparing for eighth grade right now. This was the difference between inanimate objects and people: people change.

Loose change still sat on the counter. Mixed in with the quarters, nickels, and pennies, there was a half roll of breath mints whose wrapping paper trailed off, and a number of matchbooks. She zeroed in on these. They were black, every one of them. Three shone with gloss and might have been new. Another was creased and weathered. The lid on the final book would not shut, and Lorraine saw that all the matches had been torn from its left side. Examining another book, she again found its matches torn from the left side. Embossed letters on the lid. A gentlemen's club on Industrial. Lorraine's first reaction was a pointed anger. But this soon faded; it made perfect sense for Lincoln to frequent strip clubs.

Still it was painful.

Disappointment grew as she thought about it—not because the husband she had spurned for almost a year had found other forms of entertainment; rather, Lorraine's disappointment was rooted in the fact that during the course of her adult life, this man had been her best friend, the lover she'd desired most, her most intimate confidant, the man she could not have more proudly called the father of her child. Even now she was sure that Lincoln was not a bad guy, far from it; he was a decent person, a man whose only guiding principles had been to do what he felt was the best thing for his wife and his family. No. Lorraine's disappointment came with the realization that this had been the case all along, but she had been so firmly ensconced in her own pain that she had not been alert to his suffering. By all rights the discovery of those matchbooks in her son's room should have been shocking; but their existence felt as logical as anything did to Lorraine these days, and this was as disappointing as anything she had to deal with.

Still, she could accept what her marriage had come to, so long as she believed her child was alive. And she was sure this was so. A mother knows. She could shut her eyes and envision the morgue and the sheet being pulled back on her son's body. She could see herself looking down at his blue-white skin and his dead stare. Hundreds of scenarios visited her, gruesome thoughts tormented her, and yet none took hold inside her heart. None of them resonated as true. The phone had rung on her birthday, hadn't it? Newell was alive and out in the world, of this his mother was sure. She wondered how much he had grown, suddenly worried that he needed clothes, and had a strange thought about the obsolescence of his wardrobe in the closet. She hoped he was warm and healthy and had food to eat. Volunteer work had given her some understanding of what possible lives he might be leading, but it was nearly impossible for Lorraine to align the grime and pain of a life on the street with the child that she had brought into this world.

How could that life be preferable to what they had given him?

Into the universe she once again gave a primal, guttural prayer, praying that caring people in a shelter had gotten him, that her son had found safety, established a new life for himself, something with some modicum of order and comfort, this even as she tried to imagine why, if his life had this comfort, he would not contact his mother.

Not for a second did she believe he had been a troubled child.

Not for a second did she believe that he had been unhappy—not in a manner that was anything more than transitory.

There was no understanding. There were no hows, no whys, no logic, no answers. There was only numbness. Exhaustion. The absurdity of this life she was in.

It was well after midnight when Lincoln got home. Lorraine heard his car pull up. By the time he opened the front door, she was downstairs, waiting. She saw he was tired, and a little disoriented, surprised to see her.

She went to him and he said "Hey," and he wrapped his arms around her and held her. "What is it? What?"

She did not answer but let him hold her and inhaled the smell of nicotine on his clothes. The stench of alcohol on his breath.

And something else.

"Lorraine?"

"The day. I, it just—"

Perfume. All over him.

The embrace ended, Lorraine removing herself, stepping back.

"There's been a mistake with the appetizers," she said. "We were supposed to have grilled shrimp with spicy cocktail sauce. But it looks like there was a misprint or something. Midge, the banquet planner. She left all these messages."

"Okay?"

"Shrimp's not part of the seventy-five-dollar menu. We can still have it but we'll have to pay."

"That doesn't sound so serious."

"It's forty dollars a dozen."

He seemed to exhale now, eyeing her with a bit of suspicion.

"Right now we're fine," she said. "We've got marinated chicken kebobs and grilled vegetable kebobs. Also these flame-roasted red peppers and smoked provolone. They're served on fresh baguettes with olive oil, they're supposed to be delicious. And there's going to be vegetable and cheese trays all around. So we can go with that. God knows there's enough other things to worry about—"

"Lorraine—?"

"But I'm telling you, Link, I was really tempted to pay for the upgrade out of our pocket, just to spite them, just to stick it to them, you know? Then we'd have the shrimp. We'd have a better cut of prime rib. I really was about to do it. And then, then I thought, *It's a fund-raiser for teenagers living on the street.*

"We're going to give these people all this food," she said, "and, and, and meanwhile—"

Her husband took her to him and he held her head to his chest and stroked her hair as he used to do a long time ago. He told her it would all be fine.

"What are we doing?" Lorraine asked. "We have to let it go. We have to. But how, how do you do that?"

Lincoln held her, and kept holding her, and they sat at the base of the staircase. He waited for her crying to subside. "Hey there. Hey." His words were slurred, a bit, but tender. She was smart to think like she did. They'd been to enough banquets. "You know how it is. You kind of assume the chicken's going to be rubber. The greens are always wilted. When we surprise them with all that fancy food, it'll knock their socks off."

She blew her nose, and wondered if he was being nice because he was embarrassed about being caught drunk. If he felt guilty about cheating on her. If he still loved her and genuinely wanted to help. If all these things could be true.

"You'll see," he said. "People get gourmet food and it makes them want to go to next year's banquet. They're happy to write a big check."

"Next year?"

The glitz and glamour shrank behind them, having given way to cluttered hucksterism—a one-story storefront hawking plane rides to the Grand Canyon; a visitors' information center where you could make show and hotel reservations. Now one of the most recognizable signs on the planet rose from a traffic median. Heading in this direction, you did not get welcomed to fabulous Las Vegas, Nevada. Instead, this side of the famed diamond read DRIVE CAREFULLY. COME BACK SOON.

Newell tightened his grip around the extinguisher's trigger mechanism. The undersides of his fingers dug into the clamp's serrated metal, and though he felt a stinging sensation, he kept squeezing.

On the other side of the street, an aboveground swimming pool sat in the courtyard of a motor lodge. The bottom of the pool was constructed out of see-through glass, and lights from inside made its water glow, and this was a momentary distraction for Newell.

The FBImobile approached an old motel and Newell held his breath. He remained breathless as the next motel went by—a split-level jobber, dilapidated, even in the night.

They weren't pulling into one of those seedy holes, but they sure weren't stopping, either. And the boy noticed the buildings becoming subsequently fewer, farther between. Cacti and tumbleweeds and dark emptiness filled the interim spaces. Behind that, the lights from nearby neighborhoods created this faint, spooky glow.

Ahead there was desert and more desert. The interstate. The mountains.

Suspense, thrilling and horrible, kept building with each second, the prospect of what could be happening, with all of its possibilities, presenting itself even as nothing happened.

Then Kenny went upright in his seat. His shoulder moved slightly.

"What's that?" he asked.

A clicked switch: the headlights became brighter, shining onto more of the asphalt in front of them, spilling onto the side of the road as well, catching the reflection of a mile marker; a bunch of gravel and brush; a sun-faded campaign placard. And something else. Up a ways.

"Dude," Newell said, leaning forward now.

In the gloom of his forty-nine-dollar motel room, Bing Beiderbixxe stretched out on a mattress that provided nothing in the way of back support. Sitting up a bit, he let himself be propped by the headboard, as well as pillows whose cases were overly starched. Bing felt roundly and thoroughly defeated, humiliated for the umpteenth time. He'd been so certain that his connection with the stripper had been real. Yep. Bing Beiderbixxe was the sucker of all suckers.

A listless point of the remote control whose batteries needed to be replaced. He fought for each click through the channels of the motel's basic cable package. Time and again Bing returned to one of those movies that always ran on cable late at night, the kind of blockbuster that had been released with all kinds of publicity, and was now constantly shown to try to get back the studio's coin. Bing had seen it, or parts of it, during many predawn hours, and knew it well enough to not pay much attention. A passably bad movie, watchable and crafted but not particularly good.

He was noshing his way through a bag of guacamole Doritos, was also down to the dregs of yet another Mountain Dew Code Red. Exhausted but nowhere near sleeping, Bing was having halfhearted thoughts, and considered whether to grab his laptop, gather his scattered clothes off the floor. The crate of his unsold comic books was in the hatchback, right where he'd left them. Ditto the cardboard fold-out, stuffed into the backseat. All he had to do, really, was go to the Pinto and get going. No need for checkout. Who gave a crap about plastic room keys.

He was going to have to skip on his electricity bill this month. Probably MasterCard too, which would do wonders for the interest. Bing's eyes were strained, fading in and out of focus. His teeth were vibrating from the accumulated caffeine. The thought of being back in Cali by morning wasn't any impetus for him to get up.

Without energy or enthusiasm he grabbed his laptop from off the stretch of bed on his right. The phone jack was still stuck into the side of the computer and soon Bing had typed in the code from his calling card, and bypassed the motel's phone charges. He logged in, checked the Knitting Room, and found there were no members inside. He vacillated, stared at the screen, and ran down his FAVORITES menu. When he couldn't avoid it any longer, he opened a word processing file. Bing typed in a stream of consciousness, without bothering to read what he was entering, without correcting his errors, leaving alone phrases that he knew were false starts. It was more important to get it all out, get it down.

]A comic book about why grown people read comic books? TOO VAGUE? 2 OVERDONE? 2 META? DO I NEED MORE SHAPE?

• Different characters have own reasons for being regulars at the comic book store. Group of f/college w/crappy jobs. Stripper who lives in dream world & think she's a movie star (remember trip! Sketch when u get home!). Each character MUST have some sort of DEFINING interest in popular culture—movies. rock & roll. Rap. Get rich schemes. Body art. Goth. Tecchie. UFOs. ETC.

Bing made a column for each character, and in this way, slowly started shaping their traits, developing ideas for them. He had some thoughts about making the stories and lives and interests intersect, and typed these out as well, under a different heading. Quickly Bing typed out a note about having different characters have overlapping interests and contrary points of view. Less quickly, he considered a follow-up: having plots and subplots based on the overlaps and contrasts. Like one story that revolves around the day a summer movie opens. Most issues would include everybody, but maybe he also could focus on one character in particular, if the situation called for it.

Bing didn't feel his headache so much. Backing up the file, he rose from the bed and stretched his arms above his head and worked the crick from his side. He paced the length of the motel room and scratched at the back of his neck.

There wouldn't be any superpowers; there wouldn't be a whole lot of escapism; but maybe it could be *about* escapism—like its place in daily life. Like what was going on with each character, what had happened to them. Why their fantasies were not just necessary but so prominent?

With a simple pull, the cloth around her wrist collapsed like wet toilet paper. Holding her newly freed hand, the girl became reacquainted with the sensation of her skin, the ebb and flow of her racing pulse. She shook her hand, trying to get back the circulation, and though it was a struggle to rise, she managed to crouch, gaining a modicum of balance. The girl began feeling her way around, groping for the side door, the handle. For precious seconds the latch did not give; but finally there was sweet release, gears shifting, a rusty, rolling groan. She did not have time to inhale, no time to let her lungs fill with the fresh night air, but hoisted herself downward, dangling her feet into the open space, then lowering herself onto the sand. The girl braced herself against the truck's hull. Before the strength in her legs had time to solidify, before she'd figured out the lay of the land, she started down the thin path between the ice cream truck and the jalopy next to it, not thinking, not stopping, not even looking up, making it down the crevice and out in front of all those parked cars, keeping on, away from the direction all the noise was coming from, away from the rumors that at that moment were spreading through the party, the whispers about a gang bang that was taking place, the ice cream truck that was rocking, *let's go knocking!*

Darkness was flat and wide and ambling in all directions. A few bright specks crawled horizontally across the flatlands, but the girl could not afford to look at them for long, just making out the cacti and tumbleweeds in front of her required concentration. She struggled over a mini-dune, lost her balance, fell to one knee and scraped herself. To the farthest left of her field of vision, the city shimmered. She took another step, felt her way along the breaks of the desert, did her best to follow whatever cues the land gave her. Geckos rustled amid the weeds; rattlesnakes burrowed, unseen. She plowed straight through the smaller weeds. Her feet dragged. She limped and held herself and ran her hands up and down her arms, the concert noise and commotion still audible behind her, but less present now than a surrounding stillness, the carrying sound of cars up ahead, whipping along that black road.

At that time of night, pretty much the only things out there were eighteen-wheelers making night runs, their head and cab and grille lights providing small markers that she could track from a distance. When one of those big rigs rumbled up and was upon her, its lights were blinding. The girl stepped off the asphalt's edge and back into the brush, and the rig slammed by with the force of an elevator in free fall, leaving her trembling for long seconds afterward. Nobody stopped. They did not slow. Not even a pulled trucker horn in warning. She thought nothing of this. She expected nothing from them, but stayed off the asphalt, and made her way down a dirt shoulder that was the width of a runner's path, the ground beneath her going hard and baked for stretches, then patchy with soft sand, then turning gravelly. The girl picked off burrs. She checked and restraightened her skirt. Her progress was meager, measured by abandoned objects, what once might have been a computer printer; the twisted corpse of a bicycle without wheels. The girl passed one thing and after a while the next became apparent: value-meal wrappers stuck in weeds; the shards of shattered amber glass; the round end of a crushed aluminum can sticking out of the ground like an artifact from a long lost civilization. She kept going and the city kept shimmering in a distance she could not touch, a faraway place that was not real to her, but that she had to move toward, her legs weary, a thigh muscle trembling involuntarily. The girl's mouth was horribly, impossibly dry. Mosquitoes had bitten the living hell out of her. The soles of her feet burned, her toes feeling as if they had kicked a wall for an hour. And there were other minor aches and inflammations and rebellions, coagulating, one skeletal throb. Though specific pains kept flaring, they were nothing in comparison to her real aches, the pains she was unable to think about, those places she was loath to address. The girl walked and stared out into the wide and dark night and it was quiet, only the slight sounds of her feet on the gravel, the give-and-take of her breathing. But the pattern of her breaths was like a lulling song, and listening to herself breathe calmed the girl with the shaved head, helped her balance on the tight thin wire, remain above the abyss from which there surely would be no return, that place where wisps of madness crashed against the gathering reality of her body's aches. The only way for the girl to survive was to stay out of that horrid place, and the only way to do this was to stay balanced on that wire, and instinctively she did this, following the line of her breaths. The margin along the shoulder of the interstate widened. Her legs were too heavy, too used. She slowed and came to a stop, and now began easing down onto a large round stone. The girl barely felt her raw knee press against jutting rock edges, and in a desiccated whisper, she repeated *Oi*, singsonging to herself, *Oi, oi, oi*. She pulled at one boot, then another, in workmanlike fashion dumping the sand and pebbles from each, then spanking their rubber soles. *Oi, oi, oi*. From below, the mingled odors of vinegar and ammonia wafted. The carriage of her ribs shuddered. The girl was still for long moments, then slowly brought her knees up toward her chest. Once again she confirmed the absence of her undergarment. Felt her pubic thatch tangled and brittle. Her sex tender, stretched and irritated.

Lestat squeezed Danger-Prone Daphney's hand and pumped his strength into her, and though Daphney's palm was limp and clammy, she was still there, squeezing back, giving what she could. Now the end of the reinforced gurney hit the double doors; Daphney whimpered and kept her eyes closed tight. The gurney continued down the hallway and underneath the fluorescent lights, an orderly kept sponging Daphney's brow, and Daphney looked calm to Lestat, like some sort of angel, and this terrified him to no end. Where Daphney's shirt had been cut open, her stomach was engorged and bright with sweat, it was rubbery and unreal. A needle had been jammed into the vein at the crook of her elbow and her arms were strapped into Velcro restraints and Lestat did not take his eyes off of Daphney, but kept gripping her hand. Presently, he spoke and it was as if he were swatting at a fly over his shoulder, and he told the ER administrator to hold off, *not* to call child welfare. This milk carton, it had Daphney's parents' address on it. Lestat swore the milk carton was in Daphney's backpack and, and, *Just give me a second, goddamn it.*

He leaned into Daphney's cheek. *"Hold on,"* he pleaded. "It's all gonna be fine. I'm here for you. Stay with me."

After some time the girl began to stir, and pulled her socks up from around her ankles and toes, where they'd bunched. She did not hurry, but felt along the ribbed stripes, delicately patting away the dust. One by one she then removed the thorns from the cotton. When she was finished, one boot went back on. Then the other. The ends of a shoelace were filthy, but she took the lace and evened it out anyway. Instead of relacing, she wrapped each end of the shoelace all the way around her boot's calf, bringing the strings back together at the front. The tongue interrupted, flopping down, getting in the way. As the girl straightened it, she constructed excuses as to her whereabouts this evening, and tried to convince herself that her lies were indeed true. Possibilities began, but were not concluded, her thoughts wandering down silent alleys, and if the wisps of madness were not exactly gathering momentum inside her, nonetheless, a withdrawal was under way.

Soon enough the girl with the shaved head would drop her old friends. Her soliloquies would give way to glares, her outbursts to empty shrugs. The girl's mother would notice the fragile shell her daughter had retreated into, and would be concerned by the absence of music from her daughter's voice. How the girl's anger had lost all traces of its former grace, her mother would want to know. Why the eloquence of her outrage had given way to such an unsteady quietude. The girl frequently stayed out late at night, there was nothing new in this; however, in future years the mother would tell a string of therapists about the morning when the aggrieved parents of a twelve-year-old boy showed up at her door with a stringy teenager in tow. They demanded to speak with the girl and, in the living room of her mother's apartment, the girl mostly stared down at the ground. Sometimes she looked over to Lincoln, Lorraine, and Kenny. In halting words, the girl told a story that corresponded with what Kenny had told Lincoln and Lorraine. The boy's parents glowered at the girl, horrified at what she might say. Frequently the girl stopped and restarted, and when she was finished, nobody in the room doubted her veracity. The girl with the shaved head would be cleared of any involvement with Newell's absence, as would Kenny, and this would be one less thing for the girl and her mother to worry about. However, this did not mean her mother was satisfied with the girl's explanation as to why she'd been walking out in the desert alone at that time of night. The party wasn't any fun, nobody would give her a ride—this is all the girl would say, telling her mother to just *drop it,* storming off or just shutting down. Something had to have happened out there, the girl's mother would conclude, and a significant amount of her next three years would be spent thinking about this night, that it had to have something to do with the change in her daughter. Even more of her time would be spent on the phone with health care representatives, discussing, for the umpteenth time, why exactly payment for the girl's psychiatric sessions kept being denied when the policy clearly stated . . . The girl with the shaved head would have her bachelor's and her master's and would be well into adulthood and still would not feel the comfort or security necessary to bring up the events that happened inside the ice cream truck. Relationships, intimate and working, with men and women alike, would be affected by her reticence, her anger, her temper, and what partners and teachers and employees would call *a difficulty with trust.* Shying away from physical contact, the girl would repel people. She would be defiant, resistant, abjectly negative. The girl with the shaved head would not be happy with all the anger that was inside of her, nor with how she moved through each day, and she would work diligently on addressing these things, and while this work would not be easy, nothing in this world that matters is easy. The girl with the shaved head would be a work in progress for quite some time, as all of us are.

For now, however, she was slipping backward, into that silence.

And, nominally, she was aware of a pair of high beam headlights.

The Plymouth slowed, veering to the right, its tires crunching softly over the gravel, the car pulling up with maybe a yard of space between the girl and the passenger window.

After all this time driving around looking for people to nail, the strangeness of her appearance—this straggly girl, served up on a rock out in the middle of nowhere—felt like it could be a big deal, although Newell did not know how. Like she had been put here for him.

"Yo."

She would tell authorities about believing the Plymouth to be the kind of car driven by the undercover drug officers at her school. She would admit to freezing up, thinking that if the cops took her in, they'd call her mom. An hour or so and she'd be home.

"Yo," he repeated. "What are you doing?"

His voice belonged to a child. And beneath this child's attempt at nonchalance, he was tense, the girl could tell that much. Keeping her head low, she raised her pupils, and made out a basic form in the window space.

Another voice now, from inside the car. "You okay?" it asked. "Need a lift or something?"

The engine lulled. The quarter moon sat luminous and large.

Her legs were bent at the knee, her heels firmly planted on the dirt. Reaching down to her untied boot, she took up its loose laces.

"We're not going to hurt you or nothing," the boy said.

She started a knot. Turned it into a bow.

"Hey."

From inside the car now, the second voice: "Newell. You better not."

"I'm not," the boy answered. *"Yo there."*

"I think we should just—" went the second voice.

"I just want to know something."

"If she's walking, we can't be too far away."

"Nothing bad, *fawck*."

A rustling in the windowsill, the boy moving something, repositioning his body. Again he addressed the girl, this time as if he were making contact with a deaf person: *"I JUST WANT TO ASK A QUESTION."*

Now her head rose incrementally, in the movements of someone betraying her better instincts. Her face remained impenetrable, the few traces Newell could make out seemed to form to a resigned and dignified grace.

This was how it worked, she thought. This world was warm promises and sweet breath on your ear and girls who got into cars and were never heard from again.

The only way to know anything, she knew, the only way to the truth, was in blood.

The look she gave caught Newell. Stopped him, even.

He had lived the great majority of his life instinctively, every movement reactive, following whatever whim captured him, saying the funniest thing that popped into his mind. Even now he had a good one ready: *You know your shoelaces are untied, right?*

"We just asked if you wanted a ride," he said. "Jesus. It's not like we're going to hurt you or nothing. Chill out. God."

He felt Kenny's hand pressing down onto his shoulder and jerked away. Newell heard his name being called and the word meant nothing. The girl's eyes were squarely on him now, staring at him in a way that showed her to be a wounded and cornered beast, combative, gathering strength. The way she was looking at Newell let him know that she saw through his lie, and probed deeper, reaching toward a bedrock place inside him. *I see what you are. I know exactly what you are.*

Newell was marginally aware of his name being called again, Kenny's hand jerking on the tail of his sleeve, jostling his arm. But it was as if these actions were being filtered through a gauze, happening to an entirely different person.

A run-down store on Industrial: Asaaf and Kunjib continued stacking the latest amateur audition duplicates. A Red Roof Inn off I-405 in the San Fernando Valley; Rod Erectile wearily strapped on the knee pads and asked if the syringe was ready. A mongrel dog whimpering, its nose pressed to the desert highway, trying to pick up its owner's scent.

Tonight Newell had already sprayed one woman with fire extinguisher foam. Tonight he had lied to his parents and broken his curfew. Newell had won money on a nickel slot machine that he was not legally allowed to play, while trespassing inside a casino that he was still a good seven years away from being legally allowed inside. Shoplifting. Vandalizing. Broken laws. Challenged commandments. None of it had caused him more than a second thought. Right and wrong had had nothing to do with whether he could get away with an act, how much trouble he might get in. But this was different. The way the girl was looking at Newell clearly let him know she understood that she would not escape, he would succeed in whatever he was about to do. Watching the girl physically brace herself, Newell felt a surge of power, and basked in her helplessness. Until he recognized that he was the source of the pain she was about to feel.

Was it possible for a good friend to make what he said was a massive mistake and still be your friend—if he said he was sorry, did that erase what he did? Was that the same as the way your parents do things that are unfair, but because they say they love you, that was supposed to make everything better? Like, because they said they knew better and said it was for your own good, it was fine they were fucking you over? And all the times when teachers and adults are right and you are wrong and this only makes you feel worse. Hassling you. Stealing from you. Motherfuckers laughing at you, doing you wrong, hurting you in deep and meaningful ways, giving you whatever reasons, whatever excuses, and you are left with shit, you are left sucking shit with a straw.

But if he unleashed the fire extinguisher on this injured girl, how was that different from any of them?

He wasn't. He wasn't any different.

Newell's hand was clammy with sweat and his grip around the extinguisher loosened just a bit and now he had the strangest sensation, a disconnect—as if all this was happening inside his head. He could feel the sweat on his hand *in his head.*

Could he really go through with this, he wondered. *Is this what people really do to one another?*

And now the girl's body language seemed to change, almost imperceptibly, she seemed to soften in a way that was victorious, defiant even, her face opening with a sickly grin. The shoelaces slipped through her fingertips.

Even when you didn't feel life was moving forward for you, there it was, happening. And if only Kenny could have reached out, if he could have grabbed this last second and held it in place, then everything would have been okay. From the driver's seat it seemed within his grasp, right there in front of him: Newell jerking, making this terrible whelping sound, as if the air had been knocked out of him; the extinguisher canister releasing, falling and hitting the Reliant's floor; the cough of white smoke weakly releasing up and out through the car. Kenny watched, uncertain, confused. He couldn't decipher exactly what was unfolding. His eyes were tearing. He coughed and coughed again. By this time the boy had pushed open the passenger door.

Eventually the face of Newell's cellular phone would be discovered in a scrap yard just outside Sedona, lying inside the trashed and stripped husk of that ice cream truck. In the time it took Kenny to get out of the car and run around the front of the Reliant, night was engulfing the boy. The sounds of Newell running through some sort of brush were still near enough, there remained a chance at catching him.

Parental neglect. Sexual abuse. Teenage girls sold from Asian farming villages. The girl with the shaved head was trying to rise from her rock, her head turning in the direction Newell had run; Kenny was close enough to see that her clothes were covered in crud. Her legs seemed to buckle, and though she did not fall, it was obvious to him that she also needed help.

And this is where it all unraveled, with Kenny on the edge of the desert, the girl with the shaved head struggling to stand, and the slight sounds of the fleeing boy growing more distant, giving way to an all but deafening gloom. The junky old car idled by the side of the road, purring and coughing up phlegm. Secular fundamentalists. Religious consumers. Commercial-free satellite radio. Noninvasive dental surgeries. The world was a pair of successfully removed breast implants and an ambitious former stripper working to rebuild her life alone. The world was an overweight artist swearing off sugar. A mother forced to deal with her grief, fighting to get beyond her anger, still waiting for the phone to ring, the door to swing open. A father exhausted by the wreckage of his marriage. The world was wandering and dirty and lost; a boy discovering a ripped concert T-shirt and, although he could not make out the name of the band, slipping the warm fabric over his head.

Each and every one of us moves toward fates we cannot possibly know. Each of us struggles against the pain of the world, even as we are doomed to join it. And for a moment Kenny wavered in his struggle. Slowing, twisting in place, he threw his hands up into the air. To no one in particular, he let out the choked, half-whispered plea that would remain at the forefront of his thoughts for years: "What am I supposed to do?" he asked. "Just what am I supposed to do now?"

AUTHOR'S NOTE

I tried to be fairly accurate in the placement of hotels, streets, et al, in my hometown of Las Vegas, Nevada. I was not always successful. In part this is because Las Vegas is a fluid city and it took me a long time to write the novel and by the time I was finished, things had changed. Sometimes stuff got moved for artistic reasons, or simple necessity (read as: the author's limitations). At the end of the day, the Las Vegas in this novel is not the actual city, but a version of Las Vegas, one created by my imagination. Vegas-o-philes are more than welcome to search the book for discrepancies between the real thing and what I came up with. Contact me about them and maybe I'll send you something, depending on my mood.

ACKNOWLEDGMENTS

This novel took a long time to write, and there's no way I could have completed it without a lot of support. From the bottom of my heart, thanks and praise to:

Buckethead. Norma Bock. Gene Santoro. Gary Libman. Slim Smith. William Kittredge. Alden Jones. Jaime Clarke. Peter Hausler. Tara Ison. Gary Giddins. Anthony Bock. Yale Bock. Slash. W. Axl Rose. John Weigund, for graciously offering me the use of his cabin for a month. William and Allison Woolston for two of the greatest summers known to man, and the most perfect place to get married that a person could ask for. Pumpkin and Hippolyte. T. J. Kenneally. Carmen Monteblanca, for shooting me full of all those drugs. Michael Neill, for the sarcasm and the cynicism and so much more. Anna Schuleit. Sue Barker. Messy Stench drew the awesomest flyer in the history of papyrus (her website, craptabulous.com, rules, go visit it).

Certain people in the world of adult entertainment were kind enough to take me into their clubs and onto their sets. You know who you are: a heartfelt thanks for letting me into your lives. Loving thanks to all the street kids I talked to, and all the ones that I didn't get a chance to talk to, and all the ones who haven't yet run: may there be nothing but peace in your futures.

The Vermont Studio Center and the UCross Foundation both were kind enough to provide me with fellowships and hospitality. The Corporation of Yaddo has been unfailingly generous to me, especially when there was no discernible reason to be. Amber Qureshi is a stone-cold joy. Marc Sapir and Isidro Blasco are wonderful, each of them, and yet for some reason I have listed them together. I need to thank everyone at the Bennington Writing Seminars for never quite running me out of town, in particular Priscilla Hodgkins, Sven Birkerts, and Askold Melnyczuk. Susan Choi is selfless and brilliant and basically awesome. Rick Moody is one of the best, most generous writers alive. To Mohammed Naseehu Ali, I make a personal promise, one day I will dance and sing for your birthday and *you* can insult *me*. Ryan Walsh, simply one of my favorite people on earth, rock on motherfucker. Mike Wise has been there for me in truly tough times, whether it was to listen to my newest and latest crazy scheme, throw me needed jobs, or just take me to lunch; I am so fortunate to have him in my life. Alison Smith is my personal corn muffin and I love her no end.

Everyone at Random House has been amazing, and I am so grateful that they have believed in my novel (*gracias,* my ruthless corporate overlords). In particular, the support of Gina Centrello has been priceless; my thanks to her are without end. Dana Blanchette worked very hard to make every page of this book a piece of art. Lynn Buckley is the genius who designed that once-in-a-lifetime cover. Diana Fox is efficient and intelligent and sweet as hell. Jynne Martin: goddess, shining and true. And as for David Ebershoff, my editor, well, there's a lot of talk in publishing circles about how editors don't edit anymore. Those comments are from people who aren't fortunate enough to have you working with them. I could not have been guided through this by a surer hand. A monstrous thank-you.

Jim Rutman at Sterling Lord Literistic: a flat-out mensch. His patience, thoroughness, commitment, brains, and complete and utter decency mark him as singular.

Mary Beth Hughes not only changed my life, but taught me how grace moves through the world.

The Great One.

Wyatt Mason possesses the finest mind I've ever known; moreover, he is the best friend I've ever had.

Crystal Bock, my sister, has been my partner in crime for as long as I can remember. She knows all the places in this novel, and many more than that.

Of course my wife, Diana Colbert, is the greatest fucking thing that ever happened to me. You make my life a joy.

Finally, my parents, Caryl and Howard Bock. For your unfathomable sacrifices, your never-ending love.

RESOURCES

If you are out on the streets, or a parent of a missing teen, here are a few places to get help:

National Runaway Switchboard
http://www.1800runaway.org
Toll free: 1-800-runaway
(1-800-786-2929)
3080 N. Lincoln Ave.
Chicago, IL 60657
Phone: 1-773-880-9860
Fax: 1-773-929-5150

Nevada Partnership for Homeless Youth
http://www.nevadahomelessyouth.org
Toll free: 1-866-U-ARE-SAFE (1-866-827-3723)
P.O. Box 20135
Las Vegas, NV 89112
Office Phone: 1-702-383-1332
Fax: 1-702-313-0216

Nevada Child Seekers
http://www.nevadachildseekers.org
2880 E. Flamingo Rd., Suite J
Las Vegas, NV 89121
Elaine Sinnock, Director of Operations

My Friend's Place
http://www.myfriendsplace.org
Membership Program
P.O. Box 3867
Hollywood, CA 90078
1-323-908-0011, ext. 110

Larkin Street Youth Services
http://www.larkinstreetyouth.org
Administrative Offices
1138 Sutter St.
San Francisco, CA 94109
Phone: 1-415-673-0911
Fax: 1-415-749-3838
mail@larkinstreetyouth.org

Covenant House
http://www.covenanthouse.org
Toll free: 1-800-999-9999

In California:
info@covenanthouseca.org
Toll free in CA: 1-866-COV-DOVE
(1-866-268-3683)

In Hollywood:
1325 N. Western Ave.
Hollywood, CA 90027

In the Bay Area:
2781 Telegraph Ave.
Oakland, CA 94612

In New York City:
info@covenanthouseny.org
460 West 41 St.
New York, NY 10036
1-212-613-0300

Also, should you happen to be driving in Las Vegas, when you need to fuel up or get a soda, may I suggest Terrible Herbst. They are a partner with the Nevada Partnership for Homeless Youth, and their stores and gas stations even serve as places where runaways can go for shelter and get a bite.

In addition, please know that I am not affiliated with any of the organizations on this list, and did not write my novel while in contact with these organizations. By no means is this list complete—it includes select national orgs, as well as groups in Nevada, California, and New York City. By all accounts, these groups do great work. However, if you or your teen is in trouble, there are excellent local recourses all over this nation. Please find them. And if you want your organization to be part of this list, contact my website (www.beautifulchildren.net). We'll confirm your info and include it in a subsequent edition of the novel. Good luck to all.

CB

ABOUT THE AUTHOR

CHARLES BOCK was born in Las Vegas, Nevada. He has an MFA from Bennington College and has received fellowships from Yaddo, UCross, and the Vermont Studio Center. He lives in New York City. Visit his website at www.beau tifulchildren.net.

ABOUT THE TYPE

This book was set in Garamond, a typeface originally designed by the Parisian typecutter Claude Garamond (1480–1561). This version of Garamond was modeled on a 1592 specimen sheet from the Egenolff-Berner foundry, which was produced from types assumed to have been brought to Frankfurt by the punchcutter Jacques Sabon.

Claude Garamond's distinguished romans and italics first appeared in *Opera Ciceronis* in 1543–44. The Garamond types are clear, open, and elegant.